Always Her Love

The Steeles at Silver Island

Love in Bloom Series

Melissa Foster

MF

ISBN: 978-1-948004-32-9

This is a work of fiction. The events and characters described herein are imaginary and are not intended to refer to specific places or living persons. The opinions expressed in this manuscript are solely the opinions of the author and do not represent the opinions or thoughts of the publisher. The author has represented and warranted full ownership and/or legal right to publish all the materials in this book.

Cover Design: Elizabeth Mackey Designs
Cover Photography: Wander Pedro Aguiar

PRINTED IN THE UNITED STATES OF AMERICA

Levi & Tara

A Note from Melissa

I love writing about single moms and dads for their strengths *and* their weaknesses, and Levi Steele is no exception. He was quite young when Joey was born, and the circumstances that brought his daughter into the world were far from ideal, but he never let that impact his love and adoration for his little girl. He isn't looking for love, but fate, family, and friends have other ideas, and of course he can't help falling for the incredible, selfless, beautiful woman who has always been there for him and Joey. All my stories are written to stand alone or to be enjoyed as part of the larger series, so dive right in and enjoy the fun, incredibly sexy ride.

If you're an avid reader of the Love in Bloom series, please note that this story takes place prior to MAYBE WE WILL, the first book in the Silver Harbor series.

I have many more steamy love stories coming soon. Be sure to sign up for my newsletter so you don't miss them.
www.MelissaFoster.com/Newsletter

Free Love in Bloom Reader Goodies

If you love funny, sexy, and deeply emotional love stories, be sure to check out the rest of the Love in Bloom big-family romance collection and download your free reader goodies, including publication schedules, series checklists, family trees, and more.
www.MelissaFoster.com/RG

Bookmark my freebies page for periodic first-in-series free ebooks and other great offers.
www.MelissaFoster.com/LIBFree

SILVER ISLAND FAMILY TREE

Extended families not noted

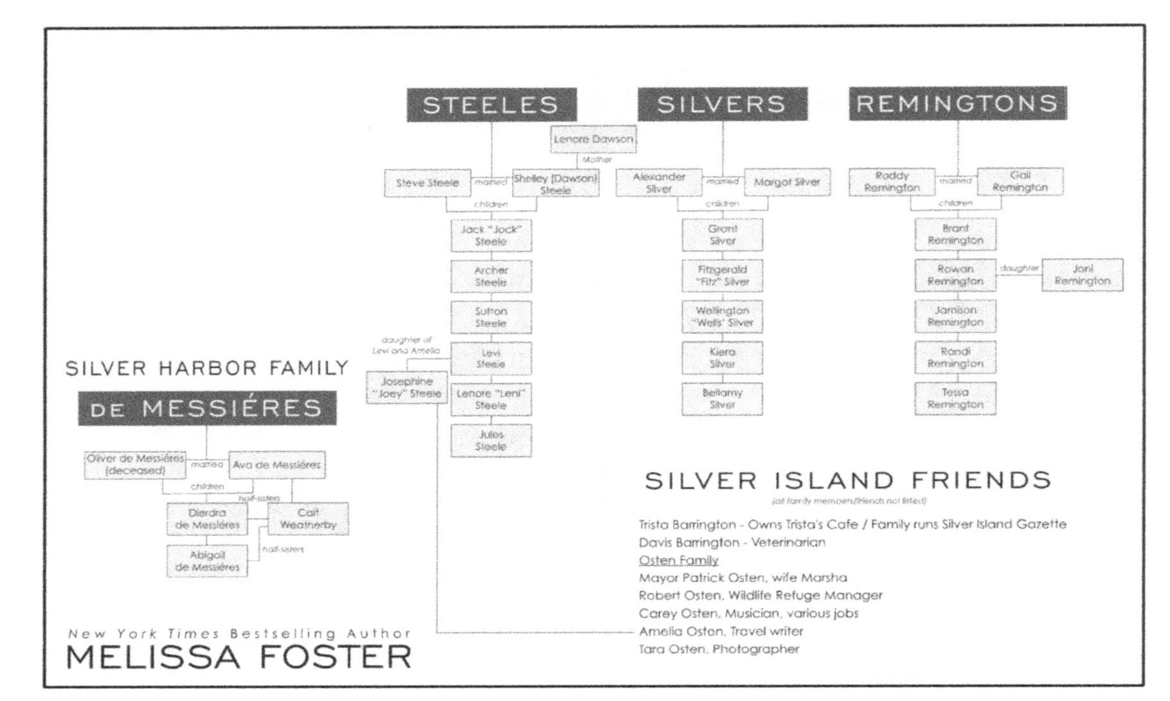

SILVER ISLAND
Wildlife Refuge
Rock Harbor
Seaport
Fisherman's Wharf
Brighton Park
Seaport Primary
Rock Bottom Bar & Grill
Trista's
Happy End
Silver Island Airport
Rock Harbor Primary
Lover's Cove
Top of the Island Winery
The Bistro
Silver Monument
Majestic Park
Silver Island Community College
Silver House
Brighton Bluffs
The Sweet Barista
Scoops
Silver Island High
Silver Harbor
Sunset Beach
Silver Haven Primary
Marina
Fortune's Landing
Silver Haven
Fortune's Cove
Chaffee
Bellamy Island
Cuddlefish Cove

Playlist

"FRIENDS" by Marshmello, Anne-Marie
"Always Been You" by Jessie Murph
"You Belong with Me" by Taylor Swift
"Light Switch" by Charlie Puth
"Crush" by Daniel Feels, Annie Schindel
"Just the Girl" by The Click Five
"Butterflies" by MAX, Ali Gatie
"Dancing Feet" by Kygo, DNCE
"Shake It Off" by Taylor Swift
"What A Time" by Julia Michaels, Niall Horan
"For The Nights I Can't Remember" by Hedley
"When You're Gone" by Shawn Mendes
"Best Part of Me" by Caleb Hearn
"I GUESS I'M IN LOVE" by Clinton Kane
"Without You" by Parachute

One

LEVI STEELE FELT like hell, and he had his older brother Archer to thank for it.

He usually slept like a bear when he went home to Silver Island to visit his parents. Being with his family and the friends he'd known forever gave him a sense of peace and reminded him of his childhood, when the worst thing he'd had to worry about was his twin older brothers, Jack, who went by the nickname Jock, and Archer, pranking him. Their pranks were wicked, but he'd take one of those any day over the way Archer had messed with his head last night, suggesting he make a move on Tara Osten, his eight-year-old daughter Joey's beautiful blond aunt. If that wasn't enough to annoy him, Archer had spent the rest of the night citing his observations about Tara smiling flirtatiously at Levi.

Levi had known Tara forever. She'd been an adorably pudgy, introverted kid and had grown into a beautiful, funny, confident woman who had earned a phenomenal reputation for her photography on and off the island, and she somehow still managed to exude the allure of the girl next door. She had an innate sweetness and innocent blue eyes that had always made Levi want to protect her. He didn't know if she was innocent or not, and yeah, he'd wondered about it from time to time, but he'd been quick to lock that shit down. She was Joey's birth mother Amelia's *sister*, for Pete's sake, and he knew better than to get tangled up in that hornet's nest. But now that Archer had opened his damn mouth, Levi couldn't stop picking apart his brother's comments. When Joey was born, Levi had purposefully closed off his heart to women, and now he wondered if it had skewed his perception. Had Tara flirted with him, and he'd somehow missed it? A zing of something hot and dark spiked inside him.

Jesus, do I want her to flirt with me?

Fucking Archer.

He went to get dressed for a run, remembering how Tara, at fifteen, had been instantly smitten with his little bundle of joy. He'd been nineteen and living with his parents when he'd found out Amelia was pregnant and twenty when Joey was born. Tara had shown up every day after school and first thing in the morning during the summer to spend time with her. Joey had suffered from colic as an infant and had loved napping in Tara's arms, holding her aunt's long blond hair in her tiny fist. She'd cried when anyone had tried to take her from Tara. Levi could still picture his honey-haired little girl at two, toddling after Tara, and Tara scooping her up, nuzzling her cherubic cheeks, sending Joey into fits of giggles. He was convinced Tara had gotten a double dose of maternal genes, since her older sister seemed to have gotten *none*.

Amelia was a year older than Levi, and they'd never dated, but they'd had sex once when Amelia was home from college for a weekend. Two months later he'd found out she was pregnant via text. The message would forever be ingrained in his mind. *I'm pregnant. It's yours. I'm having it, and unless you want it, I'm putting it up for adoption.*

Her use of the word *it* still turned his stomach.

He pulled on his sweatpants. He'd never forget how the world had stood still while he'd processed that text. He'd been trying to figure out what to do with his life while working construction. He loved working with his hands and hadn't had an interest in going to college like Jock, who'd dreamed of becoming a screenwriter and had since written two novels, or had aspirations of working at their family's winery like Archer. But from the moment Levi had read that text, he'd known that whatever career he chose would come *second* to caring for his baby.

He'd thought he knew what he was signing up for as a single father, but he couldn't have been more wrong. Between working to afford diapers, formula, and everything else a tiny human needed, while getting almost no sleep and worrying over every little thing, he'd felt like a zombie in the *Twilight Zone*. Thank goodness for his family, friends, Tara, and after a while, for her family, too. He finally understood what his mother and grandmother had meant when they'd said, *It takes a village...*

He put on sneakers, hoping running would stir up enough endorphins to overshadow the shitty night's sleep he'd endured *and* the shitstorm of mental chaos Archer had induced. Archer had never been good at understanding or dealing with emotions until his now-fiancée, Indi Oliver, had worked her magic. He'd changed a lot, but he obviously still needed help, because the more Levi thought about it, the more he realized he'd never seen Tara flirt with *anyone*. She was a consistent and important part of their lives, and Joey was lucky to have her. Hell, they both were, and he didn't need to screw that up. Archer knew they had an easy friendship, which meant she smiled at him often, and for the life of him, Levi couldn't figure out why his brother would twist it into something more.

He gazed out the window, and as if the answer had risen with the sun, he realized his pain-in-the-ass brother was intentionally screwing with his head. The bastard was pranking him.

Levi cursed and scrubbed a hand down his face, annoyed that he let his brother get to him. He inserted his phone into his armband and put the armband on, trying to push away his annoyance as he pocketed his earbuds and followed the scent of freshly brewed coffee downstairs, but frustration pecked at him like a crow to roadkill.

He heard two of his sisters talking as he came down the hall. Last night was the grand opening of Indi's cosmetic boutique, and their whole family had shown up to support her. While Jock, Archer, and their youngest sister, Jules, lived on the island, Levi lived in Harborside, Massachusetts, his twin sister, Leni, lived in New York City, and their oldest sister, Sutton, lived in Port Hudson, which was in Upstate New York.

He found Joey sitting at the kitchen table in her pajamas with his mother and Leni. Sutton stood at the counter pouring a cup of coffee. "Morning, ladies."

He kissed the top of Joey's head, giving her shoulder a squeeze, and met his mother's smiling eyes. Shelley Steele was a big, beautiful woman with a vivacious personality. She had long auburn hair, bangs that gave her a youthful look, and a heart of gold, which his father wholly and completely owned. His parents had taught him more about patience, parenting, and love than he could have ever asked for.

"Look what the cat dragged in." Sutton, a tall, sassy, and tenacious blond television reporter, carried her coffee to the table, exchanging a secretive glance with Leni.

"Grandma made blueberry pancakes." Joey tilted her adorable freckled face up to look at him with a mouthful of food. She had Amelia's fair skin and cinnamon hair, but thankfully, she'd inherited Levi's love of life and big heart. "You look funny, Dad."

"Maybe because you're looking at me upside down." He ruffled her hair and went to get a glass of water.

"Or maybe because you look like crap." Leni sipped her coffee, her auburn hair framing her snarky expression. "What happened to you last night?"

"What happened to *you* last night?" he countered, their age-old banter coming as easily as his own name.

"What did you hear?" Leni asked coyly.

He filled his glass with water, staring her down. "What did *you* hear?" If Archer said anything to her or anyone else about Tara, Levi was going to kill him. The last thing Tara needed was to deal with unfounded gossip.

"Wouldn't you like to know." Leni's lips curved slyly.

"Okay, you two," their mother interrupted with a shake of her head. "*Sheesh*, it's like you're teenagers all over again."

Joey giggled.

Levi leaned against the counter drinking his water, sharing a chuckle with his sisters. It was all in fun. They were each other's confidants. His twin was the most sarcastic of his siblings, but she was also the most practical and level-headed, making decisions with her brain rather than her heart. He was fairly certain he was the only one who knew *why* she no longer opened her heart to men, and he'd take that secret to his grave. Just as he knew she protected his secrets.

Leni was the first person he'd called when he'd gotten that text from Amelia. She'd been at college in New York City, and when he'd told her he wanted to keep the baby, she'd come home. They'd talked all night, and Leni had done what she did best. She'd made lists—dozens of them—and had forced Levi to think of everything good and bad that could possibly come from being a single parent. Even at nineteen, she'd been far more practical, and smarter, than most people their age. She'd helped him forecast budgets for raising a kid from birth to college, which had freaked him out, but then she'd helped him feel less lost and more in control. She'd believed he'd be a great father, and in the years since, when things got tough, she was always there to say, *I know you can do this.*

His mother studied him with a furrowed brow. "Actually, honey, you do look a little rough around the edges. Did you and the boys go out and have too much to drink last night?"

"I haven't had too much to drink in years. I just didn't sleep well." The conception of his daughter had knocked the urge to drink himself into oblivion to the curb. Back then he'd thought hangovers were hell, but they had nothing on Archer's ability to screw with his head.

"I'm sorry to hear you didn't sleep well," his mother said. "Joey said you have a big afternoon planned with the Venting Vixens."

When Joey was an infant, Levi had met a group of moms that got together on weekends to commiserate and hang out, and he'd dubbed them the Venting Vixens. They'd been his sanity saviors the first year after Joey was born. They understood his fatigue and frustrations and how, at times, he felt as though he'd lost his own identity. When he and Joey were in town, they still got together with some of them and their children.

"You're not going to cancel, are you, Dad?" Joey asked.

"No way, sweets. I know how much you're looking forward to showing them your new skateboarding tricks." His daughter had gone through a long princess stage, but she'd moved on to skateboarding. He loved that she followed her passions, and he did everything he could to support them, including hooking her up with skateboarding lessons.

"Don't forget my new Dark Knights stuff Uncle Brent gave me," Joey exclaimed.

"It's all in your bag and ready to go." Levi and his twin older cousins Jesse and Brent, who also lived in Harborside, were members of the Dark Knights motorcycle club. Joey had grown up around bikers, and all the guys looked out for her and treated her like she was their own daughter. She was so close to them, she called most of them her *uncles*. Jesse and Brent owned a surf shop and restaurant, and Brent had been skateboarding since he was a kid. He'd been training Joey for the past year, and he'd given her a helmet and pads with the Dark Knights emblem on them to wear to her first tournament, which was just a few weeks away. It was a big one, the fifteenth annual for their town, and Joey was determined to win a trophy.

"I'm glad you're making time to see the Vixens," his mother said. "I was talking with Grace Chabot the other day, and she told me her daughter is still single." Her brows waggled.

"Where are all the hot-single-dad groups?" Sutton asked.

"You won't find them on *this* island," Leni droned.

Levi put his glass in the dishwasher. "It's not like that with this group."

"But it could be," his mother said. "You have so much love

to give, honey. All our kids do, but not as easily as you used to. Don't you remember how you were before Joey was born? You had lots of girlfriends, and you were always loving on them and spoiling them, and every one of them added something special to your life."

He couldn't imagine trying to fit a woman into their busy lives, much less splitting his attention between his daughter and anyone else. He wasn't about to slight Joey. Her mother did enough of that.

"He didn't just have a lot of girlfriends," Leni chimed in. "Levi was a hot commodity in high school. All the girls wanted him."

He'd had all kinds of *game*, but becoming a father at twenty had given him different types of moves. Like the ability to change a diaper while holding a bottle in a baby's mouth and juggle his precious peanut and all of her accoutrements on two hours of sleep.

"He's still got game," Sutton said, as if he weren't standing right there.

"Can we *not* analyze my dating abilities? My life is fine as it is." When he needed to find a little relief, he did it when Joey was otherwise occupied, and that relief had become far less important in the last few years than it was when he was younger.

"Oh, honey." His mother got up from the table and carried her plate to the sink. She looked pretty in a rust sweater and jeans. "Is it so bad that I'd like to see you happy, with a woman to share your life with? Someone Joey can look up to and talk to?"

"You're not getting any younger," Sutton pointed out with a glimmer of *better you than me* in her eyes. "You might want to hook a bride before you lose your hair or all those muscles."

"We have Tara," Joey piped in.

"Tara's not ours in that way, peanut," Levi said.

"But she wishes she were." Leni smirked and speared a piece of pancake with her fork, popping it into her mouth.

"No, she *doesn't.* Why would you say that?" Levi glowered at her. "What did Archer tell you?"

Leni raised a brow. "What did he tell *you*?"

"Nothing. Forget it," Levi grumbled.

"Aw, come on. Now I have to know what Archer said," Sutton urged. "Was it about Mouse?"

His protective urges flared at the nickname Amelia had given Tara when she was a little girl and would hide in the pantry at parties, nibbling on snacks to avoid her mother's nitpicking. Even though her sister had started it by saying Tara looked like a cute little mouse, and his sister and their friends used the nickname affectionately, and Tara didn't seem to mind it, the nickname reminded him of the insecure little girl he'd found in that pantry too many times—and the condescending way Amelia had said it to *him* after they'd had sex. *Now every time you look at that pudgy little Mouse, you'll think of me.* He had no idea why she'd brought up Tara, and he'd never asked, but when he'd gone home that night, he'd felt used, as if he were a pawn in some type of twisted game, which made no sense, since Tara had been only fourteen years old. He didn't regret having Joey, and he wouldn't want to imagine his life without her, but he sure as hell regretted getting goaded into having sex with Amelia. The woman's heart was colder than an iceberg.

"Why *isn't* Tara ours like that, Dad?" Joey asked. "We always have fun when Tara stays with us."

"Yeah, *Dad*," Sutton taunted.

Leni put her elbows on the table and folded her hands, resting her chin on them with an expectant expression. "Do tell."

There was nothing worse than the combined annoyance of sisters. He focused on his daughter, who looked innocently confused. "Joey, Tara and I are just friends. You know that."

"I know," Joey said. "You're really good friends. You laugh a lot when you're together, and you always say she's your favorite dance partner."

His daughter had a memory like an elephant. He and Tara had been dancing together for years at events on the island. She was a great dancer, and she saved him from having to dance with single women who were just looking to hook up. He steered clear of anything that could loop him into being part of the island grapevine. "You're right, Joey, but what Grandma meant was that she'd like to see me dating someone, like a girlfriend."

"And falling in love, expanding your family together." His mother sighed dreamily. "Jock is married, and Jules and Grant are picking a wedding date, and now Archer and Indi are engaged. Can you blame me for wanting all our kids to be as happy as your father and I are?"

Levi was amazed that after raising six kids and working together at their family winery for decades, his parents still acted like newlyweds. They were always holding hands, touching, and kissing, making love look easy and appealing. But Levi had closed that door long ago to focus on his daughter.

"Sutton's older than me," Levi pointed out. "She should be next in your matchmaking lineup." He grinned at his sister.

"Sutton's not getting married until after she bags her hot

boss," Leni said.

Sutton rolled her eyes. "A body bag, maybe." She'd been less than qualified for her reporting job when her company had promoted her, and her boss had been trying to get her fired ever since.

"What's a body bag?" Joey asked.

"It's what you put arrogant bosses in when they piss you off," Sutton said.

Levi knew he should explain that his sister was kidding, but it was better to let that topic go than open a door for his sisters to add their even more confusing two cents.

"Sutton is still finding her way in her career, but your company has grown by leaps and bounds," his mother pointed out.

Levi's business, Husbands for Hire, was a franchise, originally started by a group of Dark Knights in another state. HFH was a handyman business, and Levi enjoyed helping people, but after taking on several employees, he'd expanded and now spent his time on larger projects and doing what he was most passionate about, buying houses in various states of disrepair and turning them into unique properties.

"How about Leni?" Levi suggested. "She's single."

"Yeah, right," Leni said sarcastically.

"She's married to her work right now. You know that," his mother said. "You're settled and doing well, and the right woman could add a lot to yours and Joey's lives."

She looked so hopeful, it almost made him wonder what he was waiting for.

"You could date Tara," Joey suggested.

His sisters tried to stifle their laughs, their eyes darting to him.

"No, peanut. As I said, Tara is just a friend."

"A friend who stays at your house all the time," Leni pointed out.

"I heard she'll be staying with you for two weeks over spring break to watch Joey," Sutton added. "That's a long time."

"And not at all unusual," Leni said in a tone that implied it made it even more curious.

They were relentless. He narrowed his eyes, but his sisters simply ignored him.

"That's right, she usually covers Joey's school breaks, doesn't she?" Sutton arched a brow.

"*Yes*, and I love it," Joey exclaimed. "My break starts right after the spring dance. I can't wait."

Leni glanced at him. "I bet Daddy secretly can't wait, either."

He glowered at her. He had to get out of there before he blew up. "Hey, Jo, I'm going for my run, okay? Be good for Grandma."

"Okay!" Joey turned back to her aunts. "Dad's starting a big project, and Tara said…"

Levi went out the kitchen door before his sisters started in on him again. He tipped his face up toward the sun, trying once again to tamp down his frustration. That felt like a never-ending battle today.

He put on his playlist and set out on his run. He'd always been a runner, and between that and the hard physical labor he did, he stayed in fairly good shape. He ran past his family's vineyard, Top of the Island, and through the neighborhood streets he'd biked as a kid, catching glimpses of the ocean in the distance. He waved to families washing cars and kids playing in their yards. A run was usually enough to clear his head, but even with the peaceful sights and the Strokes playing in his ears, his mother's comments still echoed in his head. Ever since Jock had fallen in love with his now-wife, Daphne, and her toddler, Hadley, and they moved to the island, Levi had noticed a *flicker* of *Maybe one day* nearly every time he saw them. But he never allowed himself to linger in those thoughts.

But now that he *was* thinking about it, Tara came to mind. *Fucking Archer and our nosy sisters.* He tried to push those thoughts away, running faster.

His phone chimed, and he withdrew it from his armband, seeing a group text from Leni sent to all their siblings, Daphne, and Indi, who happened to be Leni's best friend. He opened and read it. *Archer, what did you say to Levi last night about Tara?*

"Damn it, Leni."

Two more text bubbles popped up. The first from Jules, the original queen of group texts. *Oh! Me likey! Levi and Tara would be so cute together. I've got LOTS of ideas to help them along.* Freaking Jules and her matchmaking. Levi read the next text from Jock. *Isn't it a little early for group texts? Archer and Indi are probably busy.* He added a winking emoji. Another text from Leni rolled in. *We can wait seven seconds.* Sutton, Jules, and Daphne sent laughing emojis, and Archer replied, *I asked him when he was going to make a move on Tara. She's into him big-time. I'm turning off my phone for AN HOUR or TWO.*

Fuming, Levi muted the group text and cranked the music. He put his phone back in his armband and sprinted up the hill, wishing he could mute the voices in his head.

800 GABLE PLACE.

Even the address was unique. Only three houses boasted such an elegant street name. There were plenty of other pretty street names on the island, but to Tara, none felt quite as special or substantial as Gable Place.

She stood on the curb across the street, admiring the house that had captured her heart six years ago, when she was on her first paid photography assignment. She'd been only eighteen years old and thrilled to have been hired to photograph the most interesting houses on the island. It was no surprise that 800 Gable Place was *not* on that list. She'd gotten lost in the older section of town and had stumbled upon the house, which had gables on all four sides, two large picture windows flanking a small porch, and a red front door with black shutters, just like the carriage house out back.

The house had been in such bad shape, most people probably wouldn't have given it a second glance, and the years since had not been kind to the hidden gem. The white paint was dingy and chipped, the porch railings were missing balusters, one of the shutters on the gable windows was broken, and the other hung like a crooked tooth. Branches from an enormous, and quite gorgeous, tree shaded half the roof, which was missing shingles and covered in moss. Gutters hung in precarious positions, and one of the front windows must have had a massive crack, because duct tape ran like lightning from top to bottom. The property also looked like it had been forgotten, with long patchy grass, unkempt bushes, and a broken, weather-beaten picket fence that looked like it belonged in front of a haunted house. But for a girl who had been overweight for more than half her life and judged by her appearance first—and often last—Tara knew looks could lie as easily as people did. She judged beauty by the way people and objects made her feel, and that practice had never failed her.

Except on rare occasions when she looked in the mirror.

But that wasn't something she wanted to think about on that unusually warm, sunny April morning. She focused on the warm, welcoming feeling she got around that house, and her thoughts strolled down a hopeful path she'd toyed with too many times to count and had finally decided to try putting away for good three months ago, with a New Year's resolution. She'd always imagined living there with the man she'd been crazy about since she was eight years old, Levi Steele, the most loyal, kindhearted guy she'd ever known, and his adorably spunky, sports-loving daughter, Joey. She pictured filling the house with scents of freshly baked cookies and the warmth of family traditions and covering the walls with pictures of family and friends, bringing every room to life with colors, textures, and cozy furniture big enough for the three of them to cuddle on. She could see Joey skateboarding on the sidewalk and playing ball in the yard with Levi, the three of them going for family walks and eating meals together, and after Joey was safely tucked into bed, she imagined loving Levi the way he deserved to be loved and being loved by him the way she'd always dreamed he would love her—with everything he had.

The blare of a car horn startled her out of her fantasy, and she dropped the flyers she was holding. The car pulled up beside her, and Georgia Smythe, a friend of her mother's and the owner of a cute clothing shop in town, rolled down the passenger window and peered over from the driver's seat, her brown hair framing her friendly face.

"Hi, Tara. Everything okay?"

"Yes, thank you. I must've been daydreaming." She felt

ridiculous, fantasizing about a man, and a life, she could never have. It didn't matter that her older sister, Amelia, had chosen a career over being a mother to Joey instead of trying to do both, or that she only saw Joey a few times a year. Amelia was *still* Joey's mother, and that made Levi Steele off-limits.

"Be careful, honey," Mrs. Smythe said. "I wouldn't want you getting hurt."

And there it was, the reason those fantasies could no longer be indulged in and why she was committed to sticking to her New Year's resolution and moving on from that childhood dream. Buying a house was a good first step, and there was no harm in hoping to connect with a guy who was as wonderful as Levi, was there? A man with a similar love for family, sense of humor, and lips she wanted to kiss and lick and suck and disappear into? A man who could obliterate thoughts of him?

She realized Mrs. Smythe was still waiting for a response and shook her head to clear her thoughts. "I will, thanks."

"Okay, sweetheart. Enjoy your day."

As Tara watched Mrs. Smythe drive away, she thought about how far she'd come. She'd spent the last few years knowing she needed to stop fantasizing about Levi and had put all her energy into making a name for herself as Silver Island's go-to photographer. Her reputation had spread so quickly on and off the island, to Cape Cod, Harborside, and other nearby coastal areas, she'd never slowed down to think about a name for her business. It was a good thing she liked her given name, because *Tara Osten, Photographer* had become her brand.

If only working hard could have distracted her from thinking about Levi, too, but thoughts of him and Joey were as constant as the air she breathed. She'd added that to her *things she must accept* list, like her sister's inability to parent and their mother's nitpicking.

She touched the round silver charm with a heart cut out of the center on her leather bracelet, thinking of Joey and Levi. She'd given Joey the bracelet that had the silver heart charm that fit inside it. *No matter how far apart we are, we're always close at heart.* Unlike Amelia, and to some extent, their mother, Levi and Joey were a big part of her life, and they were going to be on her mind. There was no escaping it, and she didn't want to stop thinking of them. *That* was why she'd finally decided that enough was enough, and a resolution was in order. Resolutions were better than goals. They were firm decisions, meant to be kept. As long as she kept her thoughts about Levi in line, she'd be fine.

Except for those late-night fantasies. *Which are now out of the question*, she reminded herself.

She turned at the sound of heavy footfalls, and as if she'd conjured him, Levi was running up the hill, wearing a black tank top, gray sweatpants, and a sheen of sweat that made his skin glisten enticingly. She might not judge on looks alone, but that didn't mean she didn't appreciate the tall, broad-chested God of a man with tattoos covering his left arm from shoulder to wrist. As he neared, a sexy smile curved his lips. She was a goner for two things on Levi Steele: his black leather biker boots and that smile. She mentally added sweatpants to that list, immediately chastising herself for it.

"Hey, blondie," he said, barely breathing hard. His short brown hair was damp at the temples, dark eyes glittering in the sun. They were his superpower. With a single glance, he could stop trouble in its tracks or weaken the strongest of knees.

"Hey—" was all she got out before getting distracted as he took off his tank top and used it to wipe the sweat from his face, baring his muscular chest and ripped abs for her to admire. Or rather, lust over. Was there a sign over her head that read, *Take me to the Land of Temptation*?

"You a'right?"

Her gaze shot up to his cocky grin. *Ugh.* Her runaway hormones were going to be the death of her. She needed to find a fantasy replacement. Stat. "*I'm* fine, but you'd better put your tank top back on so you don't cause an accident. You know how the women on this island are. They see a shirtless guy and lose their minds."

"*Man*, I must be getting old if I have to take my shirt off to get women's attention."

She rolled her eyes.

"What're you doing up here? Decorating the street?"

Shoot. She'd forgotten about the flyers scattered at her feet. "You know me, always trying to make things a little prettier." Levi worked hard to make a good home for Joey, and he spent loads of time with her. But while they had a yard full of gardens and birdbaths, and one of the coolest houses Tara had ever seen, with secret hiding places, a multitude of cozy nooks, and sliding barn doors, all of which Levi had created with his own two hands, he had little time to tend to the gardens, much less think about sprucing it up inside every now and again. When Tara stayed with them, which was fairly often, she and Joey gardened, picked flowers to bring inside, and found other ways to try to freshen things up.

She crouched to pick up the flyers, and he knelt to help her. His musky scent was *not* doing her any favors. "It's okay, I've got it."

He looked at her like she was being silly and continued gathering flyers. His gaze fell to her chest, making her breathe a little harder. "You always wear that necklace, don't you?"

She touched the gold necklace he and Joey had given her last Christmas with an aquamarine infinite heart charm. "I never take it off."

"I like that," he said thoughtfully, and looked at the flyers as they pushed to their feet. "Are you taking pictures for Charmaine again?" Charmaine Luxe was a local real estate agent.

"No. I was around the corner and stopped to look at that white house. It's my favorite house on the island."

"Really?" His brows knitted. "What do you like about it?"

"Everything. I love the gables and the big windows. The whole house gives me a warm, fuzzy feeling, like it's just waiting for a family to bring it to life, and it's got that great carriage house out back, which would be perfect for a photography studio. I'm sure you think I'm crazy because you see all its flaws. But I see a diamond in the rough."

"T, how can you think that about a guy who renovates and flips houses for a living?"

"I don't *know*. I figured you'd see its faults before you recognized its beauty."

He arched a brow. "And here I thought you knew me."

She stayed with them so often to babysit Joey and when she was working with local photography clients, she knew things she probably shouldn't. Like if he got up in the middle of the night, she'd hear him walk into Joey's room to check on her, and when Joey cried, she could see his daughter's anguish mirrored in his eyes. When Joey laughed, he looked at her like it was the most glorious sound he'd ever heard every single time. She also knew that sometimes she'd find him on the back porch off the kitchen staring absently out at the water with the loneliest expression. One she'd never seen when he was on the island with his family. But she kept those things to herself and said, "I *do* know you."

"I'm starting to question that." He bumped her with his

shoulder. "Seriously, have you ever known me to judge a book by its cover?"

My gorgeous sister had an attitude bigger than the Grand Canyon and you wham-bam-thank-you-ma'amed her, so…

She couldn't say that, either, so she went with, "No. You're right. I was just being silly." She'd always wondered about the night her sister had gotten pregnant. News traveled fast on the island grapevine. Even at fourteen she'd known that Levi wasn't one of those guys who had slept around. But Levi *had* screwed Amelia at the *height* of her bitchiness. Amelia was more tolerable now, but she was still selfish, and Tara had never been able to figure out why he'd done it. Especially since her sister had always made it known that she never wanted to get tied down with *any* guy, and Levi had had other girlfriends who had each lasted a while. Tara had been a little jealous of those girlfriends, but when he'd hooked up with Amelia, her teenage heart had been crushed. Her bestie, Bellamy Silver, had told her that nineteen-year-old guys think with their dicks. As Tara grew up and had her own experiences with guys, she realized most of them thought with that particular appendage, but she'd always believed Levi was different. His banging Amelia should have been enough to stop her from crushing on him, but if she'd learned one thing over the years, it was that where Levi and Joey were concerned, her head and her heart were *not* connected. Now that she was trying to let her head take charge, she was much better off.

"I'm going to have to start taking you to see some of my projects before I get my hands on them."

"That sounds fun." She liked watching him work. Not as much as she was sure she'd like to have his hands on *her*, but she couldn't afford to fantasize about playing in a sandbox that didn't exist.

"*Great.* We'll do it." His expression turned serious, and he raked a hand through his hair. "Listen, I know Joey put you on the spot yesterday about staying with us over spring break, so if you want to back out of watching her, she'll understand."

"She didn't put me on the spot. I'm excited to spend time with Joey and watch her win the skateboard tournament. Besides, you know as well as I do, if I didn't spend spring break with you guys every year, your gardens would turn into jungles."

"That's true. I'm glad you're not backing out. I like having you around."

Her hopeful heart quickened at his words and the way he was looking at her more intently than usual.

"I mean, *we* like having you around," he corrected himself.

"Right. Of course." With her hopes deflated, her mind dragged her stupid heart back to her second resolution: to stop spending long periods of time at Levi's house. She really needed to do something about that after spring break.

"So, what's up with these?" He waved the real estate flyers.

"Nothing really. I just started looking at houses. That's why I'm up here. I was checking out the neighborhoods, so I don't waste Charmaine's time."

Surprise rose in his eyes. "You're looking at buying a house and I'm the last to know? Way to knock me off my pedestal."

"You're not the *last*. You're actually the first."

He rolled his shoulders back. "That's more like it. But a house is a big commitment."

"I know, but it's time to spread my wings. The photography studio I rent is going on the market next month, and I'm not sure I'll be able to find another, so I need a backup plan. I'm hoping to find a house with room for a studio."

"And you can afford to buy?"

Her services were in such high demand, she'd tripled her rates in the last three years. "I've never paid rent, so my money is just piling up in the bank, and real estate is a great investment. Besides, living with my parents is a little stifling."

"You mean your mother," he said knowingly. "She's a tough one. I don't know how you've lasted this long."

He knew her mother nitpicked about everything from food to clothing. But he also knew her mother wasn't malicious. She was just particular, and Tara would like to believe that her mother simply didn't realize how the things she said affected others. She'd always been one of Tara's biggest supporters when it came to her love of photography. When Tara was younger, her mother would seek out photography exhibits and take her on day trips to see them in Boston, New York, and other places that weren't too far away. Sure, that had meant dressing and acting in ways her mother deemed appropriate, but her mother had made efforts no one else had, and that was special.

"I've been too busy to think about it. But now that my professional life is on track, I can start focusing on my personal life, and I can't really do that living with my parents."

His jaw tightened. "No, I guess not. Who's going with you to check out the houses?"

She'd been thinking about asking Jules and Bellamy to go with her but hadn't gotten around to it. "Charmaine."

"No, I mean to look at the structures and make sure there's nothing wrong with them. Isn't your father or one of your brothers going to help you?"

"My father and Robert are so busy, I don't want to bother them, and Carey is helping Drake with one of his stores for the next few weeks." She was close to both of her older brothers. Robert was the manager of the island's wildlife refuge, and Carey helped his friend Drake Savage run his music shops along the East Coast and sold vinyl records and other musical paraphernalia at flea markets and other outdoor venues. He was a vagabond, and his schedule was anything but consistent.

"When are you going?"

"Next Saturday. Charmaine has a few new listings coming up on other parts of the island, so I figured I'd wait and see them all at once."

"Great. I'll go with you."

The prospect of looking at houses with Levi was as nerve-racking as it was exciting. "Are you coming back next weekend?"

"I am now," he said happily.

"You don't have to come back just to help me look at houses." *But, yes, please!*

"I want to. Houses are my jam, and Joey will be thrilled to see her grandparents and Hadley again." Jock had adopted Hadley when he and Daphne were married, and Joey adored her cousin.

"Are you *sure* you don't mind? I know how busy you are."

"I'm never too busy to help you." He set that sexy smile on her again.

It would be so easy to twist that thoughtfulness into something more…

"You're giving up two weeks to spend with us. I think I can handle checking out a few houses with you."

That made it easier. He was merely repaying a favor. Not that she needed to be repaid, but she could use his expertise when evaluating the properties. "Okay, if you really don't mind. Thanks."

"Great. What time is your first appointment?"

"Ten."

"I'll take an early ferry and pick you up at your parents'

house. Does that work?"

"Yes, perfectly."

"I look forward to it. I guess I'd better get back to my run. Will I see you tonight at Rock Bottom?"

There had been a small celebration last night at Indi's boutique for Archer and Indi's engagement, which had included family and friends. Tonight's parent-and-kid-free celebration was hosted by Wells Silver, one of Bellamy's older brothers, at his restaurant, Rock Bottom Bar and Grill, one of the hottest night spots on the island.

"*Yes.* I'm going with Jules and Bellamy. It should be a lot of fun."

"Awesome, and it's a date."

Did she miss something? "A *date*?"

"To look at houses together."

"Oh, right. *Yes.* Sorry, my mind is on a hundred things."

"Busy day ahead?"

"Yes." *But that's not what had me sidetracked.* "I'm taking pictures at the annual police and fire department car wash."

"Taking pictures of shirtless guys?" He arched a brow. "Think you can handle it without losing your mind?"

She gave him a deadpan look. "Ha ha."

"Hey, that was *your* warning, not mine."

"It wasn't meant for *me*. You're shirtless and I'm doing just fine, aren't I?"

"Yes, you are, and that doesn't bode well for my ego." He winked. "I'll see you tonight." He took a few steps and glanced over his shoulder, holding up his tank top. "Guess I'd better put this on so I don't cause any accidents." He put on his tank top and jogged down the road.

"Your ego is fully intact," she called after him. *My heart, on the other hand, is a work in progress.*

Two

THE BEAT OF the music pulsed through the air, competing with the din of the crowd dancing and mingling at Rock Bottom Bar and Grill. Levi's siblings and several of their childhood friends were sitting at a table by the dance floor. Archer hadn't left Indi's side all night, and he'd never looked happier as he joked with his buddies Brant Remington and Grant Silver, Jules's fiancé. Jock and Daphne were holding hands, chatting with Leni, Sutton, and Grant's younger siblings, Keira, Fitz, and Wells. While Levi was thrilled that three of his siblings had found love, there was only so much *nuzzling* a guy could take when he was struggling with things he shouldn't be thinking about.

He excused himself to get a drink and ordered at the bar. A cute brunette was making eyes at him, trying to catch his attention. There were plenty of beautiful women there, but Levi's focus was riveted to the gorgeous off-limits blonde dancing with Bellamy and Jules. Tara might be the epitome of sweet and careful in her daily life, but when she danced, she morphed into a pure cock-hardening seductress. He didn't think she even realized it. It was like she became possessed by the music, moving sensually in a clingy off-the-shoulder yellow top that stopped just shy of her low-waisted, curve-hugging skinny jeans, giving Levi—and too many other men—glimpses of bare flesh and her sexy belly button. Heat sparked beneath Levi's skin, simmering hotter with every rock of her hips.

Fuck.

He told himself to look away. But he couldn't. He didn't *want* to. He'd always kept a protective eye on her, so why was his mind going places it shouldn't? Places it had tiptoed over the years but he'd been quick to shut down and deny?

His damn brother had him analyzing more than Tara's interactions with him. He had Levi questioning his own motives and noticing her in new ways, and it was irritating the hell out of him.

The bartender brought his drink. Levi paid and headed back to the table, where three separate conversations were taking place. He didn't bother trying to catch up, his gaze moving back to Tara just as the song ended and she and the girls headed for the table. Ryan Lacroux, the most lusted-after policeman on the island, stopped them to chat. The guy was raising his drug-addicted brother's young son, and with his short dark hair and chiseled features, he looked like he belonged on magazine covers. In other words, he was a walking aphrodisiac for single women, and there was no mistaking his appreciative glances at Tara, which sent a hot streak of jealousy through Levi.

He gritted his teeth against the unwanted emotion. Was Ryan one of the reasons she wanted to focus on her personal life? He looked around at the other guys who were checking her out, wondering who else might be on her radar, and his hands fisted, his gaze returning to Tara as she walked away from Ryan. She glanced at Levi and smiled, a familiar jolt of happiness radiating between them. She lifted her hand in a familiar waist-high wave and wiggled her fingers, just like she usually did. There was no seduction in her eyes, no flirtatiousness in her smile. He wasn't *missing cues.*

He was just an idiot.

He wasn't usually impressionable. He was in control of everything in his life. He had to be, for his daughter's sake. How he'd let Archer's or his sisters' comments—*or my own overthinking*—awaken something in him that had the power to totally screw up his daughter's world was beyond him. It was time to shut that shit down for good.

"Hey, bro," Archer said, drawing Levi's attention to his arrogant smirk. "Thinking about what I said last night?"

"Yes, and you were dead *wrong*. Don't screw with people's lives anymore, got it?" Levi warned. Their siblings and friends were watching them with interest, but after that morning's group text, he decided it was best to ignore them *and* the rising temperature as Tara approached the table. Determined not to act any differently than he usually did around her, he pulled out a chair for her. "You were looking hot out there, blondie. I had to beat off a few guys who were prowling their way over to you."

"Thanks." Tara's baby blues filled with mischief. "But I didn't know you swung that way." She giggled as she slid into the chair. Bellamy, a petite brunette with her hair cut in a jagged bob, sat on her other side. Bellamy was an up-and-coming lifestyle influencer, and she also worked part time for Jules.

"What's everyone looking at?" Jules asked as she sat next to

Grant. She wore her long golden-brown hair loose, the sides pulled into a fountain on the top of her head, making her look more like a college kid than the adult business owner she was. Jules owned the Happy End gift shop in town.

Bellamy wiggled her shoulders, looking down the length of the table at the others. "They just can't believe the hottest girls in the place are sitting with them."

Everyone laughed.

"Now that everyone's here, I'd like to make a toast." Jock lifted his glass, looking at Archer. "Until last year, I didn't think I'd ever have a chance to hang out with everyone like this again, much less toast Archer's engagement."

Archer's jaw tightened, emotions swimming in his eyes.

As Jock went on about brotherhood and friendship, Levi's thoughts traveled back in time to years ago, when Jock's pregnant girlfriend, Kayla, who had also been Archer's best friend, was killed in a horrific accident. Levi had watched his brothers' relationship shatter, leading to a decade-long rift between them that had affected everyone in their family and had only recently healed. Levi had been about seventeen at the time of the accident, and he couldn't fathom loving anyone so deeply that losing them would change everything about himself and tear him away from his family. But the minute he'd held Joey, he'd understood. Those bigger-than-life feelings had hit him like a sledgehammer, and he'd vowed to do everything within his power to keep her safe and bring her up right. He was proud of himself, too. He'd always been careful about who he let into Joey's life, and he was raising a happy, confident little girl, despite her mother's continual disappointments.

Tara leaned closer, whispering, "Jock's toast is beautifully sincere. You can tell he's a writer."

Jock had written a bestseller before the accident, but he hadn't begun writing again until Daphne had come into his life. It was funny how certain people influenced others. Joey had several adults she looked up to, but Tara had become her *person.* The one she trusted with her secrets and called first when she had news to share or a problem Levi couldn't help her with. He'd bought Joey an iPad so she could keep in touch with her mother, and while he knew she and Amelia messaged from time to time, he also knew Joey and Tara messaged and video chatted several times a week. He realized he spoke with Tara often, too, and she was also the first person he called when he had news about Joey, but he wasn't about to start picking apart what that meant.

"Here's to Archer and Indi," Jock said, and cheers rang out.

Tara held up her glass, clinking it with Levi's as she cheered, "To Archer and Indi!" She turned to touch her glass to Bellamy's.

"I'm happy for you guys, but I still can't believe *Archer* is engaged, much less to my best friend," Leni said.

"We have you to thank, you know," Indi said. "I told you on New Year's Eve not to let me end up in his bed, and you were too busy to reel me back in."

Leni rolled her eyes. "As if anything could have stopped you two."

"I think someone's drugging the drinking water around here." Wells pushed his glass of water to the side with a distasteful look, and chuckles rose around the table. He was tall, dark, cocky as hell, and usually on the prowl.

"You might be onto something." Keira's eyes narrowed as she looked around the table at each of them. "I think it's Jock."

"*Hey.* My husband would never drug anyone," Daphne, a

voluptuous blond, exclaimed.

"I wouldn't be so sure about that. Think about it." Keira flipped her light brown hair over her shoulder. "First you two fall in love and move to the island. Then Grant *and* Archer fall, one right after the other? Two of the broodiest guys on the island? Something fishy is definitely going on."

Brant smacked the table. "Sign me up for ten cases of that water, because I'm looking for Mrs. Right." The blue-eyed, dimple-cheeked boatbuilder was one of Jock and Archer's closest friends. "I always thought *I'd* be the first to fall in love."

"I thought it would be Fitz," Levi said, referring to the clean-cut, sandy-haired charmer sitting across the table. Fitz ran the Silver House resort with his parents.

Fitz scoffed.

"Not me." Sutton looked at Levi. "I thought *you* would be the first to settle down."

"I *am* settled," Levi said.

Leni arched a brow. "She means with a woman."

"Joey and I have a great woman in our lives." Levi put his arm around Tara. "Tell 'em, T."

"I am pretty great," Tara said with a shrug.

"Pretty great? You're flat-out amazing," Levi said.

"I don't know about *that.*" Tara lowered her eyes, looking adorably embarrassed.

"I do," Levi said at the same time Jules and Bellamy said, "Yes, you are."

"No offense, Tara, but I don't think his sisters were talking about an aunt slash babysitter," Keira said.

"She's a hell of a lot more than Joey's babysitter," Levi said in a tone sharper than he meant to use, but he didn't want anyone thinking that was all she was to them.

Tara looked at him curiously.

"*Is* she?" Leni taunted.

"You know she is." Levi stared down his troublemaking sister. "I couldn't do all I do and raise Joey without Tara's help." He met Tara's gaze. His arm was still around her, and he pulled her closer. "I hope you know how much Joey and I appreciate everything you do for us."

"Of course I do," she said sweetly. "Leni just likes to get you riled up."

"I'm glad you realize my sister is an A-class pest."

Leni flashed a cheesy grin.

"All I know is, if you're going to settle down, it's got to be with the right woman." Grant took Jules's hand and said, "Nobody has ever rocked my world the way my Pixie does." Grant had lost his left leg from the knee down during a covert mission for the military and had returned to the island a changed, disgruntled man with a short fuse. Somehow Jules, a cancer survivor who spread happiness like confetti, had pulled him from the dredges of despair and showed him how beautiful life could be.

Jules was looking at Grant like he was holding a litter of puppies. "Aw, babe, you rock my world, too." She leaned in and kissed him.

"See? It's all about connection," Indi added.

"In *and* out of the bedroom." Archer winked at Indi and smirked at Levi, eyeing his arm around Tara.

Tara's eyes widened. "We're not..."

Fucking Archer. "And you thought Leni was the only troublemaker." He lowered his arm from around her.

"Being friends *is* important," Daphne said. "You've got to be able to talk and laugh as much as you...*you know.*"

"*I* sure as hell know." Jock kissed her temple, and Daphne blushed.

"All three of you newly matched couples make love look pretty darn good," Sutton said.

Levi was thinking the same thing. Maybe seeing his siblings happy and in love was making him see Tara in a new light, too.

"They make it look sickeningly good, but I'll still stick to my cupcakes." Keira owned the Sweet Barista, a coffee shop and bakery.

"I'm with my sister on this one," Fitz said. "Life's short. Why not enjoy as much frosting as you can before closing the bakery?"

"Hear, hear." Wells lifted his glass and took a drink.

Levi had been of a similar mindset before he'd found out Amelia was pregnant, but that news had changed everything. Suddenly the warnings his father had given him about sex having lifelong ramifications had become his reality, and he'd begun measuring his every move against what he wanted his child to learn from him. He couldn't be sleeping around if he wanted Joey to look up to him the way he looked up to his father.

"Hey, Levi, speaking of *frosting*," Fitz said. "Leni claims you're not hooking up with any of the single Venting Vixens. What's up with that?"

"You could at least hook *us* up with some of them," Wells encouraged.

"They're his *friends*, Wells, not his enemies," Leni chimed in. She and Wells had dated in high school, and he had a permanent strike against him for cheating on her.

Keira and Sutton chuckled.

"Seriously, Levi. I don't know how you do it, man. I love

Jules, but I would not willingly put myself in the middle of a hen party." Grant stroked his beard, his shaggy hair brushing the collar of his Henley.

"I could *totally* hang with the ladies," Brant boasted. "I love to talk, and I love women. It's a match made in heaven. All I need is a kid."

"You could borrow Hadley," Wells suggested.

"No, he cannot," Jock said.

"I know you're joking, but don't mess with single moms," Levi said. "They've got enough on their plates." A few of the Venting Vixens had gotten divorced. Parenthood was not for the faint of heart. He didn't need to be married to know that it could bring couples closer together, amplify their differences, or overwhelm an already-precarious marriage.

"As a former single mom, it's nice to hear a guy sticking up for single mothers," Daphne said.

"I'm just telling it like it is. Those women saved my ass so many times. I value their friendships." He glanced at Tara, who had also saved his ass on numerous occasions when it came to Joey.

"I get it now, biker boy. You fought similar battles. It's like a brotherhood but with women." Grant took a swig of his drink.

"Exactly," Levi said.

"Speaking of parenting." Keira looked across the table at Jules, Bellamy, and Tara. "We saw you chatting up a certain delicious single daddy."

Levi rolled his shoulders back and puffed out his chest. "I've been called a lot of things, but I think I like *delicious* the best."

The guys chuckled.

"It's a good thing you're good-looking, because that big ego takes you down a notch," Tara teased.

"*Damn*," Wells said.

"That's okay." Levi stretched his arm across the back of her chair again, grinning arrogantly. "I've got something even bigger that keeps me on top."

Tara sipped her drink, eyeing him playfully. "I see you took your parents' advice to heart when they told you to dream big."

Everyone cracked up, including Levi.

"For the record, Levi," Keira said, "you are a hot single dad, but you're also like a brother to most of us, so can we please get back to *Ryan*, the hottest cop and pop around?"

Levi ground his back teeth together as jealousy clawed at him again.

"Ryan *is* hot," Bellamy agreed. "And he was totally checking out Tara."

Fucking hell.

"He was *not*," Tara snapped. "He was asking about the pictures I took of him at the carwash."

"*Shirtless* pictures of him all wet and lickable," Bellamy added with a waggle of her brows.

"Would you *stop*?" Tara said.

"What? He *was*." Bellamy's gaze moved around the table. "And that's not all. Two guys asked Tara out at the carwash. *Two!*"

What the hell kind of torture was this? If Levi didn't know better, he'd think Archer had put Bellamy up to saying that just to mess with him. But Tara was gorgeous. Of course guys pursued her. He was just about to ask who had asked her out when Tara, Jules, and Bellamy squealed and popped to their feet, shouting, "'*Friends!*'" in unison as the song by Marshmello and Anne-Marie rang out. Levi knew it well. It was one of Tara and Joey's favorites.

"Dance off!" Jules hollered, pulling Grant up beside her, causing an uproar of commotion as Daphne and Indi tugged Jock and Archer toward the dance floor, and Bellamy ran around the table yelling, "Who's *not* my brother?"

Bellamy grabbed Brant. "You're mine!" She yanked him to his feet, dragging him out to dance.

As Keira grabbed Leni and joined Sutton in goading Fitz and Wells into dancing, Tara beamed wordlessly at Levi and held out her hand. She was so cute, knowing she didn't have to ask.

He took her hand and rose to his feet. "All right, blondie. Let's show 'em how it's done."

They'd danced together so many times, he knew her moves by heart, and they fell easily into sync on the crowded dance floor. Tara's hips swayed, her hands snaking over her head, graceful and sexy. Levi grabbed her by the hips, drawing her closer. Their bodies swayed and rocked as they had a hundred times before. Only this time, he was acutely aware of her softness brushing against his thighs and chest.

Jules danced over to them, singing, "Get that friend shit *out* of your head," and danced back to Grant. She considered herself a music aficionado, but she always got the lyrics wrong.

Tara and Levi shook their heads and fell right back into sync. Tara whisper-sang the lyrics with a taunting look in her eyes, singing about making it obvious that they were only friends. She danced even *more* seductively, turning in a slow circle, one arm above her head, her shoulders and hips begging to be touched. She turned toward him again, smirking. *You little siren.* He mouthed the lyrics about her having no shame for looking at him like that. She continued turning up the heat with her sinful dance moves, which he matched beat for beat. They'd always danced like that, knowing it was safe and done only in fun.

When the song ended, they stayed on the dance floor, dancing to the next song and the next, eyes trained on each other, bodies grazing, hands brushing. This felt different, personal, *intimate*. They danced so long and close, everything around them faded away, until Tara was the only thing he saw, her eyes at half-mast, glossy blond curls swaying over her breasts as she lost herself in the music. He itched to feel that hair tangled in his fist, to feel her naked body moving against him.

He needed to get back to that safe zone. To stop seeing her as a sensual woman and close the door Archer had opened, but no part of him wanted to.

The song "Better" by Khalid came on, and Tara wound her arms around his neck with an easy smile. She rested her cheek on his chest, her breasts pressing against him, sending heat slithering south. She felt so good, he held her tighter, wondering how he'd danced with her so many times without being lured in by her femininity. How long had it been since he'd felt the magnetic pull, the bone-deep ache of *wanting* a woman, not just needing relief? He was playing a dangerous game he couldn't afford to lose. She tipped her face up, her sweet, trusting eyes gazing at him, and he didn't see Joey's aunt or Amelia's sister. He saw a beautiful, sensual woman, and he had the overwhelming urge to lower his lips to hers and *taste* her sensuality, feel her energy from the inside out. *Fuuck*. While she was dancing like they'd always done, he was slowly losing his mind, having trouble deciphering reality from fantasy. The only thing he knew for sure was that she felt incredible, and he wished the song would never end.

Three

TARA HAD A love-hate relationship with mornings. She loved the possibilities new days held, but she hated waking from dreams of Levi and being forced to accept the reality of their platonic relationship and vow once again to honor her resolution to stop fantasizing about him. She showered, dried her hair, and put on a little makeup, and as she pulled on tan skinny jeans and a white sweater, thoughts of last night crept in and she reveled in every word, every touch, that heated look in his eyes…

She froze like a deer caught in headlights. *What am I doing? No. No. No. I am not going there.* Her resolution wasn't a fad diet or exercise routine that could be tossed away without care. This was her *life*, and she deserved to have a full, beautiful one and find the kind of all-consuming love that Jules and Grant had.

She stuffed a jacket into her tote bag and swore that after Levi and Joey came over to say goodbye to her parents this morning, she would make a valiant effort *not* to think about him again until next weekend, when he came back to look at houses with her. She shoved her feet into a pair of canvas sneakers and took a few deep breaths. Her gaze trailed over the pictures of family and friends around her room, each one in a colorful, hand-chosen frame, and lingered on a picture of Levi and Joey, taken when Joey was only six days old. She was such a tiny baby. Tara had gone to see them after school and had found Levi fast asleep on a blanket on his parents' living room floor. He was lying on his side with his head on a throw pillow from the couch, and Joey was sleeping in the crook of his arm, a half-empty bottle of formula lying beneath his hand. Joey's cheek rested on his arm. Her knees were bent, her tiny feet tucked against his side. Levi's other hand cupped her bottom. His cheeks were scruffy, his thick brown hair stuck out all over, and his shoulder had dried spittle on it, but he had a small smile on his lips.

She had no idea how Amelia could have given birth to such a precious little girl on a Tuesday and gone back to school the following week, leaving behind her infant and an incredible man who vowed to do whatever it took to raise their baby right. It still infuriated Tara that Amelia hadn't even reached out to see how Joey was until weeks later.

But then again, she'd never understood anything Amelia had done.

She huffed out a breath and took a quick scrutinizing look at herself in the mirror. Most mornings, she saw the smart, strong woman she'd become looking back at her. But some days she still saw that chubby, insecure girl who had taken comfort in food and was plagued by secretive snide comments from Amelia, who had always looked like one of their mother's perfect projects. When those mornings came, Tara spent extra time looking at the pictures of Jules and Bellamy tucked into the edges of her mirror frame. They'd always been there to pick her up when Amelia knocked her down, at least the instances she'd let them know about. She thought of all the times Levi had found her in the pantry at parties and had sat with her, sharing snacks and talking until she'd felt safe enough to come out. When she finally had, he'd stayed by her side, and he hadn't ever made her feel awkward about hiding in the first place. She'd never confided in him about her sister's comments the way she had with Jules and Bellamy. It was too embarrassing to admit to him that her own sister had found her so pathetic.

Thankfully, after Amelia went away to school, through years of working on her confidence and overall emotional and physical health, she'd developed a healthier relationship with food and learned to be kind to herself, making those more difficult mornings few and far between.

She took one last look around her bedroom to ensure she hadn't left anything out of place, her mother's lessons ingrained in her mind. *Whether we're out in public or home, we must always look our best and be ready for guests.* Her mother made more out of their father's mayoral status than it warranted. He was voted into office because he was a caring, smart businessman and always treated others kindly, not because of the way he dressed or presented his home. Her father had grown up on the island and enjoyed small-town life so much, he often shared fond memories of his youth, and he knew material things didn't matter to the people there. However, her mother had grown up with wealthy parents in a high-class neighborhood in Connecticut. She found reminiscing to be impractical and preferred to live in the present. *Why look back when you can only succeed by moving forward?*

Unfortunately, making the house perfect for guests they rarely had made it feel less like a home. As soon as Robert had moved out and Amelia and Carey had begun building lives off the island, her mother had redecorated their rooms in pristine white, tans, and blues, like the rest of the house. Her mother's need for perfection was almost as much of a bane of Tara's existence as Amelia's selfishness, but it gave her mother purpose, and she supposed everyone needed something of their own.

Too bad Amelia's *thing* was traveling rather than mothering.

Tara's saving grace was that her grandmother had moved in with them, sharing the second floor with her since her grandfather passed away a few years ago, while her parents' master suite was on the first floor. Tara shut her bedroom door and headed down the hall to Carey's old room, which she used as an office.

"Hey, *roomie*," her grandmother called out as Tara walked by her bedroom.

She peeked in and found her father's mother, Blanche Osten, standing by her dresser wearing white capris, a pink-and-tan striped shirt, and tan flats. She had many pairs of fashionable glasses, and today she sported round pink frames. Her grandmother was a sprite of a woman, at just over five feet tall and probably all of a hundred pounds soaking wet, with short white hair and a flair for rebellion. Tara *adored* her.

The first thing her grandmother had done when she'd moved in was rearrange and redecorate Robert's old bedroom. She replaced the drab decor with colorful blankets and curtains and vibrant paintings. She also belonged to the island's Bra Brigade, a group of older women who had been sunbathing in their bras together since they were teenagers and who frequented Pythons, a male strip club on Cape Cod, under the guise of playing harmless games of bingo. The group was started by

Levi's grandmother, Lenore. They'd recruited many of their daughters, granddaughters, and daughters-in-law for their sunbathing activities over the years. Tara's mother was *not* one of them, although Tara had joined in a few times at the insistence of Jules and Bellamy.

"What's up, Gram?"

She motioned for Tara to come into the room. "Would you mind if I borrowed your laptop, sweetie?"

Tara crossed her arms, setting a serious stare on her sassy grandmother. "The last time I lent it to you, it got a virus from sites I'd rather not mention."

"Yes, but you quickly rectified that. Don't be a fuddy-duddy. I'd just like to support my new friend in his business endeavors."

"What friend is that?"

"His name is Sylvester Stabone."

"Sylvester Sta*bone*?" Tara sighed. "Grandma, how old is this guy, and what does he do for a living?"

"I think he's probably in his late twenties. He'd be a good catch, sweetie. He's very talented. Sometimes he's a fireman, or a policeman, or a construction worker. I think he could be *anything* you want."

"Did you and the other Bra Brigaders meet him last weekend? Does he work at Pythons?"

"You say that like it's a bad thing. He works very hard to earn a living, and he's quite well rounded."

"And what type of business do you want to support? His OnlyFans page?"

She straightened her spine, waggling her finger at Tara. "Don't try to shame me for enjoying the human body. It's only natural. I might be old, sweetie, but I'm not dead."

"*Gram*, you really need to find a better way to spend your time and money."

Her grandmother waved her hand dismissively. "You sound like your mother. Now, *that's* a woman whose life could use a little spicing up. Speaking of spicing up lives." Her eyes widened with excitement, and she lowered her voice conspiratorially. "Did you get to dance with your man last night?"

Practically everyone on the island had known she'd crushed on Levi when she was younger, but as soon as she'd realized how wrong it was to be lusting over the father of her sister's child, she'd tried to keep her feelings under wraps. She'd never even admitted them to Jules and Bellamy, her strongholds, her safe havens. The girls who had always, and would forever, have her back. Not sharing the truth with them made it harder to hold it in. But her grandmother had never bought into Tara having outgrown her crush, and Tara had finally confided in her.

"He's not *my* man."

"Honey, that's only because you're not working your assets. If I had all that you have going for you, I'd be on his front porch wearing nothing but a trench coat and a come-hither smile."

"*Ohmygosh*. Grandma!" She laughed. "I told you, I made a res—"

"Resolution, I *know*," her grandmother said flatly, and then pointed her finger at her. "But you know how I feel about that. Levi Steele should top your to-do list, not be sworn off like a bad habit."

"*Ugh*. Gram. I'm going downstairs for breakfast. Are you coming?"

"No. I'm going to be busy helping Sylvester earn a living.

Right?" she asked hopefully.

"Fine, but if you get caught, you'd better tell Mom you stole my laptop, and stay *off* those other sites."

Her grandmother did a joyful shimmy. "That's my girl."

"Levi and Joey are coming to say goodbye before they go back to Harborside."

"In that case, when I'm done with my economic assistance, I'll come down and say goodbye. But it might be a while." Her grandmother lowered her voice. "And, honey, if Levi doesn't appreciate what's right in front of his eyes, you just let your Grammy know, and I'll hook you up with Sylvester."

"*Gram*," Tara warned.

"Just sayin'." Her grandmother hurried out of the bedroom, heading for Tara's room.

Tara shook her head and went into her office. She put her planner in her tote and grabbed her photography bag. As she headed downstairs, she heard her mother talking in the kitchen and drew in a deep breath, praying for patience.

The kitchen was stark white with light bamboo floors, varying shades of tan and blue accents, and bouquets of fresh flowers her mother picked up in town every week decorating the counters. Tara loved the flowers, even if her mother hadn't gotten them so her family could appreciate their beauty, but rather just for guests who rarely appeared. The flowers reminded Tara of when she was young and she and her mother would go to the nursery together at the start of each season to pick out flowers and plants for the gardener. She couldn't pinpoint exactly when those trips had been overcome with nitpicking rather than fun, but eventually that had sucked the joy right out of them.

Her father was reading on his iPad at the table, dressed in a white button-down and slacks. Mayor Patrick Osten was in his late fifties, with short brown hair, a little extra weight around the middle, and a kind word always at the ready. In the center of the table was a platter of scrambled eggs with goat cheese, sliced fruit garnished with sprigs of mint, and wheat toast. *We must always be ready for guests.* Her mother, Marsha, stood at the island in navy slacks, an off-white blouse, and heels, talking on the phone and jotting notes on a pad. Her side-parted shoulder-length blond hair was tucked behind her ears. Tara shared her mother's high cheekbones and fair skin and hair, but she had her father's blue eyes and warm heart.

Her father looked up from his iPad. "There's my beautiful jelly bean." He'd called her that since she was a little girl, and it never failed to bring a little extra sunshine into the moment.

"Morning, Dad. Who is Mom talking to?" She put her photography bag and tote on the counter and poured herself a glass of orange juice.

"Goldie Gallow, over in Seaport. They're putting together a charity drive. Your mother asked me to help out, and I was thinking it would be a great time to get some community photos of your dear old dad doing the mayoral thing."

"Sure. When is it?"

"The Sunday you return from watching Joey."

"Okay. Just let me know the details when you have them." Her father was two years into his third consecutive four-year term as mayor of Silver Island, and Tara had been photographing him for the newspaper since she was eighteen.

"Great. Sit with me." He patted the chair beside him and sipped his coffee as she sat down. "Did you kids have a good time last night?"

Her father had always taken an interest in her personal life, and he'd encouraged her to strike out on her own professionally. He'd helped her set up her business and understand all the aspects that went into it, from marketing and accounting to negotiating and pricing her services appropriately. She'd balked at the high prices he'd suggested but had quickly realized that her skills warranted higher rates than less-skilled photographers.

She'd been blessed with a lot of support from her family and the community. Her mother had helped her get her first job with the newspaper, and she had always helped spread the word about Tara's services among her friends and volunteer groups. Her brothers had cheered her on, just like Levi always had. Levi had started his own company just a few years earlier, and he'd helped her navigate some of her biggest frustrations. His parents and Bellamy's parents were prominent local business owners, and they'd also stood behind her, offering sage advice and hiring her for many projects over the years, and there was no shortage of rallying friends supplying marketing and social media advice.

"Yes. We always have fun, and it's good to see Archer and Indi so happy." Archer had sported a permanent scowl for so many years, she'd wondered if he'd ever smile again.

"It sure is," her father said thoughtfully. "Their family has been to hell and back. It's tough when your kids don't get along."

"I know it is," she said apologetically.

Tara's relationship with Amelia had always been a bone of contention between Tara and her parents. Amelia's pregnancy had sent their family into turmoil, and they'd never quite recovered. When Amelia told their parents she was pregnant, their mother had been horrified that *her* daughter, the *mayor's* daughter, could do such a thing, and she'd villainized Levi. As if it didn't take two to tango. Their father had worried more about Amelia's insistence over giving the baby up. He'd been concerned she might change her mind later in life. Her selfish sister had quickly nixed that worry. But her father *had* kept a cool distance from Levi for a while. Tara didn't know how Levi had put up with it. But Levi's love for Joey, his constant efforts to include her family in Joey's life despite the way her parents had treated him, and his drive to be the best father he could be and not cut Amelia out of Joey's life had won her father over, while her mother remained a bit standoffish toward him.

"What's on your agenda today?" her father asked, cheerily changing the subject as he did so well. Although he'd been cold toward Levi at first, in general he wasn't one to linger in hard spots.

"A baby photo shoot, a family session, a new client, and then I'm going to scope out some new locations for a shoot I'm doing Thursday evening with Bellamy. It should be a great day." Bellamy was applying for a spot on *The Bachelor*, but they were keeping it on the down low because Bellamy's family would not approve. They hadn't even told Jules since she was engaged to Grant. Tara hated keeping it from her, but Bellamy didn't want to put Jules in a position to have to lie to her fiancé.

"Did I hear you say you were seeing a new client today?" her mother asked as she came around the counter after ending her call. She put her hand on Tara's shoulder, giving it a gentle squeeze as she sat down.

That was her mother's version of a hug, and it always left Tara yearning for more.

"Yes, in Chaffee." The island had several boroughs. Ritzy Silver Haven, where they lived, artistic Chaffee, with cobblestone streets and colorful shops, and two old-school New England fishing towns, Rock Harbor and Seaport. Tara loved the eclectic mix of towns on the island, and since there was only one high school serving the island, it made for close-knit communities.

Her mother ran an assessing eye over her. "Honey, maybe you should put on something a little nicer."

Tara tried not to roll her eyes. "People come to me for my photography skills, Mom, not my outfits." They'd had that annoying conversation for years. When Tara had first started her business, she'd tried to dress a little nicer when meeting clients, but as her days had gotten busier, it was more important to be comfortable during photo shoots than to try to impress people with dressy clothes.

Her father winked, as if to say, *Way to keep your cool, sweetheart.*

"Yes, well, it never hurts to outshine the competition."

"If my work wasn't better than other photographers', they wouldn't have contacted me in the first place." Tara's patience was wearing thin.

"Tara outshines others no matter what she wears," her father said.

"Of course she does. I was just trying to give her an edge. Tara, honey, have some eggs and fruit," her mother suggested as she sipped her coffee.

Tara held up her glass. "I've got orange juice."

"You know that won't fill you up, and then you'll just snack on the run, which isn't good for you."

"People my age live on caffeine. I think I'm fine."

The kitchen door opened, and Robert walked in, tall and athletic in a green T-shirt and jeans. He was carrying Joey, smothering Tara's frustration with happiness, and holding a pastry box from the Sweet Barista.

"Look who I found out front." Robert set the pastry box on the counter. He lived in Rock Harbor, and he adored Joey and Levi.

Levi stepped inside behind him, looking like sex on badass legs in his black leather vest, which had Dark Knights' patches on the back, a T-shirt, worn jeans, and black biker boots, bringing a conflicting mix of flutters and trepidation. Had he felt the connection she had last night, or was it all in her head? His dark eyes found her, and a sexy grin spread across his face, sending those flutters into overdrive.

I will not make this into something it's not, she vowed.

"There's my *Jojo Bean*," her father exclaimed as they all got up to greet them. Joey grinned at the nickname he'd called her since she was a toddler.

"Uncle Robert brought muffins and pastries!" Joey wriggled out of Robert's arms in her black leather jacket that had a DARK KNIGHTS' DAUGHTER patch on the back, which Levi called his hands-off warning. She ran straight to Tara, her biker boots—miniature versions of her daddy's—clomping on the pristine floors.

Tara gathered her into a hug. "Are you going on a motorcycle ride with Daddy today when you get back to Harborside?" She glanced at Levi as her father embraced him, and her mother gave him an awkward hug.

"*Nope*. I have a playdate." Joey ran to her grandparents. "Grandpa! Grandma! I learned a new skateboard trick…"

As Joey went on about the trick, Levi made his way over to Tara. "She's hanging out with some of the other club members' wives and kids while I go riding with the guys."

Tara glanced at her mother and lowered her voice. "I'd give anything to be on the back of your bike right now instead of here."

"I can't do anything about that now, but I'd like to make that happen when you come down for spring break."

He held her gaze, and the air hummed with electric energy between them, as if he were trying to relay a deeper message. *Nothing like a little leftover wishful thinking to drive a girl crazy.* Robert walked over, bringing her mind firmly back to reality. "I'd love that," she said. "But who will watch Joey?"

"She's already had three invitations for playdates over her break. We'll find the time."

"Hey, Levi. I'm a little offended," Robert teased. "You know how I love the wind on my face. Where's my invitation to be your back warmer?"

"When you get to be as cute as your sister, I'll give you a ride," Levi teased.

Robert chuckled. "That doesn't give me much hope, does it?"

Levi had called her *cute* many times. But cute was for little girls, which was probably how he still saw her. When she'd made her New Year's resolution, she'd listed all the things he'd said and done that she'd tried to twist into something more, and that was one of them. She'd clung to it, hoping it would help ease her out of the crazy-for-Levi zone. It had helped, and this was a good reminder.

"You should come to my tournament," Joey exclaimed to her grandparents. "I'm the best skateboarder in my age group. I'm going to win a trophy!"

"I bet you are, sweetheart. We'll try to make it," Tara's father said encouragingly.

"Skateboarding?" Her mother glanced disapprovingly at Levi and returned a strained smile to Joey. "Wouldn't you like to try dance or maybe swimming?"

"I swim all summer, and I dance all the time in our living room with Daddy and Tara," Joey said. "They're great dancers."

Levi slung an arm around Tara, pulling her tight against his side. "Tara makes us look good."

As Tara gobbled up that praise, she noticed another of her mother's disapproving expressions. She ducked out from under Levi's arm and went to check out the pastries Robert had brought.

Joey climbed onto a chair at the table. "Grandpa, if I eat eggs, can I have a pastry?"

Smart girl asking Grandpa instead of Grandma.

"Hey, Tara," Robert called over as he poured himself a cup of coffee. "Remember when I caught you dancing and singing into your hairbrush?"

Tara pretended to be studying the pastries. "No. Not really. *Nope*. I don't remember that."

Robert laughed.

Levi went to her. "This, I have to hear."

"It was nothing. I was fourteen." *And brokenhearted.*

"Fourteen and fantastic." Robert lowered his voice so their parents wouldn't hear him. "I came home for a weekend, and I thought everyone was gone, but the Taylor Swift song 'You Belong with Me' was blaring from upstairs. I went up and found *this one* dancing on her bed, holding a hairbrush like a microphone, and belting out the lyrics."

Levi grinned, and Tara pointed at him. "Don't say a word." She leaned against the counter, giving Robert a narrow-eyed look. "Thanks a lot."

"You know I love you, and you gave Taylor Swift a run for her money. I was seriously impressed." Robert grabbed the box of pastries and headed over to the table, where Joey was deep in conversation with their parents.

A sexy grin played on Levi's lips. "Why are you embarrassed to be a Swifty?"

Because I was singing about you. "I'm not."

"Good, because I'm glad you're a Swifty who likes to sing and dance. When Joey went from her princess stage to playing sports and skateboarding and those girls at school made fun of her, you really came through with your 'Shake It Off' lesson. I'd tried everything to make her feel better, and I was at a loss."

"I remember the video call. You were at your wit's end." He'd been devastated because Joey was so upset, and she'd had to talk them *both* off the ledge. Levi had wanted to storm over to the girls' houses and have it out with their parents. But Tara knew how skewed parents' views of their children could be and that confronting them could make things worse for Joey. As for Joey, Tara had given her the help she hadn't been able to give her younger self. She'd explained that some people might try to bring her down because they were jealous or intimidated. She'd been honest and had said there were also people who were just plain mean but that it was up to Joey how she let their words affect her and how she treated the people who hurt her. They'd talked for a long time about how what was said had made Joey feel and how to handle those girls. When Joey had stopped crying and was feeling better, Tara shared her secret mood booster. She and Joey had grabbed their hairbrushes, cranked the Taylor Swift song "Shake It Off," and sang and danced until they both collapsed into a giggling fit, the sight of which had soothed Levi's tension, too. Tara had gone to Harborside the next day and had been there when Joey had gotten home from school, because she'd worried about both Joey and Levi, and she'd stayed for the weekend, just to be sure they were okay.

"You knew exactly what to do. You gave her something she could relate to that empowered her, and I couldn't be more grateful," Levi said, drawing her back to the moment.

I've had a lot of practice getting over bad feelings.

"Now it's her go-to mood lifter. When she's mad at me, like if I tell her she can't do something, she cranks up that song and sings it in pure defiance."

Tara winced. That was easy to imagine. Joey had a fiery spirit. *"Sorry…?"*

"Don't be. I want her to speak up. She's lucky to have you, T." Levi's voice was low, his tone serious. "We both are."

He was looking at her the way he had earlier, as if his words held a deeper meaning. She averted her eyes, trying to calm those hopeful butterflies swarming inside her, and watched Joey chatting animatedly with her parents and Robert. "I'd do anything for her." She looked at Levi. "She's easy to love. You raised an amazing little girl who's comfortable in her own skin and wins *everyone* over."

His expression sobered. "Not quite everyone."

"Don't get me started on my sister," she grumbled.

"I was thinking of those mean girls at school, but your sister fits, too. I know she loves Joey, but not like we do."

The way he said *we* made her body tingle with the same intense energy she'd felt last night, like he was pulling her closer, only he wasn't touching her. She opened her mouth to say she should go before she started spinning dangerous fairy tales in her head, but he cut her off.

"That was fun last night, wasn't it?"

His tone was low, as if his words weren't meant to be heard by others, and *oh*, what that did to her. "Yeah. I had a great time."

"I always forget just how good a dancer you are until we're out on a dance floor. It's a lot different from when we dance with Joey in the living room."

It always is.

"You pulled out all your best moves."

Being in your arms brings out the best in me. "It must have been the wine or something."

"Or *something*," he said, low and sexy.

She was definitely losing it, because it sure sounded like he was flirting with her, and her stupid heart raced at what she swore was a flicker of heat in his eyes, as if he'd meant it exactly the way she *wanted* to take it. But that couldn't be right. "I, um. I'd better go. I have to meet a client this morning." She went to get her bags off the counter before she could misconstrue anything else. *I will not break my resolution* played like a mantra in her head.

"Are you leaving, jelly bean?" her father asked as she shouldered her bags.

"Yeah." *Before I start weaving tales of me and Levi k-i-s-s-i-n-g in a tree.* "I need to get to my studio." She put a hand on Joey's back. "Can I get a hug goodbye, cutie patootie?"

Much to her grandmother's dismay, Joey stood on her chair and hugged Tara. "I'm gonna miss you."

It never got easier to say goodbye to her or Levi. "I'll miss you, too, but we'll text, okay?"

Joey's beautiful freckled face brightened as she nodded.

"Make sure your daddy behaves." She stole a teasing glance at Levi, but his eyes were still locked on her, like heat lamps burning up the space between them. Maybe Wells wasn't so far off about someone drugging the water. Or maybe they'd slipped a hallucinogenic in the orange juice.

Joey giggled. "I will."

As Joey lowered herself to her chair, Robert stood up and pulled Tara into a tight embrace. "Good to see you, sis. You look gorgeous, as always."

He'd always been so good to her, sometimes she wondered why his and Carey's praise hadn't outweighed Amelia's cutting comments. "Thanks. You're not looking too shabby, either." She eyed the pastries and reached for an éclair.

"Honey, wouldn't you rather take some fruit?" her mother asked.

"Nope." Tara took a big bite of her éclair and headed for the door.

"I'll walk you out." Levi fell into step with her and whispered, "Shall we escape into the pantry?"

She laughed as they stepped outside, thankful for the humor. "I'll never hide again, but I'd like to put my mother in the pantry." She took another bite of her éclair.

"Are you going to share that or what?"

"I don't know," she teased, stopping beside her car. "It's awfully good. What do I get in return?"

His eyes narrowed, and he stepped closer, rasping, "You get to watch."

He wrapped his fingers around her wrist, holding her gaze as he licked the cream from the center of the éclair. Her pulse skyrocketed. His tongue slid over her fingertips, and she held her breath, mesmerized as it took a slow, deep dip into the cream. His eyes turned dark as night, and he wrapped his lips around the éclair and took a bite, making a raw, guttural, excruciatingly sexy sound. *Holy mother of hotness.* She stumbled backward, dizzy with desire, but his arm swept around her before she hit the car, hauling her against him. The air rushed from her lungs. They were both breathing hard, hearts hammering, lips a whisper apart. His brows knitted, a battle of white-hot lust and restraint staring back at her. A voice in her head chanted, *Kiss him. Just do it. Kiss him.* As if he'd heard her thoughts, the edges of his lips quirked, and he tightened his hold on her just as the kitchen door swung open, and Joey ran out, startling them apart.

Tara grabbed her car to keep from falling over, turning her back to her family as they filed out of the house, and she tried to make sense of what had just happened.

"Dad! I'm gonna get my skateboard and show Grandpa some of my tricks!" Joey ran to Levi's Durango.

"Great." Levi stepped behind Tara and said, for her ears only, "Guess I still got it, and I didn't even have to take my shirt off."

He opened her car door for her, flashed a coy grin, and sauntered away without a backward glance.

She stuffed the rest of the éclair into her mouth to keep from snapping at the frustrating hunk of a man and climbed into her car. She fumed at herself as she drove away, trying desperately to clear the lust from her brain. But Lord help her. If he could steal her ability to think when he was playing some stupid game, what would it be like if he'd really meant it?

Four

DAYS PASSED IN a whirlwind of photo sessions and editing, new client appointments, and too many dirty daydreams about Levi. Tara's thoughts swung like a pendulum between believing she'd felt a lot more than their usual friendly chemistry and the misinterpreted éclair debacle. Her head felt like it might explode. Last night she'd wanted to video chat with Joey instead of texting, but she knew if she did, she'd see Levi, and she was still trying to climb back onto the *resolution train*. The darn thing was speeding down the track, leaving her to sprint after it. Forcing herself to stick to texting felt like a small victory. One small step toward weaning herself off Levi between visits.

Go, me!

It was Thursday evening, and she was on her way to pick up Bellamy at the Happy End gift shop for her photo shoot. She drove down Main Street, trying to focus on the town she loved instead of the mayhem in her head. In a couple of weeks, the shops would stay open later, the flower boxes would be overflowing with beautiful blooms, and the sidewalks would be bustling with tourists. Tara loved everything about Silver Island, from her friends and their close-knit families to the community events and the way the air held the scents of the sea no matter where she was. She'd never gotten the travel bug, like Amelia. Her sister had wanted to see the world for as long as Tara could remember, and she was glad Amelia had left the island, since she didn't want to be a mom to Joey. Tara didn't think she could stomach looking at her every day. Although as much as she disliked Amelia, some part of her still held out hope that her big sister might one day come to her senses for Joey's sake and realize there was more to life than money, parties, and fame.

She parked in front of Jules's shop and climbed out of her car, taking in the red-framed picture windows and two iron giraffes flanking the entrance, with their pastel sunglasses and Silver Island baseball caps. Jules decorated them differently every day.

Tara peered through the glass doors at vibrant displays of beachy signs and spring decor and spotted Jules and Bellamy by the register. The tension in her neck and shoulders eased at the sight of them. She knocked on the window, and Jules waved, hurrying over in a black miniskirt and peach sweater, her golden-brown hair spilling over her shoulders.

She unlocked the door and tugged Tara inside, locking the door behind her. "You're just in time. We're taste testing the taffy we got in from a new distributor."

"*Yay*. I need something yummy. It's been a heck of a week, and I have so much on my mind, I can't think straight."

"Is what's on your mind roughly six two with tattoos down one arm and a great ass?" Bellamy asked, looking stylish in white linen slacks and a pale blue silk tank top as she hoisted herself up to sit on the counter beside the open box of taffy.

"*No*," Tara lied.

"Bellamy, she's *not* into Levi." Jules handed Tara a piece of taffy. "How many times do I have to tell you that?"

"Oh, come on. You saw them dancing together last weekend. I thought the whole place was going to go up in flames." Bellamy popped a piece of taffy into her mouth with a smug expression.

"That was just *friend* dancing," Jules insisted. "Tara wouldn't go for a guy like Levi. He's too good-looking and nice."

Tara rolled her eyes.

"You're right. That ass is too much for Tara." Bellamy giggled.

"Okay, *stop*." Tara's glowered at her besties. "You don't have to do that thing you did back in seventh grade, when you made me dance to 'Thriller' in the talent show."

"What thing?" Bellamy asked.

"I have no idea what you're talking about." Jules tried to stifle a smile.

"Yes, you do. The whole good-friend, bad-friend thing." She mimicked their voices. "*Don't ask Tara to dance with us. She hates dancing in front of people. No, she doesn't. She loves it. We can't do it without her. She's the best. Sure we can. We'll win the talent show.*" She gave them a deadpan look. "Ring a bell?"

"No," they said with a giggle.

Tara groaned. "You guys are so frustrating."

"It's working," Bellamy whispered loudly.

"I know. We're awesome at this," Jules whispered back.

"We should have tried it years ago," Bellamy said.

"You're both pains." Tara didn't know why after all these years of guarding her secret, she was seriously considering giving it up, but maybe the reason she couldn't get over Levi was *because* she'd kept her feelings a secret. Everyone knew secrets made everything more tempting.

"I told you she wasn't into him," Jules said.

"Maybe *I'll* go after Levi." Bellamy looked over the taffy selection as if she hadn't just annoyed the hell out of Tara.

"*Bellamy,*" Tara warned.

"What? You don't want him, and it's not like there are that many men to choose from around here."

"*Ugh. Fine.* I can't believe I'm telling you this, but..." She took a deep breath and blurted out, "I'm still into Levi. I lied when I said I was over him. Okay? Are you happy now?"

They both squealed.

"I knew it!" Jules bounced on her toes. "Why didn't you tell us?"

"Do you have any idea how embarrassing it is to admit that I'm into your brother?"

"Why? Jules is banging *my* brother, and she's not embarrassed by it," Bellamy said.

"Not even a little, and we do really dirty stuff." Jules giggled. "Tell us *everything*!"

"There's nothing to tell. You know I crushed on him when I was younger, and those feelings never went away. They just kept getting bigger, and the last couple of years, they've gotten *too* big."

"Because you're not a kid anymore. You're an adult with womanly needs," Bellamy said. "And Levi is *all* man."

"Do you get tingles all over when you're near him, like I do with Grant?" Jules asked.

"I get way more than tingles. I get full-on tremors."

Bellamy and Jules squealed again.

"Would you stop?" Tara pleaded. "This is hard to admit, and it's *not* a good thing."

"Sorry," they both said, and Jules whispered, "She's wrong. It's awesome."

Tara stared at her, unamused, and they schooled their expressions.

"I wish it was awesome, but trust me, it's not. I love my friendship with Levi, and I'm really worried that I'm going to screw it up and make things awkward. I made a resolution to move on from my feelings for him, but lately they're *really* hard to ignore." She paced as the confessions tumbled out. "When we were dancing last weekend, I *did* get tingly, but I don't think he felt anything, because he acted normal when he came to my parents' house to say goodbye the next morning. But then he licked my éclair *and* my fingers, and I thought he was interested, you know? I was *so* wrong. All that custard licking was a joke. He said he still *had it*, even with his shirt on. I know I need to stick to my New Year's resolution, especially after that embarrassing fiasco, but my stupid heart won't break the Levi-loving cycle, as if there's actually a *chance* he'd ever be into me. I have to *stop* thinking about him like that because he sees me as Joey's aunt, which I am, and Joey is *Amelia's*, and that makes it even weirder for me to be into him. And you *know* how my mother is around him, so even if by some miracle he drank drugged water and he gave me a second look, it could never go anywhere. But I can't stop wanting him, and I feel so out of control. I swear I need to go to Levi rehab or something."

She groaned frustratedly and stopped pacing, chancing an embarrassed glance at her friends. Jules was grinning from ear to ear. Bellamy's eyes were as wide as saucers, and she was blinking rapidly, as if she couldn't believe Tara was stupid enough to still be into Levi after all these years, despite her initial excited squeals. "Please say *something*. I can take whatever it is."

Bellamy held up her index finger. "Can we go back to the licking your éclair part? Is that code for oral sex?"

"And the shirt-on thing," Jules said excitedly. "What was that about?"

She told them what had transpired when she'd seen him jogging. "We always tease each other, and you know we don't shy away from dirty jokes. But I'm definitely losing it, because I was ready to strip my clothes off and let that tongue of his do all sorts of wicked things to me in my parents' freaking *driveway*."

"Tara, he *licked* your fingers," Bellamy said. "That's *not* how you usually tease each other."

Jules handed them each a piece of taffy. "She's right. I think my brother was testing the waters to see how you'd react."

"If he was, then he's definitely *not* interested because I acted like a buffoon. But I know you're wrong. He may not be as arrogant as Archer, but his ego is pretty darn big, and I know he was just proving that he still had it *all* going on, and boy does he *ever*." Tara fanned her face and leaned against the counter beside Bellamy. She sighed in defeat. "What should I do, you guys? He's coming with me this weekend to look at houses, and I don't want it to be weird."

"You're looking at houses?" Bellamy and Jules asked in unison.

"I'm just starting. I was talking with Charmaine at Indi's grand opening, and she said it's a good time to buy. She sent me information, and I've been checking out neighborhoods." She ate the taffy Jules had given her.

Jules and Bellamy exchanged hurt expressions, sending a pang of guilt through her.

"Why didn't you tell us?" Jules asked.

"I'm *sorry*. I was going to ask you if you wanted to look at them with me, but then Levi offered, and my stupid heart took over my brain. You've got to help me stop thinking about him that way."

"Or maybe we just need to help you get his attention," Jules suggested. "For all the toughness guys show, I think they're oblivious when it comes to women. I had to practically throw myself at Grant, and then he tried to push me away. Talk about clueless. I mean, we're perfect together."

"You are," Bellamy agreed. "I've never seen either of you happier."

Jules gasped. "I have an idea! We can ask Indi to give you a makeover and buy some sexy clothes. That'll get his attention."

"And we'll teach you to flirt really well so you're ready when you stay with him over spring break. Imagine you're making dinner, and he comes into the kitchen." Bellamy sat up straighter and pulled her tank top off her shoulder. "You have to touch him. Guys love that. So put your hand on his arm or chest and talk breathy and sexy, like this. *Hey, Levi*," she said huskily. *"The spaghetti is wet and the sauce is hot. How about I get your meatballs ready?"*

They all burst into hysterics.

"I am *not* going to ask him about his meatballs." Tara groaned. "You know I can't flirt my way out an open door. Besides, I want him to want me for *me*. Jules didn't have to change for Grant."

"I didn't mean you had to change," Jules said. "You're perfect just as you are. Some guys go through life with sunglasses on, and you have to make yourself so bright, they can't miss you."

"But that's not *me*, Jules. I appreciate the help, but I'm trying to accept that it's not going to happen, not force it to happen. That's why I made the resolution to move on with my life and try to put my feelings for Levi behind me. And before you ask, I was afraid to tell you about that, too, because it's embarrassing to need a resolution to get over a guy who's never looked at me like that."

"We're your best friends. We'd never judge you," Bellamy said.

"I know, but I still felt foolish."

"What does this resolution entail?" Jules asked.

"Well, the first step is setting up my life in a way that allows me to wipe the slate clean and start over. I figured I'd buy a house and focus on making it mine, turning it into a home, and maybe put myself out there a little more and be open to other guys more than I have been."

Jules gasped. "*No*. I know you never admitted it before, but I've always known you and Levi were meant to be together."

"I thought I did, too," Tara said softly. "But I was wrong, and as much as I hate it, if I'm ever going to get over him, I have to start somewhere. I also think spring break has to be my last long-term stay with them."

"*What?*" Jules said. "You can't do that to Joey."

"Or to yourself. You'll miss them so much," Bellamy said.

Tara's heart ached just thinking about seeing them less, but she saw the writing on the wall. "I know, but eventually he's going to fall in love with someone else, and if I don't start weaning myself off them now, it'll be even harder later. Who knows, maybe I've been so focused on him, I'm missing out on who I'm really supposed to be with." The attempt to convince herself only made the idea hurt worse, but she was buying into the *fake it until you make it* theory.

"I don't think so," Jules said carefully. "I know this doesn't help, but I believe our hearts know who we belong with before our heads do. Look at Jock and Daphne. After they met, he traveled for an entire *year* trying to forget her, and he couldn't even be near Hadley because of all he'd been through. And they're perfectly matched. He couldn't escape it because it was true love."

Bellamy slid off the counter and put her hands on her hips. "You're right, that doesn't help. She wants to *stop* thinking about Levi, Jules. You know what they say about the best way to get over a guy." She raised her brows. "There are lots of hot bikers in Harborside. Maybe someone else will catch your eye."

"Maybe," Tara said halfheartedly, knowing it wouldn't happen. She'd been trying to forget Levi for months, and nobody stirred butterflies like he did. "It's going to take some serious competition to get my mind off Levi. I guess I could take my grandmother up on her offer to introduce me to her friend from Pythons, Sylvester Sta*bone*."

They all laughed.

Tara caught her breath and said, "Or I could submit an application to *The Bachelor* with Bellamy."

Jules gasped, eyes blooming wide, and Tara realized her mistake.

"*Shoot!* Sorry, Bell!" Tara exclaimed. "I didn't mean to spill the beans."

"You're applying to *The Bachelor* and you didn't tell me?" Jules said incredulously. "Is *that* why Tara's taking your picture tonight?"

"Yes. I'm sorry. I wanted to tell you," Bellamy promised. "But you'd have to tell Grant, and you know he doesn't want me going on that show."

Jules crossed her arms, sadness drawing her lips into a frown. "First Tara spends years pretending she doesn't like Levi, and she doesn't tell us she's looking at houses, and now you're doing something monumental, too, and you don't trust me enough to clue me in? And here I thought we could tell each other everything."

"I'm sorry for not telling you about my feelings for Levi, and I *was* thinking about asking you guys to look at houses with me," Tara said.

"I trust you, Julesy," Bellamy said softly but firmly. "But I also respect your relationship with Grant, and I know you don't like keeping secrets from him."

"I know, but..." Jules's brow furrowed. "This is a bestie secret. I can keep it, just like I'll keep Tara's secret."

"Are you sure? Because my family will go apeshit if they know what I'm planning," Bellamy reminded her.

Jules nodded. "Yes. Unless Grant tortures me with oral sex, because I don't have any willpower when it comes to him doing *that*, and I *will* spill your secrets."

"Ew." Bellamy scrunched up her face. "I don't want to know about you and my brother doing that."

Jules rolled her eyes. "It's not like I'm telling you all the dirty details, like—"

Bellamy put her fingers in her ears. "La la la. I can't hear you."

"Bellamy," Jules said sharply, but Bellamy just sang louder. Jules tickled her ribs, and they laughed.

"I love you guys, and I promise not to keep secrets anymore," Tara said. "You always make me feel better."

"That's because we're awesome." Bellamy handed out more

taffy. "I promise, too."

"Good, because I'd hate to have to find new besties," Jules threatened.

"Do you want to come with us to take pictures for my application?" Bellamy asked.

"I would, but Grant and I have plans," Jules said cheerily.

"What are you doing?" Bellamy asked.

Jules whispered, "You don't want to know."

They talked for a few more minutes, and when they got ready to leave, Bellamy took Tara's arm, speaking quietly. "For the record, I'm willing to take one for the team if you need to go to Pythons after you come back from Harborside. We'll leave the engaged one here to do unspeakable things with my brother, and you and I can check out the potential competition, because I'm *that* good of a friend."

Five

"CHARMAINE HAS EIGHT houses lined up for us to see today," Tara said Saturday morning as Levi drove them to the first property. "Three on the outskirts of Silver Haven, two on the east side of Rock Harbor, and three in Seaport..."

Levi tried to concentrate, but it was a losing battle. She was absolutely gorgeous with her hair pinned up in a messy bun and her long-sleeve black V-neck hanging off one shoulder. It didn't help that he'd spent all week trying to convince himself that what he was feeling was all in his head, or that his thoughts kept sprinting back to the desire he'd seen in Tara's eyes last weekend. He'd had a hell of a time trying to obliterate *that* image from his mind.

It was still there, like a freaking neon billboard taunting him.

"But I don't want to take up your whole day. I can postpone seeing some of them, or go on my own."

She turned those sweet baby blues on him, and hell if that magnetic pull, that ache to be closer, didn't suck him right in.

Focusing on the road, he said, "I'm here for you, T. My entire day is yours. Joey's going to have a great time with my parents and Hadley, and I have to head home first thing tomorrow, so let's see them all today."

"Okay, but if you get bored—"

He silenced her with a sideways glance. "If I didn't want to spend the day with you, I wouldn't." She was good at taking care of him and Joey, but today was supposed to be about her, and he was going to make sure it stayed that way. He knew dozens of little things about her, and assuming he could keep his desires in check, he was looking forward to figuring out what made her tick on a deeper level.

He navigated through the residential streets to Seaside Lane. While there wasn't any notable crime on Silver Island, he wanted to be sure she was looking at safe neighborhoods, and scanned the streets for signs of trouble, like beer cans or rubbish, broken-down cars, and houses in states of disrepair. He was glad to see the older, two-story houses were fairly well kept. They had small but tidy yards and children's chalk drawings on the sidewalks, which he took as a good sign.

"There it is." Tara pointed to a cute cedar-sided home with green shutters and a weathered picket fence.

Charmaine, an attractive, leggy brunette, was waiting out front. She looked professional in a blue dress and heels, holding a folder in one hand and waving as he parked by the curb.

Tara waved, drawing in a deep breath.

"Nervous?"

"A little." Her brow furrowed. "Is that weird?"

"No. You should be nervous. This is a big step. It's easy to get caught up in the excitement of buying a house, but they can be money pits if you don't know what to look for. That's why

I'm here. Don't worry. I've got your back." He winked and went to help her out of the vehicle. Tara took his hand, and electricity skated up his arm. *What the…?* Her eyes flicked up to his as if she'd felt it, too.

"Hi, Tara," Charmaine said, and Tara quickly withdrew her hand. "Levi, I didn't expect to see you."

"I'm here for moral support," he explained.

"Levi knows a lot about houses," Tara said a little nervously.

"I've heard all about Husbands for Hire. I love the name, by the way. We could use a service like that here on the island." Charmaine handed Tara the folder she was holding. "This has listings for all the houses we're seeing."

"Thanks." Tara took out the flyer for the house.

Levi reached for the folder so she could focus on the flyer. She handed it to him with a sweet smile.

"Why don't we check out the inside first?" Charmaine suggested.

Tara nodded. "Sure."

He put a hand on Tara's back, and they followed Charmaine up the walk and into a small tiled foyer. To their right there was a moderately sized living room with awful orange shag carpet and floral curtains. There was a dining room to their right with hardwood floors, and at the end of the hall, he caught a glimpse of cabinets and assumed it was the kitchen.

"This is a three bedroom, two bath," Charmaine said. "It obviously needs some updating, but the neighborhood is nice. They haven't used the fireplace in a while, but they said it works, and they added a deck off the kitchen three years ago."

"What do the utilities run on?" Levi already knew it wasn't the right house for Tara. It was too confining. She needed an open living space with lots of sunlight where she could put plants in the windows and nurture them like she did at his place. But that wasn't his decision to make.

"It has electric heat and a propane stove," Charmaine answered.

"Great. Crawl space or basement?" he asked.

"Crawl space."

"Any updates to electric or appliances in the last decade?"

"You *are* good at this," Charmaine said. "There's a new washer and dryer in the laundry room, but that's it as far as upgrades go." She looked at him expectantly, as if waiting for more questions.

"Okay, cool. Thanks."

"I usually step outside while clients look around, but I can go through the house with you if you'd like," Charmaine offered.

Levi looked at Tara, letting her answer.

"I think we're okay, thanks," she said.

"Then I'll give you some privacy."

As Charmaine stepped out, Tara said, "I'm glad you're here. I would never have thought to ask those questions. Which is better, electric or propane?"

"That depends who you ask."

"I'm asking *you*," she said sassily.

"I like propane. It's more efficient than electric. But that's an easy modification to make. It's more important that you love the house and neighborhood."

"I agree. Let's check out the bedrooms first."

He flashed a grin, unable to hold back. "Now you're talkin'."

"I didn't mean…" Her cheeks flushed, and she rolled her eyes. "I meant, let's start *upstairs* and work our way down."

"A woman after my own heart." He motioned for her to go first and followed her up.

She looked over her shoulder. "You like starting upstairs?"

"Not with houses, but with women." *Jesus.* He had no idea where that came from, but apparently his mouth had a mind of its own around Tara these days.

She gave him a deadpan look. "I think you have that backward. Wouldn't most guys say they like to start *downstairs*?"

"Maybe, if they're just looking to get laid." They made their way into a painfully small master bedroom, which was painted yellow with white trim and had two windows overlooking the backyard.

She eyed him curiously as she went to look out the window. "How did we start talking about women?"

Shit. Thinking fast, he said, "Think about it. Whether it's a house or a relationship, the most important thing is the foundation, right? With houses, you inspect the footings, basement, or crawl space."

"That makes sense." She opened the closet and looked inside. "Then why do you prefer starting upstairs with women? *Wait.* Are you a boob man?"

"I'm an *everything* man." He loved the way her cheeks pinked up. "But I like to get to know a woman before getting down and dirty. I like to explore her mind, figure out how she thinks, what she likes, what turns her off…and *on*."

"And you just *ask* them?" she asked with disbelief.

"No. I pay attention."

She planted a hand on her hip, brows lifted, as if she didn't believe him. "To what?"

"Lots of things. Like how she kisses."

"There aren't that many different ways to kiss."

Careful, sweetheart. Now you've piqued my interest. "Sure there are. How a woman kisses says a lot about her. Does she rush, or is she into it? Is she aggressive or sensual—"

She held up her hand. "I get the idea. But according to my friends, if you can think about all that while kissing, then you're kissing the wrong women."

"Maybe your *friends* are right." He made air quotes when he said *friends*.

"For your information, I *am* talking about my friends. I've never kissed anyone who made me see fireworks the way they describe it." She cocked her head curiously. "What else do you pay attention to?"

He was still thinking about her having never been kissed in a way that made her lose her mind and how he'd like to be the one to do it. Mentally shelving those thoughts, he said, "How she reacts, the things she says, and the things she *doesn't*."

"Reacts to what?"

Seeing me lick her éclair floated into his mind, but it was enlightening to learn about her perceptions. He liked her inquisition and exploring her curiosity, and he wasn't about to walk away from *that* opportunity. "I'll show you." Their eyes locked, and he slowly closed the distance between them, loving the way her breathing shallowed. He ran his fingertips along her exposed shoulder, and she gasped the sexiest little breath. He brushed the back of his fingers down her cheek, and her eyes darkened, her lips parting with a sigh.

"What else?" she whispered.

He'd surely go straight to hell for this, but he didn't care. The lustful look she was giving him was worth it. He cupped her cheek. Her skin was soft and warm as he dragged his thumb along her lower lip, then threaded his fingers into her hair, taking hold at the nape of her neck and tugging just hard enough for her to feel it in her core, angling her mouth beneath his. Her tongue slid across her lips, leaving them temptingly wet. The heat in her eyes drew him deeper into her. Lust coiled tight and hot inside him, as visions of crushing his mouth to hers and *devouring* her made his heart thunder. His body pulsed with the need to explore more of her. To learn what turned her on and make her *see* and *feel* a hell of a lot more than fireworks. But this was supposed to be a tease, a game, a testing of boundaries, not crossing lines that couldn't be uncrossed, no matter how badly he wanted to obliterate them. He couldn't risk screwing up things with one of the most important people in his and Joey's lives. He reluctantly forced himself to release her and stepped back. It took everything he had to try to play it off casually, despite the desire blazing through him. "See? Like that."

"Uh-huh," she said breathily, blinking repeatedly.

He needed to back the hell off, but when he opened his mouth, "What about you? Where do you start with guys? Upstairs or down?" came out. *Yup. I'm going straight to hell, all right.*

Shock cleared the lust from her eyes, and an adorably sexy, flustered sound fell from her lips. "I'm not telling you *that.* Geez. I can't believe I fell for your nonsense *again.* Can we get back to looking at the house?" She sounded a little nervous as she walked out of the bedroom. "How did we get so off track, anyway?"

He was asking himself the same thing.

He struggled to force his dark desires down deep, but sexual tension crackled around them as they went down the hall. This was definitely *not* in his head, but she was averting her eyes.

Had he pushed too far? *Shit.* What was he thinking? He was there to help her find a house, not flirt with her. He needed to get back to that safe place she trusted before he fucked them up beyond repair.

As they walked into the next bedroom, a shock of pink shag carpet and bright orange walls gave him the opening he needed to dampen the heat with a little humor. "This is awesome. Perfect for your boom-chicka-wow-wow room."

"My *what*?" She laughed.

"You know what I'm talking about. A few couches, a pole in the middle, and you've got yourself a great setup for boudoir photos."

"That is *not* a boudoir." She looked around the room, mischief filling her eyes. "All it needs is a disco light, and then it would be perfect for making films like *Boogie Nights*."

"You are *not* making adult films. I need to get you out of this room."

He reached for her, but she dodged his hand, eyes twinkling with a tease. "Do you know how much those actors earn?"

He hooked an arm around her neck, dragging her out of the bedroom. "It doesn't matter. You'll be locked in my dungeon if you even think about it."

They fell right back into their usual banter as they checked out the other bedroom, which was just as hilarious. They headed downstairs, walking through the living room, dining room, and finally the bright yellow kitchen with olive-green appliances.

Exchanging an amused glance, Tara said, "Is it just me, or do you feel like we're in an episode of *That '70s Show*?"

"Definitely." With his head clearer, he focused on the reason he'd offered to come with her. "But those are just cosmetic fixes, and you've got an in with a guy who can make anything beautiful. The important thing is how you feel about the layout, the sizes of the rooms, the overall vibe of the home. What do you think?"

"I don't know. Other than my *Boogie Nights* room, there's not much to it, is there?"

The only way she was getting a *Boogie Nights* room was if *he* was starring in it. "It's a starter home. You're used to living in your parents' elegant mini-mansion, with all the finest furnishings. Is that what you were hoping for?"

She wrinkled her nose, shaking her head. "I don't want that. I want a house like yours, that feels like home, and when you walk in, you never want to leave. You know what I mean. Like Jules and Grant's place."

Jules and Grant lived in a tiny bungalow on the beach that had been in shit shape when Grant had moved in. But once Jules found her way into Grant's heart, they made it into a warm, welcoming home. *The same way you help me with my place.*

"I want a home like your parents' have," Tara added. "I've always loved being there. Your mom is always cooking and doting on everyone and telling amazing stories, and every time your dad walks by, he reaches for her or puts his hand on her back." She paused, a little dreamy eyed, and he wondered if she was thinking about how often he put an arm around her or his hand on her back. That was a look he'd like to see more of. "I could sit and listen to your mom all day long."

"You're not alone in that." His mother was loved by everyone.

"I'm sure I'm not. But it's not just her stories or cooking that make me want to spend time there or make the house feel special. It's *her*. She treats everyone like family. When I was little, my mom would make dinners or dessert and give me tiny portions and tell me I should eat only half a piece of cake or half of whatever she'd made. But your mom never singled me out or made me feel like I was different from everyone else. And I know I wasn't her daughter, so it's not the same, but when my mom did it, I wanted to eat more, even if I wasn't hungry. Your mom made me feel so happy, I wasn't as hungry. Your mom does everything with so much love. I hope you know how lucky you are to have her."

His chest constricted. There had been hundreds of times he'd wanted to step in and say something to Tara's mother for the way she picked on Tara, but it wasn't his place. He'd heard her mother say similar things to her own husband, and to a lesser degree, to Carey and Robert. Amelia seemed to have escaped the nitpicking, at least from what he remembered hearing. But she'd always been hyperaware of her own appearance.

"I know how lucky I am, but you possess those qualities too, T, and I know your house will feel that way, regardless of what it looks like."

"I hope so." She looked around the dated kitchen. "But my house is *not* this house."

"Definitely not." He slung an arm over her shoulder. "Let's see what else Charmaine has in store for us."

They toured the other houses in Silver Haven, stopped for lunch with Charmaine on their way to Rock Harbor, then checked out the houses there. They were nice, but Tara had found faults with each one, which was good, because Levi did, too. He was glad she was taking it seriously and not just jumping at one of them. But Tara had never been impulsive, and he had a feeling when she found the right house, there would be no missing it. She'd light up the way she did when she *really* loved something, the way she had when she'd been looking at the house on Gable Place.

It was after six when they made their way through the last property in Seaport. The cute cottage was just a few blocks from the water, and it was the nicest property they'd seen all day. It had gingerbread detailing around the front porch and a spacious area for gardens out back. Levi did a quick visual inspection of the foundation, siding, and windows and headed around to the front door.

Charmaine was sitting on the front steps. "How'd everything check out?"

"It looks great. This is a sweet property." He'd prefer Tara was closer to Silver Haven so his brothers and Robert could keep an eye on her, but Seaport wasn't that far from their other friends and families. "Is Tara still inside?"

"Yeah. I think she's upstairs. You guys are really cute together."

"*She's* cute," he said. "I'm just the protective friend."

"I hear ya. But if I had a friend who looked like you and made me laugh as much as I hear you two laughing, I'd do anything I could to be more than friends. You guys have great chemistry."

She wasn't going to get an argument from him on that. The question was, was she even interested? And if so, was it worth the risk to explore it? "Thanks. We've known each other forever." He lifted his chin toward the door, trying to escape having anyone else's comments emblazoned into his mind like his siblings'. "I'm going to head inside. We shouldn't be much longer."

Charmaine nodded. "Take your time."

He found Tara looking out the window of the second-story master bathroom. The sun had dipped low in the sky, illuminating her gorgeous, slim figure. She was twirling the ends of her hair, which she did when she was deep in thought.

"Hey, blondie. What do you think of the view?" *It can't be nearly as good as the view from here.*

She glanced over her shoulder and smiled, but it was a little deflated, giving him her answer before she even said a word. "It's got a nice view. I can see the water."

"But it doesn't *wow* you, does it?" He'd been sure she'd love this one, with the open floor plan, Jacuzzi tub, and sunlight-flooded morning room.

"I like a lot of things about it, but no, it doesn't wow me. I can't picture myself in it for the long term." She looked at him with a pained expression and lowered her voice. "How am I going to tell Charmaine? She spent *all* day with us. I've wasted so much of her time, I feel like I should make an offer on one."

"It's a good thing I'm here to keep that big heart of yours from getting you into trouble." He drew her into his arms, and she rested her cheek on his chest. This wasn't new for them. He'd held her spontaneously for years, but being acutely aware of just how good she felt each and every time *was* new. And dangerous. He drew back, trying to rein in his emotions. "You're not putting down an offer on anything we saw today, and you're not going to feel guilty about it. Showing houses is Charmaine's job, and you're just starting your home search. It could take months, and she knows that."

"I could never waste that much of her time."

"It's a process, Tara, not a waste. Come on. I'll break the news to her, and then I'm taking you to dinner and we can talk about what you're really looking for." He took her hand, leading her out of the bathroom.

"You don't have to take me to dinner."

He squeezed her hand. "I think I've just figured out why you've never been properly kissed."

"I can't believe I told you that," she said flatly. "Okay, I'll bite. *Why?*"

He stopped walking at the entrance to the bedroom and looked her in the eyes. "In the last few hours, you've told me I didn't have to spend all day with you, I didn't have to check out every house, I didn't have to buy your lunch, I didn't have to open doors for you, and a few other things. You're a smart, beautiful woman, and you deserve to have doors opened for you and to be treated to a hell of a lot more than just lunches and dinners."

Her face lit up, as if he'd built her the most spectacular house she'd ever seen, and man, he loved that.

"It's time to stop telling people what they don't have to do for you and learn to say *thank you* instead."

She rolled her eyes. "I'm not used to people doing things for me, and it's not easy for me to accept those offers. It feels selfish, or entitled."

"I know it's not easy for you, but you are the least selfish or entitled person I've ever met." He didn't know if it was her own insecurities holding her back or the need to separate herself from her mother or sister. But either way, he was about to make it easier for her. There was only one surefire way he knew of to get her to do anything.

She lowered her gaze, and he lifted their joined hands, using them to tilt her chin up so he could see her face. "If you won't do it for yourself, do it for Joey. You may not realize this, but you do that at my house when I offer to get you a drink or a blanket, or just about anything else. She learns from you, T. If you act like you're not worth my time or energy for those little things, she'll learn to act that way, too, and I know you don't want that."

"I never thought of it that way."

"I know you didn't." *And I never thought of you the way I have lately, either.*

"You're right. I don't want Joey to have a hard time with those things."

"Good. I want you to feel the way you want Joey to feel, so how about we practice that?" He squeezed her hand. "Now do me a favor and let me take you to dinner so the guys in Seaport think I've still got it."

She scoffed. "As if they don't already know." They headed downstairs. "You *could* just lick some woman's éclair in front of them and turn her legs to wet noodles."

He chuckled, and once again couldn't resist pushing the envelope. He tugged her closer, lowering his voice. "You're playing a dangerous game, blondie, letting me know I got you wet."

"Levi!" She swatted him, and he cracked up as they walked outside.

"What are you two laughing about?" Charmaine asked.

They exchanged knowing smiles and said, "*Éclairs*," sending them both into hysterics.

Six

"IT WAS LIKE a bad sitcom." They'd been at Whit's Pub, a rustic dive bar on the wharf in Seaport, for more than an hour, and Tara was telling Levi about some of her funniest photo shoots. "Every time the parents finally got the kids settled, the baby would cry or the two-year-old would throw sand. And the three-year-old kept shouting for no reason, which scared the puppy, and then he'd run around barking, sending the younger one into hysterics."

"And yet you love photographing kids and keep going back for more." Levi shook his head.

"I do love it." She sipped her wine and pushed her empty plate to the side.

They'd shared clams on the half shell as an appetizer and had enjoyed scallops and pasta for dinner, all of which was delicious. She and Levi had never gone out to dinner alone before, and even though this wasn't a date and she missed Joey, she was loving having him all to herself. But as much as she wanted to spin it into something more, what he'd said earlier—

If you won't do it for yourself, do it for Joey—had hit home in more ways than one. The combination of that comment and having such a great time together was the golden ticket she needed to put the nail in the resolution coffin. Their friendship was perfect. It was fun, easy, and just flirty enough to make her feel special. Okay, lately she felt a lot more than special, but she never wanted anything to ruin what they had, and she realized she'd been silly hoping for something magical to happen. She'd been looking at it all wrong. Something magical had *already* happened. Levi was a man who went after what he wanted, and even though he hadn't gone after Tara in the way she'd hoped, he *had* welcomed her into his and Joey's lives, and she loved being there. She didn't want to risk messing that up for something that would never come, and having that perspective made it easier to relax and just be herself again.

"I bet you never put your camera down when you were with that family, did you?"

He knew her so well. "Nope. I take some of my best pictures during the most unexpected moments. Like when the parents are at the end of their ropes, but they pick up their child or crouch next to them and that child smiles. I can *see* their love push their frustration aside. *Those* are some of my favorite moments. They're so real and beautiful, I get goose bumps just thinking about them. Look."

She pulled up her sleeve and held out her arm. He ran his big, rough hand down it, his eyes never leaving hers as he gave her wrist a gentle squeeze, sending electric currents all the way to her heart before letting go. She wanted to savor those scintillating sensations, but she knew better and put her hands in her lap. *I will not lust after you. I will not lust after you.*

"You've gotten great shots of me and Joey that way, but I

can't imagine juggling multiple kids and a dog."

"It wasn't easy. The puppy kept running off and the kids would chase him. We'd booked an hour, and we were there for *three*, half of which was spent listening to the three-year-old's stories, because she had *so* much to say."

"Oh, man." Levi sat back, grinning and shaking his head. "Remember how Joey used to tell stories that went on and on, and just when we thought she was done, she'd take a big breath and go right into another?"

"I loved when she did that." Tara remembered Joey's adorable antics as she waved her hands or scrunched up her face. Sometimes Levi would whisper, *I'll distract her so you can go outside before you lose your mind.* But Tara had never taken him up on it. She didn't want to miss out on that part of Joey's life. "Remember when she was four and she'd get so excited she couldn't talk? She'd fist her little hands and shake all over."

"Yeah, I worried she was having a seizure."

"No, you *didn't.*"

He shook his head. "She was so stinking cute."

"I miss those days. But she tells even better stories now."

"She sure does." He took a drink, and his expression softened, as if he was thinking about Joey's stories.

"Do you ever miss when she was little?"

He shrugged. "Maybe on occasion, like when we're talking about it, but those were tough times. I'm just glad we got through the early years in one piece."

"Oh, come on. You've always been such a good dad. You'd never let anything happen to her."

"Thanks, but half the time I didn't know what I was doing. She was so tiny and vulnerable." He took a drink. "I thought as she got bigger and wasn't quite so fragile, I'd worry less, but the worrying never stops."

"For me either, and I'm just her aunt."

"You're not *just* her aunt, Tara. You're one of the most important people in our lives."

She remembered hearing him say something similar to Keira at Rock Bottom, and as happy as that made her, she forced herself to put it into perspective. She was an important *friend*.

Their waitress, Macie Walsh, the cute single mother who had just started working a second job at Indi's boutique, came over to clear their plates. "How was everything?"

"Great, thanks," Levi said as Tara said, "Delicious, thank you."

"Can I tempt you with some dessert?" she asked. "We have a killer Boston cream pie tonight."

Levi's gaze shot to Tara, and she knew by his mischievous grin that he was thinking about the éclair, too.

"That sounds perfect," he said. "One slice, two forks, please."

"Coming right up."

As Macie walked away, Tara said, "Are you sure you want a fork and you don't want to just lap it up with your tongue?"

Those dark eyes turned sinful, just as they had in her parents' driveway, but she wasn't falling prey to *that* little trick again and steeled herself against the streak of heat that sexy look caused. Eventually putting things into perspective would get easier, right? She wouldn't need to remind herself forever, would she?

"I would," he said seductively. "But I didn't want to embarrass you by getting you wet in public."

"Shut up." She threw her napkin at him. "I'm going to be much more careful with the words I use around you."

"*Aw*, come on. Don't kill my fun. I like cutting loose with you."

"You like knocking me off-kilter."

"Yeah, well. It *is* fun. You're adorable when you're flustered, and I spend enough time watching what I say around Joey."

She sipped her wine, patting herself on her back for not clinging to the niceties he was sprinkling like moondust. The space gave her the courage to ask what she'd been wondering for a long time. "Speaking of my wonderful niece, do you ever think about having more kids?"

"Our lives are so busy, I haven't really thought about it."

"Come *on*. You haven't gone out with anyone that made you wish for, or wonder about, having more?" She couldn't believe she was asking him that, but then again, she *could* believe it. She had to know. They never talked about the people they went out with. It wasn't that she'd intentionally avoided the subject. She knew he probably went out with a lot of women, but when they were together, it was either with a group of their friends or with Joey. When their friends made references to dating, he usually brushed them off, and when they were with Joey, her thoughts rarely strayed, because she was exactly where she wanted to be. Suddenly a horrible thought occurred to her, and she wished she could take the question back, because if he told her about a woman he was going out with, or falling for, or contemplating a future with, she might just die on the spot.

He leaned forward, crossing his arms on the table. "Believe it or not, tonight is the first time I've been alone with a woman in ages."

"No *way*." She set down her glass, flabbergasted, and then she realized he might not want to talk about it with her. "You don't have to tell me. I'm sorry. I was being nosy."

"Seriously, T. When do you think I have time to go out?"

"I don't know. I figured you went out after church or on Sundays, when you go riding with the guys." Church was what the Dark Knights motorcycle club called their meetings.

"Church is on Wednesday nights. I go home to Joey afterward, and Sundays are for family. After our rides, I hang out with my cousins and whoever else wants to stick around, and Joey's right there with us."

Tara had met his cousins Jesse and Brent in Harborside. They were older than Levi and owned Hooligan's restaurant and Endless Summer Surf Shop. She really liked them. They adored Joey, and it was obvious how much they respected and loved Levi. But she wasn't buying what he was saying about not dating. Emboldened by her fresh perspective, she called him on it. "You don't really expect me to believe that you never go out with women."

"*Go out* is a relative term." He cocked a grin. "I'm no saint, but I do give a shit about what my daughter and the parents of her friends think of me. I take care of my needs when Joey isn't around, and I'm careful not to get together with anyone she knows. I don't ever want my daughter used in some sort of manipulation tactic. And like I said, it's been a while."

She didn't know what she'd expected to hear, but it wasn't such blatant honesty, and she was surprised at how it made her feel. While she didn't want to think about him with other women, she wanted him to be happy, even if it wasn't with her. "That's respectable, but it makes me kind of sad for you."

"It shouldn't," he said with a deathly serious tone. "It's how things should be. What about you?"

"What about me?"

"Have you got a guy on the line?"

"I *wish*," she said more to herself than to him.

His jaw tightened. "If it's Ryan you're hoping for, he was definitely into you last weekend."

"He was *not* into me. Bellamy was way off base."

"No, she wasn't. Guys know these things."

She rolled her eyes. "In my experience, guys are clueless to what's right in front of them."

"So you *are* into him," he said gruffly, the muscles in his jaw bunching.

"I never said that." She took another drink, wondering why he was talking about Ryan.

"Well, he's great with his nephew. You know he'd be a good baby daddy."

She choked on her wine, nearly spewing it out, and grabbed a napkin to wipe her mouth. "Who says I'm looking for a baby daddy?"

"Nobody. I was kidding," he said as Macie arrived with their dessert.

"One slice, two forks." Macie set a plate with an enormous slice of pie on it and silverware between them. "Can I get you anything else?"

"I think we're all set. Thanks, Macie." Levi handed Tara a fork as Macie walked away, his expression lighter than it was moments ago. "This looks almost as good as the éclair."

"Almost? It looks amazing." She ate a bite, and the sweet goodness melted in her mouth. "*Mm.* It's every bit as good."

"It would be tastier if you were holding it." He smirked.

She pointed her fork at him. "I'm not letting you throw me off with your ridiculous games anymore, so put away that troublemaking smirk."

He pointed his fork at her. "You know what, Osten? I think this is the first time we've ever gone to dinner alone."

"It is. It's kind of weird, right, without Joey?" She scooped up another forkful of pie.

"I don't know about that. I kind of like having you all to myself."

He held her gaze, and she wondered if he could see her swatting that sweetness away with her imaginary tennis racket.

"Now you can tell me *all* your secrets." He took a bite, dragging the fork out of his mouth slowly, his eyes never leaving hers, as if he could lure her secrets out with hotness.

If she wasn't determined not to look foolish again, she might even fall for it. "I hate to burst your bubble, but I don't have many secrets."

"Sure you do. You didn't tell me you were buying a house until I saw the flyers."

"That wasn't a secret. I had just started looking and didn't want to make a big deal out of it."

"I think it was a little bit of a secret, wasn't it? You're a private person. That's one of the things I admire about you."

She would get really good at mental tennis if he kept this up. "I guess you could say I'm private." *Considering I kept a secret from my two best friends for so long.*

"We've known each other forever, and I think you know you can trust me," he said thoughtfully. "You said you wanted to get your personal life in order, and if you're not looking for a baby daddy, what *are* you looking for?"

That was a loaded question. "Do you really want to know?"

"Yes, I really do. You're embarking on a big change and an exciting time in your life. I'd love to hear what you envision."

She took a deep breath and told him the truth. "I guess I

want what I've always dreamed of. A house full of love, with pictures of my kids on every wall, finger paintings on the fridge, and a husband who hates to leave us in the morning and can't wait to get home to us every evening. I don't want to just watch my kids grow up. I want to be *part* of that process, helping with homework and school projects and baking birthday cakes. I want to pile on the couch with my family on cold winter nights in front of a roaring fire and play silly games and roast marshmallows, chocolate, and strawberries in waffle cones, because everyone else makes s'mores. I want to sing with my kids into hairbrushes and take them for prom dresses and suits, and never, *ever* make them feel like they don't measure up."

She felt like Joey going on and on, but the words came straight from her heart, and there was no stopping them. "I want to be loved by a man who makes me laugh and will comfort me when I cry, who will embrace my favorite things even if they're weird. A man who will treasure my heart as much as I'll cherish his, and who will love me and our kids even when we don't love ourselves. And I want to be with that man *forever*, through times when life seems too difficult to go on and when we can't stop laughing and we're so full of hope we could burst. But above all, I want to be with a man who looks at me like your father looks at your mother, like your brothers look at Indi and Daphne, and like Grant looks at Jules. Like I'm everything he could ever want, even on my worst days. Like I rock his world *and* soothe his soul. I want to be the person he knows he can trust to let his guard down with and he can trust to be completely in love with him, he knows without a shadow of a doubt that it won't matter if he loses his hair or gains fifty pounds, because what we have is so much deeper than that." She felt something wet on her cheek and when she brushed it away, she realized it was a tear. She clamped her mouth shut and lowered her eyes, embarrassed. "Sorry for rambling."

LEVI COULD DO little more than stare at the beautiful, passionate woman before him, and that was *exactly* what he saw. Either she'd lifted a veil or he'd been living behind a smokescreen. He didn't know which had clouded his vision for so long, but he no longer saw Joey's aunt or Amelia's sister. He saw a *woman* with hopes and dreams of an incredible future, and when he imagined being part of all of that trust and love, he wanted everything she described. He *yearned* for it, felt the dull ache of longing, as if she'd read the pages of his autobiography that he hadn't written yet.

He was baffled. Blown away. Dumbfounded. How could he want those things with such desperation when he'd never even thought about them before?

The answer blared through his mind. *I've never had to think about them.* They'd been living it naturally, without any manipulation. He and Tara had done most of what she'd said together with Joey many times. They'd roasted waffle cones and played silly games when they'd lost power. Joey called Tara a homework whisperer because she could help without frustrating her. The list went on and on—school projects, singing into hairbrushes, buying dresses for school events, birthday cakes, and, most importantly, inherent trust.

Holy hell…

"I must sound like a starry-eyed kid," she said, snapping him out of his trance.

He cleared his throat, trying to shift his thoughts. "Not at all. You deserve all those things." *And maybe I do, too.*

That was all he could think about as they finished their pie and stayed a little longer to listen to music before driving back to Silver Haven. Tara was quiet on the way, and that was probably a good thing, given Levi's current state of mind. Maybe it wasn't all in his head after all. Could it be a coincidence that she'd said all those things? Did he want it to be? *Hell no.* But it didn't matter what he wanted or how attracted to her he was. Getting involved with Amelia's sister was walking into a hornet's nest, and he could practically hear the little buggers preparing to sting.

When they reached her parents' house, he climbed out to open her door, trying to tamp down his desires and his questions. Every step brought a tightening to his chest, an ache of need deep inside him. He opened her door and reached for her hand, her sweet smile tugging at him as he helped her to her feet.

"Thanks for dinner and for coming with me to check out the houses. I had a lot of fun."

"Me too. Let me know if you want to see more during the week. I can come back for an afternoon." He didn't want to say goodbye. He wanted to find out more of her secrets as badly as he wanted to kiss her.

"I will. Thanks again."

She hugged him, and he returned the embrace. She smelled feminine and familiar and felt incredible in his arms, awakening all his senses, but it was his heart falling prey to that inescapable pull reeling him in. He fought against it like a shark caught on a fishing line, his mind thrashing, trying to break free, but her allure was too strong. He felt her stepping back and struggled against the urge to tighten his grip and whisper, *Do you feel it, too, or am I alone in this?* He reluctantly let her go.

Her beautiful, trusting eyes gazed up at him. "See you next Sunday?"

That felt like a lifetime from now. "I look forward to it."

"Me too."

As she headed up the walkway, desperation burned through him like wildfire. He had to know if she'd felt it, too, or if his mind was playing tricks on him. "Tara" came out urgent and heated before he could stop it.

She spun around. "Yeah?"

His own words rushed back at him. *If you won't do it for yourself, do it for Joey.* When it came to his daughter, the line between right and wrong had always been clearly defined by one simple rule: Don't do anything to fuck her up. He had never wanted anything bad enough to let that line blur. Until now.

Until Tara.

Her eyes sparkled in the moonlight, and every iota of his being wanted to ask if she felt it too, but he couldn't unleash those hornets when there was so much at stake. He lifted his chin and begrudgingly closed that door. "Have a great night."

"You, too. Give Joey a hug for me."

He watched her go inside, telling himself he'd done the right thing, no matter how wrong it felt.

He picked apart everything she'd said and everything he'd felt over the past week as he drove to his parents' house, and by the time he arrived, he didn't know which way was up. His gaze swept over his family's sixty-acre winery and vineyard next door as he headed up to the rambling two-story with peaked roofs and a built-in gazebo anchoring one side of the wide front porch. Their grandmother, Lenore, lived in the carriage house around back. *This* was what Tara wanted. The safety, comfort, and love he'd grown up with and had taken for granted would always be there.

As he stepped inside, he realized he'd always thought, *assumed*, he'd have it one day. Until he'd gotten that text from Amelia and he'd closed that door.

It was late, and the house was quiet as he bent to untie his boots.

"I thought that was you," his father said from the entrance to the living room at the other end of the hall. Steve Steele was thick-chested, with short salt-and-pepper hair and a neatly trimmed beard, and he was folding a flowered blanket.

"Hey, Pop. I'll be right there."

He left his boots by the door and went to join his father. There were toys scattered around the floor and a group of stuffed animals lined up on an armchair, tucked beneath a blanket, each with a single piece of popcorn in front of it. There was a large bowl with popcorn remnants on the coffee table, four empty glasses, a handful of crumpled napkins, and one of Joey's baseball caps. Two more blankets were bundled together on the couch.

Levi grabbed a blanket and began folding. "Movie night with you, Mom, and Grandma?"

"Close. Your grandmother was playing bingo with her friends at the Remingtons' tonight." He set down the blanket and began folding the last one. "Jock wanted to do something special for Daphne, so Hadley and Joey had a slumber party. They've been asleep for a while. Your mother just went up to check on them and get ready for bed."

"Joey must've liked that. Mom didn't mention it when I texted earlier to say I'd be late."

"That's not surprising. We were pretty busy with the girls. How was house hunting?"

"Interesting. I'll put these in the hope chest." He reached for the blanket his father had folded, and as he put them away, he was struck by how different his home life was from Tara's. He couldn't imagine her mother allowing blankets to be strewn around or popcorn to be set out for stuffed animals.

His father gathered the dirty dishes and the errant pieces of popcorn. "You were out pretty late. Did Tara find a house she liked?"

"Nothing that set her world on fire." Levi followed him into the kitchen. "Relax, Dad. I'll rinse those." He began washing the dishes. "Sorry I was so late. I took Tara to dinner in Seaport, at Whit's Pub."

His father leaned against the counter. "On the wharf? That's a fun place, and I wasn't complaining. I was just curious."

"Can you believe that in all the years I've known Tara and how often she stays with us and watches Joey, this was the first time I've taken her out alone?"

His father arched a brow. "I guess that's not so unusual. How was it?"

Eye-opening. He glanced at the man who had taught him everything he knew about what it meant to be a father, and he was thrown back to the night he'd told his parents that Amelia was pregnant. He'd been scared shitless, but not about telling them she was pregnant. He'd tried to be responsible. It wasn't his fault the condom had broken, and he knew his parents would understand that. He'd been scared they might want him to marry Amelia, and that was something he wouldn't have done for all the money in the world. But they hadn't pressured him to do anything. They'd listened to what he'd had to say, and they'd run him through the wringer about what it was really like to be a parent, warning him about how his life would change, much like Leni had. But he'd been steadfast in his decision to keep the baby, and nothing would have changed his mind. They'd hugged him and told him how much they loved him and had said they'd help in every way they could. But they'd also made it clear that he would have to support his baby. He wasn't getting a free ride through parenthood while he went out partying.

His father was watching him expectantly, and he realized he hadn't answered him. "It was interesting."

"That's a lot of *interesting* for one day."

His father wasn't the type to pry into his kids' lives. He didn't have to. Levi could practically hear his unsaid offer to talk about it. He trusted his father, and he wanted his advice, but Amelia's pregnancy had changed their family's relationship with the Ostens, and he didn't want to upend that situation again. He placed the last of the dishes in the dishwasher, and as he dried his hands on a dish towel, he tried to fly under his father's radar. "It sure was. Mom said something last weekend that got me thinking about the future. Do you have a minute, or is Mom waiting for you?"

"She's probably knee-deep in a novel by now. I have all the time you need."

Levi leaned against the island, facing him. "You know dating hasn't been on my radar since I found out Amelia was pregnant."

"Yes, that's what you've said."

"Well, I'm wondering if it's time to start thinking about it, or if you think it'll be too disruptive for Joey."

"I guess that depends. I don't recommend bringing a stream

of ladies you're not serious about into her life."

"You know I'd never do that. I'm not looking for hookups, Dad. I'm so far past that, sometimes I feel like I just turned fifty instead of twenty-nine."

His father nodded. "Parenting does that to you, and I'd imagine as a single parent it's twice as exhausting. But you're a responsible guy, Levi. When Joey came along, life kicked the hell out of you, and you always got up without ever complaining. You've put Joey first and set your own needs aside for a long time."

"That's what parents do. You taught me that."

"Not all parents, but I'm glad you have. You're Joey's white knight, son, and you always will be. You know what's right for your daughter, and you don't need my, or anyone else's, permission to date. But you had a crash course in figuring out who you were going to be *for* Joey, and while you aced it, you've never had the chance to figure out who you were for yourself. To play the field, or cut loose and have a fling, or fall in love."

"I don't regret raising Joey."

"I know you don't, and we couldn't be prouder of you. You've gone above and beyond as her father. A lot of men would have pushed Amelia out of Joey's life for the way she treats her like an afterthought. But you have tried to keep those lines of communication open for the good of your daughter, and I know that can't be easy."

"Nothing about parenting is easy, except loving your kid. I can't imagine it's easy for a little girl to grow up without a mom. That's why I try not to let my feelings toward Amelia get in the way of her and Joey's relationship. I don't want Joey growing up with abandonment issues because of her mother." That was the sole reason, despite the cold manner in which

Amelia had delivered the news of her pregnancy, Levi had hoped she'd want to be involved in Joey's life. But Amelia had made no effort toward Joey for the first three years, seeing her only when their paths crossed on the island. Even then, there hadn't been any intentional visits. She'd seen them around town and had remarked about how cute Joey was, but her tone had made it clear that she had better places to be. It wasn't until Joey was four or five, and could communicate more effectively, or as Amelia had so rudely put it, *had finally become a person*, that she'd begun to take more of an interest in her. She'd started sending birthday gifts and holiday cards and had called to speak with Joey a few times a year. Levi had invited her to birthday parties and school events, but she was usually too busy traveling for her job to show up. She'd made a name for herself, and a few years ago, her *Girl's Guide to Traveling* had hit every bestseller list out there for several weeks. Amelia was like a distant aunt to Joey, and on the rare occasions she had shown up, Joey had been thrilled to see her. As much as Levi hated Amelia's priorities, he knew that connection was important for his daughter.

"I don't know if I'm doing the right thing where Amelia is concerned. She was honest from the start about not wanting to be a mother. But I've got to believe that on a close-knit island like this, some contact is better than none, especially since Tara and her parents are involved in Joey's life."

"I think you're doing the right thing. You're doing all you can, and Joey has a lot of women in her life who adore her. Hopefully that will ward off any issues." His father's expression softened. "But your child cannot be your whole world, Levi, or all of that helping will turn into smothering. I can't tell you what you should do about your personal life, but as your father,

I hope you won't miss out on dating and falling in love, because no matter how much you love Joey, trust me when I tell you there's a space inside you that she can't fill."

He'd never let himself think about that before Archer's comment had slapped him upside his head. "I'm starting to realize that."

"Good. It's about time. I know it seems like you have forever to think about yourself. But time goes quickly, son. It won't be long before Joey's social calendar fills up with school dances and dates. You'll be surprised at how often you're sitting home alone at night waiting for her. It might be nice if you had someone to share that time with." His father paused, no doubt letting that sink in. "Have you been feeling lonely lately?"

"Not really, but I think I know *why* I'm not."

"Care to enlighten me?"

His father had been standing next to Archer when his brother had made the comment about making a move on Tara, and he had quickly excused himself. Levi hadn't been sure how to take his quick exit, and because of that he was careful not to mention Tara.

"Your eyebrows are twitching, son. Stop overthinking and spit it out," his father said, pulling him from his thoughts.

"Joey and I have a close friend, and when she's around, she makes everything better. But she's got a busy life of her own, and I recently realized that when she's not around, I haven't been looking for someone to fill that gap, and I don't think Joey has, either."

"Is this friend someone you've been romantically involved with?"

Levi shook his head. "No. I haven't even thought about it until recently."

"Why do you think that is?"

"I *know* why it is. I put blinders on when Joey was born, and I've never taken them off. I didn't want to get caught up in anyone or anything that could derail us. Then someone took a cheap shot and knocked those blinders off, causing a tidal wave of thoughts and emotions I hadn't known existed."

"I know that feeling well. The moment I set eyes on your mother, I was a goner."

"I never said I was a *goner*. I'm not even sure I can afford to take the risk to find out if she feels the same way. Her relationship with Joey is more important than my own selfish desires."

His father clapped a hand on his shoulder, shaking his head. "And here I thought you were going to stop putting yourself last. Only you can decide which way to go, but in my experience, if what you're feeling is the real thing, you won't be able to put those blinders back on."

Seven

LEVI RARELY HAD shitty days, much less several in a row, but by Wednesday evening he was fit to be tied. He'd made enough stupid mistakes to piss off one client, two employees, *and* himself. He needed to get his head on straight and stop thinking about Tara. The situation was beyond frustrating. While she was putting her wheels in motion toward building a future and eventually having a family, he was trying to imagine his and Joey's life without her as entrenched in it as she'd always been.

He couldn't picture it, and he sure as hell didn't want to.

He'd barely gotten to speak to her Sunday when she'd stopped by his parents' house to give Joey an Easter basket, and he'd picked up the phone a dozen times since then to text her, only to put it back down without doing a damn thing.

He wasn't a pussy. If she were anyone else, he'd text or pick up the phone and call. Hell, he'd have said something Saturday night or taken the kiss he'd wanted and let their bodies figure out the rest. But she *wasn't* anyone else, and he couldn't afford to say or do the wrong thing. The trouble was, *no* part of him wanted to do the right thing, which made it impossible to concentrate on anything else, including his sunshiny girl sitting across the table at Hooligan's yapping his ear off about the kids at school and the dance he'd agreed to chaperone this weekend.

"And then Chelsea told Billy that Sara liked him, and now Sara and Billy are going to the dance together, and she said she wants to marry him." Joey threw her hands up. "I don't know *why* Sara likes *Billy*. He can't even skateboard. The only boy I've ever wanted to marry was Maverick, but now he's married to Chloe, so I'm *done* with boys..."

His buddy, Justin "Maverick" Wicked, was a Dark Knight from the Bayside chapter, and Joey had crushed on him for more than a year, telling anyone who would listen that she was going to marry him. Including Chloe when she and Maverick were dating. Joey's friends had been crushing on boys for the past few months, and he was ruing the day she'd confess to another crush.

There were certain stages of his daughter's life that had thrown him for a loop, like the first time he'd dropped her off at a friend's house and hadn't stayed for the playdate. That had been like leaving a piece of himself behind. When she'd insisted on riding the school bus, he'd followed it all the way to school, and her first slumber party away from home had been excruciating. What if she'd woken up scared or the other kids weren't nice to her? He'd called twice that night and first thing the next morning to check on her. He was *that* annoying, overprotective father, and he didn't give a damn who knew.

But Joey had come through each of those events unscathed.

It was the dangers that had been lurking in plain sight that he'd never seen coming that had turned his brave, strong little girl into a blubbering mess. When the girls at school had made fun of her for playing sports and had stopped calling for playdates, Joey had been heartbroken, and he'd been like a grizzly wanting to tear someone apart. That was only one of the many nights he'd turned to Tara for advice. He didn't know when it had happened, but somewhere over the years he'd started looking to her for help with Joey before his mother or sisters. Tara was level-headed and always seemed to know just what to do. That was how he knew that when Joey eventually confessed her first crush, it might be to Tara and not him. And if it was to him, Tara would be his first call, because he was pretty sure threatening a little boy would land him in jail.

"*Dad*," Joey said exasperatedly, startling him from his thoughts. "Your phone is ringing."

"Sorry. Thanks, peanut." He pulled it out of his pocket, seeing Tara's name on the screen, and like a freaking schoolboy, his heart tripped up as he answered it. "Hey, Tara, miss me already?"

"It's Tara?" Joey bounced on her seat, eyes shimmering with delight. "I want to talk!"

Levi held up a finger and mouthed, *In a minute.*

"Yes, *terribly*," Tara said cheerily. "How'd you know?"

Her sweet voice unraveled the tightness in his chest, but it also brought rise to more of the conflicting emotions he'd been battling for days. He tried to ignore them. "I felt it in my bones."

"Such a charmer," she teased. "Did you miss *me*?"

"More than you can imagine, T" came out so honestly and raw, he worried she or Joey might pick up on the difference from his normal tone and quickly added, "Have you gotten leads on any more houses?"

Joey leaned over the table with her hand outstretched. "I want to talk to her."

He held up his finger again.

"Not yet," Tara said. "But I'm sure there will be more soon. Where *are* you? It's so loud."

"We're at Hooligan's, having dinner."

"*Dad!* Please?" Joey pleaded.

"Oh my gosh, it's dinnertime," Tara said. "I'm sorry. I just finished a shoot and thought I'd catch up with you guys. I didn't even look at the time. Tell Joey I'll call her later."

"And deprive you of speaking to the coolest eight-year-old around? No way." He winked at Joey. He didn't want to stop talking to Tara, but Joey looked like she was going to jump out of her skin if she didn't get to speak to her soon. *I feel your pain, sweetheart.* "She's right here. Hang on."

Joey snagged the phone, excitedly repeating the latest gossip about her friends and the dance to Tara. "And Dad is chaperoning…"

Levi sat back, an idea forming in his mind as Jesse stopped by their table. His tattooed, bearded cousin was in his midthirties, with thick dark hair that brushed his collar. Like Levi, he wore his black leather vest over a T-shirt. When Levi had first come to Harborside, Jesse had suggested he prospect the Dark Knights, and it had been the second-best decision he'd ever made. The first being raising Joey.

"Hey, Jesse. I didn't know you were working tonight."

"I've got to take care of a few things in the office." He glanced at Joey, who was still chatting happily with her aunt, and looked amused. "Has she ditched you for the cool kids already?"

"Nah. It's Tara."

Jesse smirked. "Sorry, cuz, but I'd ditch you for Tara, too."

"Back off, old man. She's far too young for you."

"Hold on, Tara." Joey bounced onto her knees on the chair. "Hi, Uncle Jesse!" She hugged him. "Guess what! Tara's coming Sunday for *two* whole weeks."

"That's awesome. Save me some of her cookies this time, will ya?" Jesse ruffled Joey's hair, and she giggled.

"Dad, Tara wants to talk to you, and look, Emily is here." Joey pointed across the restaurant at her classmate. "Can I go say hi?"

Emily was waving from a table where she sat with her younger sister, Annie, and their mother, Lauren. Lauren tilted her head, smiling flirtatiously. The curvy brunette could make a career out of hitting on him. He was used to it from her and a few other single moms in their mid-to-late thirties, including Joey's teacher, a gorgeous redhead. There had been a time when Levi had been attracted to women who aggressively pursued him. It had fed his teenage ego, but Amelia had turned that attraction into inherent distaste, and he'd never gotten over it. He lifted his chin in acknowledgment to Lauren and realized that was another reason he was so attracted to Tara. She'd never once come onto him. The way his feelings had rushed in, he wondered if she'd had his attention all along, and he'd just been suppressing those feelings.

"Sure, peanut. Give me the phone, and don't stay at her table too long." He reached across the table. Joey gave him the phone and made a beeline for her friend.

As Jesse lowered himself to the chair she'd vacated, Levi put the phone to his ear. "Hey, blondie."

"She's so excited about the dance. I'm glad we found that dress for her last month." Joey didn't love wearing dresses, but she'd wanted one for the dance that she could wear with her skateboarding sneakers. Tara had taken her shopping while Levi was at work, and they'd found a cute dress that had a sleeveless denim top with sparkly embellishments on the collar and a fluffy, colorful jagged-edged skirt that went perfectly with her sneakers. "But we'd better keep our eyes and ears open where boys are concerned. It sounds like peer pressure is nipping at her heels."

"I'm trying not to think about that."

"I figured as much, but don't worry. She's got a good head on her shoulders, and she talks to us. That's what's important."

Us. They used that term often when talking about Joey, but it hit differently tonight. Just like his need to see Tara's beautiful face and every other thing where she was concerned. "I was thinking, are you busy Friday night?"

Jesse arched a brow curiously.

"Not really. Why?" Tara asked.

"Want to be my date for the school dance?"

Jesse chuckled, shaking his head. Levi glowered at him.

"Your *date*?" Tara asked.

"Yeah. You know how the single moms are always after me. You can help me fend them off." *I sound ridiculous.*

"You want *me* to be your *chick repellant*?" she asked with sheer disbelief.

No. I can fend for myself, but I want you by my side. He needed to feel out the situation before he could put those cards on the table. "Something like that. What do you say? I'm sure I can get them to play Taylor Swift for you."

"You're *serious*?" she asked softly.

"Hell yes. You know we'll have fun, and don't even try to pretend that you have a better offer than going to an elementary school dance with the hottest guy in Harborside and your favorite niece." There was no shame in his game.

"Well, if you put it that way, how can I say no?"

"Yes!" His overzealous exclamation earned another head shake from Jesse.

"Those women must be really pushy for you to be that happy," Tara said.

He was so excited, he'd already forgotten the ruse. "They are. You'd better stay close to me at the dance."

She was quiet for a second, and he wished he knew what she was thinking. "I just realized that I have an early-morning shoot Saturday."

Is that an excuse to blow me off? "I promise to get you to the ferry right after the dance, and I know a certain little girl who will be psyched to hear you're joining us."

"Great. Now I just have to find a dress."

"Short and sexy for the win." Levi could practically hear her eyes roll, and he freaking loved it. They talked for another minute, and he ended the call feeling like he'd won the lottery.

"Dude, I had no idea you were into Tara," Jesse said.

"What makes you think I am?"

"That goofy grin you're sporting. But *that's* your move? Asking her to your kid's dance?"

"It's complicated." He scrubbed a hand down his face, but the stupid grin was plastered there.

Joey returned to the table with Emily and Annie. "Dad, can I play pinball with them in the game room if their mom comes with us?"

Lauren was heading to his table, openly devouring Levi.

"Sure, baby." He dug a couple of dollars out of his pocket and gave them to Joey. "You know the rules."

"Stay together, don't go to the bathroom alone, and don't talk to any strangers," she recited dutifully.

"Hi, Levi. Care to join us?" Lauren asked without acknowledging Jesse.

"Thanks, but my cousin and I are having an important discussion. Maybe another time."

"I'm holding you to it," Lauren said, then followed the girls toward the game room.

"Isn't that the woman who tried to get you to go out with her after the winter festival?" Jesse asked.

"Yeah, that's her."

Jesse clasped his hands behind his head and sat back. "Things are starting to make sense."

"What are you talking about?"

"Women hit on you all the time. I've been wondering why you haven't been into them. Now I know. You've been bullshitting me about not being into Tara. So, how long has this thing been going on?"

"There's nothing going on, and I never bullshitted you."

Jesse cleared his throat. "Then what am I missing? If there's nothing going on with you and Tara, why are you turning down beautiful women?"

"I'm not into aggressive women."

"And Tara?"

His jaw clenched as he briefly debated denying his feelings, but they'd already become too big for that. "She has no idea I'm into her, which is good for now, because of Joey and Amelia." *And her family and probably a hundred other reasons I haven't thought of yet.* Levi told him about Archer's comments and the domino effect they'd caused.

"*Ah*, she's your forbidden fruit."

"That's not what this is." He'd been picking apart his feelings for days, and they were far deeper than wanting what he couldn't have.

"Sure it is," Jesse said. "Everyone has that one person they're dying to get their hands on, but they convince themself otherwise and do such a great job of it, they forget they're doing it. But when that switch is flicked, there's no turning it off, because in here"—he patted his chest over his heart—"and in here"—he tapped his temple—"they've been comparing every other man or woman to that person. How long they've been doing it is different for everyone, but I think it's been at least a few years for you and Tara."

Levi had come to the same conclusion.

"But it wouldn't matter if it's been only a month or a week. The bottom line is always the same," Jesse said. "No one else will ever do."

Levi chewed on that for a minute, taking a swig of his beer. "What makes you such an expert?"

"I've seen it happen a million times."

Levi studied his cousin, mentally paging through his women friends and ex-girlfriends. Jesse had a few crazy-ass exes, and he was wicked close to Brooke Baker. Brooke owned Brooke's Bytes, an internet café on the boardwalk, and she co-owned a party-planning and catering business with their friend Cassidy Lowell, a photographer. But Jesse was close to a lot of women. He was a great listener, and that drew them like flies. "Who's your forbidden friend?"

"Wouldn't you like to know?" He grinned, but his expression turned serious again. "So, what's the dilemma? Amelia's barely in Joey's life, and your history together was nothing more than one night, right?"

"Yeah, but that doesn't matter. She's *still* Joey's mother, and Tara's still Amelia's sister and Joey's best buddy…who I just asked to a freaking elementary school dance just so I could see her face." He sat back, shaking his head. "Jesus, I'm pathetic."

"You're into a gorgeous blonde who looks at you like you've hung the moon and loves your kid. Yeah, man, real pathetic," Jesse said sarcastically.

"You think she looks at me like that?"

"Like all the other women do? Like you've got a golden dick?"

Levi shook his head. "Just answer the question. I need to find out if this is one-sided and all in my head before I lose my mind, but asking her if she's into me will open up a can of worms that could ruin our relationship and her relationship with Joey."

"Then it's a good thing you've got a golden *rod*, because when you're around, I'm pretty sure you and Joey are *all* she sees. Don't you notice the way she looks at you?"

"Lately I think I do, but I'm so into her, I don't trust my judgment."

"Either you've been out of the game too long, or you're being humble, and we both know you're not *that* humble. *Yes*, she looks at you like that. What's your plan once you get her to the dance? Ask her if she wants to go steady and sneak her into a janitor's closet to feel her up?"

Levi would never live down being caught in the janitor's closet with Iris Simmons, the lucky recipient of his first sloppy kiss and nervous, sweaty hands. Luckily, it hadn't taken him long to master the art of making out. "That's about how ridiculous I feel. Like I'm back in seventh grade, with all these feelings and no clue how to handle them."

"Hey, seventh-grade Levi was the hottest bad boy around. If you could tap into him again, you might have a chance."

Levi thought back to that awkward year when he'd been into boy bands and had wanted to dye his hair blond. Archer and Jock had offered to do it for him. Little did Levi know his helpful older brothers had planned on pranking him. They'd dyed his hair pink and, unbeknownst to him, had shaved a penis into the back of his head and somehow managed to keep him away from everyone until he'd gone to school the next day. It would have been an epic prank, if not for his mother saving his reputation by shaving his head after he was sent home from school. The girls had gone crazy for his new look, calling him a rebel and a bad boy. He'd gone from feeling like an awkward kid to the toughest guy in school with nothing more than a new haircut and bolstered confidence. He'd eaten up the attention of his instant harem, and that had been the start of Levi Steele figuring out who he was and where he fit in. He'd asked for a leather jacket for Christmas and had never looked back.

"Seriously, man," Jesse said. "What's your plan with Tara?"

"I don't have a clue. There's a lot at risk. I guess I'll figure it out when I see her."

Jesse smirked. "If all else fails, there's always the janitor's closet."

Eight

"MY FRIENDS ARE excited that you're coming to the dance. They *all* want to dance with you." Joey sat on the upstairs bathroom sink in her pretty dress and skater sneakers, fidgeting with her bracelet and watching Tara put on her makeup before the dance. Tara had offered to do something special with Joey's hair, but in true Joey style, she said she was going to *rock it* just as it was, glossy and straight.

"I'm excited, too." The *old* Tara would have tried to twist Levi's invitation into anything other than being his personal woman repellant. But the new Tara, the one with a realistic perspective and a plan for moving on, tried not to waste her brainpower on such futile thoughts. Instead, she decided to simply do as he'd asked and pretend they were together. Acting like she was into Levi would *not* be a hardship. She'd gone shopping with Jules and Bellamy and had bought a sexy sleeveless olive-green dress with a formfitting tank-style bodice and a flowy jagged skirt, like Joey's. Jules and Bellamy had assured her it was school-dance appropriate, and Joey was excited that they were wearing similar dresses. She'd worn dangling gold earrings to go with her infinite heart charm necklace.

"Daddy said you have to go home after the dance, but you'll be back Sunday, right?"

"I sure will." Tara finished applying her eyeliner and began putting on blush. "Have you thought of anything else you want to do during spring break?"

"Uh-huh. *Lots* of things. Go skateboarding, and to the movies, and the boardwalk. I want to have lunch at Brooke's Bytes so I can see Brooke."

"That sounds great. Your dad might want to join us on the boardwalk. You know how much he loves playing in the arcade."

Joey giggled. "He's like a big kid. Okay, he can go. Emily, Avery, and Robby want to have playdates, and I want to watch *Just Desserts* and make something yummy." Emily and Avery were her friends from school, and Robby was one of her skateboarding buddies. "Daddy said we should cook him dinner from my cookbook like we did last time."

"Sounds like we're going to be busy."

"Are you girls almost ready, or do I need to come up there and get you?" Levi hollered upstairs.

"*Don't,* Daddy! You know Grandma's rules!" Joey shouted. "The Steele ladies *always* make an entrance!"

That rule was another thing Tara loved about the Steeles. For as long as she could remember, Levi's mother and sisters would get ready for events together, no matter how big or small, and every single time, Levi's father would wait at the bottom of the stairs praising them as they each made their way down. They'd included Joey in their pre-event ritual since she was an infant, when one of Levi's sisters had carried her downstairs, and he would gush over both of them. Tara was pretty sure it would be impossible to grow up in the Steele household and not be self-confident.

She tried to ignore the flip-flopping of her stomach as she tapped Joey's nose with her makeup brush. "You're going to be the most beautiful girl at the dance, cutie." She lifted Joey off the counter and set her on her feet.

Joey smiled up at her. "Ready?"

"I sure am. We just need to grab our sweaters from your room." Tara took her hand, remembering the first time she'd helped Joey get ready for an event in Harborside. Joey had been four, and the Dark Knights had been hosting their annual charity ball to fund their literacy and anti-bullying programs. Joey had beamed up at her then, too, and said, *Time for our Steele-lady entwance.* Tara had tried to explain that she wasn't a Steele and had encouraged Joey to make her entrance alone, but Joey had gotten so upset, she'd relented. Levi had been waiting at the bottom of the stairs and Tara had quickly tried to explain, but he'd cut her off and he'd said, *All beautiful ladies get to make an entrance in our house.* Being called beautiful by Levi had set her nineteen-year-old heart aquiver.

Now her heart was beating rapidly for a whole different reason. She grabbed their sweaters from Joey's room, hoping Levi liked her dress.

"Here we come!" Joey yelled.

As they made their way downstairs, Levi's admiration was clear as a summer sky. He turned his attention to Joey. "Wow, sweets. You look beautiful."

"Thanks, Daddy."

His dark eyes shifted to Tara, holding her gaze for a few

heart-thrumming seconds before raking slowly down the length of her. She steeled herself against the heat slithering through her, refusing to give in to her childish fantasies.

He met her gaze again, a coy grin lifting his lips. "I'm going to be the luckiest guy at the dance, with a gorgeous girl on one arm and a stunning woman on the other."

Tara's cheeks heated.

"Come on. Let's go!" Joey ran to the door.

He put a hand on Tara's lower back, speaking quietly as they followed Joey. "That's quite a dress."

"Is it too much?"

"It's *perfect.* But I'm glad I'm the only dad who signed up to chaperone. I'd hate to have to take a man down for ogling you."

The old Tara would have swooned over those words, wrapped them up in pretty little bows and ruminated over them for weeks. But not the new Tara.

She actually had no idea what the new Tara would do, because she was too busy trying not to drool over Levi as they made their way outside. He looked unfairly hot in a black button-down with the sleeves rolled up, revealing his muscular forearms and tattoos, dark jeans that hugged his ass, and those badass biker boots that always did her in.

Damn him.

Thankfully, she'd managed to pull her head out of the clouds by the time they reached Joey's school. They'd been there for an hour and the dance was in full swing. Pastel balloon arches crisscrossed over the gymnasium floor, and twinkling lights gave the room a magical feel. A SPRING FLING banner hung across the stage, where a DJ was playing pop music. Kids were running around in cute outfits, dancing, eating goodies from the snack table, and taking pictures at the framed photo stand, where they'd provided props on sticks like funny hats, glasses, ties, mustaches, and bunny ears. Tara and Levi had just finished dancing with Joey and her friends, and they were watching the kids run around.

"Incoming," Levi warned, sliding his arm around Tara's waist.

He'd stuck to her like glue. Not that she was complaining. She was having a fantastic time, even if they were getting curious looks from the other chaperones. She followed Levi's gaze to Joey's teacher. Joey raved about her. "You've got to be kidding. Miss Moore hits on you?"

"She sure does. Just watch."

Tara's nerves prickled. She'd seen a few of the other women checking out Levi, but she hadn't seen any hit on him. She smiled at Miss Moore, who returned the smile as she strolled past them, heading for a group of kids. "I don't think you need my help. Nobody's hitting on you."

"That's because it's working."

She rolled her eyes.

He tightened his grip on her waist, making her even more aware of the heat spreading beneath his hand as he pulled her closer, speaking low and all too seductively. "Roll your eyes all you want, but they know there's no competition for you, especially in that killer dress."

She kept her eyes trained on Joey, afraid if she looked at Levi, he'd somehow see, or sense, the thrills ricocheting through her like a pinball. She scrambled for a response that wouldn't reveal her swooning. "They're probably thinking I'm closer in age to the kids than the adults."

"That's called jealousy, T, and it's written all over their faces. Look at the women by the entrance to the gym."

She glanced in that direction, catching Emily's mother, a beautiful brunette she'd met once or twice, a tall, thin blonde, and a petite blonde watching them. The women quickly looked away. Were there that many single moms around there? *They don't have to be single to appreciate how good-looking Levi is.* "Okay, so maybe some of them have the hots for you."

"I told you. I bet they're thinking, *She's gorgeous, and his daughter loves her. We might as well give up even trying to get his attention.*"

"How can that possibly be *good* for you? Shouldn't you be reveling in their attention?"

He stepped in front of Tara, blocking the other women's view, his gaze pinning her in place. "I'm too busy reveling in yours."

He really needed to stop saying nice things tonight, because they were landing like warm summer breezes, making her want to close her eyes and disappear into him. She was getting too caught up in him again, and she couldn't afford to backslide. Breathing space. That was what she needed to rein in her emotions. *Lots of it.*

A group of kids ran past, heading for the snack table.

The perfect escape.

"I'm going to grab a snack. I'll be right back." Before he could offer to go with her, she hurried away, chased by the heat of his stare. Was this all in her head? She tried to stop the mental tug-of-war she was having with his comments and what felt like possessiveness rather than his usual protectiveness. But she couldn't escape them any more than she could shake off the feeling of him watching her.

The urge to look back was so strong, she couldn't resist stealing a glance over her shoulder. His dark eyes were still trained on her. He winked, his lips quirking up, sparking a torrent of confusing, and equally exciting, thoughts. Was he just playing her again, or was this something more? *Ugh.* She wished she could turn off her brain.

She spun around, nearly barreling into another chaperone. "I'm so sorry. I was"—*losing my mind.*

"It's okay. If I could get my husband to come to the dance, I'd have a hard time concentrating, too," the woman said kindly, and walked away.

Tara didn't have the bandwidth to correct her. She stepped up to the snack table and focused on the cupcakes instead of the man who was driving her nuts either for his own amusement, or—Levi's voice trampled through her mind. *I like to explore her mind, figure out how she thinks, what she likes, what turns her off…and on.*

Could he be…?

Her nerves flamed, and she stole another glance at him. He was talking with Emily's mother. She must have practically run across the room to him when Tara walked away. Jealousy clawed up her spine, and she turned back to the snack table, only to find herself standing between the other two women who had been ogling Levi with Emily's mother.

"Now, *that* looks delicious," the petite blonde said.

"Too good to resist," the taller blonde said.

Like a certain man I know. Wait. Were they talking about Levi or the cupcakes?

The petite blonde smiled at Tara. "You're here with Levi, aren't you?"

As if you weren't watching us five minutes ago. "Yeah. I'm Tara."

"The nanny, right? Here to take care of Joey for spring

break?" the taller blonde asked, giving Tara a condescending once-over.

"No, she's her *aunt*," the other woman corrected her. "At least that's what Emily told Lauren."

"Emily's right. I'm Joey's aunt." *And I'm really not in the mood for twenty questions.* She picked up a cupcake.

"Oh, well, you and Levi seem *awfully* close," the taller one said, as if that fact irritated her.

"Unless you're his sister?" the other woman asked hopefully.

"They seem oddly close for siblings," the taller blonde said.

Levi wasn't kidding. They were like well-orchestrated vultures. These two were sent to pick the meat off her bones while the curvy brunette looked like she wanted to eat Levi alive. He was nodding appreciatively at the brunette.

Was he into her?

The green-eyed monster perched on her shoulder, its talons digging into her skin.

If he wanted her to repel women, she was about to do one hell of a job. Emboldened by her frustrations, she met the two blondes' curious gazes. "I'm not his sister, and we are *very* close." She scooped frosting onto her finger and raised her brows. "Like icing on a cupcake." She sucked the icing off her finger, thoroughly enjoying their jaw-dropping expressions, and peeled the cupcake liner off, dropping it in the trash can beside the table. "If you'll excuse me, Levi's waiting."

She stalked across the room, as irritated with the women as she was with Levi and herself. Emily's mother threw her head back, laughing in that fake way women did when they were trying to impress a guy, and Levi gave Tara a *save me* look.

Drawing on the advice Bellamy had given her, she used her sexiest breathy voice and turned up the heat. "Sorry I took so long. I know how much you like sharing desserts, and I wanted to pick the perfect one." She put her hand on his chest, feeling his heartbeat quicken, and boldly turned to the other woman. "Sorry. This will just take a second. He goes *wild* for sweet treats." She held up the cupcake. "Open up, big boy."

Flames flickered in his eyes as his fingers circled her wrist. His eyes remained trained on hers. His lips brushed her fingers as he bit into the cupcake. Holy cow, watching him eat was like an aphrodisiac. Or maybe that was the way he was looking at her, like he wished he were licking *her* from his lips instead of icing. Tara was vaguely aware of Lauren saying something and walking away, but Levi was sliding his other arm around her waist.

"Guess I nailed it," came out a little shaky.

"You little siren. Where have you been hiding?" He pulled her closer, guiding the cupcake toward her mouth, his eyes turning volcanic. "Your turn."

Like a kitten offered milk, she lapped up his gruff demand and took a bite of the sugary treat. She could barely hear past the blood pounding through her ears, much less swallow. When she finally managed to gulp it down, she licked her lips, and his eyes turned impossibly darker. Forget swallowing. She needed to remember how to *breathe*.

"Dad! Auntie Tara!" Joey shouted as she ran toward them with three of her girlfriends.

Tara tried to pull out of Levi's grip, but he kept her close.

"Finish your cupcake and come dance with us!" Joey said.

"Please?" her friends pleaded.

"We'll meet you on the dance floor in a sec," Levi said casually, as if he weren't holding Tara hostage against his smoldering body.

"Okay!" the girls said in unison and ran toward the stage.

Levi didn't say a word as he finished the last bite of the cupcake, his mesmerizing eyes scanning the area around them. He turned their backs to the rest of the party. Still holding Tara tightly, he gazed deeply into her eyes as he lifted her hand to his lips and licked the frosting from her fingers. *Sweet baby Jesus.* Could he feel her burning up inside? Sense the needy pulse between her legs? She was sure everyone there could see sparks flying, but she was powerless to break their connection. When he reached up and slowly dragged his thumb over her lips, *Kiss me,* whispered through her mind.

A slow grin slid across his handsome face. "Time to dance, secret siren."

He took her hand and started walking toward the kids. But her feet were rooted in place. She was afraid her noodle legs wouldn't hold her up if she moved. He turned back to her, and she must have looked as light-headed as she felt, because his grin turned devilish. "Guess there's no denying it now."

"Denying what?" she asked so hopefully she felt like she might burst.

He stared at her for a beat before saying, "That I've still got it."

That snapped her from her trance, and in the space of a second, disappointment was kicked to the curb by annoyance. "I *hate* you right now."

"You know you love me." His words oozed with charm, and that devilish grin turned boyish and playful, tugging at her stupid heart that had liked him for far too long. "Come on, blondie. Let's go have some fun."

As he dragged her toward the dance floor, she said, "You are no longer allowed to use me as your woman repellant *or* your gauge for if you still have *it* or not. Got it, Steele?"

"Got it, blondie." He winked as Joey and her friends squealed and grabbed their hands, pulling them into their circle to dance.

Levi immediately fell into goofy dance moves, and Tara joined him, earning soul-healing laughter from the girls and other kids who were standing nearby watching them. They danced with the girls, and with each other, to one song after another, leaving no room for overthinking, or anything else other than pure, unadulterated joy.

When "Butterflies" by MAX and Ali Gatie came on, another of Joey's favorite songs, Levi reached for her. "Come dance with your dear old dad."

"Let's go take pictures!" one of Joey's friends shouted, and her friends took off for the photo booth.

"Sorry, Dad!" Joey ran after her friends.

Levi locked eyes with Tara. "You know what that means." He crooked his finger.

Tara put her hand on her chest, feigning surprise and looking around before mouthing, *Me?*

"Get in here." He tugged her against him.

Her arms circled his neck, and they fell into an easy slow dance. There were a few kids on the dance floor, but Tara felt the stares of the other chaperones. "Is it okay that we're slow dancing? Everyone's watching us."

"I told you they're jealous. Forget them. Focus on me."

"Every time I do that, you leave me weak-kneed." She was surprised the truth came so easily.

"You have no room to complain after what you did to me with that cupcake."

"What I did to *you*?"

"Don't pretend you don't know."

She wanted to believe he meant that she had the same effect on him as he had on her, but she wasn't going to play that game or she'd end up with another case of whiplash. Instead, she threw his words back at him. "Guess I've still got it, too."

"Hell yeah, you do."

And there it was, that seductive lilt to his voice that brought as much hope as butterflies. She mentally swatted them away.

"Are you having a good time?" he asked.

"*Mm-hm.* You?"

"This is the best time I've ever had at a school dance."

"At any school dance, including your own?"

"Easily. Dances were nerve-racking when I was a kid."

"I don't believe that. You were the cool kid."

"Just because I was cool doesn't mean I wasn't nervous. Being a cool kid is tough, trying to say and do the right things to impress your friends *and* girls."

"Tell me about it," she said flatly. "School dances kind of sucked when I was Joey's age."

"You were a bit of a wallflower, but then 'Thriller' girl showed up and threw everyone for a loop."

"Jules and Bellamy can get me to do just about anything." She was pretty sure he could, too.

"You were cute and gutsy back then, but I liked the rendition you did at the Field of Screams Halloween party last year." He held her tighter. "You've refined your moves, or maybe it was the *sexy* mouse costume."

A little thrill darted through her. She'd bought that costume hoping he'd think it was sexy. "You mean I didn't look like an uncoordinated, flailing kid?" she joked.

"Hardly."

"You can thank your sisters for that. I spent a lot of time watching Sutton and Leni dance at community parties when I was growing up. I thought they were the coolest girls around."

"So did they," he joked. "Speaking of my sisters, want to hear something crazy?"

"Sure."

He held her a little tighter. "They think you and I should go out."

A surprised "*Oh*" came out before she could stop it. *Holy crap.* He said sisters, *plural,* which meant he wasn't just talking about Jules. "Really?"

"Crazy. Right?"

And there it was. The way he felt about it, with no pretense. Just his honest feelings. "Yeah, crazy," she said softly, trying not to give in to the crushing feeling in her chest.

Thankfully, the song ended, and Joey and her friends barreled into them, tugging them apart and away from the dance floor. "Come take pictures with us!"

The rest of the evening was a blur of photo booth pictures and dancing with Joey and her friends, all of which only mildly distracted Tara from the ache in her chest. She didn't know why she was so devastated. She'd made a resolution and had already given up the idea of ever having anything more than friendship with Levi. So why did it hurt so bad to finally know exactly where he stood? She struggled against the reality that she'd thought she'd already accepted, reminding herself that it was okay. That *she'd* be okay and that friendship was what she'd decided she wanted anyway.

By the time they left the dance, she'd *almost* put that sadness away. But it lingered, clinging like humidity before a summer storm.

"That was *so* fun," Joey exclaimed, holding Tara's and Levi's hands as they walked out of the school. "I'm glad you came, Aunt Tara."

"I am, too." *Now I know for sure where I stand with your daddy.*

"That makes three of us," Levi said. "What time will you be here Sunday, T?"

Somehow staying with them was easier before she'd known for sure that her feelings would always be unrequited. She wouldn't even have time to mourn her dreams of having something more. Maybe it was better this way. It would force her to pull herself up by her camera strap and see the truth through her lens, instead of the beautiful fantasies she'd been weaving forever. "What time do you need me?"

His lips quirked, and if she didn't know better, she'd swear that was a flirtatious glint in his eyes. But she *did* know better. It was time to refocus on her goals—buying a house, finding a studio, and getting over Levi—and let him know this would be her last long-term stay with them.

"Daddy's going riding at noon, and I'm hanging out with the other kids. Then we're all meeting at the Taproom. Can she meet us there, Dad?" The Taproom was a rustic restaurant and bar that was family friendly during the day, adult oriented at night, and owned by two of Levi's friends, twins Wyatt and Delilah Armstrong.

"That's up to Tara." He opened the back door of his SUV for Joey and helped her in. She scooted over to the other side of the bench seat. "What do you think, T? We're meeting up around four."

"That's fine."

"Yay!" Joey cheered. "Aunt Tara, will you sit back here with me?"

"Sure." She climbed into the back seat, relieved not to have to sit up front and talk with Levi. She didn't think she could pull off pretending to be happy.

Levi put his hand on hers, giving it a gentle squeeze. "Are you okay? You're kind of quiet."

"Mm-hm. I'm just tired."

Joey yawned and leaned against her. "Me too."

Levi's expression turned serious, and he looked at her for a long moment before closing the door and climbing into the driver's seat.

Joey fell asleep on the twenty-minute drive to the ferry, and Levi must have glanced at Tara in the rearview mirror about a hundred times. She looked out the window to avoid the spear of longing those glances caused and gave herself a much-needed pep talk, reminding herself of all the reasons she'd made that resolution in the first place. She could live without his love, even if it left her feeling empty inside, but she couldn't give up his friendship, and she needed to be in Joey's life. Those two things were nonnegotiable.

She rested her head back and closed her eyes, thinking of Jules, Indi, and Daphne. She wanted what they had. A man who would go to the ends of the earth for her, not toy with her emotions. She reopened her eyes, gazing out the window as they drove down to the pier, willing herself not to cry because that man would never be Levi. Why was being just friends with Levi so excruciating when it had seemed acceptable the night they'd had dinner together in Seaport?

Sadness pressed in on her as he parked. He left the SUV running as he got out to open her door. She kissed the top of Joey's head, whispering, "I love you. See you Sunday."

Joey mumbled a sleepy, "G'night," and closed her eyes again.

Tara took Levi's hand and stepped out. He closed the door, drawing her into his arms for their typical goodbye hug. Bringing a car on the ferry was expensive, so she brought hers only when she was working or watching Joey. Not when she was there for only a few hours with both of them. Now she wished she had brought it, to avoid this very moment.

A boarding announcement rang out for the ferry, and instead of letting her go, Levi held her tighter. When his grip finally eased, he kept one arm around her and his gaze bored into hers, stirring butterflies despite everything. He put his warm, rough hand on her cheek and dipped his face beside hers, whispering, "Maybe my sisters' idea isn't so crazy, after all."

The air rushed from her lungs. Had she heard him right? His lips brushed the edge of her mouth as he kissed her cheek, sending shivers of heat skating down her chest. When his eyes found hers again, she couldn't breathe, couldn't think, could barely stand. A last call for boarding the ferry rang out, and she managed, "I'd better—"

He nodded, stepping back. "I'll see you Sunday."

"Okay," she said, or at least she thought she did as she headed for the ferry, praying her legs wouldn't fail her. Levi's voice echoed in her head—*Maybe my sisters' idea isn't so crazy, after all*—as she boarded, clinging to the railing. She collapsed into the first seat she saw, like an automaton. But those words were too much to take, and she went to stand at the railing, gulping the brisk night air into her lungs, as the ferry pulled away from the dock. She looked back at the parking lot, and her heart stumbled at the sight of Levi standing in the ray of his headlights, watching her go.

Nine

TIME HAD NEVER moved so slowly. It was Saturday night, and Levi was sitting on Joey's bed with his daughter tucked under his arm as he read three chapters of one of her Unicorn Academy books. They'd had a great day together, but the look on Tara's face before she'd left last night was etched into his mind, and he couldn't read what he'd seen beyond shock. Hell, he'd been shocked, too. It wasn't like he'd planned on saying that. It had come without thought or warning, and then it was out there. Lodged between them like a double-edged sword.

He'd wanted to reach out to her today, but he hadn't wanted to do it while he was with Joey. He'd never forgive himself if he screwed up their friendship, and if he didn't talk to her soon, he was going to drive himself insane, and then it wouldn't matter, because he'd be locked in an asylum and Joey would be with his parents.

Could he go any farther down a rabbit hole?

He finished reading the end of the third chapter and closed the book, anxious to get downstairs and text Tara. But he and

Joey had a bedtime ritual, and he wasn't going to rip her off just to put his own mind at ease. *Or break my own damn heart.*

Holy shit. Since when did he think of that particular organ?

"I wish unicorns were real," Joey said as he set the book on her nightstand.

"I wish they were, too, so you could have one. But you can dream about them. That'll make them seem real."

"Da-ad."

She'd begun stretching his name into two exasperated syllables a few weeks ago, and he'd wanted to make her take it back. To turn back time to before she'd learned to roll her eyes and think Daddy was anything short of magical. After the things his father had said about Joey eventually having too busy a social life to include him, he saw that time coming far too quickly. The truth was, Levi wouldn't trade her growing up and coming into her own for anything, but that didn't mean he wouldn't feel his losses along the way.

"If only dreams *could* make them real," Joey said. "That would be cool."

"If only…" Then he'd have seen lust on Tara's face instead of shock. He didn't even know what to make of that shock. Had the idea of going out with him horrified her? Or had it stunned her into silence because she wanted him *that* badly? *Please be the latter.*

He kissed Joey's forehead and climbed off her bed.

"Don't forget my stuffies."

He arched a brow. "Do I ever forget?"

She shook her head, grinning as he began placing her menagerie of stuffed animals around her. "Mr. Bear needs to sleep here tonight." He tucked the brown bear under her right arm. "Olive wants to snuggle with Mr. Bear." He put the stuffed hedgehog beside the bear.

"Snout wants to be here!" Joey reached for her dalmatian and tucked it under her right arm. "Do Peanut next."

He pretended to walk Peanut the piglet up her leg, and she giggled. "Where to?"

"Next to Snout of course."

"Of course." Her stuffies slept in different places every night. They continued the ritual until she had stuffed animals lined up along her right and left sides and one over each shoulder. Levi kissed her forehead. "I love you, sweets. Get some sleep. You have a big day tomorrow."

"Auntie Tara is coming," she said excitedly. "Maybe she'll go on an adventure with me while she's here. I love her adventures."

"I'm sure she'd love to." Tara had a great imagination and had been making up adventures for Joey with elaborate maps and scavenger hunts since Joey was old enough to follow along. There had to be some sin wrapped up in the fact that he was wondering if Tara was adventurous in the bedroom, too.

He tried to push that thought aside as he leaned down to give Joey another good night kiss. "I love you."

"Love you, Daddy. Have good dreams."

"You too, baby." He turned out her light and pulled the door behind him, leaving it ajar.

Tara remained on his mind as he went downstairs, his gaze sweeping over the open living room and kitchen, taking in the little touches she'd added over the years, like the plants she'd taught Joey to care for that sat in nearly every window and the framed picture of Joey's handprints that Tara had started a week after Joey was born and had added to every year on her birthday. How had a fifteen-year-old girl known to do something so special? He looked at the old wooden ladder in the corner of the room that she and Joey had found at a yard sale when he was at work. They had painted it red with gold stars and draped throw blankets over each rung, brightening the entire room.

His phone rang, jarring him from his thoughts. He pulled it out of his pocket, hoping it was Tara, and saw Leni's name on the screen. He shoved his disappointment down deep and answered the call. "Hey, Len."

"What is *wrong* with your species?"

He flopped onto the couch. "How much time ya got?"

"I'm serious. I spent forty-five minutes every night for the better part of a week talking to this guy, and he asked me to meet him for dinner. You know I always meet guys for coffee first, to make sure they pass muster, but we got along great, and I figured I'd go for it. I had to rearrange my schedule, because you know, *work*, and then he doesn't show up and doesn't call. What the hell? Is it so hard to pick up the phone and call?"

"I'm sorry that happened, but you know guys can be dicks."

"No shit. I have no idea why I agreed to go out with him. *This* is why I don't date. What are you doing tonight?"

"Driving myself insane." He kicked his feet up on the coffee table, crossing his legs at the ankles. His arm brushed the colorful father-daughter pillow Tara had given him for his second Father's Day, and as he moved it, his gaze caught on the enormous collage on the wall by the kitchen table that Tara and Joey had made. They'd painted and decorated old picture frames—more yard sale finds—then glued them together at interesting angles and filled them with pictures Tara had taken of Levi, Joey, and their family. The night they'd made it, he'd secured their glued frames, which had already started coming loose, with hardware before hanging them up. He'd since swapped a few of the pictures for one of Tara holding Joey as a baby, swimming with her at the beach, and for one Jesse had taken of the three of them on a hayride during a Dark Knights fall festival a couple of years ago.

"Over what?" Leni asked.

"A woman, believe it or not." Her little touches were everywhere, and each one brought warm memories.

"No way. This I *have* to hear. Who is it?"

He scoffed. He wasn't that stupid, but he could use some advice. "Let me ask you something. If you've been friends with a guy for a while and he tells you he thinks there might be something more between the two of you, how would you react if you were into him?"

"*Might* be? I'd tell him to kiss off. You know there's nothing I hate more than a wishy-washy guy."

He bit out, "*Great.* Guess I screwed up that friendship."

"Oh *God*, Levi. What did you do?"

"Apparently the wrong thing. When did dating become so complicated? What happened to the days when you could look at a girl and be like, *Hey, you're cute, want to hang out?* and the next thing you know you've been dating for three months, having a good time, and enjoying great sex."

"First of all, don't call a woman cute. *Cute* is for Joey."

Strike two.

"Second of all, you were nineteen the last time you really dated. While your peen has been on hold, petering along to elevator music instead of rocking out to hip-grinding tunes—"

"Shut up. I get plenty of action. I just don't talk about it."

"Watching porn after Joey goes to bed doesn't count as action."

He grimaced. "Forget I said anything. I don't know why I thought I could talk to you."

"Because you trust me. I'm just giving you shit. Which friendship did you screw up?"

"Never mind."

"No, really. I promise not to be my jaded self."

"Not possible. I'll figure it out."

"*Fine*, but let me explain a few things. Dating has gone from face-to-face flirting to sexting and naked Snapchats, and women don't just chat with one guy anymore. So if this friend of yours is on dating apps, like most women, then chances are she's chatting with at least a few guys, maybe more like a dozen. Women these days have rosters, and you're lucky to make it off the bench."

"Rosters? A *dozen* guys? Shit." He was definitely not into that, and he couldn't imagine Tara was, either. "I don't think she's on dating apps."

"Don't kid yourself. Most women our age are on them."

"You're not."

"Because I don't have time to weed through a river of sludge."

"Christ, Leni. If I don't stand head and shoulders above *that*, then something's seriously messed up, and you're not making me feel any better."

"Gee, sorry about that," she said sarcastically. "Did you want me to say that any woman would be crazy not to fall at your feet? Because for that you'd have to call Jules."

He leaned forward, resting his forearms on his thighs. Jules would know if Tara was on dating apps. Maybe he should ask her.

Was he *really* thinking of calling his baby sister to chase down answers about a woman? Fuck that, and the hell with trying to figure this out with Leni. "Never mind, Len. I'm going to call her."

"I wouldn't do that."

"Why the hell not?"

"Because nobody talks on the phone anymore, especially if you're not dating or pre-screening to see if you want to date."

"Pre-screening? Is that really a thing?"

"Hell yes. So is video chatting before meeting in person, to be sure you're not being catfished."

"This is a *friend*, remember? We know each other."

"Okay, so forget pre-screening and catfishing, but you can probably count on her app chatting."

"I'll ask her if she's on dating apps."

"Sure, if you want to look like a possessive, insecure asshole."

He leaned back with a sigh and stared up at the ceiling. "You know what? This is all too complicated. I don't want any part of it. She's either into me or she's not."

"Good luck with that."

"Yeah, thanks. I hope your night gets better."

"Oh, it already has. I have a bottle of Archer's award-winning wine and my laptop—"

"Stop right there. I don't want to know the rest. See ya, sis." He ended the call and navigated to Tara's contact info. His thumb hovered over the call button, but after what Leni said, he thought better of it and thumbed out a text. *Hey. Hope your shoot went well. Have you thought about what I said?* He stared at the message for a minute, then deleted it, not wanting to put her on the spot, and typed, *Hey. We're looking forward to seeing you tomorrow. How'd your shoot go?* He read the damn thing three times, finally decided texting was for the *sludge* of the world, as Leni had so gracefully put it, and called Tara.

Her phone rang so many times, he wondered if she was screening her calls. Just as he was about to hang up, she answered, and the sounds of music blaring and loud people assaulted him, nearly drowning her greeting.

"Hey," he said tightly. "I just thought I'd see how your photo shoot went."

"My what?" she practically yelled.

"Your photo shoot."

"*Oh*. It was great. Sorry, I can hardly hear you. I'm out with Bellamy."

He steeled himself against the jealousy pummeling him. What the hell did he think she'd be doing on a Saturday night? Sitting around pining for him? She was young, gorgeous, and single. *And I'm a fucking idiot*. Tara was in an entirely different time and place in her life than he was. She loved Joey, and she gave up her time to be with her, but that didn't say shit about what she thought about him. He had no business going after her when she was unencumbered, free to party in the evenings, and he had a daughter to look after. "I'm glad to hear it went well. Have fun. I'll see you tomorrow."

"*What?*" she practically shouted.

"See you tomorrow," he said louder, and ended the call, wishing he'd never made it.

Ten

TARA DROVE OFF the ferry in Harborside late Sunday afternoon and headed to the other side of town with her heart in her throat to meet Levi and Joey. She'd never been so nervous. It didn't help that she'd barely slept since the dance or that Bellamy had dragged her out last night. Tara had hoped it might take the edge off and give her something to focus on besides the fact that Levi had opened a door she wanted to sprint through and wasn't sure how. But she hadn't been able to hold in her thoughts, and she'd confided in Bellamy about what Levi had said. They'd talked almost all night. Last night it had seemed like everything she wanted was within her grasp, and all she had to do was reach out and take it. But while Bellamy's excitement and support had bolstered her confidence when they were together, now that she was alone and here to stay with Levi and Joey for two weeks, she felt like she was holding herself together with Scotch tape.

She had no idea what to say to Levi, or what to expect when she saw him. Should she bring it up? Just throw it out there, like, *Hey, you know that thing you said Friday night? I'm here for it!* Or should she wait until he brought it up? What if he didn't bring it up? What if he regretted saying it? What if that was why he'd called last night?

Her stomach knotted, and she felt a little woozy.

She gripped the steering wheel tighter, her hands sweating despite the cool temperature as she drove through the quirky beach town, remembering the first time she'd come to see Levi and Joey there a few weeks after they'd moved. She'd gone with Jules, Sutton, and Leni and had instantly fallen in love with the laid-back vibe of the small surfing town, so different from touristy Silver Island. She hadn't been able to picture Levi living so far away from his family after relying on them for the first year of Joey's life, but later that afternoon they'd met Jesse and Brent for lunch, and his cousins had been with a number of other Dark Knights. Tara had been wary at first of the rough-looking men wearing black leather vests with scary skull patches on the backs. She'd never been exposed to bikers before, and some of them looked like they could crush a man's skull with one hand. When Levi had said he'd begun prospecting the club to become a member, she'd worried for his and Joey's safety. But the guys had treated Levi like he was already one of them, like a brother, and they'd fawned over Joey with so much love and tenderness, it had endeared them toward her. They'd wrapped Levi's sisters and Tara in warm embraces as if they'd known them their whole lives and had said things like, *You ever have trouble, you call us and we'll take care of whoever's bothering you.*

She'd wondered what kind of place they thought Silver Island was and exactly what *take care of* had meant. Leni, being the aggressive, afraid-of-nothing young woman she'd always been, had asked just that, and Jesse, Brent, and two of the most intimidating guys Tara had ever seen—Ozzy, a massive man with a thick beard and coal-black eyes who looked like he ate small children for breakfast, and Forge, another mountain of a man, who was half Samoan and half Italian with pitch-black hair and a mile-wide chest—had sat them down and patiently explained what the Dark Knights stood for. *Love, loyalty, and respect for all.* They'd explained the differences between a motorcycle club like the Dark Knights and biker gangs. Tara had been relieved to learn that their club did good things for the community, like spearheading literacy and anti-bullying campaigns.

It hadn't taken long for Tara to understand how Levi had made his life work without his family around or to realize she'd broken her own rule and had wrongfully judged the men who had already become Levi's brotherhood and family by their appearances alone.

She'd been careful not to make that mistake again.

Tara pulled into the parking lot by the long pier that jutted out into the ocean, at the end of which was the Taproom. Motorcycles lined the edge of the lot. It was easy to spot Levi's shiny black Harley. It had several of the colorful braided necklaces and bracelets Joey had made for him over the years wound around the handlebar. Tara had been helping Joey make gifts for Levi since Joey was a toddler, and he'd kept almost every one of them, which just added to the long list of reasons she was crazy about him.

She parked and wiped her sweaty hands on her jeans as she gazed up at the weather-beaten wooden building at the end of the pier. A light shined down on the large driftwood TAPROOM sign on the side of the building. Even from that distance she could see people milling about by the outdoor seating, many wearing black leather vests. She didn't need to see the Dark Knights patches on the backs to recognize them.

Stepping from her car, she inhaled the crisp sea air in a futile attempt to calm her nerves. She pocketed her phone and grabbed her small purse, putting the strap across her body, hanging her camera around her neck. The camera was her safety net. A ready excuse to extricate herself from conversations. She wished she was more like Leni, able to face anything that came her way without so much as a hesitation, but everything she wanted was up on that deck, and there were so many things that could go wrong, she was afraid to face the music.

But she had no choice, and she forced herself to move.

A few minutes later she was on the pier, following the din of deep voices, laughter, and guitar music as she walked past the entrance to the Taproom, toward the crowd. She scanned the deck for Levi, catching sight of Brandon Owens playing the guitar. Brandon wasn't a Dark Knight. He was a graphic designer and musician, and he was sitting a few feet away from where Levi stood talking with Joker, another Dark Knight. Joker was a shameless flirt who looked like Charlie Hunnam and worked for Levi's company.

"Aunt Tara!" Joey burst through the crowd, running toward her in her black leather jacket, pink leggings, and black boots.

Levi looked over, their gazes colliding for one heart-stopping moment before Joey launched herself into Tara's arms. Tara hoisted her onto her hip, hugging her. She smelled like strawberry shampoo and French fries.

Tara marveled at how one little girl could help soothe hours of anxiety. "Are you having fun?"

"*Yes*. Guess what!" Joey exclaimed.

"Hm. Let's see. You and Caleb are getting married?" she teased. Caleb was the nine-year-old son of Cannon and Debra Wheaton. Cannon was a Dark Knight.

Joey giggled. "No, silly. Daddy said we could watch a movie on the wall tonight." Levi had a projector he hooked up to his laptop to show movies on the living room wall, and Joey loved making forts and watching from within them.

"Did he?" She saw Levi and Joker headed her way. Joker was grinning and rubbing his hands together like he was up to something. Levi's jaw was tight, his eyes too serious. Tara swallowed hard, worried he'd changed his mind.

"Uh-huh. Can I sleep in your room tonight?" Joey pleaded.

"Sure. We'll have a slumber party after the movie."

"We're gonna have so much fun!" Joey wriggled out of Tara's arms and ran to Levi.

"There's my favorite blond bombshell," Joker said as he swept his arm around Tara and kissed her cheek.

"Hi, Joker. Your stubble tickles."

"It'll feel even better on your thighs."

"You're too much." She laughed him off, but Levi looked like he was chewing on glass.

Levi lifted his chin. "How's it going?"

Apparently not very well, since you usually hug me, and your hands are fisted. "Good."

Joker put his arm around her shoulder. "Her week is about to get a whole lot better. How about you let me take you out one night?"

He flashed a panty-melting smile that probably earned him all sorts of sexual favors, but Tara's panties didn't melt for anyone but the suddenly brooding biker who had one hand on his daughter's shoulder. She thought Levi would shut Joker down like he usually did when he hit on her, but he didn't, and the realization hit her like a bullet train. *You changed your mind.* Gutted but acutely aware of Joey watching her, she refused to fall apart.

"Thanks, Joker, but I think I'm going to be pretty busy with Joey," she finally said.

"Not twenty-four-seven. Levi might have to be in bed before he turns into a pumpkin, but he'll let you out to play with me." Joker looked at Levi. "Right, old man?"

"You heard the woman," Levi said sternly. "She's gonna be busy."

She glanced appreciatively at Levi, and he gave a single curt nod, twisting the knots in her stomach tighter.

"A'right." Joker raised his brows at Tara. "Babe, if you change your mind, I'm your guy."

Ozzy walked up to them, towering over Tara as he dropped a kiss on the top of her head. "Hey, sweetheart. Good to see you. Let me get the riffraff out of your hair." He grabbed Joker by the back of the neck, dragging him away.

"Is that my girl Tara?" Brent said as he and Jesse came out the back door of the restaurant.

"Yes!" Joey yelled, running to Brent.

Jesse waved, then stopped to talk with someone. Although he and Brent were twins and shared similar collar-length dark hair and athletic physiques, they were as different as Levi and Leni. Jesse's face was harder, his disposition more serious than jovial Brent, and even in the dead of summer, Jesse wore jeans, his leather vest, and boots, while Brent wore board shorts and flip-flops and more often than not was shirtless. Although since they'd just returned from a ride with the club, like Jesse and the rest of the guys, Brent sported jeans, a T-shirt, boots, and his leather vest.

Brent scooped Joey up in one arm, giving Tara a hug with the other. "I hear I'll be seeing a lot of you at skateboard practice with my little skater queen."

"She'll be at them for two whole weeks," Joey exclaimed as he set her on her feet.

"That's right, and I can't wait to see her new tricks," she said as Jesse hugged her. She saw Levi talking with Forge and a few of the other guys. Tara wanted to go talk to him, but Brent was filling her in on skateboard practices, and Joey was tugging them both toward a table with her friends and some of the other members and their significant others, who were getting up to greet Tara.

Tara sucked up her heartache and put her best face forward, spending the next few hours chatting with Joey and catching up with Tonya, Forge's beautiful dark-skinned, hazel-eyed girlfriend of two years, and Leilani, his four-year-old daughter, as well as the rest of Levi's friends. She caught a few cursory glances from Levi and the snarls he directed at the guys when they flirted with her, but she was used to that. What she wasn't used to was every time their eyes connected, either his jaw clenched or his lips twitched, like he wanted to smile but he was holding back. By the time they were ready to sit down to eat dinner, Tara's nerves were on fire.

Joey sat next to Levi, and he patted the chair on his other side for Tara to join them. She thought they'd finally have a second to talk, or at least to acknowledge what he'd said after the dance, but other than making a few minutes of the type of small talk a person made with someone they'd just met, asking about her ferry ride and commenting on the beautiful day, he went over his and Joey's schedule for the week, and then remained close-lipped. Joey having a sleepover at her friend's house Wednesday night *was* important, but it was *not* what she wanted to talk about.

His shoulder brushed against hers, and sparks skated down her arm. She looked over and smiled, but the muscles in his jaw bunched, making the fissure between them even more painful.

She wasn't a needy person, but she felt awkwardly disconnected from him, and she hated it. She missed his smile and their easy friendship and wondered what it was about her that had turned him off before they'd even had a chance to talk.

How was she going to survive two weeks of this?

LEVI COULD COUNT on one hand the number of times in his life he'd wanted to strangle someone. He wasn't a violent guy, but by the time they left the Taproom, he wanted to kick the asses of most of the guys he trusted to always have his back. If he'd had to watch one more of them flirt with Tara, he didn't know what he would have done, but it wouldn't have been good, and that was totally messed up since he'd decided to back off from Tara. She was better off with a guy who wasn't tied down and could go out on the town and have a good time whenever she wanted to.

He carried Tara's bags, following her and Joey into the first-floor guest bedroom. Joey was rattling on about making a fort so she could lie in it to watch the movie, and sweet, beautiful Tara, who had managed to burrow beneath his skin without even trying, was talking with his little girl with a strained expression that was no doubt caused by his assholish behavior.

As if he could help it. He'd never felt like this about a woman before, and he didn't know how to turn those feelings off. Even now the thought of Joker's hands on her made him want to rip Joker's head off, and he liked and trusted the guy.

"Thanks," Tara said softly as he set her bags down.

Her eyes flicked up to his, the light in them dimmer, hesitant. He hated that he'd done that to her. He wanted to pull her into his arms and kiss her until her legs gave out, obliterating her memory of tonight, and he didn't trust himself not to do just that, so he ground his back teeth together and headed out of the bedroom. "I'll get the projector ready."

"I'll get my pj's on," Joey said.

"Wait one sec. I picked up something for you." Tara opened a suitcase and withdrew a gift-wrapped box.

"Thank you! What's this for?" she asked as she tore it open.

"Do I have to have a reason to buy my favorite niece a present?"

Joey gasped and held up a pair of pink flannel pajama shorts and a long-sleeved black cotton top with a sleeping unicorn on it, above which SLEEP SQUAD was written in pink. "Daddy, look!"

His chest constricted. "That's really special, sweets." *Like the woman who gave it to you.* Tara was looking at Joey, at her suitcase, the bed, the floor, anywhere but at him, while he couldn't take his eyes off her. How could he have messed things up so badly that she couldn't even look at him? Thank God her discomfort didn't carry over to her relationship with Joey. *Yet*, stomped through his mind, bringing a sinking feeling to his gut.

"Thank you." Joey threw her arms around her. "I wish you had one, too."

"*Oh*," Tara said sadly. "If only I knew you liked to match."

"You *do* know," Joey insisted. "We have matching sweatshirts and Valentine's Day socks and Dark Knights T-shirts."

"You're *right.*" Tara's brows knitted. "Maybe..." She dug through her suitcase and whipped out a matching outfit.

"I *knew* it." Joey hugged her again.

"That was really nice of you, T."

She finally looked at him, that strained expression returning as she reached into her suitcase again. "The pajama fairy might have brought you something, too."

She tossed something at him, and he caught it with one hand, self-loathing eating away at him. "You didn't have to get me anything."

She shrugged, but she didn't look away, and in those few seconds before Joey exclaimed, "What is it, Daddy?" discomfort wafted off Tara like the wind. She looked away, but he kept looking at her, a dozen apologies flying through his mind, followed by just as many reasons he needed to keep his distance.

"*Dad,*" Joey urged.

He tore his gaze away and held up the incredibly soft black T-shirt that had a badass-looking muscular unicorn on the front. It was standing on its hind legs, wearing a leather vest and black boots, and its front legs were crossed over its broad chest. Its horn was gold and black, the colors of the Dark Knights. SLEEP SQUAD BODYGUARD was written above it in bold gold letters. He planted his feet more firmly on the floor, fighting against the magnetic pull drawing him toward Tara. "I love it, T. Thank you."

"You're welcome," she said without looking up as she picked through her suitcase.

"You're our bodyguard," Joey said excitedly, but it was followed by a yawn. "Let's go put them on." She grabbed his hand, dragging him out of the guest room and down the hall toward the stairs.

"I'll get the projector ready while you change," he said as they went upstairs.

"Okay," Joey said. "I'm glad Tara's here."

"Me too." That tightening sensation filled his chest again. He needed to clear the air and make things right with Tara.

While Joey changed, he retrieved the projector from the hall closet and headed downstairs. He set the projector on the coffee table and started down the hall toward the guest room, trying to figure out what to say. He had no idea where to start. *I'm sorry I said what I did the other night?* But he couldn't say that, because he wasn't sorry. He didn't want to take it back even if he knew he should. *I meant what I said, but you deserve someone who isn't tied down?* His jaw clenched. He didn't want to cut her loose, either. But he had to.

Tara's door was closed, and he heard her talking. Was she telling Jules or Bellamy that he'd been a prick? Or was she talking to some guy she'd met when she was out last night?

"Fuck."

"Dad?"

He spun around, finding Joey in her new pajamas with her comforter wrapped around her and her arms full of stuffed animals. "Hey, peanut. I was just going to tell Tara that you'd be right down. But now that you're here, let's get the projector ready." He put his hand on her shoulder, guiding her back toward the living room.

"Why'd you say the F word?"

Because I suck. "I just remembered something I forgot to do."

She crawled onto the couch and began setting out her stuffed animals as he hooked up the projector. "Do you need to do it before the movie?"

He wanted to, but with little ears around, he wouldn't have a chance. "Nah. It can wait. But I would like to shower before the movie."

"I know." She rested her head on the father-daughter pillow and lay down, snuggling beneath her blanket.

"How do you know?" He finished hooking up the projector and kissed her forehead on the way across the room to move the oversize chairs away from the wall so they could see the movie.

"Because you always shower after you go riding with the club," Tara said as she walked into the living room wearing the pink flannel sleeping shorts that showed off her long, sexy legs, and the unicorn shirt that clung to her small, perfect breasts.

Levi forced himself not to stare and moved the chairs as she crouched beside Joey and said, "Do you want to make a fort in our nook?"

Our nook. She and Joey had names for all of the hidden spaces in their house. *Our nook, our reading hideout, our leave-me-alone spot*...For the first time ever, Levi wished their use of *our* included him. What the hell was that about? He didn't need hideouts or special spots, but he was beginning to think he needed Tara.

"Yeah," Joey said sleepily. "But can I lie here and watch you make it?"

"Sure, cutie." Tara went to the wall behind the couch and slid open the hanging wooden barn doors Levi had stained dark to stand out from the buttercream living room walls, revealing their queen-size nook.

He had built a platform for a queen-sized mattress, with pullout steps for Joey to climb up, and built-in drawers for her toys. When she was younger, those drawers were full of diapers, extra clothes, and anything else a little one might need while they were downstairs. The platform was buttercream to match the living room, and the walls of the nook were dark blue. When Joey was little, she liked to nap in the nook. Back then he'd had railings to keep her in. The first time Tara had seen the nook, she'd cut out cardboard stars, covered them with tinfoil, and asked if she could hang them from the ceiling. He'd been afraid thumbtacks might come loose, so he'd fastened iron rods close to the ceiling, and they'd tied silver ribbons through tiny holes in the stars and hung them from the rods.

Those sparkling stars were still there, along with pictures of gorgeous sunsets over the water that Tara had taken from his back patio, pictures of Levi reading to Joey, and various other photos that Joey and Tara had added over the years of the two of them doing what Joey called sleepy-time things. Levi had taken pictures of her and Tara lying on the grass out back beneath the real stars while Tara told Joey stories and one of them cuddled on the couch watching a movie, and a favorite, which he'd taken last year when Tara was there during winter break: Joey had come down with a stomach virus, and Tara had refused to keep her distance from his little girl and had caught the virus. The two of them were sleeping in the nook, foreheads touching, Tara's arm wrapped protectively around Joey. He'd never known why it was his favorite until this very second. It took a lot of love to willingly step into the ring with a cranky, puking child, and Tara had done it more than once without concern for her own health.

His heart squeezed as he watched her setting up the fort, those feelings he'd been trying to tamp down clawing their way to the surface. He had to get the hell out of there. "I'm going up to shower."

"Okay," Tara said without turning around.

This officially sucked.

Eleven

LEVI GAVE HIMSELF shit for the position he'd put them in as he stepped into the shower. The evening at the Taproom played in his mind like a rerun from hell, assaulting him with images of his buddies' arms around Tara, offers for motorcycle rides and dates flinging at her from every direction like she had a HIT ON ME sign around her neck. Had they always flirted with her like that? He was strung so tight, he felt like a time bomb waiting to blow. He pressed his hands to the wet shower tiles, letting his head fall between his shoulders, and closed his eyes, hoping the warm water pelting his back might loosen his muscles. But behind his closed lids, he saw Tara gazing up at him with desire in her eyes when they were looking at houses. He could still feel her lips against his thumb as he'd dragged it across them, still feel the hitch in her breathing in her parents' driveway as he'd licked her pastry. She was so sexy, his cock hardened greedily.

He angrily shut off the hot water and tilted his face up to the icy stream raining down on him, doing mental math to try to quell his urges. But Tara was front and center in his mind, feeding him the cupcake at the dance, looking at him like she wished his tongue was between her legs when he'd licked the frosting from her fingers. He couldn't take it. She was everywhere. He fisted his cock, working it tight and fast, visualizing his hand as her mouth, her lustful eyes staring up at him, until he was so worked up, his hips thrust violently. His teeth clenched as his orgasm gripped him, and he grunted out her name with every pump of his dick. Fantasies of her naked, on her knees, pummeled him, making his climax go on and on, the last of it leaving him with an unstoppable, "*Fuuck.*"

He leaned back against the wall, eyes closed, breathing hard, aftershocks jerking through him. His dick was so sensitive, the slick of the water drew curses.

"*Jesus,*" he panted out. It'd been too damn long since he'd been with a woman.

When he finally caught his breath, he soaped up, and like metal to magnet, his mind skated back to Tara, and his greedy cock rose for the occasion.

This was going to be the longest two weeks of his life.

When he finished showering, he turned off the water and reached for a towel, swiping nothing but air. He looked around the bathroom, remembering he'd done laundry that morning and hadn't had a chance to get it out of the dryer. *Great.* He ran his hand down his chest and arms, wicking the water away, and stepped out of the shower, cracking the bathroom door open. "*Joey!* Can you bring me a towel, please?"

He brushed his teeth while he waited, telling himself to pull his shit together.

"Joey's sleeping, so—"

He opened the bathroom door further at the sound of

Tara's voice, peering out from behind it, and their eyes connected with the heat of a thousand flaming suns. The air between them crackled as those gorgeous baby blues trailed down his wet body. His damn dick saluted her from behind the door.

She thrust a towel at him.

He snagged it and quickly wrapped it around his waist.

Her eyes were fixed on his chest. "I'll—" She absently pointed behind her but made no move to leave. He stepped around the bathroom door, and her gaze trailed down his body to his erection straining against the confines of the towel. She licked her lips, lust pooling in her eyes.

"You're not going anywhere. We need to talk." He stalked toward her. Her gaze flicked up to his, full of want and need, her fingers fidgeting like she wanted to rip his towel off. Her nipples pressed against her thin cotton shirt. She never wore bras under her sleeping shirts. How had he ever resisted her? He backed her up against the wall, mentally cursing himself for doing it, but he *couldn't* stop. "You sure Joey's asleep?"

"Uh-huh," she said breathily.

"I'm sorry for being an ass earlier," he said, rough and angry at himself. "I didn't mean to make you uncomfortable by saying what I did after the dance. But I meant what I said that night, and I'm *not* going to deny it."

She blinked several times, those gorgeous eyes narrowing in concentration, as if she suddenly realized how lost she'd been in him. "What you said didn't make me uncomfortable."

"Then why couldn't you look at me tonight?"

"Because *you* couldn't look at *me*," she said sharply.

He put his hands on either side of her head, boxing her in as the truth roared out. "No shit, because you've got me tied in knots. I feel like I'm going insane. I can't fucking see straight around you. All I can think about is kissing you, getting my hands on you. I *fantasize* about how you taste, how you feel, the sounds you'd make if we were together, and seeing the guys hit on you made me want to tear them to pieces."

Their lips were an inch apart, and she was breathing in short, fast bursts, her breasts brushing against his bare chest with every inhalation. He ached to feel her against him, and it took everything he had not to push his hands into her hair and *claim* her.

"Put me out of my misery, T," he demanded. "Tell me whether I'm alone in this or if you feel it, too."

She opened her mouth to speak, but no words came. Her hands rose between them, coming to rest on his chest, and that light, nervous touch sent shock waves through his core as she went up on her toes and whispered, "I've wanted you for as long as I can remember."

Something inside him snapped, unleashing desire so primal he couldn't hold back. His hands dove into her hair, fisting as his mouth crashed over hers, fierce and possessive. She tasted like wickedness and innocence, and he wanted it *all*. He wanted to strip her bare, lay her out, and taste his way down her body. He imagined crawling over her and burying his mouth between her legs while she sucked his cock until they both came so hard they couldn't remember their names. He'd never felt so much from just a kiss, and he told himself to slow down, to give her a chance to breathe, but she was rising higher on her toes, arching into him, returning his efforts rough and hungrily. She dug her nails into his back, moaning needily into his mouth. Her desire electrified him, and he growled against her lips, "Fuck, T." He pressed his hips forward, grinding against her, and slid one hand down her hip, squeezing as he kissed her deeper, harder. Exploring, *taking*, reveling in her sinful sounds, each one stoking the inferno inside him. He pushed his hand beneath her shirt, palming her breast, and she moaned, long and low. He brushed his thumb over the taut peak, and her hips pressed forward. *That's it, baby. Show me what you like.* He rolled her nipple between his finger and thumb, and her head fell back with a greedy noise that seared through him like lightning.

He felt untethered, animalistic, feasting on her mouth, tugging at her hair, and she was just as into him, clawing at his back, rubbing her body against his like she couldn't get close enough as he kissed her cheek, jaw, and blazed a path to her ear, growling, "I need my mouth on you."

"Ye—"

He'd pushed up her shirt with both hands, lowering his mouth over one breast and groping the other before she even finished the word. He sucked hard, and a high-pitched, "*Ah*," fell from her lips.

He winced. "Too hard?"

Her eyes narrowed, and she grabbed his head with both hands, pulling his mouth back to her breast. *"Again."*

The siren he'd glimpsed was coming out to play, and she was *hot*.

He sucked her nipple to the roof of his mouth, and her hips shot forward with a long, sensual moan. He did it again, and she writhed against him so enticingly, he continued taunting her, grinding against her center. Every slick of his tongue, every suck, nip, and bite earned needier pleas. Her skin was hot, her heart hammering against her chest, as he lavished her breasts with openmouthed kisses. She was trembling, her fingernails slicing into his arms. He welcomed the pain, magnifying the pleasure of finally getting his hands and mouth on her. He lifted his face, needing to see her eyes, which were at half-mast as he pushed his other hand down her back and into her shorts, grabbing her ass, holding her tighter against him.

"*Levi*," she panted out, and he captured her mouth in another demanding kiss.

Her mouth was exquisite, kissing him eagerly, her hips moving in sync with his as his tongue delved deeper, and he tested her boundaries, his fingers dipping lower. He brushed his lips over hers. "Are you wet for me, baby?"

Her breath hitched, and her body tensed as her eyes opened. The embarrassment in them tugged at something deep in his chest. "It's just you and me, T. What's said between us stays between us." He kissed her again, slow, sensual, reassuring, and felt her relax against him. He drew back, gazing into those deep pools of desire, though the flush on her cheeks told him she might feel safer, but the embarrassment lingered. "Want me to stop?"

She shook her head, whispering, "I just don't want to answer."

Laughter bubbled out before he could stop it, and he touched his forehead to hers. "You're killing me, blondie."

She giggled. "Same."

"*Christ*, I like you." He reclaimed her mouth in a deep, passionate kiss that quickly turned urgent, and they both went a little wild, pawing and devouring. When he pushed his hand into the front of her shorts, beneath her panties, she inhaled sharply, and he slowed their kisses. His fingers dipped low enough to feel that she was waxed bare. Salivating, he stopped just short of that magical spot, giving her time to either change her mind or get comfortable with the idea of him touching her.

He dragged his tongue along her lower lip. "How could I have been blind for so long?" He kissed her tenderly. "I want to make you feel so good, you'll forget that I was an idiot."

She smiled and rocked her hips, giving him the green light he'd hoped for. He didn't want to further embarrass her or make her nervous, but he wanted to see her face as he touched her for the first time. He kissed her softly, drawing back just far enough to hold her gaze as his fingers slid over that magical detonator, and through her wetness, then back up, moving in slow circles. Her eyes widened, brimming with desire. She clutched his sides as he brushed his lips over hers again, sliding his fingers between her legs, then back up again, continuing in an agonizingly slow pattern, causing her to gasp and pant. Her eyes closed, and she bit her lower lip.

"Eyes on *me*, beautiful."

She opened her eyes, and "*Levi*" fell from her lips.

"Trust me?"

She nodded, her eyes so dark and needy, he wanted to tear off her shorts, spread her legs, and drive his cock into her until he was buried to the hilt. He craved the feel of her slick heat surrounding him, desperate to make them both lose their minds. But that would have to wait, because *needy Tara* was the sexiest thing he'd ever seen.

"I'm gonna make you come, but I'm not going to rush." He kissed the corner of her mouth. "And after you come on my hand, you're going to come on my *mouth*." Her eyes widened again as he rained kisses down her neck and pushed her shirt up, licking, sucking, and biting her nipple as he stroked her until she was whimpering, rocking, pleading, clinging to him like he was her lifeline, and man, he wanted to be.

When he pushed two fingers inside her slick heat, they both

moaned. He crooked his fingers, seeking that hidden spot that took her up on her toes, and used his thumb where she needed it most. Her hands slid down his torso, knocking his towel loose, and it fell to the floor, freeing his cock. She looked down, shock and appreciation glowing in her eyes. He'd gotten lucky in the endowment department.

"Touch me," he coaxed, and she wrapped her fingers around his cock, sending rivers of heat through his body. She began stroking him, and he worked her faster. "Give me your hand." She did, and he guided it between her legs, wetting it with her arousal, then wrapped her fingers around his cock. With his hand over hers, he gave it two tight, hard tugs, groaning with restraint. She continued to stroke him, and he shoved her shorts and underwear down, taking a long, lascivious look. Her cheeks flushed. "You're absolutely gorgeous. *Look.*" He nodded toward the mirror on the wall to their left. "You're fucking beautiful, T."

He brought his hand back to her glistening sex, another sexy gasp escaping her lips as his fingers entered her.

"Watch us." Her eyes shifted to the mirror, and he nipped at her neck. "Stroke me as I make you come. I want you to see what you do to me."

He lowered his mouth to her breast, working her faster between her legs, and she matched his pace. "Don't stop," he said gruffly.

She continued driving him out of his mind, taking him right up to the edge of madness. He applied more pressure to her clit, and her legs tensed, her hand stilling on his cock, as "*Ohmygosh*" fell from her lips.

"Hold your shirt up." When she did, he fisted his cock, still working her with his other hand as she watched. He lowered his mouth to her neck, kissing and sucking, until she was shaking and begging. He grabbed the base of his cock to stave off his release and sank his teeth into her neck. She cried out as she rode his hand, and he covered her mouth with his, swallowing her sounds as her hips bucked, her inner muscles pulsing tight and hot around his fingers, and she grabbed his dick, stroking the come right out of him. Maybe his blue-eyed girl wasn't so innocent after all. He came so hard, it felt like it was ripped from his soul. He groaned into their kisses, coming on her stomach as they rode out their pleasure. There was total cavemanish gratification in claiming her that way, branding her with his seed, and he fucking loved it. When she went boneless against him, both of them panting, he held her, his hot, sticky come binding them together.

"Jesus, T." He drew back to see her face. She looked dazed, utterly blissed out. "You okay?"

"*Fireworks*...still going off," she said just above a whisper.

"We're just getting started." He kissed her softly and used the damp towel to clean her up before tending to himself.

"Daddy?"

They both froze for a split second at the sound of Joey's voice, before their lust-addled brains kicked in. Tara scrambled into her clothes, and he grabbed shorts from his drawer.

"Be right there, sweets!" *Fuck.* Had they woken her up? He'd been so caught up in Tara, he hadn't even thought to close his bedroom door. But his lack of fatherly brainpower wasn't his biggest problem. How could he tell Tara that they shouldn't let Joey know without sounding like an ass? There was no time for a discussion, so he went with, "We should lie low around Joey."

"Yeah, okay."

He pulled on his shirt. "Good. We're on the same page."

As they headed out of the bedroom, she whispered, "I can't believe my legs are working."

"They won't be after Joey goes to bed."

HOLY SHIT. WHAT just happened? Did that really happen? Tara wasn't sure who that girl was upstairs, but she *liked* her, and Levi seemed to *really* like her, too, so she hoped she'd stick around. But how could she do those things with the door wide open? What if Joey had walked in? Her only explanation was that her brain had ceased working the second she'd seen him fresh out of the shower, and she *loved* the result. Levi awakened the confident, desperate, sexual woman in her who must have been hiding her whole life. Even though she'd been embarrassed that he'd seen her nearly naked and they'd done filthy, dirty things to each other, she was aching to do it again! To *explore* with him. To let him show her everything there was to know about touching and *taking*. She'd never seen him like that, all sexy and demanding, crossing boundaries she had never even contemplated. God, she'd loved it. She'd never forget how his hand looked wrapped around his magnificent cock, and when he'd come on her stomach? *Ohmygod.* That sight alone could have taken her over the edge.

If not for her body still vibrating after nearly an hour, she might think she'd dreamed the whole thing up.

They were lying in the nook fort, leaning against pillows with Joey between them, curled up against Levi's side. His arm was around her, but his hand was resting on Tara's shoulder. His long, *talented* fingers had slipped beneath the neckline of her shirt and were tracing slow circles on her skin, wreaking havoc with her nerves. She stole a glance at him, catching him watching her. A slow grin lifted his lips, as if to say, *That's right, blondie. I'm thinking about you, too.*

Heat crept up her neck and cheeks. He squeezed her shoulder and winked with the most sinful smirk. *God,* she wanted him. Where did this insatiable appetite for sexy stuff come from? She'd had Scooby-Doo roller-coaster-quality sex *once,* with a guy she'd dated for four months, and here she was, chomping at the bit for Levi to throw her over his shoulder, carry her up to his bedroom, and take her six ways to Sunday. They weren't even dating, and she'd let him do anything he wanted to her. What did that say about her? Did she care what it said about her? The man she'd wanted forever had given her Magic Mountain and with nothing more than his hands and mouth. She didn't even know her body was capable of such sensations.

A better question was, could she ever survive *more*?

As if he'd read her thoughts, he tangled his fingers in the back of her hair, giving it a gentle tug that seared down her core, making her burn with anticipation. Her gaze shot to his, and he made a show of licking his lips and dragging his teeth over his lower lip, his dark eyes relaying how much he wanted to get his mouth on her. *Yes, please…*

She tore her eyes away, trying not to think about it, wishing Joey had chosen a shorter movie.

She finally understood what Jules had meant when she'd said that kissing the right guy would make her see fireworks. She wanted to go for a full-on nuclear explosion, and she didn't care what that said about her, because she was pretty sure she'd be dead by the end of the night anyway.

Death by orgasm.

What a great way to go.

Tara had thought her body was vibrating before, but the rest of the movie was a blur of secret sensual touches, winks, and mouthed promises that had her heart hammering and lust coursing through her like a raging river. She was pretty sure if she opened her mouth to speak, she'd sound like a cat in heat, begging to be touched.

Levi turned off the projector with the remote and climbed out of the nook, reaching for Joey's hand, overzealously urging her toward the stairs. "Come on, peanut, up you go. I'll tuck you in."

Tara was glad to see she wasn't the only one desperate for more.

"I'm sleeping with Aunt Tara tonight," Joey said as he helped her out of the nook.

Tara's stomach sank. She'd completely forgotten her promise.

"How about you sleep with Aunt Tara tomorrow night?" He winked at Tara.

"But she *promised*." Joey looked pleadingly at her. "Right?"

"She's right. It must've slipped my mind." Her heart broke, and the disappointment on Levi's face made it hurt even worse. But she wasn't about to prioritize sex over keeping a promise to Joey, no matter how much she wanted to.

"A'right." His gaze locked on Tara. "Looks like Daddy's tucking himself in tonight."

"*Da-ad*, you tuck yourself in every night," Joey said.

He hugged Joey. "You've got me there, sweets. Don't keep Aunt Tara up too late. I have a feeling she's going to need her energy while she's here."

Oh boy…

"I won't," Joey promised.

He hugged Tara, and she wanted to melt into his strong arms as he whispered, "Guess I'm going to bed without dessert."

Her sex clenched longingly.

He brushed his scruff along her cheek, sending titillating sensations skittering down her chest, and kissed her cheek. "Sweet dreams, T."

"You too," Tara managed.

"I have a feeling mine'll be anything but *sweet*," he said as he headed upstairs.

A little while later she was lying in the guest bed with Joey sleeping beside her, surrounded by a dozen stuffed animals, wondering how she was going to sleep when she was all revved up. She'd never felt like this—high on heady anticipation. Was it normal to want a man so badly?

Her phone vibrated on the nightstand. She picked it up and saw a text from Levi. Her heart beat impossibly faster as she read it. *Well, that's a first. Cockblocked by my daughter.* She smiled, thumbing out, *Sorry. I totally forgot I promised her a slumber party.* Joey stirred beside her, and she turned the screen away so the light wouldn't bother her.

Another text from Levi rolled in. *I've never been jealous of Joey before.*

Tara's heart soared. *I've never wanted to break a promise to her before.*

His response was immediate. *I'm glad you didn't. You're mine for two weeks. We've got plenty of time for our own sleepovers.*

Her eyes flew open wider, every ounce of her silently celebrating but also freaking out. Nobody had ever talked like that to her before. How was she supposed to respond? *Good?* That seemed too small a word for what she felt. She typed, *I look forward to it.* Did that make her sound more experienced? Her thumb hovered over the send icon. For the hundredth time that night, she couldn't believe this was really happening. Did she sound like she was used to this type of texting? He knew her better than that, didn't he? *Ugh.* She was *not* going to chicken out. She hit send and held her breath.

Seconds later, another text bubble popped up. *Me too. How am I supposed to sleep knowing you're right downstairs? Knowing what your mouth tastes like and how your body feels? I'm hard just thinking about you.*

She bit her lower lip, need stacking up inside her. She peeked at Joey, fast asleep cuddling her bear, and typed, *Cold shower?* He replied with an eye roll emoji and, *It didn't even take the edge off last time.*

She loved knowing that. *Your hand?*

His response was immediate. *Only if I pretend it's yours.*

She was pretty sure her heart was going to pound right out of her chest as she sent a begging emoji followed by an angel and clutched her phone tighter as his response rolled in. *You naughty thing. You really want me to go there?*

She couldn't type *hell yes* any better than she could say it, so she sent a cheesy-smile emoji and squeezed her eyes shut, unable to believe she was going there. Another message rolled in. A devil emoji and *Turn your ringer off.* She quickly thumbed out, *I can't talk. Joey's asleep.*

His response stole her breath. *You won't have to.*

She couldn't silence her phone fast enough. His call came through a minute later, and she put the phone to her ear, his gruff voice giving her goose bumps. "You have no idea how much I wish this was your hand."

She couldn't resist whispering, "Me too."

A rough growl came through the phone. "Or your *mouth*."

A needy whimper escaped, and she clamped her mouth shut.

"God, Tara, the sounds you make drive me wild." His voice was full of restraint. "Have you done this before?"

"*No*," she whispered. "You?"

"Hell no. I've never wanted to, but with you…" His voice trailed off, and he was quiet for a second. "You bring out the animal in me. I have a feeling we're going to need a safe word before these two weeks are up."

She knew he was kidding, and she'd never been interested in being dominated in that way, but she trusted Levi and felt so much for him, even that wouldn't be a dealbreaker.

"I want you to close your eyes and imagine my fingers inside you."

She closed her eyes, her inner walls clenching.

"I can still feel how tight and wet you were, feel you squeezing them as they fucked you."

She'd had no idea how much of a turn-on this would be, but hearing him say those dirty things, his voice dripping with desire, and picturing his thick cock pushing through his hand made her wet.

"I can still taste the desire on your skin when I sucked your tits."

Her nipples throbbed, aching for his touch.

"I want my mouth on you, T. On *all* of you."

She made a desperate sound, squeezing her thighs together, fisting her hand in the sheets, shocked by how turned on she was.

"Are you wet for me, baby?"

"*Yes*" came without thought. She should be embarrassed, but she wasn't. She wanted this piece of him that nobody else had ever had, and she wanted to give this *first* of hers to him, too.

"*Jesus.* I'm so hard for you. But this isn't fair, is it? I should stop so I don't leave you hanging."

"Don't you *dare* stop," she warned in a harsh whisper as she quietly climbed out of bed. "I'm sneaking into the bathroom." She hurried on tiptoes into the bathroom and locked the door, panting out of sheer desperation.

"Fuck, T. You're going to be the death of me. Lean against the wall and push your hand into your panties. Touch yourself like I touched you. Make your clit swell for me."

She followed his command, his dirty demands as addicting as his kisses. As her fingers slid through her wetness, a moan escaped, and she clamped her mouth closed.

A potently masculine, guttural sound rumbled through the phone. "*That's it,* baby. I wish I was sucking your nipple right now, tasting my way down your body."

Delirious with desire, she closed her eyes and leaned her head back against the wall, more needy noises vying for escape.

"Imagine you're in my bed, naked, your legs over my shoulders as I feast on your pussy." His words came faster, emphasized with each stroke. "I want to feel you lose control with my mouth on you. I want to hear you scream my name uncontrollably as I drive my cock into you."

Emboldened by the distance and the darkness, she whispered, "Tell me what you're doing to yourself."

"I'm stroking my cock, tight and fast, picturing all the ways I want to take you and all the things I want you to do to me."

"I want to do it *all.*" She quickened her efforts between her legs. "Tell me *more.*"

"Picture me lying on top of you, buried so deep, you feel every inch, and you know you'll feel it tomorrow, too."

Lust billowed and burned inside her, swelling and pulsing until her skin felt like it might melt off.

"Can you *feel* me inside you, T? Feel my weight on top of you?"

"Yes." She breathed harder, imagining his thick cock moving inside her, his powerful thighs pressing her into the mattress.

"I'm pinning your hands beside your head, lifting your knees so I can take you deeper."

She moved her fingers faster on her clit, curling her toes.

"I'm close, baby. *So* close."

"Me too," she panted out.

"I feel your fingernails clawing at my back, feel you arching beneath me."

"*Levi,*" she whisper-pleaded, bowing off the wall, clutching the phone so tight her fingers hurt.

"Let go with me, baby. Close your eyes and picture us naked, your legs around my waist. My mouth on your neck, sucking and biting so hard you—*Fuuck.*"

Her eyes slammed closed as he grunted out her name, and pleasure crashed over her. She turned to the side, curling into herself against the wall to keep from crying out as his moans wound around her, seeping beneath her skin, until she slid down to the floor, utterly and completely lost in him.

Twelve

THE SWEET SOUND of Tara's voice Monday morning brought an onslaught of dirty thoughts and images and a gust of unexpected emotions so fierce, Levi stopped at the bottom of the stairs to try to get a grip on them. He never imagined he and Tara would be so combustible. He was into her for far more important reasons than sex, but he couldn't stop thinking about how she'd blown him away last night in his bedroom and on the phone. Hell, he'd shocked himself. He didn't think he'd ever trust a woman enough to put himself out there like that, much less with his daughter sleeping beside her. But with Tara, it hadn't taken any thought. *She'd* planted the seed—*your hand?*—and he'd felt her eagerness to watch it grow. He'd wanted to fulfill that fantasy for her as much as he had for himself, and once he'd started, there was no holding back.

His cock twitched. He'd be hard all day thinking about his sweet, sensual, secret siren. He saw Tara rinsing strawberries in the kitchen sink, gorgeous in black leggings and a denim button-down that was knotted at her waist. Her hair was still damp from her shower, and the ends were curling. Now that he knew how her thick hair felt tangled around his fingers, his hands curled with the urge to touch it.

Come on, man. Get your shit together.

"Can we go on a picnic before skateboarding practice?" Joey was kneeling on a stool by the island wearing one of her favorite outfits—blue leggings with skateboards on them and a long-sleeved yellow shirt that had SKATERGIRL printed in different colors all over it. She was cutting a banana with a plastic knife from the chef kit Tara had given her last Christmas.

"Sure," Tara said. "I was thinking we'd go to the nursery after practice and try to whip the front gardens into shape."

"Yay!" Joey exclaimed.

Tara and Joey had been gardening together since the first spring break Tara had spent in Harborside, when she was eighteen. He'd never forget the first time Tara had brought up the idea of creating gardens in their yard. He'd been so busy trying to stay on top of single parenting and work and hadn't even thought about gardens. Joey had been so excited, she'd immediately started drawing pictures of what she wanted. Together, the three of them had come up with plans, starting small, with two flower beds against the house. Every time Tara came to visit, she and Joey would add a little more to them, until they took up most of the front and much of the back yard. Joey loved hunting for cool birdbaths, and Levi had set up an account at the nursery long ago so Tara could buy whatever they wanted, and he loved that she no longer felt funny about putting things on that account.

"I want to look for a hummingbird feeder like Emily's," Joey said. "It has to be red, because most of the flowers they like are red, and Emily's mom said we have to clean it every few days or the nectar will spoil and the birds won't ever come back."

They hadn't spotted him yet, and he liked witnessing their relationship like an outsider might. It was so pure, it was beautiful.

"Are you willing to clean it when I'm not here?" Tara asked. "Because your daddy already has a lot on his plate, and I'm not sure he'll remember to do it."

There she went, watching out for him again. When has anyone else outside his family done that in the last decade? The intense *need* to be closer to Tara was inescapable. That allure was her superpower, and as his legs carried him through the living room, he had no idea how he'd ever been able to shut it out.

"I promise I'll do it," Joey said. "I want the birds to keep coming back."

"Then I'm all for it." Tara turned with her hands full of strawberries as Levi stepped into the kitchen, and their gazes collided.

He swore the world stood still, save for the space between them buzzing like live wires. He half expected Joey to get burned by their sparks. Tara's cheeks were beet red, and he wondered if it was caused by the heat between them or from last night's *activities*.

"Morning!" Tara said too energetically as she dropped the strawberries on the cutting board in front of Joey, nervously trying to catch the ones that rolled away. "Shoot!"

"I've got it." He gathered the berries. Her eyes flicked up, nervousness staring back at him. He focused on Joey to give Tara a minute to regroup.

"You both look extra beautiful today." He kissed the top of Joey's head. "I like your pigtails."

"Auntie Tara did them for me," Joey said. "We're making

strawberry-banana pancakes."

"I see that." Most people mashed bananas for pancakes, but Joey preferred them sliced. He put his hand on Tara's back, feeling a slight tremble. "How are you this morning?"

"Good. You?" She shoved a strawberry in her mouth.

"Never been better." A quick glance at his daughter confirmed that she was focused on cutting the rest of her banana. He slid his hand down Tara's back and squeezed her ass.

Her eyes bloomed wide, then narrowed, their warning coming across loud and clear, but when she spoke, her nervousness betrayed that warning. "Are you hungry?"

"Very." He held her gaze. "I could eat for *hours.*"

"Then we'll make you pancakes," Joey offered.

That's not exactly what I had in mind. "Thanks, peanut, but as good as that sounds, I need to grab a protein bar and some coffee and get over to the job site."

Tara went into the walk-in pantry, and Levi followed.

He wrapped his arms around her from behind, kissing her neck. "How's my secret siren?"

"She's going to catch us," Tara whispered, turning in his arms.

"Then you'd better kiss me quick." He kissed her smiling lips. "Are you okay, or are you going to be embarrassed every time you see me?"

"Yes, and...*probably.*"

"It's just me, T." He framed her face in his hands, whispering, "If I went too far, you need to tell me."

"You didn't. I'm the one who initiated it," she whispered harshly. "But it's not like I'm used to doing stuff like that."

"Neither am I, but you have some kind of spell over me. You infiltrated my dreams. I had to take things into my own hands just to make it through the morning. I've had more right-hand action this past week than I've had in the past year."

Her cheeks flamed again. "Don't tell me *that.*"

Oh, sweet darlin'. I'm going to have fun getting under your skin. He lowered his mouth beside her ear, whispering, "Then maybe I shouldn't tell you that tonight I'm going to make up for last night's one-handed activities, so don't plan a sleepover with you-know-who." He pressed a kiss to her cheek. "Hey, Joey, how're the strawberries coming along?"

"Fine," she called out. "I'm halfway done."

"Perfect," he said loudly, then whispered to Tara, "I need my hands on you." He grabbed her ass, holding her against him, and lowered his lips to hers in a long, slow kiss. When she went soft in his arms, he drew back. "Mm-mm. Tonight cannot come fast enough."

"Done!" Joey exclaimed. "What are you guys *doing* in there?"

"Looking for pancake mix," Tara answered hurriedly as he reached past her, pressing himself against her as he grabbed a protein bar from the shelf. She glowered at him.

"It's on the counter," Joey said.

Levi arched a brow at Tara. "Did you come in here to *avoid* me?"

"Not *you.* Just the butterflies you give me," she whispered. "But you caused a swarm anyway…and *maybe* I was hoping you'd follow me in."

Did she have any idea how much of a turn-on that was?

"Stop looking at me like that," she hissed, pink-cheeked again.

"Like what?"

"Like you want to *eat* my *butterflies* for breakfast."

He grinned.

"*Ohmygod.* Get outta here." She shoved him out of the pantry.

LEVI TOSSED ANOTHER load of paneling and other scraps into the dumpster outside the house he was renovating and wiped the sweat from his brow. He'd been at it for hours, hoping physical work would take his mind off Tara. But it would be a cold day in hell before that happened.

He'd been excited when he'd accepted the job. The money was good, and he loved nothing more than stripping a house down to its bones and doing a complete renovation. But that was before Archer had uncapped a freaking geyser of desire for the sweet blonde who now consumed Levi's every thought. He'd give anything to have these two weeks free to spend with Tara and Joey. They really did have a beautiful relationship, and he suddenly wanted to be an even bigger part of it. He didn't care what they did. He just wanted time with them, to share in their enjoyment of each other.

But that would be torture, too, because even though he was sure his feelings for Tara had been brewing for a while, he couldn't risk getting Joey's hopes up until he knew exactly where Tara stood and where they were headed. Tara had said she'd been into him forever, but that could've been a heat-of-the-moment comment, and he couldn't afford to speculate. He'd already crossed lines he could never uncross, and he wanted to cross even more of them. But he needed to minimize the damage, to keep Joey away from any potential fallout. He and Tara needed to talk, but talking was the *last* thing he wanted to do when he got her alone.

He pulled out his phone to check the time and saw a missed text from Tara. He quickly opened it, and a picture of Tara and Joey making faces at the camera popped up, sent two hours ago. He wished he hadn't missed it. Another text rolled in of Joey at skateboard practice, followed by, *We're having a great day. Hope you are, too.* They were pretty typical texts from Tara when she was with Joey. But the red heart emoji that followed was new, and hell if it didn't bring a goofy-ass grin to his face.

He wanted to see her, to get the words out before they were alone, and skateboard practice was the perfect place to make that happen because Joey would be busy.

Yes. That was exactly what he needed to do.

He shook his head at himself, knowing he'd just whipped up an excuse to go see Tara. He told himself the unrelenting urge to drop everything and go see the woman he was into was normal, and maybe it was. But it had never been normal for *him*.

He squinted against the sun and hollered up to Joker on the roof, "How's it looking?"

"Good, boss. It'll be done before the rain comes. Don't worry." They were calling for rain later in the week.

"Great. I'm taking off for a bit. Need anything while I'm out?"

Joker peered down at him with a troublemaking grin. "You could bring Tara back for me."

Levi glowered at him. "You trying to get thrown off that roof?"

Joker laughed.

Asshole. Levi climbed into the pickup truck he used for work and headed over to the skate park.

Last summer, Joey had wanted to learn to surf, but Levi wasn't sold on the idea of his daughter's fate left up to a fickle bitch like Mother Nature. He'd talked with Jesse and Brent about it. They were avid surfers and had been teaching kids to surf for years. Brent had suggested that she start with skateboarding to perfect her balance and build muscle, and once she mastered that, they could talk about surfing. Levi figured he'd bought himself a year, maybe more if her interests changed. His determined little girl had gone online and read up on skateboarding. She'd quickly become enthralled with skateboarder Naila Blue, the youngest professional skateboarder in the world. Naila had learned all her tricks from YouTube, and a couple of years ago, she'd competed in the Olympics and had won a bronze medal, making her the country's youngest medalist. Joey had instantly come up with a new goal—to be an Olympic skateboarder—and she was putting her all into it.

He pulled into the Harborside Skate Park and parked by the entrance. As he climbed out of his truck, he spotted Tara standing in the grass, and he felt lighter, as if he were illuminated from the inside out. Just being around her did that to him. No wonder she was so addicting. He drank her in as she looked through the lens of her camera at Joey. Joey was skating the halfpipe with half a dozen other kids, practicing her newest trick, a Miller Flip, which was a frontside handplant where she flipped all the way around to a fakie, which meant she landed in her normal stance, but skated backward. It was a hell of a trick, and with Joey's other tricks, Levi was pretty sure his little girl would place in the top three at the tournament.

Brent skated over to Tara, flipped his board, and caught it with one hand.

Tara lowered the camera, and Brent said something Levi couldn't hear. Tara waved her hand, shaking her head. He could tell Brent was pouring on the charm. His coaxing expression had Levi's muscles tensing. He wasn't jealous of his cousin, was he?

Man, he was really losing it, but he continued watching with interest as Brent put the skateboard down and Tara crouched to put her camera in the bag at her feet. She smiled up at Brent as he reached for her hand. *What the…?*

His cousin helped her onto the skateboard and placed his hands on her waist. Levi's eyes narrowed, watching him like a hawk. She kicked off with her right foot and sailed forward. Brent let go, walking beside her as she put her hands out, wobbling.

Levi strode through the gate just as Tara lost her balance and landed in Brent's arms, both of them laughing. Levi closed the gap between them and tried to mask his ridiculous jealousy. "You okay, T?"

"Yes," she said lightly.

"Hey, man." Brent put his hand on Tara's back. "I've got her. No worries."

No worries, my ass.

"I told him I was too uncoordinated to skateboard," Tara said.

"He's seen you dance. He knows you're not uncoordinated." *And if he doesn't take his hand off you, we're going to have trouble.*

"That's what I told her," Brent insisted.

"You're both off your rockers." Tara shook her head. "I think I'll stick to taking pictures."

As she walked back toward her camera bag, Brent splayed

his arms and cocked a grin. "Aw, come on, Tara. I'll ride *with* you."

"Like hell you will." Levi went after her, ignoring Brent's curious glance. He caught up with her, the caveman in him clawing his way out. "We need to talk."

Worry rose in her eyes. "Did you change your mind? It's okay if you did." She lowered her eyes. "I understand. I'm probably nothing like the women you usually hook up with."

"What?" Had she lost her mind?

"I've been thinking about it, and if you just got carried away—"

"*Stop*. Jesus, Tara, that's the farthest thing from what I wanted to say." He stepped closer, wanting to take her in his arms and kiss her worries away, but he couldn't with Joey around. He put his hands on her waist, reclaiming that piece of her. Apparently his feelings for her turned him into a possessive Neanderthal. "I take hooking up with you very seriously. I don't know what this is between us yet, but I have never thought about a woman as much as I think about you. I couldn't even stay away for a full workday today."

"Oh." Relief washed over her. "*Good*. I was worried."

"We both know how much is at stake if this goes sideways. I don't expect it to, but it's new and complicated, and there's a lot we don't know about each other. That's the only reason I want to keep it from Joey. But you need to know that I wouldn't have kissed you or let things escalate if I didn't want there to be more between us."

She smiled, loosening the knots in his chest.

"Things are happening fast, and I'm not sure who I am with you because I've never been jealous before, especially over one of my cousins. I know Brent was just playing around, but I *hated* seeing his hands on you, so I want to make something very clear. If we're together, I don't want anyone else touching or kissing you."

A nervous laugh fell from her lips. "Darn it. I had big plans with this guy I met earlier."

"Please tell me you're messing with me."

She rolled her eyes. "Do you really think I'd let someone else touch me when I *finally* got together with the guy I've wanted forever?"

"I hope not, but you're a gorgeous woman, and the world's full of horny young guys."

She put her hand on her hip. "Have I ever gone out with a guy while I'm here?"

"No, but that doesn't mean anything."

"Well, maybe it should." She took a step away, then turned back with a sassy smirk. "Let me make *this* very clear. I have a thing for one *older* horny guy, who I assume will not be touching anyone else, either. And if you have any doubt about who he is, just look for the guy who's still got it *all* going on."

She spun on the heel of her tennis shoe and sauntered away, leaving him falling that much harder for her.

Thirteen

TARA WAS ON cloud nine as she and Joey made their way through the nursery after skateboard practice. She'd been thrilled when Levi had shown up at the skate park, but that was nothing compared to how she'd felt when he told her he didn't want anyone else touching her, because she sure as heck didn't want anyone else touching *him*. She didn't want to get her hopes up too high or make too much out of what was going on between them. Well, that wasn't really true. She wanted to make *everything* out of it, but she was trying her best to keep her expectations in check, which was easier said than done when he called her gorgeous and acted jealous.

Levi could have any woman he wanted, and he wanted *her*. That was unbelievable. *No*, she corrected herself. It wasn't unbelievable. He *should* want to be with her. She was a good, honest, loving person who worked hard and adored him and Joey.

Amelia's evil whispers trampled through her mind. *Who'd want a chubby little mouse like you?* Tara swallowed against the sinking feeling in her stomach, but it didn't last long. She'd made up her mind long ago that she wasn't going to let Amelia put a damper on her happiness anymore, and she reminded herself that she had a whole community of people who liked and appreciated her and had done so even when she was a chubby, confused little girl.

At the top of that list were Levi and Joey.

"Look how pretty this one is." Joey held up a bright red hibiscus. "Can we get it?"

"You have good taste. I think it'll look great in the yard."

They loaded up the cart with beautiful flowers and lush plants, chatting about where they wanted to put each one and how great their gardens would look. Then they went on the hunt for a hummingbird feeder.

"Look how many they have!" Joey ran toward the rather large display of hummingbird feeders made of various materials in different sizes and shapes, but they all had one thing in common—the color red.

"How did you know hummingbirds liked red?"

"Emily's mom told me. I'm spending the night at Emily's Wednesday." Joey walked along the aisle, inspecting each feeder.

"I know. Are you excited?"

"Yes. Want to know a secret?"

"If you want to share it." Joey's secrets were usually about how she and her friends snuck extra cookies or how her friends' mothers let them stay up late during sleepovers.

"Emily's mom likes Dad."

She looked over the feeders, answering absently. "I don't blame her. He's a likable guy." But as she said it, she remembered Emily's mother was *Lauren*, the woman who had flirted with Levi at the dance. That should make Wednesday's drop-off fun.

"No, I mean Emily says she *really* likes him, like she wants to be his *girlfriend*."

"Oh." Hit with a pang of jealousy, Tara suddenly knew just how Levi must have felt when he'd seen her land in Brent's arms. Hopefully Levi's possessiveness and Tara's cupcake seduction had put a stop to Lauren's flirting. Although she couldn't blame her for being interested in him. He was kind, sexy, and an incredible father.

And now he's mine.

"But I can tell Daddy doesn't want to be her boyfriend."

I hope not, after the things we did and what he said to me. "How can you tell?" she asked as nonchalantly as she could.

"Because he never looks happy to see her like he does with other moms."

Moms? Plural?

"Or like he does with you. He's always happy to see you, but I know he doesn't want to be your boyfriend because he said it's not like that between you two."

Tara wasn't going to touch that subject with a ten-foot pole. She tried to steer the conversation back to birdfeeders. "Do you see any birdfeeders you like?"

"Uh-huh. The one with all the pretty colors." She pointed to a blown-glass feeder with swirls of red, green, and blue on the bulb that held the nectar.

"It's beautiful, but maybe we should start with a plastic one until you get used to cleaning it."

"Okay, then how about this one?" She ran farther down the aisle and pointed to a feeder that looked like a giant strawberry, with a green base and a hanger with fake leaves on it.

"That one looks perfect."

"And here's the food." Joey grabbed a big jug of nectar from the shelves.

They paid for their purchases and headed home. After putting everything they'd bought on the porch, they stood in the front yard studying the jungle of long grasses and weeds that had taken over the gardens the last few months. When Tara and Joey had first started gardening, she hadn't known anything about plants. She hadn't grown up picking out pretty flowers with her mother so each one would be special to them, or planting a tree—as she'd done with Joey—so she could watch it grow as she grew. She and her mother had picked out flowers and plants that her mother had seen in magazines and thought would make their yard stand out from the rest. It wasn't the picking of plants that Tara had enjoyed. It was the only time they'd spent together when her mother would set her nitpicking ways aside. At least they'd enjoyed a few years of picking out flowers together in peace.

But just like when she'd first seen the house on Gable Place, the first time she'd visited Levi and Joey, the cedar-sided house had felt *right*, and a little familiar. It had felt like Levi—comfortable, safe, and masculine. She'd envisioned the yard with a plethora of gardens overflowing with a colorful mix of flowers, shrubs, and plants. She pictured gardens that looked a little wild, like they'd sprouted organically, and she'd thought it would be easy. After all, her parents' gardeners made landscaping *look* easy.

But she'd quickly learned that gardens were a labor of love, and for Levi and Joey, she had plenty of love to go around.

As she stood thinking about the past and seeing how their visions had bloomed to life, she realized that she'd done photo shoots all over the island and Harborside and had seen a multitude of gorgeous homes, but she'd never experienced connections with any of them the way she had with Levi's and the one on Gable Place. She'd never stood before any of the others champing at the bit to get her hands in the dirt or spruce up the interiors. With the exception of Levi's parents' house, she'd never felt much of anything. She wasn't sure what that meant, or if it meant anything at all. But it felt significant.

She looked at Joey and said, "What do you think?"

"This is a *big* job." Joey took her hand. "Look at all the weeds."

"I always forget just how big a job it is until our spring cleanup days. But nothing's too big for us. We'll crank up the music and have these gardens looking good as gold in no time. Right?"

"Right!" Joey beamed up at her.

"Let's get our gardening tools and get started."

They headed around to the backyard. Levi's house sat high on a hill and had glorious views of the water in the distance. Tara loved the privacy of his property. There were other homes on the street, but they weren't close, and each was shrouded with trees on either side, buffering them from their neighbors.

She and Joey had also put their green thumbs to work on the backyard. But they knew better than to try to tackle the front and back in one afternoon. They'd make time later in the week to go back to the nursery and make those gardens beautiful, too. She glanced at the screened-in porch off the kitchen, thinking about all the times she'd found Levi sitting there, gazing out at the water, deep in thought. Off the living room was a stone patio with a built-in firepit. She had fond memories over the years of Joey bundled up in her coat, hat, gloves, and a scarf covering all but her eyes, cuddled on Levi's lap by the fire, insisting she wasn't cold, and of summer bonfires, when Joey would run around trying to catch fireflies and when she'd get too pooped to run, she'd cuddle on a lounge chair with Levi or Tara, and they'd tell her stories.

She tucked away those sweet memories and crossed the yard to the enormous garden shed that had been Levi's workshop before he'd grown his business to the point of needing to rent space for his equipment. The shed had windows, two large barn-style doors, and a whole lot of crap inside. It had become a catchall for everything from old furniture and Joey's baby stuff to discarded tools, boxes of Levi's belongings he'd moved from his parents' house but had never gone through, and Lord only knew what else.

They pulled open the doors, and Tara stared at the mess she'd told herself she'd clean up every time she saw it. She and Joey sighed.

"It's a good thing you're wearing sneakers," Tara said. "Looks like you'll have to climb over the boxes and the lawn mower to get to the gardening tools."

"And pass it to you in the bucket again?"

"If you can find it."

They looked at each other and laughed.

"Next time I'm bringing you a Wonder Woman outfit so you can fly through the shed, picking up what we need."

"That would be *cool*," Joey said. "We could get you one, too!"

Tara eyed the mess again. "I think I should try to take the mess off your dad's hands and tackle the shed while I'm here. We can have a yard sale and get rid of the things you guys no longer need."

"That sounds fun. I'll help."

"That'd be great."

"Can I sell lemonade at the yard sale and use the money I earn to get stickers for my skating helmet?"

"I think that's a great idea. But first we have to make sure it's okay with your dad if I clean it out."

"He hates how messy it is. Every time he takes out the lawn mower, he says bad words. He thinks I don't hear him, but I do."

She made a mental note to mention that to Levi. "We need to find out if he wants to keep any of this stuff."

"He doesn't. He's always talking about cleaning it out. I'm gonna get our gardening tools." Joey squeezed between the lawn mower and an old dresser.

"You want help getting through?"

"Nope. I've got it." Like a mountain climber, Joey scaled boxes and ducked beneath a tarp that must have come untucked from the rafters. She disappeared behind Levi's old ten-speed bike and a filing cabinet and popped up with a bucket in her hand. "Found it!"

Twenty minutes later they had their gardening gloves and tools and had extricated the wheelbarrow. Tara queued up one of Joey's favorite playlists and blasted it while they weeded the front gardens. They sang and joked around, and Joey talked about the tournament, which was taking place that weekend. She wanted to practice every day, which was fine with Tara, except that they were calling for rain Thursday afternoon.

Joey looked over as she tugged at a hunk of weeds. "I'll get up early and practice before the rain starts."

"That's a good idea. Maybe we can go to the movies in the afternoon." She tossed a handful of weeds into the wheelbarrow.

"Can I invite my friends to go with us?" Joey asked excitedly. "Remember Emily, Avery, and Robby want to have playdates. I told them you or Dad would call their parents."

Oh joy. I get to talk to Lauren. "I don't see why not. I'll call them when we go inside."

"Can we cook dinner for Daddy after the movie?"

"I think he'd love that. We should pick out what we're going to make tonight or tomorrow so we can get groceries."

As Joey went on about the movie she wanted to see and the other things she wanted to do over break, they finished weeding, which took forever. They dumped the weeds at the edge of the woods behind the house and finally began planting. It was always fun letting Joey pick the spots where she wanted to put the flowers and plants and working together to get them right.

When they finished, their knees and faces were dirty, and the sun had colored their cheeks. They stood back to admire their hard work. It was still a little too early for most of the bushes and plants to flower, but bright clusters of daffodils and tulips peeked out among the greenery, and gorgeous white bloodroot and trout lilies, were scattered around massive hydrangeas, whose big brown *puffs* would bloom in a few short weeks. Pink, purple, and white blunt-loped hepatica created a halo around the leafy hostas and ground coverings. Bluebells and white wood anemones, with their beautiful petals and lush green leaves, covered the ground at the base of a pink-flowering dogwood tree and around the long grasses, bright hibiscus, and fringed bleeding hearts they'd planted today.

"Daddy's gonna be so *happy*!" Pride glittered in Joey's eyes.

This was what Tara loved most. Making memories they could look back on and feel good about. Traditions Joey could carry forward, and maybe one day she could make gardens with her own children. Later in the week, Levi would bring home a truck full of mulch and help them put it down, making those memories that much sweeter. This was what a childhood should be like, not riddled with anxiety over what an older sister might do or say or hoping a mother wouldn't call her out in public for wearing the wrong shoes or eating too much dessert. Joey would be a great big sister one day. She was sweet and caring with Hadley. Tara stumbled over the thought.

Why am I thinking about Joey being an older sister?

She shook it off. "We did a great job. Now we just need to water them."

"I'll get the hose!"

Joey ran toward the house as Levi's work truck rumbled down the street, stirring those butterflies to life again. Tara waved as he pulled up behind her car and went to him as he climbed out. His T-shirt strained against his biceps and broad chest, bringing images of last night when they had their hands all over each other. His dark eyes roved hungrily down the length of her, sending shivers of heat from the top of her head to the tips of her toes and every needy place in between.

"Where's Joey?" he asked gruffly, taking her aback.

"Getting the hose." She barely had time to register his wolfish grin as he hauled her into his arms and his mouth came urgently down over hers. His tongue delved deep, his strong arms holding her gloriously tight and wickedly possessive. She went up on her toes, her hands pushing into his hair, holding on for dear life because this stolen kiss, this enticing man, was *everything* she ever wanted. Then his hands were on her upper arms, pushing her away, leaving her breathless and desperate for more. Restrained desire stared back at her, and she knew she wasn't alone in her agony.

"Daddy!" Joey exclaimed, dropping the hose and running to him.

With one quick squeeze, Levi released Tara and turned to scoop Joey into his arms. "Hey, sweets. How was your day?"

"Good. Did you see the gardens?"

"How could I miss them? They're almost as beautiful as you and Aunt Tara." Levi shifted Joey to his right hip and slung his left arm around Tara, drawing her against his side.

While Joey would see what she always had, her daddy being his loving self toward her aunt, Tara was eating up the feel of him, her body still humming from his kiss.

"I need to water the flowers!" Joey wriggled out of his arms and ran back to get the hose.

Levi kept his arm around Tara. "This place looks incredible. You two must have worked all afternoon."

"We had a good time."

His eyes found hers, his gaze softening, moving slowly over her face. "You've got some dirt on your cheek." His warm fingers brushed her cheek. His brows knitted, and his jaw tightened.

"What's wrong?"

He shook his head. "You're just...The way the sun's hitting your face, your hair, and eyes...You're beautiful, Tara."

Embarrassed, she looked down, scrambling for a change in subject. "Joey was glad you stopped by to watch her practice."

He stepped closer, bringing her attention back to his handsome face. "You know I love seeing my daughter skate, but I went to see you." Electricity arced between them, hot and sharp and titillating. Just when she was sure they'd combust, he cleared his throat and put space between them again, glancing at

Joey as she watered the plants. "How do you feel about pizza for dinner? We can use the firepit and make a night of it."

It took a second for her to climb out of her lustful state. "If Joey's up for it, I'd love to. Can we get half—"

"Olives and half pepperoni? I've got you, blondie."

She smiled as they made their way to Joey.

"Hey, Joey," he said.

"Yeah?" Joey turned, spraying him with the hose. "Oops! *Sorry!*"

"You're going to be sorry, all right." He ran toward her, and she shrieked, dropping the hose and sprinting across the yard with Levi on her heels.

"Aunt Tara! *Help!*" Joey shouted.

Tara sprinted toward them to block Levi, but he didn't even slow down. He lowered his shoulder and threw her over it like a sack of potatoes. Tara squealed, arms and legs flailing as he closed in on Joey and hoisted her over his other shoulder with a sinister laugh, making them all crack up. Tara looked at Joey, hanging upside down over his back beside her, and pointed to Levi's butt. They banged it with two hands like a drum.

"Hey!" Levi complained.

Tara felt his big hand clamp down on her ass, and she *yelped.*

"Better watch yourselves, or I'll cook you in the firepit," Levi threatened.

"No!" Joey shrieked.

"Or in the oven like Hansel and Gretel," he teased.

"Daddy!"

He lowered Joey to the ground, but he kept Tara over his shoulder and headed for the house.

"What are you doing? Put me down," Tara shouted.

"Da-ad!"

"I'm taking her to my lair," he said huskily. "Bad girls need to be punished."

A thrill darted through Tara, even though she knew he was kidding.

Joey ran to the porch steps and put her arms out to the sides, blocking his way. "Put her down!"

"Or else?" he asked with amusement.

"Or else I'll pants you!" Joey warned.

Tara laughed, but Levi's muscles tensed.

"Where did you learn about pantsing people?" he demanded.

"Robby's older brother did it to him," Joey explained.

"You better not have seen that. I don't want your hands on any boy's pants, you hear me?"

"Da-ad." She grabbed Tara's foot and yanked.

"Whoa!" Tara held on to Levi as he lowered her to the ground.

"You're lucky she's on your side," he said. "She saved you from a butt whooping."

Tara tried to stifle the intrigue skating through her and narrowed her eyes. "You wouldn't dare."

He arched a brow with a devilish grin. "Wouldn't I?"

"You *wouldn't*," Joey said. "You don't believe in spanking." She took his hand, pulling him toward the gardens. "Come on. I want to show you which flowers we planted."

"I'll order the pizza," Tara called after them, pulling out her phone.

"Please don't forget to call my friends," Joey said.

Levi glanced over his shoulder and winked, catching Tara taking a picture of Joey and her very hot daddy walking away hand in hand.

AFTER ALL THE plants were watered, the hummingbird feeder was hung, and the pizza devoured, Levi sat with Joey and Tara bundled in sweatshirts around the fire. As the sun went down, they filled waffle cones with fruit, chocolate, and marshmallows and heated them in grilling baskets over the flames, and Joey told him about the plans they'd made.

She and Tara were sharing a lounge chair and finishing each other's sentences as they traded chocolate for strawberries and ate their desserts. It was about the best thing he'd ever seen. He'd been right when he'd told his father he thought he'd figured out why he hadn't been lonely.

This was why.

When Tara was there, their world felt complete, and they made the most out of every moment. In all the years she'd been staying with them, they'd never *just* gotten through nights like they sometimes did when she wasn't there. It was easy to fall into routines and feel that way. But she brought extra light and energy into their home, and he and Joey *wanted* to be with her every minute they could. It was no wonder he hadn't gone looking for something special with a woman these last few years. Tara's energy lingered even in her absence. She'd said she'd been into him forever, but she'd never competed with Joey for his attention the way other women had tried to, even if only in conversation, and he had a feeling she never would.

Tara broke off a piece of her waffle cone and used her fingers to sever the long, gooey marshmallow tail. "I was thinking about cleaning out the shed and having a yard sale for the things you don't want to keep."

"And I want to sell lemonade at the yard sale." Joey had marshmallow on her chin and cheek. She licked her fingers. "I'm gonna use the money I make to buy stickers for my helmet."

"I like the lemonade idea, peanut, but, T, you don't have to spend your time cleaning up our messes. I don't even know what's in there."

She finished her bite and said, "It'll be fun, and if you don't know what's in there, this is a great way to find out."

"Then I'll help you do it."

"The idea was to take the job off your plate," Tara pointed out. "You've got enough to do."

"I appreciate that, but there's a lot of heavy stuff in there, and I don't want you getting hurt."

"Me and Tara are strong, Dad," Joey interjected. "We can do it."

"That's right. We are women, hear us roar," Tara teased.

Joey put her hands up like claws and *roared.*

He eyed the two of them acting like teammates or co-conspirators. He should feel outnumbered, but he didn't. He knew why Tara had offered to clean out the shed. For the same reason she gardened and was always willing to put her own work off to help them. Because nothing was more important to her than Joey's happiness, and she knew that making time to do those things after work would take his attention away from Joey. Tara wasn't just sweet, beautiful, and smart. She was selfless, and in today's world that was a rarity.

"Fine, but don't prioritize it above all the fun stuff you have planned." He would damn well make sure they didn't get hurt. He'd start moving the heavier things tomorrow morning before work and would clear a path so they could get to the lighter boxes and whatever else was hidden behind them.

"We won't," they promised, and began making plans as they finished dessert.

As it neared nine, he offered his hand to Joey and said, "Come on, sticky face. Let's get you in the shower and off to bed."

"*Da-ad*," she complained. "It's spring break. Can we just play one round of ghost story first?" Ghost story was a game where one person started a story, and the next person added to it, and so on.

He was dying to be alone with Tara, but Joey was looking at him pleadingly, and Tara looked as torn as he felt. They were both softies for his little girl. "One game."

"Yay! Thank you. I'll go first." Joey sat up, her little brow furrowing. "It was a cold, dark night. The kind Grandma Shelley calls a hot-chocolate-and-fuzzy-blanket night. The wind was howling."

Tara made a howling noise, which thrilled Joey.

"And the trees were blowing," Joey said.

Levi made a wind noise.

"But the man hobbling down the road wasn't cold." Joey lowered her voice. "Because he was a *zombie*."

"And everyone knows that zombies aren't afraid of anything," Tara added. "Or are they? Only the witch flying on her broom knew the answer…"

An hour, and many spooky lines later, after Joey got cleaned up and went to bed, Levi finally showered, put on sweats and a T-shirt, and went in search of Tara.

Fourteen

LEVI FOUND HER in the kitchen, putting away the remainder of the berries, humming and bopping her sexy little ass to some imaginary tune. The ruffled tie-dye sleeping shorts she wore barely covered her ass, and the matching long-sleeve shirt bared one sleek, kissable shoulder. Her hair was damp, and as he closed the distance between them, he smelled the fresh lavender scent of her body wash. He nipped at her earlobe and wrapped his arms around her from behind.

She gasped, turning around and putting her hands on his chest. "You *startled* me."

"You turned me on in those sexy shorts."

"How is that even a response?" she asked with a laugh.

"Because I couldn't help myself." He slid his hands down her back, along the curve at the base of her spine, and grabbed her butt. "You've messed with my head, blondie. I can't stop thinking about you, and when I see you, all I want to do is touch you."

Her smile lit up her eyes. "I love hearing that, but…" She

whispered, "This is kind of weird, right?"

"What is?" He knew what she was asking, but he wanted to hear her say it.

"This. *Us.*"

"I think it's perfect." He really did. They had a lot to figure out, and they were moving fast, but it didn't feel *weird* to him.

"I'm serious. It doesn't feel a little strange to you?"

"It's definitely a different dynamic for us, but I like it. I like *you*, T, and I like how I feel when I'm with you. You don't feel that way?"

"No. I didn't mean anything bad by it. I feel good about us, too. I meant a *good* kind of weird. Like you said, a different dynamic."

Thank God. "I get it. We've pushed some boundaries, and it's happened fast. Do you need to slow down?"

"No," she said quickly, and put her arms around him.

"If you do, just tell me. I like you for a lot more than sex, T."

"I know you do." The honesty of her words was underscored by the trust in her eyes.

He brushed her hair away from her face. "I know we don't have it all figured out, and we don't know what'll happen between us in the long run, but didn't you say you've had a crush on me forever?"

She touched her forehead to his chest for a second, then smiled up at him. "Don't you ever forget anything I say?"

"Nope. Why didn't you ever tell me?"

"Are you *really* asking me that?"

"*Yes.* I had no idea you were into me. Archer noticed how you looked at me and said something at Indi's grand opening."

"Archer?" Confusion riddled her brow.

"Yeah, believe it or not. He said a lot of things, actually, and it made me question everything I thought I knew about us. That's when I started realizing there was more between us than I'd let myself see."

"What do you mean?"

"I think I've been into you for a few years, but I suppressed it." That earned the most magnificent light in her eyes. "I closed the door to relationships after Joey was born to focus on her, and it wasn't until Archer said those things and opened that door that I really *saw* you, all of you, and our friendship, for what it was, and then I couldn't unsee it or unfeel the things I felt. So, yeah. I want to know why you never clued me in when you *knew* how you felt about me for so long."

"Isn't it obvious? The whole Amelia-Joey thing, and our age difference, not to mention that you're *you*, and you can have any woman you want, and sure this turned out well for now, but what if I'd tried to tell you and you didn't want me? Everything would've changed."

"Those are the reasons I hesitated when I first realized how much I liked you." The last thing he wanted to do was talk about Amelia, but it was inevitable. He braced himself for an uncomfortable conversation. "But what happened between me and Amelia was a onetime thing, and the condom broke. There was never anything special or meaningful between us, and that's horrible to say because that's how I got my daughter, but you need to know the truth."

"I figured that much. She's not one for emotions."

"Do you want to talk about it?"

"At some point, yes. But not now."

"Okay." Relieved, he kissed her softly and tried to lighten the mood. "Then tell me, blondie, exactly how long *have* you been into me? How long is forever?"

She looked just as relieved to set thoughts of her sister aside as he was. "Embarrassingly long."

"A year?" He brushed a kiss to her lips.

"Longer."

He kissed her again. "Two years?"

She shook her head and pointed to her neck.

God, he liked her. He lowered his lips to her neck in a sensual, openmouthed kiss.

"Oh, boy. If you do that again, I might not be able to answer."

"Then I'll withhold it until you do."

"When did you get so mean?" she teased.

He licked his lips lasciviously.

"Since we were kids, *okay*?" she relented. "I mean, not in this way, obviously, but I've crushed on you since I was Joey's age, and as I got older and started noticing guys in a different way, you were this amazing, kind, smart, funny person who would do anything for his daughter. And let's face it, you're ridiculously hot."

He laughed.

"By the time I was twenty, no other guy stood a chance."

"Aw, blondie." He hugged her, wishing he'd known sooner. "You've wanted me for that long and you just lived with it? That must've been torture. I nearly lost my mind wanting you for a *week*. In that regard, I'm glad I suppressed it for so long, or I might not have survived."

"It wasn't easy. I had a plan to get over you, but it wasn't working very well."

"A get-over-Levi plan? This I've got to hear."

"Shut up." She swatted his chest. "You owe me." She tapped

the other side of her neck.

"Next time I pick the spot." He sank his teeth into her neck and sucked *hard.*

"Ohhhh, *fudge.*"

He arched a brow. "Fudge?"

"I'm not big on the F word, and it's not my fault you scramble my brain with that wicked mouth of yours."

"I'm going to do a lot more than that after you tell me about your evil plan to forget your crush on me. What did you do, throw darts at my picture?"

"No."

"Make a voodoo doll and stick me with pins?"

"That's a good one. I'll have to keep that in mind."

"The hell you will." He kissed her lips. "You don't have to tell me if you don't want to." He dragged his scruff down her cheek, and she inhaled sharply as he spoke into her ear. "But my mouth is off-limits until you do."

"I'll keep that in mind, too, for when I want something from *you,*" she teased. "If you must know, I promised myself at the beginning of the year that I would move on from my feelings for you. That's part of why I'm looking at houses. I was going to tell you after these two weeks that I couldn't stay over for extended periods anymore because it was too hard for me to keep pretending that I don't want you."

His chest constricted. "You would've broken Joey's heart."

"I would've broken my own," she said quietly.

"I've got news for you, blondie. You'd've broken mine, too, so get that plan out of your head. Maybe you should ask Charmaine about checking out rentals instead of buying while we figure things out." He kissed her softly and lifted her onto the counter, wedging himself between her legs. "How do you really feel about what's happening between us?"

She ran her fingers down his chest. "Like it's scary and wonderful."

"How about if we concentrate on the wonderful and hope that scariness subsides with time?" He slid his hands up her legs and beneath the hem on the sides of her shorts, brushing his thumbs over the tops of her thighs.

She put her arms around his neck. "I like that idea."

He kissed the edge of her mouth. "Me too. How can I miss touching you this much?" He trailed kisses down her neck and along her collarbone.

"I don't know, but don't stop." She tipped her head back, giving him better access. He continued kissing, whispering against her skin, and slid his thumbs between her legs. She spread her legs wider, sighing longingly as he teased her.

"*Mm,* baby, you're already wet for me."

She rocked her hips, and he moved his thumb in slow circles over her most sensitive bundle of nerves. Sweet, sexy sounds of desire tumbled from her lips. He teased her center with his other thumb, and she rocked harder, pushing her hands beneath the waist of his sweatpants, holding his ass over his boxer briefs.

"*Mm,* that feels good, but I want your hands on my skin."

Her hands pushed beneath the thin material and grabbed his ass. His hips thrust, and he quickened his efforts between her legs. Her moan sent a rush of heat to his dick.

"Give me your mouth," he demanded.

She gripped his ass tighter with one hand and used the other to pull his mouth to hers, kissing him like she needed him to survive. Their tongues battled, teeth gnashing as he teased, until she was whimpering, rocking. Her fingernails dug into his ass cheek, and she spread her legs wider, her desperation magnifying everything. He pushed two fingers inside her, crooking them. She gasped, and he breathed air into her lungs as he fucked her with his fingers, still rubbing her swollen clit.

"Come for me," he growled against her lips, and reclaimed her mouth. He quickened his efforts, loving the feel of her tight heat, the taste of her exquisite mouth. When she cried out, her nails carving into his flesh, he stayed with her, stroking and teasing, until she went soft against him. He drew back on a series of tender kisses. "I want my mouth on you right here and now, but I know I won't want to stop there, and with—"

"*Joey*," she said at the same time he did.

"Yeah. We can't be reckless like last night. How do you feel about moving our party to your bedroom?"

"I want you, Levi. *All* of you."

With seven little words, she annihilated his ability to speak. He lifted her into his arms, covering her mouth with his as he strode toward the guest room. He set her on her feet, and as he turned to lock the door behind them, he realized his mistake and bit back a curse.

"What's wrong?"

"I left the condoms upstairs."

She hooked her finger into the waistband of his sweatpants, tugging him closer. "I'm on birth control."

His entire body flamed. It took every ounce of his restraint not to take that invitation and run with it as he pressed his hands to her gorgeous cheeks and gazed deeply into her trusting eyes. "As much as I want to be inside you with nothing between us—and I *do* want that more than anything—we're just getting started together, and I've already got Joey. I don't want to take any chances."

Hurt rose in her eyes. "Do you think I'd trick you into

getting me pregnant? Did my sister?"

"*Hell no* and *no*, she didn't. I told you the condom broke. I trust you explicitly, T. I just want to spend the little free time I've got after Joey's asleep focusing on *you*, not juggling an infant. I know it sounds ridiculous to double up on birth control, but I'm trying to protect us both, for now."

Her gaze softened. "It's not ridiculous. It's thoughtful." She went up on her toes and kissed him. "Hurry back."

He was back in her room in a flash, locking the door behind him.

"Wow, you were like a ninja on speed."

"I wasn't about to give you time to change your mind." He tossed the unopened box of condoms toward the nightstand and drew her into his arms. "Now, where were we? Oh yeah, getting you *naked*."

Her cheeks flamed. "I'm not getting naked alone."

"Hey, babe, that's *not* a problem." He stripped off his shirt and sweats, feeling the heat of her gaze as she drank him in. *That's right, beautiful. I'm all yours.* He reached for his boxer briefs, and his cock jerked in anticipation. "I'd better leave these on." He stalked toward her.

"Why?"

"Because I have plans for you." He kissed her shoulder. "And once I set that monster free, he's going to want to get in on the action."

"*Ohmygosh*. As if I'm not nervous enough?" She covered her face.

He lowered her hands and kissed her lips. "Were you nervous last night?"

"*Yes*, at first," she confessed. "But you weren't looking at me, and it was dark."

There were no lights on in the bedroom, but moonlight spilled in through the open curtains. "It's pretty dark in here, T, and I *want* to look at you. I want to see *all* of you, taste you, touch you, and make you feel better than you ever have." Her eyes sparked with desire, and he brushed his lips over hers. "Do you want that?"

"*Yes*," she said fast and heated, with a thread of nervousness.

He kissed the corner of her mouth. "I know you're nervous, but I also know you trust me."

"I do," she whispered.

"Then it's time to trust yourself. To *know* you're beautiful inside and out and to own the power of that knowledge and follow your intuition without fear of judgment, because there is no right or wrong in this. I loved the way you touched me last night, and listening to you getting off over the phone was the hottest thing I've ever heard." He lowered his mouth to a whisper away from hers and threaded his fingers through her hair, grabbing tight as he'd learned she liked. He was rewarded with a sharp, gratuitous inhalation. "Do you want to feel that free and powerful with me and let your inner siren out to play?"

"*Yes*," she said pleadingly.

"Good, because I've been looking forward to fulfilling my promises." He crushed his mouth to hers in a penetrating kiss that had her practically climbing him like a tree. "Oh yeah, baby. Let's have some fun." He stripped off her shirt and tossed it across the room, earning the cutest giggle. He started to take off her shorts and panties, but her foot got caught, and she lost her balance, taking them both down to the bed, cracking up.

"Sorry," she said between laughs, kicking off the offending clothes.

"That's one way to get me in your bed." He kissed her smiling lips, taking it deeper, turning their laughter into greedy moans. Skimming his hand up her side, he brushed his thumb over her silky breast, and she sucked in a breath. He pressed a kiss there and another beside her necklace, which glittered against her flawless skin. "I love seeing that on you," he whispered as he dipped his head and slicked his tongue over her nipple. A long, lustful sigh left her lips. "*Mm.* My girl likes that."

She closed her eyes.

"Open those baby blues, blondie. I want you to watch me drive you wild."

Her eyes opened, and her cheeks flamed. "Is this like exposure therapy?"

He wondered if she had any idea how magnificent she was. "That's one way to look at it." He nipped at her breast, and she gasped. "Or you could just enjoy the ride and not try to define it."

"Okay, let's go with that."

He grazed his teeth over her nipple.

"Levi—"

The plea in her voice spurred him on, and there was no holding back. Using his mouth and hands, he loved her breasts, teasing and taunting, sucking and nipping, making her writhe and moan. He kept his eyes trained on hers, flames igniting the space between them. He leaned up on one hand, watching his other hand slide down her breast. Her nipples were red from his mouth, her skin flushed, and as he lowered his mouth over the taut peak, their eyes met, and hers closed. He sucked hard. "Eyes open, blondie."

Her eyes flew open. "It's *torture.*"

"Do you want me to stop?"

"Are you *insane*?" They both laughed. "Do you have any idea what it does to me to see you doing that?"

He grinned arrogantly, making them both laugh again. "Trust me, T, when you put your mouth on me, I'm going to watch every second. I want to see you suck and lick and touch me, and I won't want to miss a second of it."

She covered her face with one hand. "The things you say…"

He pressed a kiss between her breasts and moved over her so he could look directly into her eyes. She lowered her hand, smiling up at him.

"You bring this out in me, T. *Only* you, and I don't want to hold back. But I will if it's too much for you."

"It's not. I like it. It's just embarrassing how *much* I like it."

"Own it, baby. There's nothing sexier than knowing you're watching me and enjoying it." He lowered his lips to hers in a long, passionate kiss, and then he shifted lower, taking a good long look at her feminine curves. "You are stunning, baby." He licked and sucked his way down her beautiful breasts, eliciting more enticing noises, and trailed openmouthed kisses over her ribs and down her stomach. When he slowed to drag his tongue around her belly button, she fisted her hands in the sheets, bowing beneath him.

"*God*, that feels good," she said breathily.

He took his time, savoring the taste of her sweet, hot skin. She arched and mewled as he tasted his way south, lingering with his mouth hovering just above her clit, his hot breath making her squirm. She rocked her hips, the scent of her arousal making his mouth water. Her eyes were closed, and he let them remain that way while he looked his fill at his sweet, trusting Tara giving herself over to him. "You're fucking beautiful." He kissed her stomach. "You're so much more than that." Emotions whirled inside him, winding him up like a top until his whole body buzzed with them. He needed to see her eyes, to know if she felt it, too. He opened his mouth to speak, but her eyes opened, swimming with so much emotion, he could drown in them.

"I'm so lucky you're *mine*." He dipped his head, dragging his tongue along her slick heat and over her clit.

"Levi—"

The desperate plea tugged at something deep inside him. "Don't worry, baby. I won't leave you hanging, but I'm not going to rush." He spread his hands on her thighs and licked along her sex, making her pant and moan. She tasted like warm, sweet honey, and he couldn't get enough. He feasted on her, licking and sucking, fucking her with his tongue. She rocked and moaned. When he took her clit between his teeth, her hips shot off the mattress. He guided her legs over his shoulders, licking from her sex to her clit, lingering there, then doing it again, finding a rhythm, and loving her with his mouth until she was shaking and begging, desperate sounds filling the room. She clutched the sheets so tightly her knuckles blanched. He reached up and, using one hand on her breast, rolled her nipple between his finger and thumb.

"LeviLeviLevi."

"Watch me, baby," he commanded, and she did so with a whimper.

Those beautiful pools of blue were utterly enraptured as he pushed two fingers inside her and lowered his mouth over that magical bundle of nerves. Her brows furrowed and her jaw clenched. *"Le…"*

He crooked his fingers, finding that hidden spot like a heat-seeking missile, stroking her fast, as he squeezed her nipple and sucked her clit until she detonated, crying out with pleasure. She clapped a hand over her mouth, her body bucking and pulsing. He moved his mouth lower, needing to feel her quake and quiver. *Sheer fucking heaven.*

"Don't stop." She grabbed his head, holding him there.

She moaned and rocked, digging her fingernails into his scalp, sending exquisite pain and pleasure straight to his dick. He wanted her hands and mouth all over him, but he needed to be inside her more than he needed the air he breathed. When she finally collapsed breathlessly to the mattress, her arms falling limp beside her, he rained kisses on her inner thighs as he lowered her legs from his shoulders.

"You're too sexy. I need to be inside you." He stripped off his boxer briefs, kissing his way up her body, the length of his cock resting on her wetness, making him want to forgo the condom and drive into her and feel her slick heat gripping him. He'd never felt a need so strong, like talons clawing at him, but then her eyes opened, a sated smile curving her lips, and she whispered, "Kiss me."

The sweetness of her request sent his protective urges surging, and he kissed her deep and slow, pouring all the emotions that were stacking up inside him into their connection. When their lips parted, the gravity of them hit him full-on, burrowing into his chest.

"You okay?" he whispered. "Or do you want to stop?"

"If you stop now, I'll have to kill you."

She said it so seriously, he couldn't hold back a laugh, and smothered those sounds with a kiss. He reached for the box of condoms, and when he rose onto his knees to open it, she reached up and stroked his length. His chin fell to his chest with a hiss.

"*Mm*. My guy likes that," she teased, using his words.

"You have no idea what your touch does to me."

She licked her lips. "I wonder what my mouth will do to you."

"Shit, baby. You wanna find out?"

She nodded, eyes lustful and wide.

"Sit up against the headboard."

She sat up fast, with the biggest grin, reaching for him like he was her favorite dessert, looking sexy, adorable, and so *hot*, he knew that moment would replay in his fantasies forever. He put down the box of condoms, and she fisted his cock, tugging him closer. He straddled her on his knees as she stroked him. She ran her tongue along the broad crown, and that first slick had his hips thrusting. His entire body flexed, trying to hold still as she licked him from base to tip repeatedly, then circled the head again.

"You're so big. I might not be very good at this."

Christ…"Baby, just touch me. You don't have to do anything more."

"I want to. I want to explore with you."

Did she have any idea the doors that opened in his mind? And then that word hit him. *Explore.* "T, have you done this before?"

"Define *this*," she said softly.

"Any of it. What we just did?"

She nodded. "A couple of times, but it wasn't anything like that. It was…" She wrinkled her nose and shrugged.

"And what you're about to do?"

"Once. Same with having sex. But the guy I was with was a lot smaller than you, and it wasn't fun."

He cursed. "You're not doing this."

"*Yes*, I am," she insisted. "I didn't feel for him what I feel for you, which I think is the reason it wasn't enjoyable."

"*Jesus*. Please tell me he wasn't just some random guy."

"He wasn't. We went out for a few months, and I kept thinking if we did those things, feelings would come, but they didn't, and the one time we had sex, I was hoping for Magic Mountain and I got the Scooby-Doo roller coaster. Then *you* gave me Magic Mountain without even having sex. I *want* to do this with you, Levi. I've wanted to do it for so long, if you don't let me"—she paused, arching a brow—"I'm going to be really mad."

He shook his head. "You're killing me."

"You can't die before we do the dirty deed."

"The *dirty deed*?" he repeated with a chuckle.

"Yeah, you have to be around for that. Afterward, I'll probably be dead anyway, because I barely survived the orgasms you gave me so far. Now can we stop talking about my ridiculous lack of experience and see if I'm any good at this or if I should throw in the towel and become a nun?"

"Baby, I think we both know there'll be no throwing in the towel."

"That's what I'm counting on. Now, can you please kiss me again and turn my brain off?"

"There's nothing I'd rather do." He lowered his mouth to hers, trying to go easy, given all he'd just learned, but, as their tongues tangled, their kisses intensified, and their hands were everywhere at once. She fisted his cock, working him so perfectly, he tore his mouth away with a curse. He rose onto his knees and her eager tongue went to town on the head of his dick, driving him out of his mind. Every slick sent heat sizzling through him. She licked his length, torturing him with long, slow strokes, lingering around the broad crown until his entire body caught fire. It was like her mouth was made just for him. She knew *exactly* how to drive him wild, teasing and taunting until he was cursing with restraint. When she took him in her hot, wet mouth, stroking him with her hand as she sucked and licked, he fought against the heat pooling at the base of his spine. His gaze locked on hers, and what a beautiful sight she was with her plump lips wrapped around his cock, her delicate hand sliding along his shaft. The urge to thrust was so strong, he grabbed the headboard with one hand to steady himself, grabbing a handful of her hair with the other. Her eyes flicked up to his, dark with lust and sparkling with appreciation. *Yeah, baby. You love this as much as I do, don't you?*

She drew his length out of her mouth slowly, making a show of licking him again, and a groan escaped his lips.

"I guess I'm doing okay?" she asked so innocently it got him twisted up inside.

"There's nothing *okay* about how you make me feel. You're unbelievable. It's taking every ounce of my restraint not to come. But what matters is how you feel doing it. If you don't enjoy it, you can stop."

A big-ass grin lit up her face. "I'm doing it to *you*, and I knew that would make the difference. I like pleasuring you, and I like when you pull my hair."

"*Jesus*, T." He grabbed the base of his cock, squeezing to stave off his release.

"What's wrong? Am I not supposed to tell you that?"

Her innocence wasn't feigned, and that made him want to claim her, to protect her from everything and everyone, even more. "No. I want to know what you like, but you can't say shit like that when I'm this close to the edge."

She giggled. "Okay. Can I do it one more time?"

"*Fuuck*" fell from his lips. "You're amazing, but you're playing with dynamite, baby."

"I'll just do it for a second," she said sweetly. "I like making you crazy."

"I'm starting to wonder if *I'll* survive tonight." He scrubbed a hand down his face and grabbed the headboard again, clenching his jaw as she took him deep in her mouth, working him faster. Their eyes locked, and he could feel her measuring the effect she had on him as she stroked him faster, sucked harder, his entire body flexing with restraint.

"*T*," he warned. "I want to be inside you when I come."

She pulled him out of her mouth, flashing a sassy smirk. "Technically, you *are* inside me."

"You're definitely going to be the death of me." He swept her away from the headboard, trapping her on her back, and crushed his mouth to hers, kissing her until the urge to come wasn't so dire. He drew back, kissing her softer. "I have a feeling I'm never going to get enough of you."

"Yay for me." She leaned up and kissed him.

Man, he loved that little act of possession. He grabbed the box of condoms and tore it open, withdrawing one. She watched him roll it on, and as he came down over her, she reached for him, spreading her legs wider. His heart hammered against his ribs. What the hell was that about? Why was he nervous? As he aligned his cock with her entrance, her trusting eyes stared up at him, full of want and need and something so much deeper, it drew the answer from somewhere deep inside his chest. He'd never given two shits about sex before. It was a primal urge, easy to satisfy. But this wasn't *just* sex on any level, and Tara wasn't just important to him because of Joey. She was important to him because of how he felt about her, and he didn't want to let her down. He knew he was good at sex and he hoped he'd rock her world, but that wasn't enough. He wanted to be more than she hoped for, which added a heightened level of pressure. He wanted to *take* and *give* and let her feel what she did to him. He wanted to leave her craving his touch, his kisses, his *mouth*, and above all else, he wanted her to feel what he *felt* for her, and that was what was messing with his head. He'd never cared enough to want to do that before, and he could only hope he didn't screw it up.

She pressed her hand to his cheek, drawing him from his thoughts. "Stop overthinking."

"How do you know I'm overthinking?"

"Because your eyebrows twitch when you do."

The fact that she'd noticed something as intimate as his *tell* did him in, and he could no more think than speak. His mouth came hungrily down over hers, and he angled his hips, entering her slowly, carefully. She was so tight, it made him hyperaware of this being only her second time, adding more self-inflicted pressure.

He wanted to make this special…for *both* of them.

When he was buried to the hilt, the gloriously tight pressure, and the complexity, the weight, and the realness of his emotions were so intense, he broke their kiss, needing to concentrate, and clenched his teeth.

"*Levi,*" she said low and breathy.

"Too much?" If he hurt her, he'd never forgive himself.

"*No*. I didn't expect it to feel so good."

He touched his forehead to hers, breathing her in. "Neither did I."

THE EMOTIONS IN Levi's voice nearly stopped Tara's heart, but when he lifted his face, the restraint in his muscles and the raw, unadulterated pleasure brimming in his eyes brought a gust of energy. She wanted to see more of that, to feel all the power he was holding back.

"You feel phenomenal, baby. *Too* damn good," he said huskily.

He laced their fingers together, pinning her hands to the mattress just as he'd said he would last night, and she loved it, but she *needed* to touch him, and she didn't want to hold back. "I want to touch you."

"I want that, too, but if you touch me now, while you're locked around my dick like a vise, I'm liable to blow like a volcano."

She giggled. "I guess you were right, and I won't be throwing in the towel."

"Definitely not. My sweet siren is here to stay."

He kissed her again, tenderly at first, but as he began to move and they found their rhythm, the pleasure was too intense. She met his quickening thrusts with a rock of her hips, and their bodies took over. Her hips moved in ways she hadn't expected, pumping and grinding, and there was no stopping the needy sounds spilling into their kisses. This was *nothing* like the first time she'd had sex, and it far surpassed what she'd imagined being intimate with Levi would be like. *Need* and *greed* twined together, coursing through her veins, making her feel bold and sexy. She reveled in the weight of him bearing down on her, the pressure of his shaft filling her so completely, she knew she'd not only feel him tomorrow but for the rest of her life, as if he'd imprinted that part of himself on her, the way he'd already been imprinted on her heart.

"*God, T.* Do you feel that?"

"*Us.* It's us," came out of nowhere, but it was true. Their connection was what made this feel so unbelievably good and right, and she wanted *more.*

He said, "I need your hands on me," as she said, "I need to touch you."

He released her hands, and she touched him with a desperation she'd never imagined, exploring his hot flesh, the hard planes and deep ridges of his muscles, intensifying her desire. Their kisses grew messy and frantic, and he lifted her legs at the knees, driving in deeper. Hot sparks radiated from her core, shooting up her chest and down her limbs. She wanted to live in that exquisite, tumultuous state. She clawed at his back, begging, "*Harder…Faster.*" Their bodies slickened with their efforts. The harsh sounds of flesh against flesh filled the room, chased by their sinful pleas and lustful moans.

"*So good,*" he said gruffly. "I want you in every way possible."

The thrill of that proclamation sent her emotions reeling. *"Yes."*

She bowed off the bed, and he reclaimed her mouth, pushing his hands beneath her ass, lifting and angling, taking her impossibly deeper. She was grasping for sanity. *More, more, more* playing in her head. When he flipped her onto all fours, kneeling behind her, it felt taboo. She clawed at the sheets, feeling dirty and thrilled at once. She had a fleeting worry about where he was planning on putting his pleasure-inducing cock, but then she felt it at her center. Relief came with a hint of longing and of *shock* at the exhilaration at even the thought of letting Levi touch her in places she'd never imagined.

He wrapped an arm around her middle, holding tight, and pressed a kiss to her back. "Can I take you hard, baby?"

"*Yes.* Do it."

His hips shot forward, and she cried out in pure, toe-curling pleasure. His hand moved down her belly, between her legs, as he pounded into her from behind, masterfully touching her until the world exploded into a fiery crash of light and dark, hot and cold, sending her soaring, his gruff, sexy voice taking her to new heights. *"That's it, baby...So tight...Hell yeah...Milk my cock."*

She was suspended at the peak, breathless and so full of him, when she finally floated down from her high, she was sure she'd died and gone to heaven.

He slowed his thrusts, murmuring against her skin, "*God, T.* I didn't hurt you, did I? You felt so good, I couldn't hold back."

She shook her head, and he gently rolled her over. She was shocked that he was still hard, and, as he came down over her, the way he was looking at her had her heart turning over in her chest. "You didn't...?"

He shook his head. "I wanted to see your face."

"Wow. You're some kind of sex god. Did you have Viagra for dinner?"

"No, babe. You've got it backward. You're a sexual goddess, and you've enslaved me with your magical pussy."

She gasped and laughed, closing her eyes.

"You love my dirty talk." He kissed her, and she opened her eyes.

"You think so, huh?"

"I pay attention, remember?" He nipped at her shoulder, sending prickles of heat down her body. "I feel the way your body reacts when I tell you I like eating your pussy and tasting your tits and mouth." He guided her legs around his waist as he spoke, sliding both hands beneath her head, cradling it as their bodies came together again.

His eyes brimmed with emotion as he gyrated his hips in slow, erotic circles. Prickling sensations climbed up her legs, gathering low in her belly. She closed her eyes, wanting to memorize the feel of him, but the need to see him was too strong, drawing them open again.

"Does that feel good, baby?"

"*So good,*" she panted out. "Kiss m—"

Her words were smothered by the hard press of a passionate kiss as he gyrated and then thrust, then did it again and again in a mesmerizing pattern. The prickling in her lower belly consumed her, burning and billowing. Building like a turbulent wave as he kissed her rougher, more demanding. She met his efforts with fervor, rocking her hips, feasting on his mouth. His muscles flexed, guttural noises seeping from his lungs into their frantic kisses. His unrelenting desire intensified every sensation, the feel of his strong body on hers, the sounds of pleasure they made, taking her up, up, *up*, until she was standing on the edge of a cliff, clinging to him as their bodies rocked and pistoned, tongues battling. His fingers tangled in her hair and he thrust harder, rougher. She wanted that roughness. *Craved* it. He reared up, as if he felt her need, driving into her from a new, tantalizing angle that sent pleasure rocketing through her. An orgasm sped up her limbs, catapulting her into ecstasy, and he was right there with her, grunting out her name as the world spun away. And then he was kissing her again, sweet and slow and oh so perfect, cradling her beneath him, anchoring her to the spinning world around her as his handsome face came back into focus.

"*Jesus,*" he said in one long breath.

"I didn't think anything could surpass Magic Mountain, but *wow.*"

He laughed and kissed her soft and slow. She reveled in those deep kisses, in the exquisite feel of him, of *them*, wishing he could stay buried deep inside her forever. They kissed until he had no choice but to take care of the condom.

"Don't go anywhere," he whispered, and climbed out of bed.

"Where would I go? To the store? Out for a jog?"

He grinned over his shoulder and headed into the bathroom.

She stared up at the ceiling in blissed-out glory, but she couldn't hold in her elation. She closed her eyes, grinning like a goof and wiggling in a butt-shaking happy dance. When she opened her eyes, Levi was standing in the bathroom doorway buck-naked and amused.

Mortified, she rolled over and buried her face in the pillow. He chuckled and she felt the bed dip beside her. "You can go upstairs now," she said into the pillow.

"And miss this? Not a chance." He pulled down the blanket and smacked her ass.

She let out a shocked gasp and glowered at him. "Do *not* spank me."

"Then don't try to get rid of me."

"If you wouldn't sneak out of the bathroom, I could do my happy dance in private. You must think I'm such a child."

"If you saw me doing a fist pump in the bathroom, you wouldn't say that." He lay beside her, gathering her in his arms, so her head rested on his shoulder.

"You did *not.*"

"Want me to pull up the video feed?"

Panic sent her up on her elbow. "You have *cameras* in there? Do you have them in here?" She looked around frantically.

He chuckled, shaking his head.

She swatted him. "You gave me a heart attack." Flopping down beside him, she put his hand over her heart. "Feel that?"

"Sorry, blondie." He rolled onto his side and pressed a kiss over her racing heart. "But you're not embarrassed anymore, are you?"

She rolled her eyes.

"Maybe I can make it up to you." He leaned down and kissed her.

He moved his hand lower, fondling her breast, and her body sprang to life again, nipples pebbling, goose bumps chasing up her flesh. "*Maybe*," she taunted, feeling him get hard against her. She ran her fingers through his hair. "Did you really do a fist pump?"

"Yes."

"Was it accompanied by *I've still got it*?" She giggled, and he glared down at her.

"You think you're funny, don't you?"

"Admit it. You said it, didn't you?" she teased.

"So what if I did?" He tickled her ribs, and she drew her legs up, laughing.

"Now I *wish* you had video."

"How about we make a video?" He pressed his erection against her, his gaze turning seductive. "Your fist can do the pumping, and I'll record it all?"

"You wouldn't *dare*."

"Wouldn't I? It could be fun, blondie. What do you say?"

Before she could respond, he covered her mouth with his. She never imagined herself to be a sex-video type of girl. But with Levi she had a feeling nothing was off-limits.

Fifteen

WEDNESDAY EVENING, LEVI sat at a table with Joker, Ozzy, and Forge at church, the weekly meeting of the Dark Knights. Their clubhouse was located a few blocks from the main drag in the old brick post office building. The windows were blacked out, and the Dark Knights' emblem—a skull with dark eyes, sharp brows, and jagged fangs—was prominently displayed above the front door. The club had originated in Peaceful Harbor, Maryland, decades ago, and they had chapters all over the country. Harborside was one of the smaller chapters, with only twenty-two members, but the close-knit group was well respected by the community for their efforts to keep Harborside safe and their literacy and anti-bullying campaigns. The Harborside chapter was founded by Jesse and Brent, the president and vice president, a little more than a decade ago. Originally from Trusty, Colorado, they'd been members of the Redemption Ranch chapter in Hope Valley, Colorado, where Finn, one of their older brothers, remained.

Levi looked around the room. Those men had been there

for him at a time when he'd been a little lost, and they'd become the brothers he'd been missing after moving away from his friends and family. Levi had always looked forward to church. It was the one place he could unwind and just be one of the guys instead of *Dad* or *Boss*. But tonight, as Jesse reminded them about Joey's tournament and Brent went over details for their upcoming rallies, Levi was eager for the meeting to end. Joey was sleeping at a friend's house, and he and Tara had his place to themselves. She was editing photos tonight, and he wondered if she'd been as sidetracked by thoughts of him as he'd been with thoughts of her.

He checked the time again.

He should be exhausted after two nights of getting little sleep, but he felt rejuvenated, like he was eighteen years old again, only better. Since Joey's conception, sex had become nothing more than an act of release, a means to an end that was anything but *fun*, because in the back of his mind were worries about unplanned pregnancy and clingy women who might complicate his life. He'd wondered if he'd ever be able to relax and enjoy it again. But from the moment he'd kissed Tara, he'd been so caught up in her, there had been no room for those cold, uncomfortable feelings. When they'd had sex Monday night, he'd thought the reason he'd been able to let loose was because of how much he trusted her. But last night, as Tara had dozed in his arms after two hours of the most intense foreplay and sex he'd ever experienced, he'd realized that there was something much deeper than trust going on, and *that* was what had led to a whole new level of intimacy.

Unfortunately, that also made it harder to be apart. He'd messed up last night and had fallen asleep in her bed, wrapped around her warm body. They'd almost gotten caught this morning when Joey had knocked on Tara's door looking for him. He'd sprung out of bed, thrown on his sweats, and climbed out the freaking window. He'd had to use his hidden key to come in through the front door, acting like he'd just gone for a run.

He knew they were doing the right thing by keeping their relationship from Joey until they were sure it would last, but he hated every second of it. He was in a relationship for the first time in his adult life, and he was with the most spectacular woman he knew. He wanted to take Tara out and treat her like his girlfriend, not hide their relationship from the people he loved. But protecting Joey had to come first.

"Hey, Steele, what's up with you tonight?" Forge's deep voice drew Levi from his thoughts. "You got a date?"

"Something like that," Levi said as Jesse finally wrapped up the meeting.

"Does that mean Tara's home alone?" Joker took a swig of his beer. "Because I'll be happy to keep her company."

Levi leveled him with a narrow-eyed stare. "What'd I tell you about staying away from her?"

"Dude, have you seen the way she looks at me? She wants a piece of this, and I'm ready to share." Joker motioned toward his body. He glanced at Forge and Ozzy. "Am I right, or what?"

"He's not wrong," Ozzy said. He was an ornery fisherman in his early forties who lacked social graces but always had their backs. If he wasn't on his boat or with the club, he was taking care of his elderly mother or enjoying the company of one of his many women. "But a sweet piece like that can have any man she wants, and you're a squirrely one, dude."

"I may not be a giant like you, but I've got a freakishly large dick that'd leave her unable to walk for days," Joker boasted as

Cannon, a tall, beefy guy with dark hair and a hairpin trigger strode over to the table.

Cannon palmed Joker's head and gave it a shake. "Sorry to tell you this, Joker, but six inches is *not* freakishly large."

"It is if she uses her zoom lens," Forge offered.

The guys laughed.

"Y'all are just jealous because Tara wants me," Joker said. "You can take a shot at her when I'm done."

Levi fisted his hands to keep from losing his shit.

"That sweet young thing doesn't need a boy. She needs a man, and I'd be happy to let her call me *Daddy*," Ozzy said.

Over my dead body.

Joker cocked a brow. "How about you put your money where your mouth is. Fifty bucks says one night with me, and Tara comes crawling back for more."

Levi shot to his feet, sending his chair skidding backward. "The next asshole who opens his mouth is going to get a fistful of teeth."

"Whoa, man." Forge rose to his feet. "Calm the hell down."

"Back off, Forge. If they were talking shit about Tonya, you'd've slaughtered their asses already." Levi pinned a threatening stare on Joker. "One more word about Tara, and it'll be the last thing out of your mouth."

"What the hell's going on over here?" Jesse asked as he and Brent headed over.

"*Nothing*," Levi bit out.

"Didn't sound like nothing." Brent's dark eyes moved between Levi and Joker.

Joker stood up, flashing a cocky grin. "Levi's got a bug up his ass because I want to get down with Tara."

Levi drove his finger into Joker's chest. "If you value your life, you'll set your sights on someone other than *my* girl."

"*Your* girl?" Joker said with amusement. "Did you hear that, guys?"

"Sure sounded like Levi's staking claim to Tara," Cannon said.

"No way," Ozzy said. "He doesn't do the same woman twice."

"Or women who know Joey," Forge added.

"Well, I do now," Levi fumed.

Joker crossed his arms and lowered his chin. "Then I'd say our job here is done, boys."

The guys high-fived each other.

"What the hell is going on?" Levi snarled.

"Man, it's been like watching a reality show the way you two have danced around each other these last few years," Cannon said. "We had to do something."

Jesse clapped a hand on Levi's shoulder. "Sometimes you gotta give a brother a nudge, or he might miss out on the best thing that ever came his way."

"So we did a little harmless flirting," Brent explained.

"I don't know about harmless," Joker said. "I thought I was a dead man last weekend after our ride."

"Yeah, Levi looked like he was going to tear you apart," Ozzy said.

Levi cursed under his breath. "Whose bright idea was this? Please tell me Jules didn't get to y'all."

"I'd like Jules to get to me," Ozzy said with a sly grin.

Levi set a dark stare on him. "I *will* tear you apart, and then Grant will eat you for dinner."

"Ozzy, cut the shit," Brent said. "It wasn't Jules, Levi."

"It was our *Pres* and Tonya," Forge clarified.

"Tonya?" *What the hell?*

"Yeah, man. You're gonna want to thank her," Forge advised. "She knows all about matters of the heart. Jesse's original plan called for Joker taking Tara out, and Tonya knew that shit wouldn't fly."

Levi looked at Jesse. "You'd have him take Tara out after everything I told you?"

"You're a stubborn guy." Jesse splayed his hands. "I thought we might have to take it a little further. Now go get your girl and meet us at the Taproom to welcome her into the club the right way."

As much as Levi wanted a night alone with Tara, the idea of bringing her into the club as his woman filled him with pride. "A'right, but we're keeping our relationship on the down low around Joey until we're sure about things." He looked at Joker. "Think you can keep your mouth shut around my daughter?"

"Hey, I put my life on the line to get you and Tara together." Joker banged his fist over his heart. "I think it's safe to say I've got your back on this."

IT HADN'T TAKEN any coaxing to get Tara to go to the Taproom. She was as thrilled about going out with Levi as he was about going out with her. He filled with pride as he walked in with his beautiful woman on his arm. His buddies cheered and clapped louder than the blaring music, waving him and Tara over from the far end of the bar.

Tara leaned into his side. "Why are they clapping?"

"Because they're fools." He kissed her, loving that he didn't have to hold back. "They're happy for us. Hell, T. I'm happy for us. We have to be careful until we're ready to tell Joey, but I want to treat you like you're my girl outside the bedroom. I want to take you out and show you off when we can." The joy in her eyes brought his lips to hers again, and they went to join his friends.

The guys hooted and hollered, called out, "Congratulations!"

"You act like we're getting married," Tara said, her cheeks pink with embarrassment. She looked at Jesse. "I can't believe you played matchmaker and got all the guys to go along with it. You could give Jules's matchmaking skills a run for her money."

Jesse laughed. "I've got about a decade of practice on her. You guys belong together. I'm glad it finally happened."

"*Finally*, being the operative word," Brent said. "It took you two long enough to figure it out. I had you two pegged as a couple three years ago."

"Three *years*?" Levi asked.

Brent nudged him. "I didn't think you'd touch her before she was twenty-one."

He was right about that.

"If I had my way, we'd have gotten together ages ago," Tara admitted, making Levi feel like a king.

"Get over here, gorgeous." Ozzy hugged her, winking at Levi over her shoulder as he said, "If he ever keeps you waiting again, you let old Ozzy know, and I'll beat some sense into the nitwit."

Joker got his arms around her next. "I wouldn't've kept you waiting."

"I have a feeling there's a long line of women waiting for a chance with you," Tara said.

"Blow-up dolls, maybe," Cannon said. "I can't hang around. I promised Caleb I'd help him with a model he's building tonight, but I wanted to say congratulations."

"Thank you," Tara said. "Please tell Deb and Caleb I said hi."

"Will do," Cannon said as Forge and Tonya sidled up to Tara.

"Congrats, girl," Tonya said, hugging her.

"*Thanks…?* It's so weird to hear congratulations because we're dating."

"You're dating one of the hottest bachelors in Harborside," Tonya said. "Be proud of it."

"I am. Where's Leilani tonight?"

"She's with my sister." Forge put his arm around Tonya. "You'll see her this weekend at Joey's tournament."

Excitement sparked in Tara's eyes. "You guys are coming?"

"We wouldn't miss it," Tonya said. "And don't worry. We won't let the cat out of the bag around Joey." She leaned in to hug Tara.

"Hey, where's my hug?" Levi teased.

Tonya planted her hand on her hip. "Hold your horses, Steele. I'm getting to you." She turned back to Tara. "He's a pushy one, isn't he?"

"He can be." Tara glanced at Levi. "I kind of like him that way."

Kind of didn't come close to how much she enjoyed his demands in the bedroom. Levi wondered if anyone else could see the heat in her eyes.

"You did good, Levi." Tonya embraced him. "Treat her well, you hear me?"

"Yes, ma'am." He drew Tara into his arms and kissed her.

He couldn't imagine being anything *but* good to her.

"How about a round of shots for the couple we've all been waiting for?" Wyatt Armstrong said from behind the bar as he poured shots of tequila. Wyatt and his twin sister, Delilah, were in their midtwenties, and they'd had it rough the last few years, having inherited the bar after their parents were killed. Wyatt was a hardworking guy, about six foot two, with light brown hair and green eyes that had been so filled with grief when he'd first moved to Harborside, Levi had wondered how he'd ever move past it. He and Delilah had come a long way from the grieving, naive kids they'd been. Wyatt was engaged to his best friend, Cassidy, and Delilah was in a long-term relationship with her best friend, Ashley.

"The couple we've *all* been waiting for?" Levi arched a brow, wondering if he was the only person who had missed Tara's interest in him and how everyone else had seen his interest in Tara when he'd suppressed it so deeply, even *he'd* missed it.

Wyatt crossed his arms. "Am I supposed to pretend we haven't been rooting for you two?"

"*No*," Tara interjected. "I like knowing I wasn't alone in rooting for us. How's Cassidy?"

"She's having a great time planning our wedding with Brooke and Delilah. She'll be glad to hear you're in town. She's been talking about getting in touch with you."

"I'd love to see her."

"Maybe we can all get together one evening when Joey's got a playdate," Levi suggested, although if another opportunity arose to have Tara all to himself, he wasn't sure he'd want to give it up.

"Sounds great." Wyatt pushed the shot glasses across the

bar, and Tara, Levi, and their friends reached for them.

Everyone held up their shot glasses as Wyatt said, "Here's to finding love and happiness with someone who's seen you at your best and your worst and still thinks you're cool enough to sleep with."

"Hell yeah," Forge shouted, and everyone cheered.

Levi pulled Tara closer as the others drank their shots, and he said, "Here's to us, blondie. If only I'd gotten my head out of my ass sooner."

"I think you're doing just fine making up for it." She went up on her toes and kissed him. "To us."

They clinked glasses and did their shots as more cheers rang out.

"Hey, Forge," Wyatt called out. "When are you going to make an honest woman out of Tonya and put a ring on her finger? Give us something else to toast?"

Forge put his arm around Tonya. "I'd do it tomorrow if she'd have me, but she wants to wait."

"Men are like wild animals. Once they're caged, all they want is to get out." Tonya gazed up at Forge like he was her entire world. "I'm in no rush to tie this tiger down."

"Bullshit," Cannon said. "I *like* going home to my wife."

That started a loud debate about love, loyalties, and wandering eyes that spread beyond Levi, Tara, and his buddies to other bar patrons. But as Levi listened to Tara debate the merits of marriage with his friends, his mind traveled back to his daughter. He'd often thought about the things Joey would go through as she grew up. He wasn't one of those fathers who pretended he'd never let his daughter date. But he hated the idea that one day, some kid would probably break her heart, even though he knew heartbreak was part of growing up, a rite of passage into adulthood. He might not have experienced the heartbreak of losing a first love, but he'd experienced the heartbreak of losing his youth. Just because he didn't regret it didn't mean he wasn't aware of it.

He glanced at Tara, now deep in a private conversation with Tonya, and he wondered who her first love was and if he'd broken her heart. *By the time I was twenty, no other guy stood a chance.* Had she been open to love before that? He wanted to know all the little things about her that he might have missed over the years.

Jesse and Brent sidled up to him and Brent said, "Are you around next Thursday?"

"Yeah, why?" Levi asked, his eyes still on Tara.

"We're going out on our boat and thought you and Tara and Joey might want to make a day of it with us," Brent said.

"That sounds great. I have to check with Tara and Joey, but I think they'd love it."

"I hate to tell you this," Jesse said, "but I think you're going to have a hard time hiding your feelings for Tara from Joey."

"You're wearing 'em like a second skin, bro," Brent added.

"I'm sure I am, but I'll make it happen. I have to. We've got a lot to figure out."

"I get why you're being careful, with Amelia hanging out there in the wings and all." Jesse crossed his arms, eyeing him. "I just wish you didn't have to."

"That makes two of us."

As the evening wore on, Levi took full advantage of the freedom to kiss and hold Tara whenever he felt like it, which was a hell of a lot more often than he'd realized. He couldn't get enough of her touch, her kisses, her smiles and laughter, and the way she tossed sassy banter like she'd known his buddies her whole life. It dawned on him that she practically had. His cousins, and most of his buddies, had watched Levi, Tara, *and* Joey grow up over the years. Tara truly had seen him at his worst, during the year after Joey was born, when he was sleep deprived and trying to hold his shit together, and at his best, *now*. She'd seen Joey at her best and worst, too, but she remained a shining light and positive influence, making sure Joey knew how much she was loved despite Amelia's disinterest and Tara's mother's apprehension and telling him how great a father he was even during those first harrowing weeks, when he was sure he'd done everything wrong, and through the toddler years when he was busting his ass and too many of his little girl's meltdowns had nearly broken him.

She'd given so much to them, and he wanted to give back. He wanted to know her hopes and dreams and be the one to make sure they came true. But right now he wanted her in his arms. She was talking with Joker, who was trying to convince her they needed to make a biker calendar. Levi draped an arm over her shoulder and said, "I don't think we need to sell ourselves in that way."

"Women eat that shit up," Joker argued.

"Like I said, I don't think we need that kind of exposure," Levi reiterated.

"You might be taken, but I'm free to *take*, *taunt*, and *please* as many women as I'd like," Joker reminded him. "The Bayside chapter takes part in Gunner Wicked's calendar every year, and they raise all kinds of money for his animal rescue." Gunner Wicked's father and uncle were the founders of the Bayside chapter, and he and his brothers and cousins were all members. "We could do that for our literacy and anti-bullying campaigns."

"He's got a point," Tara said.

"Do you *really* want my picture hanging on other women's walls?" Levi asked.

"No, but it could be good for fundraising, and it's just a picture. It's not like you're in their bedrooms."

"I'll take the bedroom hit for the team," Joker offered with a waggle of his brows.

"Talk to Jesse and Brent about it," Levi suggested. "If they like the idea, they can bring it up and take a vote at the next meeting. But I'm not doing it. I don't want Joey thinking it's okay to sell herself in that way. Now, if you'll excuse us, I want to dance with my girl." Levi took Tara's hand and led her out to the dance floor.

As he drew her into his arms and they fell into sync slow dancing, she said, "Sorry about the calendar thing. I wasn't thinking about how Joey might see it."

"That's okay. I don't know what's right or wrong where that's concerned. I really just wanted to get my arms around you."

"I'm glad you did. There's no place else I'd rather be."

He kissed her tenderly. "Are you having a good time?"

"Yes. You know I like your friends, but I really like being with you, like this."

"I do too, babe. I didn't realize how much I was holding back to keep things in check in front of Joey until tonight. I *like* holding your hand, kissing you, and pulling you close whenever I feel like it. I want more of this, T. More of *us*."

"Are you saying you want to tell Joey? Because it's not just her I'm worried about. Our families might not be okay with us being together." She stopped dancing.

"I realize that," he said reassuringly, and held her closer, swaying to the music. "My family will be cool with it, but I know yours probably won't, and we need to talk about that."

"I know we do, and I want to, but…"

"But we just got together, and you want to be sure about us before we say anything?"

"No. It's not that. I feel good about us. I'm just not ready to deal with my mother yet, and I know my dad is okay with you *now*, but this might set him off, and my parents and my grandmother are coming for Joey's tournament. If we tell Joey, we *have* to tell them because you know Joey will say something, and I don't want it to be uncomfortable for us or for her." Her words, and her beautiful face, were riddled with tension. "Can we please just wait until after her break is over to tell our families?"

"Sure, babe. We can wait." He held her tighter, swaying to the music, trying to ease her mind. "But you need to know that I *want* to tell the world you're my girl. I've wanted you to be mine since the last time we danced together at Rock Bottom."

"You did?" She gazed up at him. "I wanted to *be* yours. I woke up the next day still reeling from everything I'd felt when we were dancing."

"That makes two of us."

"Was *that* why you got all flirty and licked my éclair the next morning?"

He grinned. "I had to test the waters to see if you were into me."

"And then torture me by saying you've still got it?" she asked with amusement. "Do you know how awkward that was, getting turned on and thinking you weren't interested in me?"

"It was just as bad for me." He held her closer, lowering his voice. "But look where we are now. You've gotten so deep under my skin, I can't keep my hands off you."

A tease sparked in her eyes. "So you just want me for sex, huh?"

"I'm not going to lie and deny that I'm addicted to being inside you. Making you come has become one of my greatest pleasures."

Crimson spread over her cheeks. "*Levi*," she whispered, her gaze darting around them.

"Nobody can hear me but you, and I hope you know I want more than that. I want to get to know all of you, T, so I can tell what you're thinking and how you feel about *everything*, big and small. I want to know how your days go and what your dreams are. Where you see yourself a few years from now."

She looked longingly at him. "I want that, too, but I can't tell you where I'll be in a few years, because someone has recently upset my life plan of getting over them, which puts me in a new position."

"I've got lots of new positions for you." He pressed his lips to hers. "Then we'll start small. Who was your first love?"

"That's not *small*. Who was *your* first love?"

He'd never been in love before, but he was pretty sure he was getting there. "You're right. That's not small." The song changed to a faster beat, but he kept her close. "How's this? I know you had a great day with Joey, but how did your photo editing go?"

"Really well. I got some great shots last week, and I think my clients will be happy with them. What about you? How was your day?"

"Long and lonely without you in it."

She touched her forehead to his chest, then smiled up at him. "I want to gather the things you say and bottle them up so

I can keep them forever."

"How about you just keep *me* forever?" He couldn't believe he'd said it, but he didn't want to take it back. Her expression was a mix of disbelief and hope, and he was sure she saw the same thing in his expression. *Hold on to that hope, baby. I sure as hell am.*

A nervous laugh fell from her lips. "I'd do that in a heart-beat. Pack you in my suitcase and take you home. But I think my mom might have an issue with that, so stop making me wish for things I can't have right now, and stick to the small things. I was serious about wanting to know about your day. I know your project is important. Is it going well?"

He wanted to tell her he'd been serious, too, but they weren't there yet. "Yeah. You'd like the place I'm working on. It's got a lot of character."

"I'd love to see it sometime."

"Really?"

Her eyes lit up. "You know I love that stuff."

"It's right around the corner, and vacant. What do you say we get out of here and swing by on the way home?"

THEY PULLED UP in front of a small Victorian a little while later, and even in the moonlight Tara could tell it had seen better days. Levi climbed out of the SUV, and she watched him in his jeans and leather vest coming around to her side, *How about you just keep me forever*, whispering through her mind. The man knew how to set her heart aflame, and she'd already bottled up those words and tucked them away with the other sweet things he'd said.

He opened her door and took her hand, helping her to her feet. "We'll be quick, but I'm glad you want to see what I'm working on."

He laced their fingers together as they headed up the walk. Becoming a couple felt easy and effortless, but she knew once their families found out, that might change. She was glad he was willing to wait. She didn't want anything clouding their happiness.

She looked up at the house, imagining him working there. The roof looked new, in stark contrast to the rest of the neglected though unique property. The wraparound porch was rounded on the left and squared off on the right. A large boarded-up picture window anchored the left side of the first floor, and on the second floor was a massive bay window that was also boarded up. Just above it was a gabled roof with a half-moon window in what must be the attic. The right side of the front of the house had only one small, square window on the first floor and a tall window on the second. The trim was an ugly rust color, and much of it was broken or missing, just like the severe brown siding, but with the funky porch and odd windows, it felt special.

"You weren't kidding about the house having character. It reminds me of some of the homes on Silver Island."

"I knew you'd appreciate it, even in its current state."

"Whose house is this?"

"Autumn McConnell, a single mom from Boston. She's had it rough. Her husband passed away last year after what sounded like a horrific battle with cancer, and she was his caregiver."

Her heart broke for them. "Oh my gosh, that's horrible."

"I know. I can't even imagine what she's gone through.

That's one of the reasons I took the job. I didn't want her to get screwed over by a half-ass contractor."

He unlocked the door and followed Tara inside. Several of the walls had been stripped down to studs, giving them a view of what lay beyond the front parlor. The framing showed arched entrances to the rooms, and there were several long stretches of elaborate crown molding laid out on the scuffed and marred hardwood floors. The wide wooden staircase took up the right half of the hallway, with its ornate wooden banister and elegantly carved balusters, some of which were broken or missing. The high ceilings made the rooms feel bigger, which was good, because Tara didn't see any windows on the sides of the house.

"Wow, this is incredible. It's easy to imagine a family livening up the place and sunlight spilling in through the windows."

"There'll be a lot more windows and natural light when we're done with it. We'll be adding windows to most of the rooms, repairing and refinishing the original flooring, updating the kitchen, which has a cool dumbwaiter, and renovating the bathrooms, but we're leaving the clawfoot tub in the master. Come on. I'll show you around."

They started upstairs, where Levi showed her the two rooms he was going to combine to create a master suite with a full bath and two smaller bedrooms that would share a Jack-and-Jill bathroom. As they made their way back downstairs, he told her all about the work he had planned for the first floor. She loved the passion in his voice as he described the built-in bookcases he'd planned for the office, behind which he was going to build a secret playroom for Autumn's son. He'd built Joey a secret space behind her closet where she liked to hide when she was upset.

"Secret rooms are so fun, and it sounds like the whole house is going to be gorgeous." Tara walked to the slider at the back of the house, gazing out at the night sky, thinking about the woman who'd bought the house. "Does Autumn have family here?"

"No. She said she wanted a fresh start to get out from under her grief and that it was hard to do with friends and family coming around to check on her all the time."

"I guess I can understand that on some level, but it sounds lonely."

His expression was thoughtful as he put a hand on her lower back. "It's hard to be lonely when you have a kid relying on you and you're trying to figure out your new life."

If anyone knew what that was like, it was Levi. "Can I ask you something about when you moved here?"

"Of course."

"I know you said you moved off the island for more work and higher pay, but I never understood how you could move away from your family when they were so good to you."

"That was the hardest thing I've ever done. I thought I'd be on the island forever, and I still miss being around my family. Especially now that Jock and Archer have reconciled and Jock and Daphne are living there. But after Joey was born, even though my friends and family supported me raising her, it was tough being looked at by other people like I'd done something wrong. I didn't want Joey to grow up with that hanging over her head. That's why when Metty told me about the construction opportunities in Harborside and offered to let me and Joey stay at her place while I found my footing, I jumped on it." Metty Barrington was an elderly rock gardener whose family had deep roots on Silver Island. The Barringtons ran the local newspaper, among other businesses. Metty had grown up with Levi's and Tara's grandmothers. She'd moved away as a young adult and had eventually settled in Harborside, but rumor had it she still had her fingers in many pots on the island.

Levi had moved because of the gossip? Sadness and annoyance tangled together inside Tara. "Because of my parents?"

"Partially." His jaw tightened. "I don't know if you remember, but our parents were pretty good friends before Amelia got pregnant."

"I remember. They were never as close as your parents are with the Silvers and Remingtons, but they were closer than they are now."

"Yeah, well, the pregnancy took care of that and left my parents being given sideways glances by a lot of people, as if it were their fault I got Amelia pregnant."

"I think you mean *my mother* took care of that." Anger flared inside her. "She told anyone who would listen that you seduced Amelia."

His jaw clenched tighter.

Gathering all her courage, Tara asked the question she wasn't sure she wanted to know the answer to. "Is that what happened?"

He took a step back, the muscles in his jaw bunching as he dragged a hand down his face. "Does it matter?"

"I'd like to know. I've only heard my mother's version of the story, and I'd rather hear it from you."

His eyes narrowed. "Your sister never told you what happened?"

She'd never forget the smug look on Amelia's face when she had sauntered into her bedroom and asked, far too nonchalantly, *Can you see the dark circles under my eyes? Levi and I hooked up last night, and I got in really late. I don't want to look tired when I go back to school today.* Tara had been devastated and hadn't been able to string together a sentence. She'd just stood there with her mouth hanging open and her heart shattering into a million little pieces. Amelia had shrugged and said, *You know what? It doesn't matter if I look tired. Levi was definitely worth it*, and had smiled so evilly, Tara remembered thinking her sister had fangs.

But Levi didn't need to know those gruesome details, so Tara pushed them down deep and said, "She rubbed it in my face that you two hooked up, but she's never told me what happened that night."

"Why would she rub it in your face?"

"*Why?* Because up until about a year ago, when she suddenly stopped being an outright bitch to me, Amelia's life goal was to make me miserable. The only time she spoke to me was either to put me down or to brag about herself, and after you two hooked up, I found out she'd read my diary and knew I had a *huge* crush on you."

His brows slanted angrily. "Are you fucking kidding me?"

"Why would I kid about something like that?"

"You wouldn't. I'm just trying to understand. I know she's always been selfish, and you two aren't close, but I had no idea she ever put you down. She's the one who started calling you Mouse, isn't she? I remember her telling everyone that you were like a cute little mouse hiding in the pantry. She said it sweetly, like she thought you were adorable."

Tara rolled her eyes, anger rising to the surface. "That's what she *wanted* you and everyone else to believe, but she spent my entire childhood telling me I was worthless and I didn't deserve the attention I got, as if I got a lot of it. *She* was the reason I hid in the pantry at parties."

"I thought you were hiding from your mother because she picked on everything you did, and you didn't want to eat in front of her."

"My mother's comments were nothing compared to my sister's." She looked outside again, not wanting to look at him as she confessed her secrets. "She used to tell me I'd never have a boyfriend because I wasn't pretty or smart. She'd follow that up by telling me not to worry about it, because boyfriends weren't all they were cracked up to be, and she'd feed me junk food to make me feel better, which was why I spent my childhood eating my way through my emotions." She looked up and found Levi's hands fisted, his nostrils flaring. "It's okay. She doesn't make those comments anymore."

"It's *not* okay. How could I have been so blind?"

"You weren't blind. She was cunning and manipulative and careful not to let people hear her condescending comments. My own parents didn't believe me when I told them."

"Why didn't you tell *me*? We were friends."

"I was too embarrassed to tell anyone, but Bellamy and Jules got it out of me, because I needed someone's shoulder to cry on, and I made them promise to never tell anyone. You have to understand that by the time Amelia left for college, I was an emotional wreck. She was my big sister, and I was twelve, and I had this confusing love-hate thing going on with her. But after she moved away and I was finally able to breathe, I realized how much she'd hurt me. But then my mom was still nitpicking, which didn't help. But *eventually* I started dealing with my emotions rather than eating them, really talking with Jules and Bellamy about how I felt instead of holding it in, and without Amelia shoving food into my hands, the extra weight came off. As I lost weight, my mom made fewer comments, and without a constant barrage of negativity, I started to figure out who I really was, and I liked myself. That was a huge revelation. But just when I finally found my confidence, Amelia told me she was pregnant with your baby, and it broke my heart."

"I had no idea," he said angrily, and pulled her into his arms. His heart thundered against her cheek. "To answer your question, I did *not* seduce your sister."

She tipped her chin up, and the agony in his eyes cut like a knife. "Then why didn't you deny it back then when my mother started those rumors?"

"Because I saw how your mother was toward you, and I didn't know if Amelia had told your parents that I'd done it just to keep them off her back."

"So you let the whole island think you seduced her to *protect* her? To protect my selfish bitch of a sister?"

His jaw muscles flexed angrily. "At the time it seemed better than the truth."

"Which is…?"

"I'm ashamed to admit it, but you deserve to know. We were at a party, and she was hitting on me all night. I don't like who she is, and even back then she rubbed me the wrong way, but she was relentless. She goaded me in front of my buddies, talking shit to the point where I *stupidly* felt like my nineteen-year-old manhood was on the line. I'd been drinking, and I didn't want to seem like a loser to the guys, and she was a year older, gorgeous…" He shook his head. "Looking back, it was a pathetic thing to do, but as much as I wish I'd never hooked up with her, I don't wish away Joey."

"Of course not. I can see Amelia doing that to you. She's always gotten whatever she wanted."

"It gets worse, T. She said something to me afterward that I never understood—until now—and it shows just how fucked up she was."

"What did she say?"

He closed his eyes for a second, inhaling deeply, and when he opened them, a different type of anguish stared back at her. "Tara..." He shook his head.

"*No*, you can't do that." She took a step back. "You have to tell me."

He reached for her hand, sorrow washing over his features. "She said, 'Now every time you look at that pudgy little mouse, you'll think of me.'"

Tears sprang to Tara's eyes. "She *said* that? She hated me *that* much? I was only a kid."

He pulled her against him, resting his cheek on her head. "I'm sorry, baby. I shouldn't've told you."

The regret in his voice brought another wave of anger, but Amelia had taken enough from her, and an icy indifference toward her sister shoved that sadness and anger aside. Tara drew her shoulders back as she regained control. "Honestly, it's not that surprising. It just hurt to hear it. I can't believe she said that to you, especially under those circumstances. I have no idea what I ever did to deserve to be despised like that, and it pisses me off that she used *you* as a weapon to hurt me. But that's Amelia."

"I'm sorry, T."

"Don't be sorry. You had no idea what she was really like. But she did me a favor, because having you and Joey in my life has helped me move past all the pain she caused. You appreciate me for who I am, and I'm glad you let me be close to Joey. I think a big part of me wanted to make sure she never experienced what I did with Amelia. I wanted Joey to know how special she was from the time she was a tiny baby so nobody could *ever* make her question her self-worth. Caring for her and watching her grow into such a sweet, capable little girl has helped me in so many ways, including validating who I am in my own head."

"Babe, you're an amazing woman with a huge heart. Did you doubt that?"

"I didn't really doubt it, but after years of being told I was worthless by the sister I was supposed to look up to, it was nice to see that my love mattered. I kind of feel like Joey and I grew up together."

"Your love matters a hell of a lot to more people than you realize. And for what it's worth, I feel like Joey and I grew up together, too. I was a kid raising a kid."

"And you became an amazing father. Joey's lucky to have you."

"We're both lucky to have you, T. I've always felt that way, even when we were young and there was nothing there but friendship between two kids." He wrapped his arms around her. "Maybe we were always meant to end up together."

"I'm bottling up those words," she whispered, and wound her arms around his waist, pressing a kiss to the center of his chest. "Know what I think?"

His brows rose in question.

"We have one night alone, and I don't want to spend any more of it talking about all the ways Amelia has hurt us."

His expression warmed, and his hands slid down to her bottom. "Then how about I take you home and make you forget all about her?"

"Think you're up to the challenge?" she teased.

He pressed a tantalizing kiss to her lips. "Baby, we've got the house to ourselves, which means lots of rooms to christen and no reason to be quiet. When I'm done with you, you won't remember your own name."

Sixteen

TARA WOKE TO the soothing sound of rain hitting the window and an empty bed. She reached for her phone on the nightstand to check the time: *3:22*. Levi had fulfilled his naughty promises with vigor. They'd barely made it inside before they'd ripped off each other's clothes. He'd taken her against the front door, over the back of the couch, *on* the couch, and that had only whetted their appetite. When they'd finally made it upstairs, she lay in his arms, cocooned by his strong body, and his sweet whispers had coaxed her into sleep.

So where are you now?

"Levi?" She sat up, pulling the sheet over her bare chest as she looked around his dark bedroom. The bathroom door was open, but the light was off. She climbed out of bed and pulled on the T-shirt he'd worn last night, inhaling his masculine scent.

She padded out of the bedroom and into the dark hallway. "Levi?"

Answered with silence, she made her way downstairs and

followed the sound of the rain through the living room toward the open door to the patio in the kitchen. As Tara entered the kitchen, she saw a flash of memory from earlier in the evening, when Levi had hoisted her up on the island and done all sorts of dirty things to her. A shiver of heat skated down her back despite the cool air coming through the open door.

She looked out at the rainy night and saw Levi sitting on a chair, shirtless, leaning forward with his forearms on his legs. How many times had she seen him sitting like that and walked away to let him be? She pondered leaving him alone with his thoughts, but she was drawn to him, wanting—*needing*—to know if he was okay after everything she'd revealed. After all, it had to be hard learning the mother of his child had been a monster to her own sister.

She went to him and trailed her fingers along his bare shoulder. His skin was warm, his muscles taut. He was wearing only dark boxer briefs, and when he looked up at her, his eyebrows twitched, and then a small smile appeared.

"Hi, beautiful."

She hugged herself, warding off the chilly, damp air and wondering which part of her confession he was overthinking. "Couldn't sleep?"

"I get a little restless when Joey's not home." He pulled her down onto his lap and wrapped his arms around her, his body heat enveloping her.

"I can understand that, but is that the only thing keeping you up?"

He shook his head. "I can't stop thinking about how Amelia treated you. I wish you had told me what was going on back then. I could have saved you from it."

She shifted, straddling his lap, and put her arms around

him. "You did."

"No, I didn't," he said vehemently.

"Don't you remember all those times you sat and talked with me in the pantry and stayed with me after you convinced me to come out?"

"That didn't stop her from putting you through years of emotional abuse."

"I don't think anything could have stopped her. But you reminded me that I didn't suck, and you soothed the pain she caused." She kissed him. "Want to know a secret?"

He pushed his hand beneath her hair, palming the nape of her neck. "I want to know all your secrets."

She traced the tattoo on his shoulder and chest as she spoke. "I went into the pantry a few times, hoping you'd eventually find me there."

"So you've always been into older guys."

It was good to hear the tease in his voice. "I've always been into *you*, but back then it was an innocent crush on a cute boy who was nice to me."

"I have a secret to share." His thumb caressed her cheek. "It's going to sound creepy, and I promise it wasn't."

"Hm, you've piqued my interest."

"After the first few times I found you in the pantry, not a single party went by where I didn't look for you."

Her heart squeezed. "That's not creepy. It's sweet."

"*I* know that, and *you* know that, but to someone else it might sound like I was a thirteen-year-old boy with bad intentions toward an eight-year-old girl."

"If anyone ever thinks that, I'll tell them they've got it all wrong. You didn't even realize your naughty intentions until now."

He touched his forehead to her chest, and when he spoke, his voice was rich and husky. “I’m crazy about you, T, and I hope I never make you feel anything but good about yourself.”

She kissed his head, and he looked up at her as she said, “Considering that being here with you and Joey is where I feel the most comfortable, I think you’re doing a good job of it.”

“Is that true?”

She nodded. “More so now that we’re together, because I don’t have to hide my feelings for you, but I’ve always been more comfortable here with you guys than at home. I’ve always been able to be myself with you and Joey.”

“We like who you are.”

“I’m glad, and I like being in Harborside, away from my mom’s watchful eyes, where nobody thinks of me as the mayor’s daughter.” His eyebrows twitched, and she pressed a kiss between them. “What else are you overthinking?”

“You don’t miss a thing, do you?”

“Not when it comes to you and Joey.”

He pressed his lips to hers. “There is something else. This was the first night we didn’t have Joey, and I’m sorry I didn’t plan a real first date for us. I should’ve given you a night of romance that you could brag about to your friends.”

“What makes you think I won’t brag about tonight?” She’d been elated at the prospect of going out with him, but she’d wondered how he’d treat her around his friends. Would it be weird for him? Awkward for her? But he’d been so excited to take her out when he’d come to pick her up, he’d glowed with it, leaving no room for worries. While they were out, he’d been attentive and caring, asking if she wanted a drink or something to eat and kissing her cheek, temple, or lips every time he got pulled away. Even from across the room she’d felt the heat of his stare, the surety of their connection. Each time he'd gotten her back in his arms, he'd whispered sweet or naughty things, both of which had thrilled her. It had been a perfect night.

"Hanging out with a bunch of bikers isn't exactly romantic."

"I guess we see romance differently." She traced the tattoos down his arm. "I think it's romantic when we're with Joey and you look at me with that secret smile that only I can read, or you walk by and touch my back in a way that says you wish you could do more. And tonight I got to kiss you in public and let all those other girls who were checking you out know that you're taken." She ran her finger just above the waistband of his briefs, feeling his arousal swell beneath her. His eyes darkened, his piercing stare making her hungrier for him. "I got to see the project you're working on, too. Someone else might not think that's special or romantic, but I do, because I know how important your work is to you and how you put everything you have into the jobs you take on." She trailed her fingers up his abs, feeling them flex, his jaw tightening. "We got to clear the air about important things, and that makes us even stronger." She teased his nipple with her fingers. He rocked his hips, making a gruff rumbling noise in his chest. "And you gave me several mind-blowing orgasms, which tops off our perfectly romantic date."

"*God*, Tara. How did I get so lucky?" His hands slipped under the back of her shirt, and his big, rough palms clutched her bare ass. His eyes burned with white-hot desire. "You naughty little thing."

"Mm-hm." She dipped her head, kissing his neck with her teeth and tongue as she rocked against his erection.

"*Christ*, baby."

"That's kind of what I had in mind," she whispered.

He pulled off her shirt, and the brisk air prickled her skin for only a second before he palmed one breast and captured her mouth in an excruciatingly deep kiss that set her body ablaze. His hand was hot and rough, his kisses penetrating and possessive. His other hand dove into her hair, angling her mouth as his tongue plunged deeper, exploring every dip and curve as he kissed her thoroughly. Pleasure surged through her in tumultuous waves. She moaned and rocked, his tongue masterfully mesmerizing her with every stroke until she was breathless and desperate. His hand dropped from her breast to between her legs, his thick fingers sliding through her wetness, gentle and forceful at once, moving at the same maddening pace as his tongue.

She clung to him as she tore her mouth away. "I *need* you."

"You've got me, baby." He kissed her again, lifting his hips off the chair to push off his boxer briefs, and stilled, cursing under his breath.

It took her a second, but she realized what was wrong. The condoms were inside. She whispered in his ear, "Birth control can't break like condoms can. We're protected."

She felt the restraint in his jaw, neck, and shoulders, and the second their eyes locked, she knew he wanted this as much as she did. He crushed his mouth to hers, rough and wild, his hands pushing through her hair and down her back, grabbing her ass *hard*, as if he were wrestling with his own desire, battling inside his head. He broke the kiss abruptly, his dark eyes drilling into her. "I will *never* get enough of you."

He pushed off his boxer briefs and clutched her waist as she rose onto her knees. Their gazes held, emotions swamping her, drawing heavy breaths and a rampant heartbeat. His tight hold told her he felt it, too, as she lowered herself onto his cock, taking every hard inch of him. He felt bigger, thicker, and buried *deeper* than ever before, and they both moaned.

"*Jesus*, T." He wrapped one arm around her middle, holding her still as his mouth covered hers so sensually and sweetly, it made the pressure of being filled so completely even more excruciating. She rocked her hips, trying to move along his shaft, but he kept her still, remaining in control, his mouth never leaving hers as he kissed the ever-loving *hell* out of her. She whimpered in desperation, her nails digging into his skin, and he drew back, biting her lower lip, eliciting a sharp gasp and sending pinpricks racing down her limbs.

He squeezed her ass. "*Mine*," he growled.

"Yes, *yes*, I'm yours, and you have no idea how hearing you say that turns me on, but I'm going to lose my freaking mind if you don't start moving."

His fingers dove into her hair, and that wicked mouth reclaimed hers as he thrust beneath her. She clung to his shoulders, using them for leverage as she rode him, urgent and frantic, her body craving him with every upward slide. Their skin dampened despite the cool air. His thickness slid and his hips gyrated in a perilous rhythm as they feasted on each other's mouths. When he reached between them, his touch sent lightning through her core, and she cried out, arching back.

"I love watching you come."

His praise spurred her on, and she rode him harder, grinding her hips, arching and moaning. His mouth covered her nipple, sucking so hard, pleasure tore through her. She cried out again, the sound echoing in the pounding rain. His hands and mouth moved over her in rough gropes and erotic bites, their bodies rocking and thrusting. Their untethered pleas rang out in the night as they gnawed and licked, driving each other right up to the verge of release. She tried to resist, to make it last, but the pleasure was too intense.

"I can't hold off, baby," he said against her breast. "You feel too good."

"Thank *Go—*"

He bit down, thrusting so brutally, her thoughts fractured. Pleasure erupted inside her, hot and sharp and wicked. Her body pulsed and bucked, and he crushed her to him, burying his face in her neck as he surrendered to his own release. Ecstasy consumed her like powerful waves, taking her up, then swallowing her whole. When they finally collapsed into each other, the last of their shudders jerking through them, Levi held her tight, kissing her cheek, neck, and lips, murmuring, "How am I going to hide the way I feel about you?"

She closed her eyes, the sweet agony in his voice burrowing deep inside her chest.

He drew back, brushing his knuckles down her cheek, the tenderness in his eyes almost too much to bear. "You don't need to gather up my words, blondie, because I'm never going to stop saying them."

Her emotions whirled and skidded. He really did pay attention to every little thing.

He kissed her softly, whispering, "You take my breath away."

She gathered those sweet sentiments and tucked them away despite his promise, and she rested her head on his shoulder. Serenaded by the cool spring rain and comforted by the feel of their hearts beating as one, she whispered, "*Same.*"

Seventeen

LEVI AWOKE IN his bed with Tara cuddled against him, her softness molding perfectly to his hard frame. As he lay listening to the peaceful cadence of her breathing, he thought about what Amelia had put her through. He'd known Tara was strong, but he'd never realized how strong she'd had to be as a young girl. The idea that Amelia had goaded him into having sex as some sort of twisted plan to get one up on Tara made him as angry as it made him sick. He'd always known he was lucky Joey wasn't like Amelia, but he'd had no idea just how lucky he was.

He looked at the sleeping beauty in his arms who poured her love into his little girl despite Joey being the daughter of the person who spent years torturing her, and his heart overflowed for both Tara and Joey. *This* was what he wanted, to wake up every morning with Tara in his arms, to see that light in her eyes at the end of a long day and his daughter's smile, knowing she'd been with the aunt who had adored her since she came into this world. He wanted to hear Tara's sated sighs as she fell asleep in his arms every night and those whispered sounds she made while she dreamed. It was crazy to feel so much so soon, to be gluttonous for more when they'd only just begun. But those feelings were as real as the twitching of his cock as Tara snuggled deeper into the curve of his hips, making an *mm* sound. Whoever said guys hit their sexual prime at nineteen was way off base.

He kissed her shoulder. "Careful, blondie. You'll wake the viper."

She turned in his arms. "Who are you kidding? That viper never sleeps."

"He's not used to having a gorgeous naked woman in his den." He brushed his lips over hers. "Last night was incredible. I was hard all night just thinking about you riding me."

Her pink cheeks brought his lips to hers. "I *might* have dreamed of wild pythons invading my body."

He feigned a stern expression. "Hopefully you mean *one* wild python."

"I'll never tell."

He nipped at her neck, and she giggled.

"The way you marked your territory, you know you don't have to worry about anyone else seeing me naked."

He looked at the love bites he'd left on her chest and dipped his head, tenderly kissing each one of them. "I'm not sorry about that." He slicked his tongue over her nipple, and she bowed off the mattress. "Are you sore? We went at it pretty hard."

"Let's just say I'm aware of muscles I never knew I had." Her eyes turned seductive. "But I hear the best way to get over muscle aches is to use them again."

"I might never let you out of my bed, blondie." He moved over her, feeling her slickness against his erection.

"Are we riding bareback from now on?" she teased.

"Now that I've felt all of you, nothing else will ever do. You've made a risk taker out of me."

"Then we're even, because you've made a sex fiend out of me."

His mouth covered hers as their bodies came together, and the emotions of the last few days took over. Amelia's spite made him want to cherish Tara even more, to show her how precious she was so she never doubted it again. He moved slowly and sensually, caressing and kissing, murmuring his adoration against her warm skin, loving her with everything he had.

A long while later, as they lay sated and spent, time ticked away too quickly. Tara had a few hours before she needed to pick up Joey, but he had to leave earlier than usual to stop by one of the job sites where his guys were working before heading to Autumn's house to work. Tara lay curled up against the confines of his body again, eyes closed, her golden waves draped over her breast. He ran his fingers through her hair, placing feathery kisses along her shoulder. "I am obsessed with your hair, baby. I love the feel of it, the thickness, the way you let me tug on it."

"I'm obsessed with other parts of you."

He laughed. "I've got to get ready for work."

"Just one more minute?" She sprawled over his side, her arm draped across his chest, her leg over his.

He kissed her forehead, wishing he could blow off work. "What are you doing today?"

"Since it's raining, I thought we might go through a few boxes from the shed this morning."

"I'll carry some in before I leave so you don't have to do it."

"Thanks. We're meeting Joey's friends at the movies after

lunch, and then we're going to the grocery store to pick up a few things so we can make you a delicious dinner and yummy dessert tonight. Joey's super excited."

"No need to make dessert. I'll get mine in bed later." He smacked her ass.

She sat up, glowering at him as he got out of bed. "Don't *smack* me, or I'll smack you."

"I might like it."

"We'll see about that." She jumped out of bed and chased him, giving his ass a hard crack just outside the bathroom door.

He turned on her, and she squealed and tried to run. "You're mine now, blondie." He caught her around the waist and swept her off her feet, carrying her toward the bathroom.

"It stings, doesn't it?" she said between laughs.

"Feels good. Just like you're going to feel when I take you against the shower wall."

Her eyes flamed. "I'm going to have to spank you more often."

TARA AND JOEY made good use of the rainy morning. As promised, Levi carried a number of boxes into the house before leaving for work. After a few games of tic-tac-toe while eating breakfast, Tara watered the indoor plants, and Joey turned the planters to ensure one side didn't get more sunlight than the other, and then they went through the boxes. They found pictures and yearbooks from when Levi and Leni were in school. Joey laughed a lot as they went through them, picking out several to frame and put up around the house. Even though

Tara had a good memory of what Levi had looked like throughout the years, she saw him differently in those pictures now that she knew those brown eyes didn't just see what was before them. They saw straight into her heart. And his lips weren't just kissable. They whispered the sweetest, and the *dirtiest*, things she'd ever heard.

Tara set aside two pictures she wanted to make copies of. In one, his siblings and a couple of their friends were fishing off the Rock Harbor pier. Tara looked to be about six years old in the picture, which made Levi about eleven. She was holding a fishing rod, looking up at Levi as he showed her how to use it. There was something innocent and intense about the way she was looking at him. Like he had all the answers she might ever need. The other picture was taken when she was nine. She remembered that sunny afternoon. She and Jules, Bellamy, Levi, Leni, Wells, and Keira were sitting on a dock, their toes dangling over the water as they ate ice cream cones. The boys wore only shorts, their slender, sun-drenched bodies covered in drips of ice cream, and the girls were wearing tank tops and shorts, all bony knees and elbows, except for Tara, who was pudgy faced and chubby limbed. The sun was setting behind them, and everyone was smiling at the camera except Levi. He was leaning down with his mouth wide open like he was going to eat Tara's ice cream. His other arm was tucked protectively around her, which he'd done a lot, even back then. But now that she saw the picture, she wondered if he was just holding her still so he could eat her ice cream.

"Did Daddy always steal bites of your dessert?" Joey said.

"He's been a pretty consistent dessert stealer."

Joey studied the picture. "Did you mind that you were bigger than the other girls?" She'd seen pictures of Tara when she was heavier before, but she'd never said much about them.

"I wish I could say no, but the truth is, it made me uncomfortable sometimes."

"Grandma Shelley is bigger than most of the other grandmas, and she doesn't care."

"Grandma Shelley is the smartest, most amazing woman I know, and I wish I'd had her confidence when I was younger. But the truth is, I wasn't uncomfortable just because I looked different. It's complicated, but it was more because of the *reasons* I was eating too much." Careful not to reveal anything bad about Amelia, she said, "Someone was mean to me, and I didn't know how to handle it, so I took comfort in food and ate enough for two or three little girls. That's why I was so heavy. When I got older, I realized why I was eating so much and paid more attention to when I was hungry and when I was eating to avoid something else."

"Like being sad?"

"Yes. I learned how to eat healthier, and eventually my body settled where I guess it was always meant to be."

"But you still eat a lot," Joey pointed out. "Sometimes you eat four pieces of pizza."

"I *do* eat a lot," Tara said with a laugh. "But I'm usually running around and burning off calories. And you know what?"

"What?"

"It wouldn't make me uncomfortable if I got heavier now, because being heavier wouldn't change who I am, and I wouldn't be overeating for the wrong reasons." Tara set the picture aside. "We should get ready for the movies."

"Is that person still mean to you?" Joey asked.

"Not really." *But it hurts me when she disappoints you.* "Why don't you grab a sweatshirt in case it's cold in the theater, and

I'll get my things so we can go meet your friends."

As Joey ran upstairs, Tara put the box against the wall with the other boxes and went into her bedroom to use the bathroom and get her own sweatshirt. She was surprised to see a note tucked into the bathroom mirror. *Blondie* was scrawled across the front of the folded paper in Levi's messy handwriting. Her heart skipped as she snagged it and read what he'd written. *How will I ever shower alone again? I can't wait to get my hands on you. I mean my mouth. I mean I can't wait to see you tonight. Try not to miss me too much. Levi*

Tara couldn't stop smiling as she pulled out her phone and texted him. *Just found your note. Too late. I already miss you too much.* She added a smile emoji with three hearts around it, then typed, *We could shower at night.* She sent it, then sent a second message. *Can't wait to see you. I mean have your hands and mouth on me. But isn't it my turn to get my mouth on you?* She could hardly believe how bold she was with him, but it felt natural, like her heart had finally regulated itself. She sent the message and immediately worried that Joey might see his phone at some point and texted, *DELETE THAT MESSAGE so Joey doesn't see it! Delete the messages from the other night, too!*

With a rueful pang, she deleted all the dirty messages from her phone. She used the bathroom, and as she grabbed her sweatshirt, her phone vibrated. She opened Levi's message, and a GIF of a man yelling *Delete. Delete. Delete!* popped up.

She sent a sad-face emoji, followed by a heart, and headed out of the bedroom.

JOEY HAD A great time at the movies with her friends, and she invited them to her skateboarding tournament. After a quick stop at the grocery store, they had a short reprieve from the rain. Tara offered to take Joey to the skate park, but once Joey schooled her in all the bad things that can happen if a skateboard gets wet, like bearings deteriorating, grip tape peeling, and the deck losing its *pop*, they opted to skip the park and went home instead. Joey played on her iPad while Tara returned a couple of messages she'd received about photo sessions. Thinking about what Levi had suggested, she sent an email to Charmaine asking her to check out the rental market for houses and studio space.

About an hour before Levi was expected to come home, they prepared chicken Parmesan, and while the oven preheated, they began making miniature no-bake raspberry cheesecake bites for dessert, as they'd seen on *Just Desserts*. Joey sat on the counter beside the stove in striped leggings and a long-sleeve green top, helping Tara stir the chocolate as it melted.

"I *really* want to put my finger in it," Joey said.

"That's a great idea if you want to get burned."

"I'm not *doing* it. I just want to. Is it almost done?"

"I think so," Tara said.

Joey peered into the pot. "Are there any lumps?"

"Not that I can see." Tara scooped chocolate into the mixing spoon, and they watched it pour back into the pot.

"I think it's ready."

"Me too."

Joey climbed off the counter and knelt on a chair at the table in front of one of the ice-cube trays they'd set out, while Tara poured the chocolate into two bowls and carried them to the table. Joey scrolled down on her iPad to the next part of the directions they were following and read them aloud. "Coat the ice-cube tray with chocolate and freeze it for five minutes." She looked at Tara. "What does coat it mean?"

"I think we're supposed to put a thin layer of chocolate on the bottom of each of the cubes, but not too much. We need room for the raspberries and cheesecake mix."

"Like this?" Joey filled a small ladle with chocolate and poured a little into one of the cubes.

"Perfect."

As they coated the bottom of each cube, Joey said, "I hope Daddy likes them. Grandma Shelley says people like to eat things that are made with love, and everything we make for Daddy is made with love."

"Everything your daddy makes you is made with love, too."

"Except when he pranks me."

Levi and his brothers were major pranksters, but Tara didn't realize he pranked Joey. "Your dad pranks you?"

"He did one time, after me and Grandpa pranked him," she said as she coated another cube.

"Grandpa Steve taught you to prank your dad?" She laughed. "That sly dog."

"It was fun! We got up early and moved Dad's truck way down the street. When he woke up and went outside, he thought someone took it. We pretended we didn't know anything about it, and he thought someone stole it, which made him say the F word. He was going to call the police, and Grandpa said we had to tell him the truth."

"That's a great prank. How did your dad get you back?"

"He got us good. When me and Grandpa were watching a movie, he put water in cups and turned them upside down on plates. Don't ask me how the water stayed in, because he wouldn't tell me. Then he put whipped cream all over the tops, which were really the bottoms of the cups, but we didn't know it. He called us into the kitchen and said he made us hot chocolate, and when we picked up the cups, water went *everywhere.*"

Tara laughed. "Your dad's had a lot of practice pranking people, but he only pranks the people he loves."

"Has he pranked you?"

Thinking of the éclair, she said, "Yeah, he has." *But I think that was out of lust, not love.* "I think we should get him back. What do you think about putting an olive inside one very special cheesecake bite instead of a raspberry?"

"Yeah! Let's do it!"

They finished coating the ice-cube trays, and as they put them in the freezer to chill, the doorbell rang.

"I'll get it!" Joey ran to the door, and Tara followed. Joey peered out the sidelight. "It's the UPS guy." She opened the door and said, "Hi."

"Hi." The delivery man looked at the package, then looked at Joey and Tara. "I have a package for Tara Osten."

"That's me." Tara took the package and thanked him.

"Who's it from?" Joey asked before Tara even got the door closed.

Tara looked at the return address, which read *J&B* and had Bellamy's address. "It's from Aunt Jules and Bellamy."

"Open it!" Joey bounced on her toes as Tara opened the box. "What is it?"

Tara pulled back the box flaps and found a note folded on top of a bundle of tissue paper. She opened it and read it. *Hi! Give Joey the yellow gift bag to distract her while you peek in the black bag. We're rooting for you! Jules and Bellamy.* Her heart leapt, and then she remembered they didn't know she and Levi were together yet.

"What does it say? Can I see what they sent?" Joey reached into the box.

Tara quickly pulled it away. "Hold your horses. They sent you something." She pulled out the yellow gift bag and handed it to her.

While Joey dug into her bag, shouting in excitement as she found skateboarding stickers, a notebook with skateboards on it, and a set of colorful markers, Tara peeked into her own gift bag, spying something pink and lacy and something else that was silky, along with another note. She stuffed the bag into the box and read Jules's curly handwriting. *Here's the plan. One night after Joey's asleep, saunter out of your bedroom wearing the lingerie under the satin robe and let the front of the robe fall open. Oopsie! Levi won't be able to resist you!* Below Jules's note was Bellamy's left-leaning script. *Remember to use your sexy voice and touch him!*

Feeling giddy that her friends had planned a night of seduction for her and Levi, she put the note in the box and closed the top. "I'll be right back."

She hurried into her bedroom and shoved the gift bag and notes into a drawer, excited to play out the fantasy one night soon, and texted Jules and Bellamy. *I just got the box. I love it, and I know Levi will go wild for it.* She sent it and immediately realized her mistake. They didn't know about her and Levi yet. She began thumbing out a message to cover her tracks, but a video call rang through from Bellamy. Shoot! Tara answered, and Jules's and Bellamy's elated faces appeared.

"You *know*?" Bellamy said.

"Did you and Levi have *spaghetti* and *meatballs*?" Jules's eyes were wide with excitement.

"I definitely smell spaghetti sauce," Bellamy exclaimed.

Tara's cheeks burned.

"She *did*!" Jules did a happy dance.

"I bet Levi devoured her *sauce*," Bellamy added. "Did you *slurp* his *spaghetti*?"

"Ohmygod, you guys, keep it *down*." Tara shut her bedroom door. "Joey doesn't know, and I don't want my parents finding out yet, so you can't tell anyone."

"We won't, but I want details. How did you two get together? Was it better than Scooby-Doo?" Bellamy coaxed.

"Of course it was," Jules said with irritation. "Steeles have all kinds of *game*."

"*Ew*," Bellamy said. "How do you know that about your brothers?"

Jules's brows slanted. "I *don't*. I just assume they do because Daphne and Indi were teasing each other about who was getting better sex, and—"

"You *guys*," Tara whispered sharply. "I can't talk about this right now. Joey's going to come looking for me."

"Just tell us if it's serious between you two, or if this is just a fling for him," Bellamy said. "It better not be, because that would just piss me off."

"It's not a fling," Jules chided her. "I *know* he's crazy about her. I can feel it in my bones."

"We're both pretty crazy about each other," Tara said quickly, worried she was taking too long. "He wants to tell everyone about us, but I'm worried about my parents, so I *really* need you to keep this to yourselves."

"We will," Bellamy promised.

"Jules?" Tara pressed.

"I swear I won't say a word." Jules leaned closer to the

screen, speaking quieter. "But I'm so happy I could shout it from the rooftops!"

"*Don't*," Tara and Bellamy both warned.

"Thanks again for the gifts, but I really have to go," Tara said. "Love you guys."

"We love you, too," they said in unison.

"I'll see you Saturday," Jules said.

Tara ended the call, thrilled about sharing her happiness with her besties. She took the box outside to the recycling bin in the garage, remembering how exhilarating it was waking up in Levi's arms and how different sex had been that morning. They'd been totally consumed with each other, but not in the frantic way they'd been the last few nights. It had been even more passionate, slower, deeper, *sweeter*. She wanted that tenderness as much as she craved the animalistic sex they'd had in the shower afterward.

While Levi was wondering how he'd ever shower alone again, Tara was thinking about how they'd make things work once she went back to the island. She couldn't give up every weekend to go see them. She had clients booked, and with Joey's friends in Harborside, she knew they couldn't come to the island every weekend, either. But she was getting way ahead of herself. They still had ten more days before she had to go back to the island, so she tucked those questions away for now and headed inside.

"I think it's been five minutes," Tara said to Joey, who was busy putting stickers on her skateboard by the front door.

"One second," Joey said.

Tara's phone vibrated, and she read the text from Levi. *Missing my girls. I need to stop at the shop, then I'll be home.*

Tara thumbed out, *We miss you too*, added a kissing emoji,

and sent it, then pocketed her phone. She put the chicken in the oven and turned on the timer. As she set out the rest of the ingredients for dessert, including a jar of olives, Joey ran into the kitchen.

"Ready!"

"Great, because your dad will be here soon, and we need to get his *olive* treat made."

"We're gonna get him so good!" Joey climbed onto a chair at the table, reading the instructions on her iPad as they mixed the cream cheese, powdered sugar, and vanilla. When it was properly mixed, they added the whipped cream. "Now we're supposed to put some in each cube." After they did that, she giggled as she put an olive in one of the corner cubes. "How will we know this one is his?"

"Good question. We'll have to remember where it is when we freeze them, then we can use the decorating gel we use on cupcakes and write our names on a few of them, like two each, and those are the ones we'll serve tonight."

"Okay. Can I write it?"

"Absolutely. Do you think you can add raspberries to the others and fill the cubes with the cream cheese mix while I take a quick bathroom break?"

"Yup."

Tara went to use the bathroom, and when she came back, Joey had filled almost all of them with the cream cheese mix. "Good job."

They melted more chocolate and poured it on top. Tara put them in the freezer. "Your dad's is in the back left of the tray on the left. Think you can remember that?"

"Back left on the left," Joey said as a video call came through on her iPad. "It's Amelia!"

Anxiety hit Tara like a gust of icy wind as her sister's flawless and perfectly made-up face appeared on the screen. Her sky-blue eyes were expertly defined by thick, dark lashes. Not a single cinnamon hair was out of place. She wore something sparkling gold and strappy. Against the backdrop of a deep blue sea, she looked like the picture of elegance, which brought an infuriating feeling of *less than* to Tara, and *that* bothered her to no end. But all those old insecurities were shoved to the side by her protective instincts toward Joey, and she listened carefully.

"Hi, Amelia," Joey exclaimed.

"Hi, Joey. How are you?" Amelia spoke in a measured tone, as if she were doing one of her travel videos instead of seeing her daughter's adorable face for the first time in months.

"Good! Me and Aunt Tara just made dessert, and we're going to prank my dad."

"*Oh*. Aunt Tara is there?"

The disappointment in Amelia's voice sent a pang of hurt through Tara. She hated that, too, and tried to ignore it as she stepped behind Joey, putting a protective hand on her shoulder. "Right here."

"Aunt Tara is staying with me for spring break," Joey explained.

"How nice. You look good, Tara."

Amelia smiled, and not for the first time, Tara wondered when her sister had become such a good actress. "Thanks, so do you."

"We've had so much fun! Today we…"

As Joey shared the litany of things they'd already done and what they had planned for next week, Tara watched her sister's eyes skim off-screen and the barely visible nod Amelia gave to someone who was obviously waiting for her. Tara made a point not to look at her sister's social accounts, watch her videos, or read her articles, but she went so long between visits, there had been moments when Tara had given in to her curiosity. She'd seen pictures of her sister in Spain, looking regal in a blue-and-white-striped bathing suit, wide-brimmed sun hat, and big sunglasses; in Israel, standing among a field of sunflowers wearing a linen dress and holding a woven purse, her hair braided in a complex updo that probably took hours to achieve, but on her, it looked casual and easy, like she'd woken up that beautiful. Her face was tilted up toward the sun, and she was smiling brightly. In those moments of weakness, Tara had searched those pictures for signs of loneliness or regret, but all she'd seen was the model-perfect sister who had forsaken her daughter to fulfill her own dreams.

"Did you get the message about my skateboard tournament? Can you come watch me?" Joey asked, bringing Tara's attention back to their conversation.

"That's why I'm calling." Amelia set her eyes on Tara, sounding uncharacteristically enthusiastic. "I wouldn't miss it for the world. I'll be there early Saturday morning."

"Really?" Joey beamed at Tara. "She's coming!"

"It's a miracle," Tara bit out, and quickly realized how sarcastic she sounded. "I mean, that you're able to get away with your busy schedule."

"It took some rearranging, and it'll be hard to leave the beauty of the French Riviera, but I'm looking forward to spending time with Joey."

"Me too! Will you stay overnight? *Please?*"

"I wouldn't have it any other way," Amelia said.

Tara pried her gritted teeth apart long enough to say, "*Great.*"

LEVI HAD BEEN in a great mood when he'd gotten home, and dinner was phenomenal, made even better by the fact that Joey and Tara had made it. But after learning Amelia was coming, his mood had soured. They were almost done with dinner, and Joey had talked about nothing else since they'd sat down.

"Can I stay up late when Amelia's here?" Joey asked.

"We'll see." He glanced at Tara. She hadn't eaten much of her dinner, but she was trying her damnedest to feign a pleasant expression. He wanted to give Amelia hell for what she'd done to Tara and take Tara in his arms and promise he'd never let Amelia hurt her again.

"*Please?*" Joey begged. "I never get to see her."

That's on her, not me. "I said we'll see."

"You let me stay up late when Tara first got here," Joey snapped.

"Watch your tone, young lady," he warned.

Joey slumped in her chair and crossed her arms sullenly. "But Amelia *never* stays over. I promise I won't get cranky."

Levi's frustration mounted at the idea of Amelia sleeping under his roof, but that wasn't Joey's fault, just like it wasn't her fault that he didn't trust Amelia not to let her down. "You're right, sweetheart. She doesn't come that often. If she's up for it, then it's okay with me."

"Thank you!" Joey got up and threw her arms around his neck. She sat down to finish eating. "Guess what else happened today."

"You mean there's more?" He looked curiously at Tara and

winked, and she flashed a genuine smile as Joey told him about the gifts Jules and Bellamy had sent her.

"That was nice of them," he said.

"I'm done eating. Can I get my skateboard to show you the stickers they gave me?"

"Carry your plate to the sink."

She did as he asked, then bolted out of the room.

"Think we can move before she gets here?" Levi leaned closer to Tara. "I'm sorry, babe. Are you okay with this?"

"She's Joey's mother. I have to be. Where does she usually stay?"

"She doesn't. I'm shocked she's coming, much less that she wants to stay over."

"Joey asked her to. I'll move upstairs to the extra bedroom while Amelia's here so she has her own bathroom."

"I'd rather you were in *my* bedroom." He kissed her quickly, giving her hand another squeeze, and released it as Joey's footsteps neared.

"*Look.* Aren't they cool?" Joey showed him her stickers.

"The coolest," Levi said.

"The rain is supposed to stop tonight, and we're planning on hitting the skate park early tomorrow and staying until Joey's sick of it." Tara flashed a sweet smile at his daughter. "Right, cutie? We need to make sure you're all set for Saturday."

"Right," Joey said emphatically.

"Speaking of Saturday," Levi said. "Jules sent a group text to see who's coming, and everyone except Sutton, Daphne, and Indi will be here. Unfortunately, they have to work."

"*Aw.* Will Hadley be there?" Joey asked.

"Yup." He tapped Joey's nose. "She's coming with Uncle Jock and both sets of grandparents, and both of your great-grandmothers are coming, too. Everyone's meeting us at the tournament."

"Maybe everyone can sleep over," Joey suggested.

Levi and Tara exchanged *hell no* glances.

"I don't think that's an option, peanut," Levi said. "They all have to get back to the island."

"I was thinking we could have everyone over for lunch after the tournament," Tara suggested. "We can get deli meats and sides for a sandwich bar, and make cookies or brownies for dessert."

"Can we make *both*?" Joey asked.

Loving that Tara was still willing to go the extra mile for Joey even though her sister would be there, he said, "Sounds great to me. Just let me know what you want me to pick up at the store."

"You have enough on your plate. Joey and I can do it."

"Can we have dessert now?" Joey asked. "We made you something *really* special, Dad."

"I don't think Aunt Tara's done eating yet."

"I'm done," Tara said. "I wasn't that hungry."

He tapped Joey's skateboard. "Why don't you put that away while I clear the table?"

She ran out of the kitchen, and Levi pulled Tara up to her feet and kissed her. "Saturday will probably suck, but we'll get through it."

"I know we will."

"I, on the other hand, have no idea how I'll keep my lips off you—"

"Ready!" Joey said as she zoomed into the room and looked at them with disappointment. "You didn't even *start* clearing the table yet."

"I was busy tickling Tara." He grabbed her ribs, making her squeal and back away from him.

Joey laughed. "*Da-ad.* I'll get dessert while you guys clear the table."

He clapped his hands together. "Sounds like a plan."

While they cleaned up, Joey set out dessert and told him about the box of pictures they'd gone through. "I know you'll want to steal a bite of Tara's dessert like you ate her ice cream when you were a kid, but we made you your *own* mini cheesecakes, so you have to eat them."

He could tell the news of Amelia's visit still had Tara on edge and tried to lighten the mood. "Maybe Tara will share her sweets with me later." The slight flush of her cheeks told him she'd received his message loud and clear.

"Maybe," Joey said. "But you have to eat yours first."

He couldn't help teasing Tara. "What if Tara wants to eat mine?"

Tara's eyes widened, cheeks flaming.

"She can't," Joey insisted. "I made her special ones, too."

Joey took their hands, tugging them over to the table, in front of napkins with two chocolate squares on each, their names written messily in gel on the tops. "*These* are yours." She pointed to the ones that had DAD written on them. "And those are Tara's, and those are mine." She went to the other side of the table to stand in front of her own.

"These look amazing. But this feels very official. Like we're taste testers," Levi said.

"Joey worked hard on them," Tara said.

They all picked up chocolates, and Joey looked like she was going to burst, waiting for him and Tara to eat theirs. They put them in their mouths, and the sweet chocolate melted on Levi's tongue. He bit into it, and a disgusted sound escaped before he could stop it. At the same time, Tara spit hers into a napkin, and Joey doubled over in hysterics.

"You tricked me, you little traitor," Tara said, giving in to her own fits of laughter.

"*What* did I just eat?" Levi guzzled water.

"An olive," they both said, cracking up.

"I pranked you both, Daddy!" Joey said proudly. "I can't wait to tell Grandpa Steve!"

"And I can't wait to get you back," Tara warned.

And just like that, a couple of olives saved the day.

Eighteen

"HOW LONG UNTIL Amelia gets here?" Joey hollered from upstairs.

"Five minutes less than the last time you asked," Levi called up to her. It was almost nine o'clock Saturday morning, and Joey had already asked a dozen times. Amelia hadn't returned Levi's texts since Thursday night, when she'd confirmed that she'd be arriving by nine.

He and Tara had spent the last two nights in her room and had set an alarm for four in the morning so he could go upstairs before Joey woke up. That extra time together made it even harder for him to keep his distance in front of Joey. Last night the three of them had put together platters for the sandwich bar. They'd turned on music and sang off-key, making up funny dances, and laughing their asses off as they made brownies and cookies and decorated them with messily drawn skateboards. Joey had said it was the best night of her life, and Levi had felt the same way.

This morning they'd moved Tara's things upstairs to the

extra bedroom. He hated putting her out of the room that had been hers since she'd first stayed with them years ago, but Tara insisted she didn't mind because it put her closer to him and Joey. She was so selfless, it made him loathe what Amelia had done to her even more.

He heard footsteps and saw Tara coming downstairs, gorgeous in a thin white sweater rolled up to just above her wrists, gray skinny jeans, and white tennis shoes. Her hair fell in loose waves over her shoulders, and she looked like she was either going to kill him or cry.

"What did I do?"

"It's not you." Her voice was pained, but there was an angry edge to it as she handed him her phone.

He read the text from Amelia. *Something came up and I can't make it. Tell Joey I'm sorry, and I'm sending her a big present.*

Anger flared in his chest, coupled with the sadness his daughter was sure to feel. "Did you tell Joey?"

She shook her head.

"I should've known Amelia would do this."

"She was in *France* when she called Joey Thursday," she seethed in a hushed voice. "She *had* to know she wasn't going to make it before now, and she didn't even have the guts to tell Joey herself. I'm so mad I could punch something."

He pulled her into his arms. "I'll tell Joey."

"How can she do this to her *daughter*?"

"I've been asking myself that for years."

Tara looked up at him as she stepped out of his arms. "I'm sorry, Levi."

"You have nothing to be sorry for."

"She's my sister."

"That doesn't make you responsible for her actions. If this is anyone's fault other than Amelia's, it's mine. I need to do what I should've done from the get-go and set up a visitation schedule with set dates and times. If she can't make it, then she loses out. This'll be the *last* time she hurts Joey."

"I'm ready!" Joey bounded downstairs in her black leggings, long-sleeve black shirt with the Dark Knights logo on it, and her skating sneakers. Her face was as bright as the morning sun. "Is it time yet?" She ran to the front window and looked out. "I wonder what kind of car Amelia rented this time. Maybe it'll be that cool black one she had last time."

He fucking hated this. "Honey, come here for a second. We need to talk."

Joey skipped across the room to him. "Yeah?"

"Sweetheart, we just got a text from Amelia. She had to work and couldn't get away." Watching the light drain out of his daughter's eyes cut him to his core. "I'm sorry, peanut."

"But she said she wouldn't miss it for the world," she said incredulously.

"I know, baby, but you know how important her job is. I'm sure she would be here if she could."

Joey looked like she was going to cry, but her voice was tough as nails. "*Whatever.* I don't even care."

"Joey, it's okay to be upset," Tara said softly.

"I'm *not* upset," she snapped.

"Josephine Steele, watch your tone," he said sternly. This was the part of parenting he hated most, reprimanding when she was already upset. "It's not Aunt Tara you're mad at."

"I said I'm not *mad!*" She ran upstairs and slammed her door.

"Shit."

Tara was shaking as she pulled her phone from her pocket.

"I'm going to make Amelia pay for this."

Levi covered her hand. "That's my job, and I'll do it right after I put my daughter's heart back together."

Her expression softened. "Want me to go with you?"

"No. I've got this." He trudged upstairs and knocked on Joey's door. "Honey, open the door."

She didn't respond.

"I'm coming in." He opened the door, swiftly taking in the skateboarding posters and pictures Tara had taken of the two of them and of Joey with her friends, grandparents, aunts, and uncles scattered along the walls. He glanced at her empty bed and the loft hideout he'd built for her fifth birthday, with bookshelves on the sides and curtains across the front. The curtains were open, and the loft was empty. Beneath the loft was her beanbag chair, and the notebook Jules and Bellamy had sent her lay open on her desk, but there was no sign of Joey.

A sliver of light peeked out around the hidden panel in the back of her closet. Emotions stacked up inside him as he crossed the room and crouched beside it. "Peanut?"

"Go away."

He could hear tears in her voice, and his throat thickened. "I'm sorry about Amelia, honey."

"I told you I don't care about her."

"I heard you, but I also know it hurts when someone breaks a promise."

She sniffled.

"You know, you have a lot of people who love you, and they're all coming to see your tournament."

"I don't care," she snapped. "I don't even want to go anymore."

He pinched the bridge of his nose, trying to rein in his anger at Amelia for single-handedly ruining his daughter's day. "Baby, I know you're hurting, and you're confused, but you've worked so hard for this. Please don't let Amelia's absence take that away from you."

"I don't care that she's not here. I never want to see her again!"

He pressed his hand flat against the hidden door, fighting the part of him that felt the same way she did. The part that believed Joey would be better off without Amelia's half-hearted efforts. "I understand why you feel that way. It's hard to forgive someone when they've let you down, but we can't turn our backs on people forever just because they make a mistake or a bad choice."

"Yes, I *can*." Her sobs came through the door. "It's *my* choice if I like someone or not."

"That's true, but do you remember how Uncle Archer and Uncle Jock weren't friends for a really long time and how Uncle Jock didn't come back to visit very often?"

She didn't respond.

"I was mad at Archer for not talking to Jock, and I was angry at Jock for staying away from the island just because Archer didn't want to see him. But I was also really *sad*, because I missed them so much. I thought the rest of us weren't important enough to them, and *that* broke my heart. We lost a lot of time with them during those years, and we could have lost forever if we all hadn't found ways to forgive each other. And now we don't just have Jock and Archer back in our lives. We also have Daphne, Hadley, and Indi. So I guess what I'm saying is that I understand what it's like to be so hurt and disappointed, you want to walk away from the person who hurt you and *never* look back."

More sniffles came from behind the wall.

His muscles tensed as he went to bat for Amelia in order to save his daughter. He touched his forehead to the door and closed his eyes. "I know Amelia's job makes it hard for her to get here to see you, but she called you, and she *tried* to get here, and that should count for something. I think shutting her out will only hurt you more in the long run, and I have a feeling if you don't go to the tournament, you're going to be even sadder."

She was quiet, but he still heard sniffles.

"This is your day, peanut, and I will support your decision to go or skip the tournament. I'm sure the other kids will be happy if you don't show up. I mean, less competition for them, right?"

The door opened slowly, and Joey's teary, red-rimmed eyes peered out, breaking his heart anew.

"Come here, sweetheart." Levi opened his arms, and she climbed into them, clinging tight and sobbing on his shoulder, making him even more determined to put a stop to Amelia's disregard for her feelings. Wishing he could take her pain away, he told himself this would make her stronger, and although he knew it was true, this was one lesson he wished she could have skipped. "I love you, Joey, and I'm so sorry."

He held her until she stopped sobbing and her tears ran dry. Then he wiped her cheeks with the pads of his thumbs. "Do you want to talk about it?"

She shook her head, her lower lip trembling.

"You have a lot of people coming to watch you today. Do you want to go to the tournament?"

She nodded.

"Good. I'm proud of you, peanut." He kissed her forehead,

needing to do more difficult parenting. "I know you were upset when you snapped at Tara, but she didn't deserve that. She loves you, and she's never let you down."

Fresh tears spilled from her eyes. "I'll say I'm sorry."

"That's my girl." He hugged her again. "What do you say we wash your face and go down together?"

As they washed her face, he tried to lift her spirits by talking about how great she was going to do in the tournament, but it would take more than a few words to heal this hurt.

Tara was ending a phone call when they went downstairs. She turned with a smile. "How're you feeling, cutie?"

Joey ran to her and threw her arms around her waist. "I'm sorry I snapped at you."

"It's okay." Tara crouched to hug her, and when she looked her in the eye, she wiped Joey's tears and said, "I know you were upset, and I'm sorry Amelia couldn't make it. But you know what? I'll take lots of pictures, and we can send them to her."

He felt like he was watching the very definition of love unfold before him. Watching Tara put aside her feelings about the sister who had been nothing but rotten to her, and to do it with the sole purpose of consoling his daughter was *everything*.

"Joey, why don't you go through your gear and make sure you've got everything you need. I've got to get something from the garage. I'll be back in a few minutes." He pulled out his phone as he headed outside and called Amelia.

"How'd she do?" Amelia asked when she answered, pissing him off even more.

"The tournament isn't for another hour, and you made Joey so upset, she was going to skip it." He paced beside his motorcycle.

"Didn't Tara tell her that I'm sending her a present?"

"When are you going to get it through your head that Joey doesn't want gifts. She wants you to keep your promises. And why did you text Tara instead of me?"

She sighed. "Because I knew you'd get dramatic, and I was right."

"Make no mistake, Amelia," he seethed. "This isn't me being dramatic. I'm *pissed* that you have no regard for our daughter's feelings."

"If I didn't have any regard for her feelings, I wouldn't send presents. God, Levi. I'm not a total monster. You *know* I never wanted to be a mother."

"No shit, and I'm the idiot who made the mistake of trying to keep some form of communication between you two so Joey wouldn't grow up feeling abandoned or unworthy of her mother's love. So when she ran into you on the island, it wasn't uncomfortable for her, and so she wouldn't have to spend her whole life wondering why her own mother never spoke to her. Big fucking mistake on my part." It took everything he had not to give her hell for the way she treated Tara, but he wasn't going to breech Tara's confidence, no matter how much he wanted to.

Amelia scoffed. "Would you calm down? I had to work. There's a big dinner party I have to attend to secure a new sponsorship. It's called *responsibility*."

"You don't know the first thing about responsibility, and for Joey's sake, I'm sorry it's taken me this long to finally get that. But you've hurt her for the last time. From now on, any and all communication goes through *me*. If you want to speak with Joey, you call me first. If you want to see her, text her, video chat with her, or even write her a letter, you clear it with me first. Do you understand?"

"Hey, that's no skin off my back, but how do you think

she'll feel when she messages me and I don't respond?"

"About as good as she does when you say you'll see her and you don't show up." He'd deal with that, just like he did all of Amelia's other shortcomings.

"Wow, look at you going all daddy bear on me. That's kind of *hot.*"

"Cut the shit, Amelia, and remember what I said." He ended the call and pocketed his phone, wishing he had time to beat his heavy bag or go for a run. But the roar of motorcycles sounded in the distance. He didn't have the luxury of time to deal with his feelings.

His little girl had a tournament to get to.

He got out their motorcycle helmets and Joey's riding harness and headed inside. Joey and Tara were watching a video on Tara's phone, and Joey was giggling. Filled with relief for his little girl's smile and gratitude for his sexy woman's loving heart, he snuck up behind them and hugged them both at once.

"*Da-ad,*" Joey said with a laugh.

"I couldn't help myself." He kissed Joey's cheek and planted a kiss on Tara's, too. "Are you ready to rock and roll?"

Tara glanced toward the front of the house, the rumble and roar of motorcycles fast approaching, and looked knowingly at Levi. "We went through Joey's gear. She's all set."

"Awesome. Then we can head out."

There was a knock at the door, and as he went to answer it, Joey ran past, yelling, "I'll get it," just as he'd hoped she would.

She opened the door, and Jesse and Brent stood on the porch, wearing their leather vests, jeans, and boots, helmets in hand. The rest of the Dark Knights stood by their bikes lined up along the street, each wearing a black leather vest.

"Hi," Joey said. "Dad can't go riding with you guys. We're

getting ready to leave for my tournament."

"We're not here to take your dad, sweet darlin'. We're your escorts," Jesse said.

"Escorts?" Confusion rose in her eyes.

"That's right, peanut. This is your big day, and you're going to arrive in style. You and I are taking my bike and leading the guys straight through town to the tournament."

"Like a *parade*? What about my skateboard and gear?"

"I'm taking it in my car," Tara said, lowering her camera. Levi was glad she thought to capture that moment.

"Your competition has no idea they're about to lose to a Dark Knights princess," Brent said.

Joey was absolutely glowing. "I need my leather jacket!" She bounced on her toes as Levi got her jacket from the coat closet and helped her put it on. "This is gonna be so cool!"

"Why don't you go with Jesse and Brent and get your helmet and harness on. I'll be there in a second." Levi gave his cousins a thankful nod. When Joey ran out, he closed the door and drew Tara into his arms. "Sorry for the rough morning."

"I'm just sorry for Joey."

"Me too, but she'll be okay. She's seeing a lot of people who love her today, and I won't let Amelia hurt her again. She canceled to attend a party to chase down a sponsorship. I told her that from now on, all contact with Joey goes through me. She won't be able to say she's coming without having firm plans in place."

"I think that's smart. I'm sorry Amelia's like that."

"She is what she is." He framed her face with his hands. "I'm so glad you're in our lives, blondie. It's going to be torture not kissing you today."

"*Same*," she said softly, eyes brimming with emotion.

How could one word touch him so deeply? "I promise to make up for it tonight." He kissed her slow, sweet, and long enough to leave her breathless and him craving more.

"Let's go give our girl a great day."

"Slow down, big boy. You're the best father Joey could ever ask for, and having all the guys show up to escort her is the kind of thing dreams are made of for little girls. I want to make sure she has more than just memories." She shouldered her camera bag, reaching for the doorknob. "Give me a five-minute head start, so I can get pictures of you and Joey and her entourage riding into the park."

"God, I'm crazy about you." He pressed his lips to hers.

She pushed back with a grin. "Same, but if we don't get out there, Joey's going to miss her tournament."

THE PARKING LOT was packed. Cars and trucks spilled onto the streets, lining the curbs. Balloons bobbed from long tails tied to the fence surrounding the skate park, and a banner hung over the entrance announcing the 15th annual skateboard tournament. There were mobs of people milling about and excited kids carrying skateboards.

With no time to waste, Tara turned down a side street and found a spot a block away. She grabbed her camera bag, Joey's gear bag, and her skateboard, and ran to the park entrance. She dug out her camera just as the sound of motorcycles broke through the din of the crowd. She lifted her camera to her eye, her heart racing as she focused on Levi and Joey, taking care to get pictures from different angles that included all the motorcycles behind them and the people on the sidewalk watching in awe. The powerful set of Levi's shoulders and the way Joey held her head up high resonated with the pride she was sure they felt. What a magnificent sight it was to see her beloved niece supported by so many people.

As Tara took pictures of the man who had the weight of his little girl's world on his shoulders and managed to carry it without ever faltering and the little girl who never had to worry about being the center of his universe, she too was in *awe*—of the lengths Levi went to, and had always gone to, for Joey.

Levi led the pack of bikers around the block, presumably looking for parking, and Tara reached for her bag.

"Tara!"

She looked up and saw Jules running toward her, holding a wide-brimmed hat on her head, cute as ever in rust pants with white polka dots, a cropped white shirt, and a short, faded jean jacket. She looked like a college kid even though she was a year older than Tara. Behind her, Leni was hurrying to catch up, holding an identical hat to her long, auburn hair, with a matching hat in her hand.

"Hi," Tara said as Jules barreled into her, hugging her so tight she couldn't breathe.

"You look different, like you've got a yummy secret," Jules said in a singsong voice.

"*Jules*," Tara warned. "Cute hat."

"What happened to promising you weren't going to run?" Leni said, glowering at Jules.

"I wasn't going to run, but I saw Tara and got excited," Jules explained.

Leni rolled her eyes and gave Tara a quick once-over. "Girl, spring break agrees with you. You look great."

"I told you," Jules sang.

"Thanks. I like your hats."

"Good, because Jules insisted on bringing you one." Leni plopped the extra on Tara's head.

"*Oh*, okay." Tara caught a *just go with it* glance from Leni. "Thanks, Jules."

"Aren't they the cutest?" Jules gushed. "I just got them in at my shop, and I bought one for all the girls in our family, and since you and Bellamy are my sisters from other mothers, I thought we could all wear them when we're out sunbathing or walking through town."

"Because we walk through town as a group so often," Leni said sarcastically.

"Well, I love it," Tara said supportively. She was used to her friend's whimsical ideas.

"Is Joey excited?" Jules asked.

"She is, but she had a rough morning. Amelia canceled at the last minute, and Joey was heartbroken."

"That selfish bitch." Leni pressed her lips together. "My brother is a saint for putting up with her. I know he keeps hoping she'll grow up, but people like her don't change."

Tara wasn't going to get into that and let Amelia ruin any more of their day. She saw Levi holding Joey's hand as they crossed the street with the other Dark Knights. Levi looked over, stirring those butterflies she'd come to expect. She was sure his sisters could feel the earth move beneath their feet, too.

"Looks like Joey's bad morning got a whole lot better," Leni said. "I'd like to be escorted by a hoard of hot bikers. Come on. Let's catch up to them."

They helped carry Joey's skateboard and gear, and as they went to join Levi, Joey, and the others, Tara fretted over how she was going to hide her feelings for Levi when they felt bigger than life. If that wasn't bad enough, Leni was watching him like a hawk, and Tara was pretty sure his wolfish grin and the way his dark eyes were trained on her were giving everything away.

Jules looked like she wanted to jump for joy, but she managed to play it cool as she scooped Joey into a hug. "There's the star of the show."

"Good luck today, kiddo." Leni ruffled Joey's hair.

"I'm gonna win a trophy," Joey exclaimed confidently.

"I bet you are," Jules said, and went to hug Brent and Jesse.

Leni eyed the other bikers, all of whom she knew well. "So, let me get this straight. All I have to do is learn to skateboard and big, badass bikers will come running?"

Ozzy sidled up to her. "Baby, you just say the word and I'll be there. No skateboard required."

"You might be a bit too *much* man for me, Oz." Leni ran her gaze down his body. "You look like you could eat me for dinner."

The corner of his mouth quirked up. "That's right, sweetheart. Breakfast and lunch, too."

"Settle down, Ozzy," Levi warned, and glowered at Leni. "Stop asking for trouble."

Leni laughed.

"Why are you even bothering them? You're always saying you have no time for men. You're *all* about work," Jules pointed out.

"Get over here, troublemaker." Jesse pulled Leni into a hug, then passed her to Brent. "Keep this one busy, will you?"

"No prob, bro." Brent cocked a grin at Leni. "So, *cuz*, you got any cute single girlfriends?"

"Dad, there's Grandma Lenore and Grandma Blanche."

Joey pointed into the crowd. "And Uncle Archer and Hadley..."

As Joey ticked off names, Tara followed her gaze. Lenore and Blanche were talking with Tara's and Levi's parents. The mere sight of her mother made her stand up straighter, and those butterflies in her belly morphed into bees. Archer was holding Hadley, standing off to the side with Jock, Grant, and much to Tara's surprise, her brother Robert. She was happy he'd come to support Joey. Tara lifted her camera to take a few shots, hoping it might ease the anxiety climbing up her spine. Her attention was drawn to her mother, with her perfect posture, pristine slacks, and expensive blouse. She looked out of place chatting with Shelley, who was dressed appropriately casual in jeans and a T-shirt with a maroon cardigan overtop. Tara's father, on the other hand, appeared as relaxed as Steve Steele. Both men wore button-downs and jeans. Tara wondered why her mother felt the need to stand out, or rather tried to stand *above*, everyone else. It had to be exhausting to put so much effort into her physical appearance and mannerisms. She felt an unfamiliar pang of compassion for her mother.

"Can I go over there?" Joey asked, drawing Tara from her thoughts.

"Sure." Levi let go of her hand, and Joey sprinted toward the group. He sidled up to Tara and put his arm around her. "Miss me yet?"

"Miss you? She sees you all the time." Leni lifted his arm off Tara's shoulder and moved between them. "Let the girl breathe. We are literally surrounded by man candy. How's she ever going to meet a guy with you acting like she's yours?"

Levi's jaw clenched, and Tara stifled a laugh.

"What makes you think Tara's single?" Joker walked over

and put his arm around Tara. "Didn't you know about me and my photo girl? We put that camera to good use." He nuzzled against Tara's neck. "Right, babe?"

Levi looked like he was going to blow a gasket.

Tara ducked out from beneath Joker's arm. "Aren't we here to focus on Joey?"

"Yeah," Levi said gruffly, taking Tara's arm and leading her away from Joker. "If I get arrested for killing someone today, you're bailing me out."

"There he goes again, making all the guys think she's taken," Leni called after them as they went to join their families.

Levi stuck by Tara's side while everyone greeted each other. She was glad he didn't head right over to their parents. As Levi's brothers caught up with their cousins and Grant gave Levi props for Joey's escorted arrival, Tara hugged Robert. "I'm so glad you're here. I didn't expect to see you."

"I wasn't sure I could make it, but I was able to move a few things around." He nodded toward their grandmother and Lenore, surrounded by Dark Knights. "Think they're trying to talk the guys into working at Pythons?"

"Or opening a Pythons here in Harborside." Tara waved to Tonya and Leilani, and just beyond them, her father waved. "I'd better say hi to Mom and Dad."

"Want reinforcements?" Robert asked.

"No, but thanks." She made her way over to hers and Levi's parents, every step amping up her anxiety.

"Hi, honey." Her mother leaned in to kiss her cheek. "Joey sure is excited."

"Yeah, she is. No thanks to Amelia's last-minute cancellation."

Her father hugged her. "She told us." He shook his head. "I

wish Amelia would stop making promises she can't keep."

"It's such a shame," Shelley said, drawing Tara into a warm embrace.

"You know how busy Amelia is," her mother said. "She barely has time to breathe."

"I can't imagine how she does it all," Tara said sarcastically. "It must be hard traveling to exotic locations, living in luxurious hotels for free, and attending parties with the elite. It sounds super stressful."

"Exactly," her mother said.

"Luckily, Joey has a lot of other people here for her today," Steve said, embracing Tara.

Shelley touched Tara's hand. "Honey, I want you to know how much we appreciate you putting your life on hold so Joey could have fun with her friends and be in the tournament."

"It's not that big a deal, and I love being with her."

"Two weeks is a very big deal for a busy woman like yourself," Steve said, smiling at Levi as he and Joey walked over. "Levi, I hope you realize how lucky you are to have our island's best photographer all yours for two weeks."

"Joey and I both do," Levi said, turning a warm smile on Tara's parents. "I'm so glad you could make it."

"So are we," her father said. "We're proud of our Jojo Bean."

"I'd like to see her do something a little less dangerous," her mother said.

"I'm careful, Grandma," Joey exclaimed. "Grandpa Steve, guess what! Aunt Tara showed me how to prank Dad, and I pranked *her*, too."

"Oh my goodness," Tara's mother said, while everyone else chuckled.

"She got us good, Pop," Levi said.

"Attagirl." Steve high-fived Joey.

Jock joined them and clapped Levi on the back. "You're bringing her up right."

"She's got to carry on the Steele tradition," Levi said.

"Here come Archer and Hadley." Shelley took Steve's hand and said, "Honey, there's Brent and Jesse. We need to give our nephews a squeeze. Marsha, Patrick, would you like to come say hello?"

"Yes, we would," Tara's father answered, while her mother gave a tight smile.

As they walked away, Hadley called out, "*Jo-ey*," and wriggled out of Archer's arms, toddling over to Joey. Hadley was adorable in a pink-and-white cheerleading skirt, a matching sweater, and white sneakers with pink laces.

"Hi, Had," Tara said. "I love your cheerleading outfit."

"Check this out." Archer tapped Hadley's shoulder. "Hey, squirt, what do we do when it's Joey's turn to skateboard?"

Her little fists shot into the air, and she stomped her foot. "Go, Joey! Go, Joey!"

Everyone clapped and commended her.

"Awesome job, Had!" Leni said as she and Jules joined them.

"That's adorable," Tara said. "Did Daphne teach her that?"

"She sure did," Jock said proudly.

"But I taught her this," Archer said. "Hadley, what do we do when other kids take their turns?"

Hadley's face morphed into a scowl and she crossed her arms, making a growling sound. Tara and the others tried to hide their amusement as Jock shot Archer a death stare and Jules swatted Archer's arm, admonishing him. "Don't teach her to be a poor sport."

Archer smirked. "Hey, someone's got to carry on my tradition."

Jock picked up Hadley, explaining why she shouldn't behave that way.

An announcement rang out calling all contestants to the skateboarding area, and commotion ensued as everyone wished Joey luck.

Levi put his hand on Tara's back, leaning in close. "You okay?"

"Yeah. Totally fine."

"Okay. I'll catch up with you after. I'm dying to kiss you right now."

"Same."

He winked and went to talk to Jesse. A few moments later, Joey went with Brent and Levi, escorted by half of the Dark Knights toward the skateboarding area. Tara grabbed her camera, catching Levi, Brent, and Joey leading the way and the crowd parting for the adorable little girl and her burly, leather-clad protectors.

"I need to find a spot to take pictures of the tournament," Tara said to Jules and Leni. "Want to come with me?"

"Sure," they said in unison.

"We've got you covered. Follow me," Jesse said.

Tara and the girls went with Jesse, and as if he'd put out a silent call, the rest of the Dark Knights fell into step with them.

The tournament was rowdy and exciting as kids took to their skateboards doing tricks and taking spills that had to hurt despite all their safety gear, making the crowd cheer and gasp. Between Levi's and Tara's families, and the boisterous brotherhood of bikers, nobody was cheered for louder than Joey, as she expertly executed each of her tricks. The crowd *whoop*ed, hollered, and applauded, and Tara took picture after picture of Levi's confident little girl whose resilience and fierce determination never failed to amaze her.

Joey flashed blinding smiles after nailing each trick, her gaze finding her daddy's every single time, with no hint of the heartbreak she'd faced earlier.

When the tournament was over and the judges' votes were tallied, the winners for the eight-to-ten-year-old beginners were announced first. Everyone applauded as the three winners ran up to the makeshift stage. It seemed the entire crowd held their breath waiting for the announcements of the intermediate-level eight-to-ten-year-olds, the level Joey had entered.

Joey stood in front of Levi, bouncing impatiently and fidgeting with her bracelet, her daddy's hands resting on her shoulders. Tara waited a few feet away, watching her through the lens of her camera, wanting to capture the very first second of excitement if she won.

"The third-place winner for the eight-to-ten-year-old intermediate group is Tyrell Johnson." Everyone clapped, and a handful of people shouted, "Way to go, Tyrell!" and "Good job!" The announcer waited as Tyrell, a cute, lanky dark-skinned boy, ran up to join the others onstage, before saying, "The second-place winner for the eight-to-ten-year-old intermediate group is Josephine, *Joey*, Steele!"

Tears blurred Tara's vision as applause and cheers exploded around her and Joey jumped into Levi's arms. Tara caught every second of their embrace, and she wasn't the only one crying. She caught a shimmer of tears in Levi's eyes as Joey ran up to the stage, and his fist shot into the air as he hollered, "Woo-hoo! That's my girl!" She also caught glistening streaks on Shelley's cheeks as their families and friends cheered.

After all the winners were announced and the kids were presented with their trophies and gift certificates, Joey ran straight to Levi to show off her prizes and then ran directly to Tara. "I did it! I won a trophy!"

Tara swept Joey into her arms and spun her around. "I knew you would, cutie pie. You're the bravest girl I know. I'm so proud of you!"

Joey hugged her tight, and as she slid down Tara's body to her feet, Tara noticed that Levi caught them with his phone's camera. He handed his phone to Archer and said, "Get a picture of the three of us, will ya?" He lifted his chin in her direction. "Get over here, blondie. You're the one who made this day possible."

Levi lifted Joey onto his shoulders and put his arm around Tara, and with their families and friends watching on, Archer took a picture of what Tara was sure was her biggest smile yet.

Nineteen

LEVI'S BACKYARD WAS buzzing with excitement. The sandwich bar was a big hit, and Tara paused to take it all in on her way outside with another container of potato salad. Joey was playing ball with Hadley and Leilani, while Jock, Shelley, Tara's father, and Tonya chatted and watched her. Joey was on cloud nine from her win, and she'd told anyone who would listen all about the yard sale and her lemonade stand. Tara spotted Robert talking with Joker and a handful of the other Dark Knights. Most of them, including Robert, had been flirting with Leni all afternoon, but Leni was back to her snarky self, being a little flirty, then yanking their chains. Tara had a feeling Leni was enjoying the game and didn't need or even want a man in her life.

She glanced across the yard at her ruggedly handsome boyfriend. What a funny word that was. Levi was far from a boy, but *manfriend* sounded even funnier, and *partner* didn't sound intimate enough for how close they'd become. He was talking with his father, Jesse, Brent, Archer, and Grant. He glanced her way, and her breath caught at how quickly those beautiful, loving eyes turned wicked. He'd taken advantage of every opportunity to drop a seductive whisper in her ear or sneak a touch as he walked by, and she'd had fun doing the same.

Jules walked into her line of sight and set her hands on her hips.

Tara hurried over to the sandwich table. Jules had been trying to corner her all day to pump her for information about her and Levi's relationship, but with so many people around, Tara was nervous about being overheard.

"You can't avoid me all day," Jules whispered harshly.

"Not if you follow me, I can't." Tara refilled the potato salad. "You know I'm dying to talk about it, but I can't."

"Well, I have a secret. I'll tell you if you share *something* with me."

Tara looked around to make sure nobody was in earshot and whispered, "What do you want to know? That I think your brother is some kind of sex god and that acting like we're not together is killing me? Because both of those things are true. He's loving and protective, and when I'm in his arms, I never want to leave."

Jules squealed and hugged her, and a handful of people looked over.

"Would you *stop*! Now, what's your secret?"

"Grant and I chose a wedding date!"

"That's *great*. When?"

"We want to say our vows at the Christmas tree lighting, because that's where we got engaged."

"That's *so* romantic. Grant is okay doing it that publicly? He's usually so low-key."

"My low-key fiancé proposed to me in front of the whole

community, remember?"

"I know. Talk about out of character."

"It just goes to show what true love can do to a person, and this was *his* idea. He knows how much I love the holidays and our community. He said he thought I'd like to give everyone a chance to be there with us."

"Aw, Jules. I love that."

"Me too." She gazed lovingly at Grant. "I fall more in love with him every day."

"I know the feeling," Tara said without thinking, and quickly snapped her mouth closed.

"I knew it! You *love* him."

"Would you be *quiet*?" Tara chided her. "I never said the *L* word."

"*Sorry*," Jules whispered. "You didn't have to. It's in your eyes, and he looks like he's going to come over here and stake his claim right here and now."

Tara stole a glance at Levi, whose piercing gaze sent her heart into a tizzy. She turned away, needing to regain control and trying to get Jules to stop talking about them. "So why haven't we received a group text about your wedding date yet?"

"We *just* decided this morning, and this is Joey's big day, not ours. Plus, I need to talk to the mayor and get his approval."

"You mean my *father*," Tara pointed out.

"*Yes*. Will you help me figure out the best way to ask him? Do I need to sweeten the pot to get his approval? Should I bring him something from the Sweet Barista or a gift certificate to the bookstore or something? Is that considered bribing a public official? Can I get fined for that? Or go to *jail*?" she asked as their grandmothers sauntered over. "What's the best time to ask your father about something like this?"

"Ask my son about what?" Grandma Blanche asked.

"Um…?" Jules clamped her mouth shut, looking guilty as sin.

"Jules was just asking me about…" She scrambled for something to say. "The charity drive Mom and Goldie are hosting."

Jules nodded emphatically. "Yes. Exactly. I was thinking about dressing up in a costume to entertain the kids, and I wanted to get the mayor's permission."

Lenore and Blanche exchanged a disbelieving glance.

"Bull hockey," Lenore said.

Grandma Blanche lowered her voice. "Tell us your secrets and we'll share ours."

"I already know some of yours, Grandma, and I don't think I can handle any more." Tara needed to get Jules out of there before their grandmothers got her talking and she accidentally spilled the beans about her and Levi. "Jules, I think Grant just waved you over."

"What?" Jules whipped around and waved to Grant. "He probably wants a kiss. See you ladies later."

As Jules hurried away, Lenore said, "What's she hiding?"

"I have no idea *what* you're talking about." Tara held the empty potato salad container against her chest like a shield. "I'd better bring this inside." She'd taken only two steps before her grandmother called her name. Tara closed her eyes, inhaling deeply before forcing a smile and turning back. "Yes?"

Her grandmother handed her the mustard container. "This is empty. Can you get another?"

Relieved, she said, "Sure."

"I can't hold it in any longer," her grandmother said giddily. "Lenore and I have a date with Joker's grandfather and a friend of his next week."

"Wow, you two didn't waste any time, did you?"

"Life's too short for wasted time," her grandmother said. "So whatever you and Julesy are hiding, you don't have to hide from us."

If there was one person who Tara believed would keep her secret forever, it was her grandmother, but with Joey's heart on the line, she wasn't taking any chances. "We're not hiding anything, Gram. I'll get more mustard."

She headed inside, musing about her grandmother and Lenore. She was throwing the empty containers in the trash when Levi walked through the patio doors. He stalked toward her like a puma on the prowl, his predatory gaze making her pulse quicken.

He didn't say a word as he took her hand, leading her out of the kitchen.

"Where are we going?"

He tugged her into the powder room and closed the door. His mouth descended on hers in a deep, delicious kiss that went on and on. When their lips finally parted, he said, "I've been dying to do that."

"Same." She pulled his mouth back to hers, and his strong hands clamped on to her waist. Without breaking the kiss, he lifted her onto the sink, wedging his big body between her legs.

"*God*, baby," he said against her lips. "How can I miss being close to you this much after only a few hours?" He trailed kisses along her jaw. "You *own* me, sweetheart."

"*Same*," she panted out, wishing she could form a sentence, but his tantalizing kisses were so much better than stringing words together. His every touch, every sexy whisper deepened her desire. When he pushed his hands into her hair, taking her in a soul-searing kiss, her thoughts fell away, and she surrendered to the need building inside her. She clung to him, wrapping her legs around his waist, and rocked her hips. He ground against her, intensifying her desperation. Their lips parted on a moan and a growl, but he kept her face close, biting her earlobe, sending fire between her legs. She gasped with pleasure, pleading, "*Again.*" He did. "*Levi—*" Her plea was silenced by another ravenous kiss. He pushed his hands under her bottom, leaning into her, and she couldn't hold back a needy moan.

The bathroom door swung open, and they startled apart.

Tara's mother stared wide-eyed and appalled, her cheeks reddening. "*Tara Ann!*"

"Mom, what are you—" Tara scrambled off the sink, but Levi moved slower, more determinedly, hooking his arm around her waist, standing tall and protective beside her.

"*You.*" Her mother glared at Levi. "It's not enough that you soiled one of my daughters? You have to go after Tara, too?" She turned that venom on Tara. "Is *this* why you're here all the time, Tara Ann?"

"*No*, but that—"

"Let's just slow down a minute," Levi said emphatically. "I will not have you taking that tone to Tara in my house. This isn't what you think it is."

Her mother scoffed. "Oh no? I think it's pretty clear what this is. I never should have trusted you around my girls."

"Would both of you *stop*, please?" Tara stormed out of the bathroom, shaking with anger as she turned on her mother. "What I do with Levi, or anyone else, is *none* of your business. I'm not a child, and Levi sure as hell isn't the kind of man who can't be trusted."

"He impregnated your *sister*, Tara. Does *Amelia* know about this?"

"It's none of her business, and *yes*, Amelia got pregnant by Levi, but it takes two people to make a baby. Amelia is *not* innocent, like you pretend she is." Tara was vaguely aware of movement in the kitchen, but she was too upset to slow down. "She slept around in high school, and the whole town knows it, whether you want to admit it or not, and yes, she got knocked up. Get *over* it already." The words flew like rapid fire. "You got a beautiful granddaughter out of it, and your precious Amelia hasn't done *shit* to take care of her. Levi gave up his life at twenty years old to raise their daughter. He has cared for her day and night and built a happy, full life for her, putting himself last in *every* way. He has done nothing *but* what is best for Joey since the day she was born, and you and your warped sense of importance have tried to tear him down for it. Well, guess what, Mom?" Hot tears streaked her cheeks.

"Watch yourself, Tara Ann," her mother said coldly.

"No. It's time *you* watched yourself," she said as Levi came to her side. "I have nothing but respect for Levi, and I don't care if you disapprove of how I feel, because I *love* him. I love him for the kind boy he was when he found me hiding in the pantry at parties because my own sister called me fat, unworthy, and ugly every chance she got, and you not only allowed it, you *taught* it to her, nitpicking at me to this day, as if I'm never good enough. And while you make me feel bad about myself, Levi makes me feel *good* every time we're together, and he always has. I *love* him for the caring friend he's always been to me and the loving father he is to Joey, and I love him for being the man I can laugh and cry with, without fear or judgment."

"*T*," Levi cautioned, taking her hand.

Tara shook her head, looking up through teary eyes. "I have

loved you since before I even understood what that word really meant, and she needs to know it."

"This is *not* happening, Tara Ann," her mother said evenly. "Not as long as you live under my roof."

Tara should have expected her to try to use the house as leverage, but it still gutted her. She lifted her chin, meeting her mother's gaze. "Then it's a good thing I've been looking for another place to live, because I will *not* end things with Levi just to please you."

Levi squeezed her hand, his expression an anguished mix of heartache and pride.

"You want to be my daddy's girlfriend?" Joey's quiet voice came from behind Tara like a knife to her chest.

Oh God. What have I done? She looked at Levi apologetically, and with her heart in her throat, she turned around, shocked to see their family and friends standing at the threshold of the living room in stunned silence. Joey was holding Shelley's hand. Tara took in Joey's confused expression, and Shelley mouthed, *Sorry*.

Swallowing hard, Tara said, "Yes, Joey, I do. More than anything in this world." She held her breath as interminable silence ticked by. Worried she'd really screwed up, she started to apologize, but Joey broke away from Shelley and ran to her, throwing her arms around her.

"I want that, too," Joey said.

More tears spilled down Tara's cheeks as she hugged her. "I love you."

Her mother huffed something and stormed out of the house.

Tara bowed her head, tears falling as Levi put his arms around her and Joey. She closed her eyes, thanking her lucky stars he wasn't pushing her away, and heard Shelley ushering everyone out of the house. Tara looked up at Levi, mortified that he and Joey, and their families and friends, had witnessed her fight with her mother. Baring her heart for him, and everyone else, to hear was nothing compared to the well-being of the precious girl in her arms. "I'm sorry. I…"

"*Shh*. It's okay, babe."

She choked out, "*Joey…?*"

Levi mouthed, *She didn't see it all.*

Tara realized that was why he'd cautioned her, and as Joey blinked curiously up at them, she tried to remember what she'd said after that warning. *I have loved you since before I even understood what that word really meant, and she needs to know it.* Hopefully she hadn't heard what Tara said about her sister and mother. "I'm sorry you saw us arguing. Do you want to talk about what you heard?"

A tentative smile curved Joey's lips, as if she were unsure if it was okay to be happy after witnessing so much strife. "Daddy, do you want to be Tara's boyfriend?"

"Yes, peanut, more than anything."

That earned a confident smile from Joey, but it quickly faltered. "Aunt Tara, was Grandma the mean girl you told me about? Was she the reason you used to eat so much?"

Tara sighed, debating if she should lie, but lies never ended well. "Sometimes."

"But it was mostly Amelia," Levi said tightly.

Tara gave him an imploring look, silently asking why he'd upset Joey any more than she already was, but the firm set of his jaw told her he had his own agenda.

He crouched beside Joey, taking her hand in his. "You're old enough to know the truth. Amelia wasn't a very nice girl when she was younger, and she made Aunt Tara feel bad about herself."

"But she isn't like that anymore," Tara said quickly, unsure why she was protecting her selfish sister.

Joey's brow furrowed. "She makes me feel bad."

More tears sprang to Tara's eyes.

"I know, and I'm sorry, sweetheart. That's my fault, and I won't let her do that to you anymore." He hugged her and drew Tara into the embrace.

"Dad, you can't make someone be nice," Joey said. "All you can do is stand up for yourself and figure out if you're going to let their words hurt you." She paused, face tight with consternation. "Maybe next time Amelia makes me sad, I'll stand up to her like Tara stood up to Grandma."

"We can talk about that another time," Levi promised. "Peanut, I want you to know that Tara and I were going to tell you how we feel about each other soon."

"But I didn't want to do it until after spring break," Tara explained. "I'm sorry we ruined your big day."

"It's okay," Joey said. "At least you guys didn't have a fistfight like Uncle Archer and Uncle Jock did."

Levi put his hand on Joey's back. "Attagirl. Always look for that silver lining."

"Can I go play with Leilani and Hadley?" Joey asked.

"Sure." Levi kissed the top of her head, and as Joey ran outside, he pulled Tara into his arms. "I'm sorry, baby. What can I do?"

"Rewind time and make me keep my mouth shut."

"You had a lot to say."

She was mortified, and the reality of what she'd said about her mother and sister, and her feelings for Levi, was hitting her with full force, and she felt the walls closing in. "I don't want to talk about it. I can't right now. I need to apologize to everyone before they think I've lost my mind."

"Nobody thinks you've lost your mind, T. You've been through enough. Why don't you relax and I'll talk to them."

"No. It's my fault. I should..." She saw her father, grandmother, and Robert walk back inside, heading their way.

Levi followed her gaze, keeping her close and standing up taller. "Tara's been through enough for today."

Her father held his hands up. "We're not here to cause more trouble. I want to apologize for my wife. I thought she'd gotten over blaming you, and I'm sorry for what she said."

"I appreciate that," Levi said, "but I'm not worried about myself."

"Jelly Bean, all I've ever wanted is for you to be happy," her father said tenderly. "I'm sorry I didn't believe you about Amelia all those years ago. There is no excuse. I guess I didn't want to believe she could be so cruel."

"A witch in disguise," her grandmother said under her breath.

Her father gave her a stern glance. "That's enough, Mother." He turned a softer gaze on Tara. "As far as you and Levi go, I've seen this coming for a while. Levi, you are everything Tara said you were, and you two have my blessing."

Fresh tears filled Tara's eyes. "Thanks, Dad." She looked at her brother.

"I'm cool with you two," Robert said. "But why didn't you ever tell me what Amelia was doing?"

She shrugged. "You're so much older than me—you weren't really around."

"Well, I am now, and if anyone hurts you..." Robert

glanced at Levi.

"Dude, don't look at me like that," Levi said. "I'd never hurt her."

"I know you wouldn't, but if you did, I'd have to try really hard to kick your ass."

"Duly noted," Levi said.

"Thank goodness you finally saw what was right in front of you," her grandmother said to Levi. "I thought I was going to have to introduce Tara to my *business associates*, and I don't need that kind of competition. A cute young thing like her can get any guy she wants." She winked at Tara. "If you're moving out, you better have a room for me."

"I will, Gram. Charmaine's looking for rentals for me."

"If you'll excuse me, I'll give you some privacy and go talk with my family." Levi kissed Tara. "I'll be right outside if you need me."

LEVI HEADED FOR the slider, but he stopped short and went out front instead. Tara's mother was sitting in the passenger seat of their car, presumably waiting for the rest of her family. He knocked on the passenger window.

She opened the door but stared out the windshield, her jaw tight, eyes glassy.

Levi leaned down, speaking kindly but firmly. "I'm sorry you had to find out about us this way, and I'm sorry you don't approve of me and Tara being together, but I didn't enter this relationship lightly, and I don't intend to walk away from it. I hope one day you'll see past the embarrassment or whatever pain you experienced when Amelia got pregnant and see me for the man I am. But, more importantly, I hope you can find a way to see Tara for the person she's always been. Your daughter is an incredible woman who loves so deeply, she puts everyone else before herself. She doesn't deserve to be pushed aside or treated like she's disposable."

Marsha's chin trembled, but she pressed her lips together and continued staring straight ahead.

"I'd like to think that Joey can grow up without feeling like the way she came into the world will always be held over our heads, but that's not something I can fix on my own." He paused, giving her a moment to speak, but she said nothing. "Thanks for coming to support Joey today. Have a safe trip back."

As he walked away, he heard the car door close and hoped to hell she'd come to her senses and do the right thing. He made his way to the backyard, where his family was waiting anxiously. Joey was playing with Hadley and Leilani, giggling and running around. Was she really that resilient? Forge and Tonya were watching over them, and the rest of his Dark Knights were talking among themselves, respectfully standing a few feet away from his family. This was all his fault, and he'd give anything to change places with Tara and be the one dealing with a hellish mother. Thank God the rest of her family wasn't like that.

"Hey, man, that was heavy," Archer said compassionately. "Is Tara okay?"

"Are you okay?" Jock asked.

Levi blew out a breath. "I'm fine, and Tara is about as okay as she can be after that nightmare." He wasn't sure she was, and he was worried about what the fight with her mother would do to her once it really sank in. How the hell was he going to fix this?

"Is it okay if I go talk to her?" Jules asked.

"Maybe we both should," his mother suggested.

"She's with the rest of her family," Levi said. "I think she needs a minute with them."

Leni crossed her arms. "I had no idea Amelia did that to her. Where is Amelia? I want to go kick her ass."

"That won't help the situation," their father chided.

"Now, hold on. I'm with Leni on this," his grandmother said. "Amelia needs a good ass whooping for treating Tara like that, as does her mother. Marsha should be ashamed of herself."

Levi tried to remain calm. "There's a lot of history there, Grandma. Tara and I will get it figured out."

"What can we do?" Jesse asked.

"Nothing, man. Thanks. I appreciate y'all sticking around, but we're good. I think I'm just going to clean up and call it a day."

"Want some help?" Jesse offered.

"Yeah, man, just tell us what to do," Brent added.

"We've got this," his mother assured them. "You boys were such great support for Joey today. She's lucky to have you both. Go enjoy the rest of your day with your friends."

Levi thanked them and said goodbye to his buddies. After they left, Jules hugged him.

"I'm sorry this is so hard," she said.

"Family shit sucks," Grant commiserated.

"We'll figure it out," Levi said.

"Guess this makes me the reigning king of the Steele family matchmaking," Archer said with a smirk.

"The heck you are," Jules argued. "You haven't done squat."

"Okay, you two. Let's go clean up and get out of Levi's hair." Grant put his hands on their shoulders, guiding them away from Levi.

Levi glanced inside and saw Tara hugging her brother. His chest constricted as her words came back to him. *I have loved you since before I even understood what that word really meant, and she needs to know it.*

"I guess Tara is the special friend you were talking about that day in the kitchen?" his father asked.

Levi nodded, his mind spinning.

"He mentioned his *friend* to you, too?" Leni asked. "Guess I'm not so special after all."

Levi gave her a deadpan look.

"Ha! I'm kidding. I know I'm special. Nothing trumps womb-mates." She held up her hand to high-five Levi, and she must have seen that he wasn't in the mood, because she wrapped her arms around him instead and lowered her voice. "I know you're worried about Tara, but she's going to be okay. I know she is. You wouldn't have it any other way."

Damn right, I won't.

AFTER ONE OF the longest days of his life, Levi sat on Joey's bed with her, reading a few chapters of one of her Unicorn Academy books. After helping clean up, his family had stayed to talk with Tara, reassuring her, letting her know how much she was loved and that they were there for her. She'd put on a brave face all afternoon and evening, but she'd made herself scarce after dinner and had gone out for an hour and a half, claiming she needed to run some errands. She'd come back with sand on her shoes, and that had made Levi ache for her. He understood her needing to be alone, but he wished she'd talk to him.

When he finished reading, Joey snuggled against his side. "Dad?"

"Yeah, peanut?"

"Is Aunt Tara okay?"

"She will be, Jo. She's just sad about what happened with Grandma." He hugged her against his side and kissed her head. He'd heard Tara showering a little while ago and hoped it had helped ease her tension.

"Do you think I should sleep with her so she's not alone?"

Her thoughtfulness hit him square in the heart, but he wasn't about to let Tara sleep alone. He wanted her safe and warm in his arms. "That's a really sweet offer, honey, but you've had a big day, too. You need to get some sleep."

"Will you make sure she's okay?"

"Of course." He climbed off the bed and set up her stuffies. When she was surrounded by her menagerie, he said, "I'm proud of you, kiddo. Congratulations on your big win."

Joey grinned. "Uncle Brent said if I keep practicing, I can enter as an expert next spring."

"You're going to take the Harborside skateboard world by storm, and I can't wait to watch it happen." He brushed another kiss to her forehead. "Sweet dreams, peanut. I love you."

"I love you, too, Dad. Tell Aunt Tara good night and that I love her."

"Will do."

He left her door ajar and followed faint noises coming from the bedroom down the hall. Tara was emptying the dresser drawers and putting her clothes in her suitcase. Her hair was piled on her head in a messy bun, a few damp tendrils framing her face, and she was wearing leggings and a T-shirt. The pit of his stomach sank. "You're not leaving, are you?"

She shook her head. "Just moving back downstairs."

He went to her, drawing her into his arms. She smelled like sunshine and flowers, but the gray in her eyes told of the storm in her heart. "I'm sorry about today. I shouldn't have dragged you into the bathroom. That was selfish of me."

"No, it wasn't. I *wanted* to be in there with you. None of this is your fault. I'm the one with the big mouth. I shouldn't have said anything. I should have let her say her piece and walked away."

"It wouldn't have ended there."

"What if my mother hates me now?"

He thought about her mother holding back tears in the car. "A mother's love doesn't turn off like that after twenty-plus years." He paused, letting that settle in. "You finally stood up for yourself, and you made your mother take a good hard look at herself and the pain she's caused. That's not an easy thing for anyone, and I'd imagine it's going to take a while for her to figure out how to deal with it."

"You're assuming she even *wants* to deal with it."

"She *does*. She loves you, Tara, and I know you believe that. If you didn't, you wouldn't still be living in your parents' house. You've experienced the sharp edge of some of your mother's worst habits, and they hurt you tremendously, but that has never stopped you from seeing the good in her and appreciating the mom who took you to photography exhibits and sparked your love of gardening and who is proud of you and the business you've built, even if she doesn't always know how to say it. She's not going to abandon you."

She shook her head and wrapped her arms around him, resting her cheek on his chest. "I don't want to talk. I just want you to hold me."

He held her, stroking her back, feeling her tension as his own. "We'll figure this out, babe. I promise."

"I don't want to ruin Joey's life or make things weird between her and my mom. That's her *grandmother*," she said shakily.

"You're not ruining her life. You make it better. She wants us to be together. She loves you, Tara." *And so do I.* That reality hit him all at once, and he wanted to tell her, to make everything better, but he didn't want such big words to get lost in everything else that was going on.

"I just can't believe I said all those things about Amelia and my mother and how I feel about you. I hope you don't think I expect you to feel the same way. You probably want to put me on a crazy train. Who says I love you after a *week*?" She didn't give him time to respond. "But in all fairness, I really *have* loved you forever, and I know it was just a crush when I was younger, but I loved you as a friend, and it was building. It became real, and now it's out there and everyone knows, and I shouldn't have said anything because now I'm embarrassed and you feel pressured, and I just want to crawl into a hole and hide." She pressed her face into his chest.

"Hey, blondie."

"Yeah," she said, muffled by his chest.

He lifted her face and kissed each blushing cheek. "If you're getting on a crazy train, then I'm riding it with you, because I didn't have years to fall in love with you. I was blinded by my own determination. But once I got out of my own way, there was no stopping what was probably there for a hell of a lot longer than I realized. I knew I was falling for you before we even kissed, and the first time I woke up with you in my arms, I didn't want to let you go. I knew then that we were exactly where we were supposed to be, and I've been falling harder and faster for you every day since."

"You're not just saying that to make me feel better? Really, honestly, truly?"

She asked so adorably full of hope, a soft laugh fell from his lips. "Really, honestly, truly."

A tear slipped down her cheek. "My relationships with my mom and Amelia are fraught with trouble. It's not going to be easy."

"Have you ever known me to take the easy route?"

She shook her head. "But—"

He silenced her with a tender kiss. "No *buts*, T. I love who you are, and I'm proud of you for standing up to your mother, even though I know it was probably the hardest thing you've ever done."

"I'm proud of myself, too, but I hated it." She touched her forehead to his chest and sighed loudly.

"Standing up to the people we love is scary, but you've spent your life *taking* the hurtful things two of the people who are supposed to protect you have dished out. You deserve to be treated like the smart, beautiful, caring woman you are and to live your life in the ways that make you happy."

She lifted her beautiful eyes to his.

"Do you want to shake it off?" he asked to lighten the mood. "I can queue up Taylor Swift, and we can get on the bed and sing into our hairbrushes."

She shook her head with a happier expression. "I think I

have to let it sink in and be a part of me, but I don't want to think about it right now. I don't want to think about anything. I just want to be with you."

He ran his fingers along her cheek and tucked her hair behind her ear. "I know the perfect way to help you relax." He brushed a kiss to her lips. "Come on, sweet thing. I'll carry your stuff downstairs."

He gathered her things and carried them down to the guest bedroom.

"Thanks. You can just put them anywhere." She waved her hand absently, and he set her bags by the dresser.

She was standing barefoot by the door, those soulful eyes pleading for him to make things better. *Don't worry, baby. I've got you.* He locked the door and hooked his index finger into the collar of her T-shirt, tugging it down just enough to place a kiss on her breastbone. "Do I get to put *you* anywhere, too?"

"I was hoping you would. I'm yours. You can put me anywhere you want."

Heat streaked through him with that open invitation. "I want you right here." He lifted her T-shirt over her head and tossed it away. Her necklace sparkled against her flawless skin. He gazed deeply into her eyes, running his finger down the center of her breastbone to the aquamarine charm, and kissed her softly, whispering, "Against the door, beautiful." He dusted kisses down her neck, stepping forward as she stepped back until her back met the door. He trailed openmouthed kisses along her shoulder as he freed her breasts, pushing her bra off her shoulders. It sailed to the floor. Her trusting eyes watched as he took a long look at her gorgeous breasts, lifted with each ragged inhalation. "So beautiful." He touched his lips to hers. "I love you, baby." She whimpered needily, and he kissed her again, slow and deep.

He drew back, holding her gaze as he skimmed his hands up her torso, his thumbs brushing her breasts. Her eyes fluttered closed, an aroused sigh falling from her lips, and he dipped his head, teasing around her nipple, along the swell of her breast, and returned to circle her nipple again. She was trembling, breathing hard.

She grabbed his head, holding his mouth over her nipple. "*Levi*," she panted out.

"I've got you, baby." He licked and teased, grazing his teeth over the peak. She bowed off the door, grinding against his cock, and he continued taunting her.

"Suck it."

The plea in her voice brought his mouth to hers in a cock-hardening kiss. "God, baby, I love that filthy mouth. I want to fucking live in it."

She reached for his jeans, but he covered her hand with his, stopping her.

"Uh-uh. Tonight is about you." He sealed his mouth over hers, tongues delving, moans slipping from her lungs to his. Kissing her had become one of his favorite things. He loved the noises she made, the way she went up on her toes, thrusting her tongue against his. He kept her there, against the door, bodies grinding, hands roaming, as they devoured each other. Lust pounded inside him, pooling hot and deep and urgent, until he couldn't take it anymore. He took off her leggings and panties and kissed his way up her legs, slowing to slick his tongue along the side of her knee. She whimpered again, and he licked her inner thigh, eating up her sinful sounds. He'd learned that she got off when he used his teeth on any part of her body, and he nipped at that sensitive flesh. She gasped, her hips pushing forward. He grabbed those gorgeous hips, licking the sensitive crease beside her sex. First one side, then the other, as she moaned and rocked, growing slicker by the second. The scent of her arousal made his cock weep. He slid his tongue between her legs, her essence spreading over it, drawing a growl from someplace deep inside him. He did it again, dragging his tongue all the way up to her clit, massaging with slow, determined pressure, a stream of indiscernible, sexy sounds sailed from her lips, her fingernails digging into his shoulders as he teased and taunted her.

"Christ, baby. I love the way you taste, the way you smell, the way you quiver when you're about to come."

"Touch me," she pleaded.

"Uh-uh, blondie. Nothing's going inside you tonight but my cock. Squeeze your thighs together."

She obeyed with an objectionable whimper.

"Trust me. You'll be so hot and tight when I make love to you, it'll blow your mind." He pressed a kiss above her sex. "Open your eyes. Watch me love you."

Her eyes found his, the heat in them branding his flesh. Her legs trembled as she squeezed them together. He used his thumbs to hold open her sex as he licked and sucked. When he grazed his teeth over her clit, she lost control, crying out as pleasure consumed her. He stayed with her, loving her until she went boneless, panting out his name.

He lifted her into his arms and carried her to the bed, stripped himself naked, and came down over her. As he gazed into her eyes and her arms circled him, there was no hint of sadness, just pure, untethered love, and it was the most beautiful sight he'd *ever* seen.

Their mouths came together without urgency or desperation. She lifted her hips, and he thrust slowly, cradling her beneath him until he was buried to the hilt, as close as two people could be. His breath became hers, their hearts beating as one as they found the rhythm that bound them together, erasing all sadness, all worries, until nothing else existed but *them*.

They moved at a pace of lovers who were sure of one another, who knew the angles and touches that made their hearts soar and their bodies combust, taking and giving in equal measure. They made love until they had nothing left to give. And then he held her as they caught their breath, whispering promises in the dark. "You are mine, and I am yours, and I will *always* take care of you."

"Always?" she whispered. "Because I need a little something more."

He leaned up on one elbow, looking down at her flushed, beautiful face. "*More?* Damn, baby. Ask and you shall receive. Give me two minutes and I'll be ready to go again."

"Not *that*," she said playfully. "I need to recover first. I'm hungry and thinking about the desserts we made."

"Aw, babe. I'm sorry, but Archer and Jock took the rest of them home for Indi and Daphne. But Archer left us a bottle of his newest wine, and we've still got a few cheesecake bites in the fridge. They might be prank bombs by *you-know-who*, but we can cut them open and check before eating them."

"That sounds *perfect*. But let's take our chances with the prank bombs. It's more fun that way."

Twenty

THEY'D BEEN GRACED with a warm, sunny morning for their boat outing with Jesse and Brent, and it couldn't have come at a better time. The week had passed with more ups than downs, but the underlying thread of sorrow remained. Tara hadn't heard from her mother, and that was weighing heavily on both of them, but they kept their minds busy. Levi was making solid progress on the renovation, and Tara and Joey had finished the gardens in the backyard in between skateboarding, playdates, and clearing out the shed to get ready for the yard sale. Levi had suggested they put it off, but Tara and Joey had been insistent. Every night, after spending the evening playing games or watching movies with Joey—and loving being able to share his feelings for Tara with his little girl, who adored her just as much as he did—he and Tara fell into each other's arms with the relief and desperation of castaways being rescued. They'd continued to fall asleep together every night and set alarms so he could return to his bedroom before Joey woke up each morning. But every day it got a little harder to leave Tara's side.

Tara was a pillar of strength, putting on a happy front for Joey. She tried her best to do the same around Levi, but he knew her too well. He knew she was worried about burdening him. He understood how difficult opening up could be when she was used to being a solo warrior, keeping everything inside and dealing with it in silence. But late at night, when she lay sated in his arms, safe and loved, her trust in him won out. Some nights they talked for what seemed like hours and others for merely a few minutes. It all helped, as did her father and brothers calling to check on her, but he knew that special spark in her eyes wouldn't return until the issues with her mother were dealt with.

And then there was the elephant in the room that neither of them liked talking about.

Amelia.

He could only assume she'd heard the news, and he was as relieved as he was shocked that they hadn't heard from her. He knew he had to talk with Amelia at some point about his relationship with Tara, but he also knew it might cause more trouble for Tara, and *that* could wait.

Tabling those thoughts, he put the bag he'd packed with towels, blankets, extra clothes, hats, and foul weather gear for all of them into the Durango. It might be sunny and unseasonably warm on land, but they could still freeze their asses off out on the water. At least they were promised a nice evening, perfect for the plans he'd made for his two favorite girls.

His phone vibrated with a text, and Leni's name appeared on the screen. His siblings and parents had called to check on them throughout the week. Even Sutton, who had heard the news of Saturday's argument from Leni. He opened and read

Leni's message. *Just wondering if I need to buy my niece earplugs so she can sleep at night.* He chuckled as he replied. *She can't hear Tara from the red room in the basement.* He added a devil emoji and sent it. Leni replied with a shocked emoji followed by a laughing emoji, and, *Seriously, how's Joey doing? Is she okay with your new lovey-dovey situation? How's Tara holding up?*

He thumbed out, *This will sound weird after everything that's gone down, but I think Joey's happier than she's ever been.* Leni's response rolled in a minute later. *I figured as much. It's kind of always been the three of you, so this makes sense in her little brain.* Levi typed, *My daughter has a big brain. She gets it from me.* Leni sent an eye roll emoji, and *I've got to run. Meeting a friend for coffee.* He typed, *A pre-date inquisition?* Another text popped up from Leni. *We can't all have single sexy friends in our guest room.*

He laughed, pocketed his phone, and headed inside.

Tara was sitting on the couch working on her laptop in the black leggings and oversize peach sweatshirt she'd put on after her shower. The leggings he'd asked her to change out of because he'd gotten his hands on her in them in the pantry, and now every time he saw her wearing them, his body ignited. It didn't matter that her sweatshirt covered her curves. He knew what was beneath it, and her smirk told him she was going to take full advantage of his lack of control.

"Hey, babe. Is Joey upstairs?"

"Yeah. She's packing a few toys."

"Good. Are you almost ready to go?"

"I'm ready. I just want to look at these last two rentals Charmaine sent over. It'll only take a minute."

He didn't want to think about what it would be like when she went back to the island. They'd had so much going on, he'd done a fairly good job of keeping those thoughts at bay. But the end of spring break was looming, and it was going to suck not seeing her every day. Not being able to hold her or take a pulse on how she was doing would likely drive him nuts. Sure, he would ask her how she was, but with Tara he needed his arms around her to really know the truth. He needed to look into her eyes and feel her heart beating steady or frantic. He hadn't been able to protect her all those years ago, and he sure as hell couldn't do it if she was on the island and he was in Harborside.

"You know you can stay with us for as long as you'd like," he said more casually than he felt.

"Thanks, but I'd never put you and Joey out like that, and I have to get back to the island and figure out my life. I've got photo shoots set up every day next week, and I have to start looking at studio space in case I decide to rent instead of buy. Jules said I can stay in her apartment above her shop, but I thought I'd see what else is out there first. I know she was toying with ideas of expanding the Happy End, and I don't want to hold her up. I'm going to see a couple of places after the clothing drive on Sunday."

"You're still thinking of buying?"

She shrugged. "I don't know. There aren't that many long-term rentals out there, and I still need studio space."

"I'm ready!" Joey hollered as she barreled downstairs in tie-dyed leggings and a black sweatshirt with pink hearts on it, backpack in hand.

"I can do this later." Tara closed her laptop and set it on the coffee table. She pushed to her feet as Joey darted past, and she scooped her up, smothering her face with kisses. "It's going to be cold on the water. Do you have a shirt under that sweat-shirt?"

"Yes." Joey lifted her sweatshirt, showing her the shirt she wore under it. "Do *you*?"

Tara peeked down the front of her own sweatshirt and whispered, "*Oops.*"

"Aunt *Tara*." Joey pointed over Tara's shoulder. "Go put on a shirt."

She set Joey down and took a step away, acting dejected, and then she spun around, lifting the bottom of her sweatshirt to show Joey the shirt she wore underneath with a "*Gotcha!*" and proceeded to tickle Joey into hysterics. Tara stopped abruptly, whispered something in Joey's ear, and Joey giggled.

"Let's see if Daddy has a shirt on under his sweatshirt." Joey walked toward him, her little hands reaching for him.

Behind her, Tara licked her lips, gathering the bottom of her sweatshirt around her waist, and with a wickedness in her grin like he'd seen last night as she'd lowered her mouth over his cock, she gave him an eyeful of her gorgeous ass as she bent over and picked up Joey's backpack.

Fuck.

Life was *definitely* going to suck when Tara left, but until then, *Watch out, blondie. I'm going to have fun paying you back for this one.*

AN HOUR LATER, as the shore faded in the distance and salty sea air stung their faces, the boat cruised toward one of Brent's favorite fishing spots. Brent was piloting the boat, which was aptly named *Endless Summer*, just like their surf shop. Levi was shooting the shit with Jesse, and Tara sat with Joey in her lap. Joey was bundled up in a blanket, and Tara was braiding her hair. Their cheeks were pink from the cold, but they were chatting happily.

Levi took out his phone and snapped a picture, capturing Tara's hair blowing in the wind and Joey gazing out at the water, seconds before Brent cut the engine, the boat slowed, and the wind died down.

"Any word from Tara's mother?" Jesse asked quietly.

"No. Tara thought about calling her, but the ball needs to stay in her mother's court. I don't get it. It's been five days. How can she do this to her own daughter?"

Jesse scoffed. "People do stupid shit. Look at Amelia, and you know about our old man."

Jesse and Brent's father, Jeffrey, was Levi's uncle, his father's brother, whom the family rarely spoke of. Jeffrey had been married to Levi's aunt Faye, one of the nicest women on the planet. Even after the divorce, she'd remained best friends with Levi's mother. Jeffrey and Faye had six kids—Reggie, Fiona, Finn, Jesse, Brent, and Shea. Jeffrey had come home one day after work and said he was leaving because their mother no longer *got* him and he'd found someone who did. Jesse and Brent had been teenagers at the time.

"Yeah. I count myself lucky to have parents who can't keep their hands off each other."

Joey popped up to her feet. "Can we fish now, Uncle Brent?"

"We sure can." Brent raked his hair away from his face.

"It's so much warmer without the wind," Tara said, already holding her camera to her eye, taking pictures of the rest of them.

"I would've warmed you up." Levi pulled her into his arms and kissed her.

"Dad, stop kissing Aunt Tara. She promised to fish with me."

"Okay, but I'm collecting interest later." He gave Tara a quick kiss and let her go.

"Let me get a picture of all of you before we get fishy." Tara motioned for them to stand close together.

"Can we do the chair?" Joey bounced on her toes. *"Please?"*

Brent and Jesse exchanged a shrug, and Jesse said, "Sure." They each held their arms straight out and crossed them. Then they took hold of each other's hands, creating a *chair*. Levi lifted Joey to sit on their arms and went to stand behind Joey.

Tara put her camera to her eye. "Say fishy wishy."

"Fishy wishy," they said in unison as she took a picture.

"Now make a funny face." Tara moved to another angle, taking the shot as Levi crossed his eyes. She had them hold up peace signs, act like pirates, and finally she said, "Just act normal," which of course caused them to act as strange as possible.

Joey pointed behind Tara and said, "Look how fast that boat is going. They must be freezing."

"That's the Coast Guard," Brent said, as a voice came over the boat's radio.

"On the vessel *Endless Summer*, this is United States Coast Guard..." They continued to give their identification number.

Brent radioed back. "Coast Guard, this is *Endless Summer*. Over."

"*Endless Summer* switch to channel twenty-two. Over."

"*Endless Summer* switching to channel twenty-two. Over." Brent changed to the requested channel and spoke into the radio again. "Coast Guard, this is *Endless Summer*. Over."

The other boat cruised closer, coming to a stop right next to them. "*Endless Summer*, stand by for a Coast Guard boarding."

"Daddy, what's going on?" Joey asked.

"I don't know, peanut. It sounds like the Coast Guard is coming onto the boat." Levi looked at his cousin. "Brent, what's up?"

"It's probably just a routine inspection. No big deal. They do them every year to just about every vessel that spends a lot of time on the water," Brent said as two rather large men wearing US Coast Guard orange-and-black float coats and holsters on their belts prepared to board the boat.

"Come on, girls. Let's get out of their way." Levi drew Tara and Joey against his sides, keeping them close as they stepped back to give the men room.

"They don't look very nice," Tara observed nervously as the men came aboard.

"Good day, skipper," one of the men said. "My name is Petty Officer Markle. The Coast Guard is here to determine the status of your vessel and to ensure compliance with applicable federal laws. Captain, do you have any weapons on board?"

"No, sir," Brent said.

"We'd like to see your identification as well as the identification of your crew members and passengers," Petty Officer Markle said.

"I didn't bring my purse," Tara whispered.

"I'll take care of it," Levi reassured her. "You stay with Joey."

"Dad…?" Joey said worriedly as Tara took her hand.

"It's fine, Joey. I'll be right back." Levi pulled out his wallet, and when the men handed Jesse and Brent back their IDs, Levi handed the unnamed man his driver's license. "My girlfriend didn't bring her identification, and my daughter doesn't have any."

The man looked at his license and put a hand on his holster. "This is our guy." He wrenched Levi's arm behind his back and slapped a handcuff on it. "Levi Steele, you're under arrest for breaking and entering on three vessels."

"*Daddy!*" Joey shrieked.

Levi forced down his ire. "It's okay, Joey. It's just a misunderstanding." His rage came out at the officer. "You've got the *wrong* guy. I haven't broken any laws."

"We'll let the judge make that decision." He pushed Levi toward the other boat.

"Whoa, hold on, Officer." Brent closed the distance between them.

"Back up, Captain." Markle moved between Levi and Brent. "There's a warrant out for this man's arrest, and we're taking him in."

"This is bullshit. He's been with us all day," Jesse said. "You definitely have the wrong guy."

"And he was with us last night," Tara added frantically. "He didn't even leave the house."

Joey ran to Levi and plastered herself to his legs. "Don't take my daddy!"

"Joey!" Tara ran after her, trying to pry her off him.

They'd piloted right into hell. "Joey, you've *got* to let go, baby."

"*No!* Don't let them take you, Daddy!"

Jesse pulled Joey off Levi, but she screamed and cried, struggling to get to him as the officer dragged Levi to the other boat.

"Just give me a second with her," Levi demanded. "She's just a little kid! She doesn't understand." He looked over his shoulder, his heart in pieces at the anguish in Joey's terrified wails and in Tara's eyes as she tried to console her. "We'll get this figured out, T! It's gonna be okay." His venom spewed at the officers. "You've got the *wrong* guy. You're going to pay for traumatizing my daughter."

"You can take it up with our boss," Markle said.

"You're damn right I will," Levi said as the door to the cabin opened, and Archer walked out with a big-ass grin on his face, followed by Jock, Brant, and Grant, who were all laughing. Fucking Brant and his Coast Guard connections.

"That was epic!" Archer shouted, holding his arms out to his sides like he was hailing a crowd.

"Get these things *off* me!" Levi glowered at his brothers and friends. "You're dead. You scared the hell out of Joey and Tara!" His nostrils flared as he fought against the handcuffs. *Fuck it.* He lowered his shoulder and charged forward, wrists still bound, but the officers yanked him back.

Tara sprinted onto the Coast Guard boat, and before Archer could say a word, she punched him in the jaw, and she didn't stop there, slapping at his chest and arms and pushing him backward. "You big jerk! Look what you did to Joey!"

Levi didn't know if he could love her more than he did at that moment.

Archer grabbed Tara's hands. "*Relax.* Joey is not traumatized." He called out, "Nice job, squirt! You deserve an Emmy for that performance."

Levi turned just in time to see his sweet, sneaky daughter high-fiving Jesse and Brent.

"You can take off those cuffs now," Archer said, and as they removed the handcuffs from Levi's wrists, Archer cocked a brow at Tara. "You might want to put a little muscle behind your punch next time, sweetheart. I've had bee stings that hurt worse."

Levi's hands fisted as he stalked toward Archer. "You want muscle, I've got plenty of it."

Jock stepped between them. "Whoa, Levi. Take a breath."

"You *know* what Tara's going through," Levi seethed.

Archer held his hands up in surrender. "Hey, man. I'm sorry. I didn't think of that. But in all fairness, Indi didn't need the prank you all pulled on her, either."

"That was *different*," Levi said sharply. "We didn't make her think you were being dragged through hell."

"And it was a great prank," Brant said, and Jock and Grant nodded in agreement.

"I heard it was *epic*," Jesse shouted from the other boat.

"I only wish we'd been there to see it," Brent said.

Tara touched Levi's arm. "It's okay. I knew you didn't do anything wrong. I was just scared for Joey. But you've got to admit, they got us good."

"Hell yeah, they did," Petty Officer Markle said. "But now we've got to get back to work, so how about you all take this party to your own boat and *don't* give us a reason to come back?"

When Archer and the others moved toward Brent's boat, Levi hiked a thumb at them. "You're leaving these guys with *us*, and you trust me not to throw them overboard?"

The Coast Guard officers shifted unsure glances to Brant.

"He's *kidding*," Brant reassured them. "Really. We're cool. Tell them, Levi."

Levi chuckled and headed back to Brent's boat.

As usual, it didn't take long to put the prank behind them. They ended up having a fantastic afternoon fishing, joking around, and playing charades with Joey. Tara got a slew of great pictures, and it was awesome being able to kiss her and hold her hand or put his arms around her without worrying about who might see them. He enjoyed paying her back for her early-morning ass wiggling with whispered dirty promises and furtive touches, getting her all worked up. He'd been happy to make up for it when Joey was busy with her uncles, and he and Tara snuck down to the cabin for a quick make-out session.

By the time Brent and Jesse dropped them off at the dock and headed to the island to drop off the others, Joey and Tara wore the glow of a day well spent. They were walking beside him, holding hands, and it was a great feeling to see Tara so happy with all that was going on.

"Who wants to go to the boardwalk?" Levi asked as he tossed their bag in the back of the Durango.

"Mememe!" Joey shouted.

Levi glanced at Tara. "Unless you're too tired?"

"When have I ever been too tired for *anything*?" she asked with a naughty smirk.

"You do have incredible stamina." He swore they were both catching up on years of repressed sexual energy, because they were insatiable for each other. He took her hand, drawing her into a kiss.

Joey grabbed Tara's other hand, tugging them both toward the boardwalk. "Come *on*. You can kiss on the boardwalk."

The boardwalk wasn't lined with brightly colored shops that sold chintzy souvenirs, like other coastal towns boasted. Instead, the shops had the charm of a New England town with cedar siding and weather-beaten wooden signs, reminding Levi of home. There were a few souvenir shops, but they sold pieces of art and other crafts made by local artisans. There were no ugly hotels looming over the beach, only two-story motels with wide balconies, built in the same fashion as the shops.

As they walked down the boardwalk, Joey moved between Levi and Tara, holding both their hands, talking a mile a minute, and letting go when they meandered into a shop, then reclaiming her position as they walked to the next one.

The smell of popcorn and the faint *ring*ing sounds of the arcade brought Levi's mind back to the moment. The arcade was just up ahead, nestled between Hidden Treasures and Sally's Saltwater Taffy & Fudge. Joey loved the arcade. He glanced at Tara, and they shared a knowing look. As if on cue, Joey said, "Can we play in the arcade?"

"You mean, can you *lose* in a game of air hockey?" Levi teased.

"I'm not gonna *lose*," Joey insisted.

"I don't know, sweets. Your old dad is pretty good."

"Then I get Aunt Tara on my team!" Joey looked hopefully up at Tara.

"Girl power." Tara high-fived Joey. "You're going down, old man Steele."

He held her gaze. "I'll gladly get down on my knees for you whether I win or lose."

She shot him an incredulous look as they headed into the arcade, instantly surrounded by the sounds of *ping*ing pinball games, computerized explosions, kids joking around, and teenagers shouting. They played two games of air hockey, each team winning one. Levi let them win the third game, and Joey cheered, "We won!" and launched herself into Tara's arms. The two of them grinned like they'd won the Olympics, making throwing the game totally worth it, even if they spent the rest of the afternoon not letting him live it down.

They played Skee-Ball, Pac-Man, raced motorcycles, and

shot basketballs into hoops. Levi pretended to be a dinosaur, distracting the girls as they shot plastic rifles in a *Jurassic Park* game, and Tara got him back when they played Whac-A-Mole and she tried to whack Levi instead of the moles. Joey thought that was hilarious.

When they walked out nearly an hour later, Levi reached for Tara's hand, pulling her into a kiss.

"*Da-ad.* Your lips are going to get worn out."

"You think so?" He grabbed her under the arms and lifted his squealing daughter over his head. "I have been kissing you since the day you were born, and my lips aren't worn out yet." She giggled as he planted a hard kiss on her cheek and set her on her feet.

"Let's go see Brooke!" Joey ran toward the blue awning above the door to Brooke's Bytes.

Levi drew Tara into a not-so-quick kiss before giving her a swat on her ass and following Joey in. Tara glowered over her shoulder at him.

Music was playing on the jukebox, and most of the tables and booths were taken by customers.

"Hey there!" Brooke said from behind the counter. The vivacious brunette wore a blue apron with BROOKE'S BYTES across her chest. Her high ponytail swung as she hurried out from behind the counter, around the customers sitting on red vinyl swiveling stools, and hugged Joey. "How are you, beautiful? Still glowing from winning a trophy, I see."

Joey giggled. "We went out on Uncle Jesse and Uncle Brent's boat, and…" She proceeded to give Brooke a blow-by-blow description of their day, including the prank and every game they played at the arcade. "And I'm selling lemonade at a yard sale this weekend. Can you come?"

"I will be there with money in my pocket," Brooke promised.

"Yay! Guess what else." Before Brooke could get a word out, Joey said, "Daddy and Aunt Tara are boyfriend and girlfriend now."

Levi laughed, and Tara blushed.

"So the rumor *is* true. It's about time you two figured things out." Brooke wiggled her shoulders and hugged Tara. "I'm so happy for you guys."

"Tara has loved my dad since before she knew what love meant," Joey said, surprising Levi, and from the look on Tara's face, surprising her, too. "Right, Tara?"

Tara looked a little embarrassed. "That's right, but I forgot you heard that."

"I didn't forget." Joey shrugged.

"That's not news to me, girl," Brooke said. "You two have been tiptoeing around what we've all seen for way too long. Which reminds me, did Cassidy get ahold of you about doing the photography for her and Wyatt's wedding in September?"

"Yes. She called me yesterday," Tara said. "Luckily, I had scheduled only one shoot that weekend, and it was on Sunday, so I can do their wedding. I can't wait."

She'd been over the moon when she'd told Levi about it yesterday. He was thrilled because it gave Tara another reason to come back to Harborside, and he and Joey would be at the wedding.

Brooke raised her brows. "It won't be long. September is right around the corner."

"And then they can have a *baby*," Joey exclaimed. "Grandma Shelley said after people get married, they have babies and she's waiting for Daphne and Jock to have a baby." She looked up at Levi. "Are you and Aunt Tara going to get married? Because I think I'd like a baby sister. I love playing with Hadley."

"*Aw*. You two would make the cutest babies," Brooke chimed in.

Tara's eyes bloomed wide. "We *just* started dating."

"So?" Joey's brow furrowed. "In *Cinderella* the prince put the shoe on her foot and then they were married, and in *Tangled*, they kissed and then they were married."

"Honey, they skipped time in movies," Levi tried to explain.

"No, they didn't," she insisted. "You two love each other, right?"

"Yes, but real life is a little more complicated than fairy tales," Levi explained.

Tara crouched beside Joey. "You know I love you and I love your daddy, but I'm not ready for babies yet, Joey. Maybe one day I will be, but how about if we just enjoy what we have right now and not try to rush it? It's much harder to do all the things we do together with a baby to care for."

"I *guess*. Can I go choose a song on the jukebox?" Joey asked. The jukebox was rigged to play without needing quarters.

"Sure," Brooke said. "I'll go with you."

Levi put his arm around Tara, pulling her closer. "Sorry about that."

"She's just trying to put all the pieces together."

"Maybe she can help us figure it out." He kissed her, and the song "Shake It Off" came on.

Joey and Brooke started dancing, and Joey yelled, "*Dad. Tara.* Dance with us!"

As they went to join them, Levi whispered, "I don't ever want to shake you off."

Tara fluttered those long lashes and squeezed his hand as she said, "Same."

AFTER EXPLORING THE boardwalk, they kicked off their shoes and played on the beach. Joey skipped and ran and did cartwheels, and when they went down by the water, Levi scooped up Tara, pretending he was going to throw her in.

Joey ran in front of him, hands outstretched, trying to stop him. "*Don't*, Daddy! She'll freeze."

"She will, huh?" He crouched like he was going to put Tara down, then swept his arm around Joey, lifting her over his other shoulder, and walked toward the water. They shrieked and pounded on his back. He laughed as he went ankle-deep in the water and they begged him to stop. The icy water swirled around his feet. "I don't know. Should I toss you in the sea and see if you turn into mermaids?"

"No!" they yelled, giggling.

"Should I feed you to the sharks?"

"No!" they said with more laughter.

"Then there's only one thing I can do." He walked in deeper, wetting the bottom of his jeans.

They shrieked. "*No, Dad!* Don't throw us in."

"*Levi!* If you do…" Tara warned.

"Fine." He feigned a sigh. "I'll guess I have no choice but to take you home, let you get dolled up, and take my favorite girls out to dinner."

As he carried them onto dry sand, a resounding "*Yay!*" rang out.

Twenty-One

TARA STOOD IN front of the mirror, assessing her outfit. She and Joey hadn't gotten ready together because they were just going to dinner and not to an event, and that gave Tara a little extra time to figure out her outfit. Levi had said to dress up, but she hadn't brought any dressy clothes with her. She'd had to get creative and wore a long light gray sweater with a thin belt around her waist. It hung to the middle of her thighs, and she'd paired it with cute black ankle boots. A knock sounded on the door. "Come in."

"Are you ready?" Joey stepped into the room, adorable in a pink sweater with a heart on the front and black leggings with pink flowers on them. "You look *pretty*."

"You think so?" Tara looked down at her bare legs, feeling a little naked.

"Uh-huh. Wait until you see Daddy. He's dressed up, too."

"Then I guess I'm ready. You look beautiful, cutie pie."

"Thanks. Daddy said I looked prettier than a skater princess. I didn't know I could be a skater *and* a princess."

"You can be anything you want."

"That's what Daddy said." She reached up and touched her headband. "Is my headband okay?" She leaned her head forward as if Tara couldn't see it.

"It's perfect." She reached for Joey's hand.

As they walked out of Tara's bedroom, Joey hollered, "*Dad*, she's ready!"

Levi met them in the living room. He looked striking in a black dress shirt that hugged his muscles and black slacks. Heat curled in her stomach at the way his gaze raked down her body, full of love and something animalistic she couldn't wait to explore. The last time she'd made any kind of entrance, the night of the dance, she'd had to tamp down her desires, thinking they were childish fantasies.

Look how far we've come, she thought as his loving eyes found hers.

"Wow, T. You look gorgeous. Almost as beautiful as Joey." He winked at Joey.

"Thanks. You're looking gorgeous yourself, Mr. Steele."

"Thank you, my sweet lady." He crooked his elbows. "Shall we go?"

They took his arms, and together they headed out the door.

WHEN LEVI PULLED into the parking lot of Crave, the fanciest restaurant in Harborside, Tara's jaw dropped. She'd read an article about the exclusive restaurant three years ago, when they were building it. She'd tracked down the owner to inquire about doing their photography for menus and advertisements, but he'd kindly turned her down, having already booked a photographer. Tara had been obsessed with the beautiful brick-and-cedar restaurant overlooking Cider Cove. Every table had a view of the water, and she'd heard rumors that it took months to get a table and nobody left without dropping a few hundred bucks. "Levi—"

"*Don't,*" he said softly and flashed that butterfly-inducing smile. "Remember how we talked about just saying thank you?"

It felt like a lifetime ago when they'd looked at houses together, and now all those touches, whispers, and boundary-testing moments made sense. Just like his words. *It's time to stop telling people what they don't have to do for you and learn to say thank you instead.* "Thank you, but—"

He pressed his lips to hers. "No *buts,* beautiful. You were enamored with this restaurant for months. It's time you enjoyed it."

You remembered. Her heart squeezed.

"I want to enjoy it," Joey chimed in from the back seat, and they both laughed.

As they walked up to the front door, Tara looked at Levi with wonder. He was always so busy with work and keeping track of Joey's practices and social calendar. How did he remember Tara poring over websites and articles three years ago?

He opened the massive arched door, and as they went inside, Joey and Tara were mesmerized by an arched pergola draped in colorful flowers and climbing vines, interspersed with twinkling lights.

"It's even more gorgeous than in the pictures," Tara said with awe.

"I want one of these, Daddy. Can you build one in our

house?"

"Maybe one day." He put his hand on Tara's back.

"Levi, we don't even need to eat dinner. Seeing this is..." She shook her head, at a loss for words. "I wish I had my camera."

"We'll have to come back sometime."

They went into the restaurant, which was even more elegant than the entryway, with brick walls steeped in greenery and vibrant, leafy plants that looked like they belonged in the Mediterranean. As they were led through a brick archway, Tara whispered, "How'd you get a reservation so fast?"

He kissed her cheek. "Where there's a will, there's a way."

They were seated in a room that had only three tables. A wall of glass gave way to a view of the cove. Soft blue and white lights led to a path from the slate patio that Tara knew they used for outdoor dining in warmer weather, through extravagant gardens, all the way down to the water's edge.

"Whoa, look." Joey pointed out the windows.

"It's beautiful, isn't it?" Levi reached for Tara's hand.

"Stunning," Tara said.

"I think it's magical," Joey said as a young, attractive waiter approached the table.

"Good evening. My name is Ricky, and I'll be serving you tonight." He placed glasses in front of each of them and filled them with ice water. Then he set champagne flutes in front them and filled Joey's with something that looked a lot like champagne.

"I can't drink that," Joey said.

"That's special champagne for kids," Ricky said.

Joey sat up taller, grinning. "Thank you."

Ricky poured champagne for Tara and Levi and placed the

rest of the bottle in an ice bucket beside Levi.

"Are we celebrating something?" Tara looked curiously at Levi.

Levi winked without answering as Ricky placed a basket of fresh bread that smelled heavenly on the table and set an enormous silver serving platter with a lid on it in front of Tara. "I'll be back shortly."

As the waiter walked away, Joey said, "What's in that?"

"I don't know." Tara looked at Levi. "What's going on?"

"Do we need a reason to celebrate?" He picked up his champagne flute and motioned for them to do the same. "Here's to feeling like the luckiest guy on earth and having dinner with the second-place skateboarding champ and the most talented—although not the most observant—photographer in Massachusetts."

As he clinked glasses with Joey, Tara said, "Not the most observant? What is *that* supposed to mean?"

"Just that you missed quite a few things, but I don't blame you. I mean, you're usually engrossed in Joey's sparkling personality, and when we're together, you're mesmerized by my good looks."

Joey giggled.

Tara's brow furrowed. "I still have no idea what you're talking about."

"Lift the lid," he said with a glimmer of mischief in his eyes.

"Lift it," Joey urged.

Excitement tingled in Tara's chest, and she glanced at Levi. "What are you up to?"

Levi shrugged, splaying his hands.

She held her breath as she lifted the silver lid, revealing a stack of photographs. On top was a picture of the three of them walking hand in hand on the boardwalk, with Joey in the middle, wearing the clothes they'd worn today. Emotions clogged her throat. "Who took these?"

"Cassidy. My house is full of pictures of the *old* us, and I adore them, but I want to put up pictures of the new us."

Tears welled in her eyes. "Oh, Levi," she whispered, admiring the picture and lifting it to see another.

"Can I see?" Joey got out of her chair and stood beside Tara.

"I haven't seen them yet, either." Levi came to Tara's other side, and they looked through the pictures.

There were several taken while they were at the boardwalk. Pictures of Tara and Joey high-fiving by the air hockey machine, while Levi looked on with so much love in his eyes, it jumped off the photo, and of Levi and Tara kissing while Joey shot a basketball, and Levi smacking Tara's butt as she walked into Brooke's Bytes.

"Daddy!" Joey giggled.

There were pictures of the three of them on the beach and of Levi carrying them into the water, and many more of Tara and Joey taken on outings over the last few days—of her and Joey on a seesaw at the park and lying on their backs on a blanket in the sand. Tara was holding up one of Joey's books, reading to her.

"I remember that," Joey said happily.

"Me too. We had fun that day."

As Tara looked through the pictures, she fell even deeper in love with Levi and Joey and the idea of them as a family. There was a picture of Joey skateboarding while Tara stood on the sidelines with her camera to her eye, and one of Levi hugging Joey in the front yard with Tara watching them, her head slightly tilted, emotions practically oozing from her pores. There was a picture of Tara watering the gardens, Joey caught midair as she jumped in front of the hose.

"You little rascal," Levi teased.

There was even a picture of Tara and Joey sitting on the grass in Levi's backyard surrounded by boxes they'd taken out of the shed, drinking lemonade and playing Go Fish. They'd worked hard to organize the shed, and Joey was so proud of what they'd done, she'd taken Levi out to see their progress each night. Tara couldn't believe Cassidy had been able to take all those photos without her knowing. In the last picture, their Harborside friends were gathered around a bonfire, and Tara was sitting with Joey in her lap, fast asleep. Joey couldn't have been more than six years old.

Tara's throat thickened with emotion. "When was this taken?"

"I took it two years ago. It's my favorite picture of the two of you. It's been on my phone and I've kept it to myself. But now that I know why it's the picture I look at when I'm having a bad day or missing home, I thought we could put it up."

Tears welled in Tara's eyes. She looked up at him, trying to blink them dry, but this was the best surprise she'd ever been given, and she couldn't stop them as she choked out, "I love them."

"I love you, T," he said softly.

"I love you, too," Joey said. "I wish you weren't leaving this weekend."

"*Same*," Tara managed, sliding her arm around Joey's waist and hugging her against her side. She had no idea how she was going to leave on Sunday. How could two weeks feel like two months? She could hardly remember what it was like before she and Levi had come together. She remembered, of course, but it felt like she was thinking about someone else's life. As if *this* was how they were always supposed to be.

She wiped her eyes, trying to pull herself together. "I don't know how you and Cassidy pulled this off. I never saw her take any of these."

"Me either. She was sneaky," Joey added.

"That was the point," Levi said, his warm brown eyes holding Tara's. "A wise and beautiful photographer once told me she took some of her best pictures during the most unexpected moments, and everything about *you*, blondie, is as unexpected as it is beautiful."

Twenty-Two

SATURDAY ROLLED IN with warm sunny skies, perfect for their yard sale. Levi had gotten up early and gone for a run to try to clear his head. The past two weeks had gone by too quickly. Tara was going back to the island tomorrow, facing her mother, getting back to work, looking for a place to live and a photography studio. He'd known the time was coming, but it still felt like it had crept up on him, and every time he tried to talk to Tara about it, she silenced him with a kiss. *I don't want to think about not seeing you and Joey every day. I just want to live in the moment.* Not that he was complaining about the kisses, but there was no avoiding the inevitable. He knew that was how she handled things, on her own, in her own head. He'd let her do that for the past few days. But he *wanted* to go back with her, to face her mother together, and when he'd finally gotten a word out about it, she'd insisted on doing it alone to show her mother she could handle anything.

He got that. He really did. But her life had imploded because of *him*, and he wanted to fix it. To protect her from any further hurt, and a phone call and a ferry ride wouldn't cut it. But she wasn't buying it, and the run hadn't helped. Neither had his shower or the blueberry waffles they'd had for breakfast. So he grabbed another box from the shed and tried not to think about it as he carried it out front, where the girls were putting out tables for the yard sale.

He couldn't believe how much crap he'd accumulated, but he'd been storing junk in the shed since he'd first bought the place. Tara had tried to get him to look through the things she'd planned to sell, but he hadn't wanted to waste what little time they had left going through discarded items he hadn't thought of in years.

"Look at my sign, Daddy," Joey said as he carried the last of the boxes out.

She and Tara were taping a posterboard to the front of the table she was using for her lemonade stand. He went to check it out, admiring Tara's long legs and gorgeous ass on his way. She looked sexy as sin in white shorts and a powder-blue long-sleeve V-neck. She flashed that secret smile that always got him going. She enjoyed torturing him like that, and he sure didn't hate it. But his daughter was watching, so he focused on the sign and not the urge to bend Tara over the table.

JOEY'S HOMEMADE LEMONADE 50¢ was written across the top of a large posterboard. Below it was a drawing of a glass of lemonade, complete with ice cubes, and beside it were rainbows, stars, and THE BEST YOU'VE EVER HAD! Joey had been so excited last night, Tara had written THANK YOU on about fifty napkins, and Joey had signed each one like she was some kind of celebrity. He loved that Tara supported his little girl's whims as much as he did, and after all their hard work, he hoped people showed up this morning. Joey had told him last night that instead of buying herself stickers with the money she earned, she wanted to buy something special for Tara.

He'd pay people to show up if that was what it took so his little girl could fulfill her wish.

If only *life* were that easy. Maybe then he could pay someone to slow time.

His fucking heart was taking a beating lately. The funny thing was, he'd only thought about that particular organ one time before Tara, and that was when Joey was born. The first time he'd held her, he'd sworn he'd felt his heart swell so big he was worried he'd have chest pain from that day forward.

"Do you like it?" Joey asked, bringing him back to the moment.

"It's a great sign, sweets," he said. "I hope you sell a lot of lemonade."

"This is my money jar." She held up a mayonnaise jar with a handful of quarters in it and a blue ribbon tied in a bow around the middle. "Tara put quarters in it so people will think I've already had customers."

He stepped closer, putting his hand on Tara's back. "That was smart marketing, T."

"We girls have to stick together. Right, Joey?"

"Yup! Is it almost ten? I told everyone to come at ten."

Tara checked the time on her phone. "How did it get so late? We only have half an hour to finish setting up. Levi, you'd better get to the bank for change and put up the signs."

"I might do it for a kiss." He'd used that line a few times Friday night, when they'd hung the pictures that Cassidy had taken, as well as the one he'd printed from his phone. Tara and Joey had found cool frames for them, and Joey had kept the one of Tara reading to her for her nightstand.

Tara went up on her toes and kissed him.

"You too, peanut." Levi crouched.

"Da-ad."

He tapped his cheek.

Joey kissed it, then pushed him toward his truck. *"Go."*

Levi spent the next forty-five minutes putting out yard signs and getting change at the bank. On his way back, he picked up a few bags of ice for Joey's lemonade stand.

When he got home, there were a few cars parked along the road and a number of people wandering around the front yard. A couple was checking out the old patio furniture and kitchen chairs he'd forgotten were in the shed, and an elderly woman was surveying a table of kitchen items. Two kids were talking with Joey and drinking lemonade, and two more were checking out a bin of stuffed animals and a table littered with old games and puzzles. Tara was taking money from a woman for a stack of books. As he headed into the garage to find a cooler, he saw Joey's old plastic push toys, her first tricycle, an old umbrella stroller, and a table of her baby clothes.

He got a funny feeling in his gut and quickly grabbed a cooler. He dumped the ice into it and carried it out to Joey as the kids she'd been talking with went to join their parents.

"How's it going, peanut? I brought you ice." He set the cooler beside the table.

"Thanks. I've sold *six* cups of lemonade already."

"That's great. I'll be back. I need to check out a few things."

As he walked away, he nodded to a couple headed back to their car empty-handed. He went to the table of baby clothes, looking over Joey's old infant dresses and little knit caps. He held up a onesie Leni had given her with pink arrows pointing to the arms, legs, and head holes and YOU'VE GOT THIS,

DADDY scribbled down the middle. He held on to it as he picked up the yellow knit hat Gail Remington had made for Joey when she was a year old and the DADDY'S PRINCESS T-shirt that Jules had given her when she was a toddler. He found the pink frilly dress Joey had worn to her second birthday party. How could Tara get rid of those things? Didn't she know how much they meant to him?

He made his way from one table to the next, picking up Joey's first plastic baby spoon and fork and her Disney-princess blanket. The familiar rumble of motorcycles came into focus, and a couple of minutes later, the Dark Knights were on the scene, climbing off their bikes in their jeans and black leather vests, making their way to Joey's lemonade stand. Her excited greetings could probably be heard on the next block over.

Levi carried his things to Tara, who was shoving something into a box. "Hey, blondie." He leaned in for a kiss, and she eyed his armful of yard sale items.

"Hi. What are you doing with all of that?"

"Keeping it. I can't sell this stuff. It has sentimental value."

"But you said you went through the boxes, and it was all okay to sell."

"Yeah, well, I might have embellished. I *started* going through them, but I didn't want to waste time doing that when I could be with you."

"*Levi*, you should have told me. I would have gone through them with you."

"Sorry, but look at this." He set down the armload of things he was carrying and began showing her each item. "NAP QUEEN, with a little crown? How could you get rid of this?"

"She wasn't a great napper," Tara reminded him.

"I know, but what if one day she has a brother or sister and *they're* a great napper? How cute would it be if they wore the same things she did?"

"Aw, I love that idea. I'm sorry. I'll get all of Joey's old clothes off the tables."

"Hey, guys. I found my new coffee mug," Joker called from across the lawn, holding up a mug that said #1 DADDY.

"Like hell you did," Levi said. "Joey gave me that when she was six."

"And I'm going to give it a whole new meaning," Joker said, and the guys laughed.

Levi stalked over and snagged the mug out of his hand.

"Dude, it's chipped," Joker said.

"I don't give a shit if it's in pieces. My little girl picked it out for *me*, not for you and your Daddy kink."

"I found a better one for you, Joker." Ozzy picked up another mug and read the side of it aloud. "*Daddy's girl.*"

The guys cracked up.

"We're not getting rid of that one, either." Levi grabbed the mug and held his hands up. "Listen up, folks. The yard sale is *off.* We're not selling anything."

"Daddy!" Joey complained.

"We've got you covered, princess," Jesse said as he pulled out his wallet, and the guys gathered around Joey's table, whipping out their own wallets.

Tara carried a box over to Levi. "You can put your stuff with mine."

"Yours?" He eyed the box curiously.

"Joey must have taken this stuff out of the pile I wanted to keep. I found them a little while ago, but don't worry. I'll pay you for them."

"In sexual favors maybe." He kissed her. "So you *are* as

sentimental as me, after all." As he put the mugs in the box, he picked up one of Joey's books from when she was a toddler. "*Wrangler and Mouse*. You gave Joey this. It was one of her favorites."

"Mm-hm."

He leaned against the table and opened the book, skimming the story about a mouse who lived under a house. Every time it ventured outside, a mean cat chased it away. The little boy who lived in the house, Wrangler, befriended Mouse, keeping her safe from the cat. *Wrangler snuck Mouse up to his bedroom and shared his snacks with her, making her feel safe, while he told her stories that made her happy. When Wrangler wasn't around and the mean cat scared Mouse, she'd run back under the house and thought about those stories until she wasn't afraid anymore.* Levi's heart took another hit. How could he have missed the similarities? Did Tara have this book *made* for Joey? He turned the page, reading more of the story. *One day, Wrangler surprised Mouse with a pretty little house of her own, which he kept in his closet, so he could always make sure she was safe. And from that day on, every night he told Mouse stories and shared his snacks, and they lived happily ever after.*

He closed the book, taking in Tara's bashful smile. "I must've read this to Joey dozens of times. You had this made for her, didn't you? How did I miss that it was about us?"

She shrugged one shoulder. "It wasn't meant to be figured out."

"Why Wrangler?"

"Because they were the only jeans you wore back then."

Christ, he loved her. "When did you write it?"

"When I was thirteen. But in the original story, the mouse lived in the pantry. When I decided to make it into a book for

Joey, I was afraid you might put two and two together, so I changed the mouse from living in the pantry to living under the house."

"Clever *and* beautiful. You're full of surprises." He put the book in the box and pulled her into his arms. "I think I just fell even more in love with you."

"In that case, maybe I'll have to write a whole series about Wrangler and Mouse."

"I'm afraid that'd be moving from children's books to erotic romance."

LEVI TOOK DOWN the yard sale signs, and though they'd had to deal with about a dozen people who had already seen them, they'd understood Levi's change of heart. His buddies had stayed for a while, and as promised, Brooke had stopped by, and she'd brought Cassidy, Wyatt, Wyatt's twin, Delilah, and her girlfriend, Ashley. Everyone helped move boxes and put away tables, and there was no shortage of fun banter.

After they left, Levi, Tara, and Joey grabbed lunch, and then they took Joey skateboarding. Later that evening, while Tara was returning work calls, Levi and Joey went to pick up dinner. Tara was booked with weddings and events for most of the summer and was already booking fall and winter sessions. She did her best not to schedule too much on the weekends, leaving her free to see Levi for a night, but some clients had only weekend availability, and events were always on weekends. She was beginning to stress over how their relationship would work. If she photographed an event on Saturday evenings, sometimes they didn't end until ten or later, and she had appointments on several Sundays, which meant she and Levi could see each other for only a few stolen hours. With the ferry rides, it didn't leave much time.

When she got a call from Carey, she was glad for the distraction. "Hi."

"Hey, sis. How's life? How're you holding up? Any word from Mom?"

"I'm okay, but she hasn't called. You know how she is. She'll just pretend it never happened."

"Yeah, that's Mom. Remember when she told me she was never speaking to me again when I grew my hair out and said I was going to live in my van? She'll get over it."

"I'm not sure I will."

"I know that feeling. Have you heard from Amelia?"

Even hearing her sister's name made her heart race. "No. Does she know what happened?"

"Yeah. Mom told her."

A pang of hurt pierced her chest. "*God*, Mom *never* protects me."

"I'm sure it feels like that. Especially after the crap she pulled. But I don't think she told her to hurt you. Amelia *is* Joey's mother."

"Still. That's *my* news to share, not hers."

"Yeah, well. I'm sorry about that. But if Amelia hasn't called you, she probably doesn't care that you're with Levi."

"Of *course* she doesn't care. Why would she? She didn't even want him when…" No, she wasn't going there. "It doesn't matter. How are you?"

"I'm cool, but I'm worried about you."

"I'm fine, or I will be."

"How're you and Levi? Is this shit with Mom coming between you two?"

"No. We're great. He's totally supportive and thinks she needs to make the next move. I'm happier than I've ever been on that front. It's just when I think of Mom that I get sad or angry. She's just so..."

"Annoying? Selfish? Mean?"

"I never thought of her as mean before, but after the things she said last weekend, I wonder if her cutting comments were purposeful after all."

"I wish I had the answers, but I haven't spent much time with Mom in years. Robert said you're going to a charity drive, and she'll be there. I'm at Drake's place in Bayside tonight. Do you want me to head over and run interference?"

Her brothers had always been willing to drop everything to be there for her if she asked. She'd never been very good at the asking part, but it felt good knowing they were there. "No, thanks. I can handle it."

"Okay, but if you change your mind, call me."

Levi and Joey came through the front door, and she said, "I appreciate that. I've got to run. Love you."

"Love you, too. Tell Levi hello and give Joey a squeeze for me."

"Will do."

As she ended the call, Joey yelled, "Be right back!" and bolted up the stairs.

"How'd your calls go?" Levi asked as he carried their dinner into the kitchen.

"Good," she said, and told him about her call with Carey.

Joey bounded downstairs. "Dad! Can we eat outside?"

They ate dinner on the deck, joking about their flubbed

attempt at a yard sale and Levi needing to build a shed just for all the old junk he wanted to keep. He teased Joey about buying the shed since she'd raked in big bucks with her lemonade stand. They played Silver Island Monopoly, which Levi's parents had given Joey last Christmas, and watched *Tangled*, and even though it was a wonderful, fun evening, Tara spent the whole time trying not to think about her departure looming like a villain in the shadows. She knew she was being silly since she was only going to be a ferry ride away, and she'd be back next weekend. She had clients Friday afternoon and Saturday morning, but she could be in Harborside by two on Saturday. Levi had offered to come to the island instead, but it didn't make sense for him to come there until she figured out her living situation.

Now it was Joey's bedtime, and she asked Tara to read to her, but she'd insisted Tara wait downstairs while she got ready for bed. Levi had gone upstairs to shower, and Tara was pacing in the living room, wishing she could get out of her own head.

"Ready!" Joey hollered from upstairs.

Tara headed upstairs and found Levi standing by Joey's bed and Joey standing *on* her bed, bouncing. Both were grinning from ear to ear. Tara let out a little laugh. "What's going on in here?"

Joey flopped down on her butt. "I got you a present!"

"A *present*? Why?" She watched Joey push a hand beneath her pillow and pull out a box with a red bow on it.

"Because you gave up your whole spring break so that I could go to my tournament."

"I don't get spring break, silly, and you don't have to give me anything. I wanted to be here with you and your dad. It's my favorite place to be."

"I know, but I want to give it to you." Joey climbed off the bed and handed her the box.

The way she said she knew, so confidently, was the only gift Tara needed, but she took the box, admiring the tiny flowers Joey had drawn on it. "Thank you. The flowers are beautiful."

"Those are our gardens. Open it!"

"She's been dying to give it to you," Levi said.

Tara untied the bow and lifted the lid, withdrawing a mug that had AUNTICORN written above a picture of a dancing unicorn, and LIKE A NORMAL AUNT, BUT MORE AWESOME written below it. "*Joey*. I love it."

"I knew you'd like it!"

Tara started thinking about when she could have bought it and putting the pieces together. "Did you buy this with the money you earned today?"

"Uh-huh," Joey said proudly.

"But you wanted stickers, and—"

"I changed my mind. Auntie Jules and Bellamy sent me stickers, remember?" She climbed back onto her bed and began bouncing again.

Tara clutched the mug to her chest, finally understanding why Levi had reacted so strongly to seeing the mugs Joey had given him on the yard sale tables. She'd never make that mistake again. "I'll use it every day. Thank you."

"Yay!" She flopped onto her butt. "Now will you read to me?"

"I'd love to." Tara sat on the bed beside her and set the mug on the nightstand, touched once again at the sight of the picture of them at the park Joey had chosen to put there.

"Go shower, Dad. You can read after you're done."

"*Hey*," Tara warned softly.

Levi arched a brow at Joey. "When did you get so bossy?"

"Sorry, Dad." Joey snuggled up to Tara. "Will you *please* read to me after your shower?"

"That's better, and yes, I will." He pressed a kiss to the top of her head, then did the same to Tara, giving her shoulder a squeeze.

As Levi walked out, Tara began reading. He stopped in the doorway and turned. He didn't say anything, just watched them for a minute, looking like he was trying to memorize the sight of them. Tara recognized that look because she'd been doing the same thing with them all day, and she planned on making her and Levi's last night together *unforgettable* by giving him *plenty* of naughty images to memorize.

WHEN LEVI CAME back to read to Joey, Tara kissed her good night and climbed off the bed, giving Levi what she hoped was a seductive look. She slowed as she walked past, whispering, "Meet me in my room when you're done."

She hurried downstairs and showered, using the lavender body wash Levi loved, and put on the pink babydoll nightie Jules and Bellamy had sent her and the silk robe overtop. She'd been saving the nightie for a special night, and although she was comfortable in her own skin with Levi, it took a different type of confidence to greet him wearing a sexy nightie with tiny lace triangles covering her breasts, a satin tie just below them, and a pleated, transparent skirt that stopped just below her cooch. It had taken some working up to it. She started to put on the pretty pink lace thong and decided against it, hoping to give

Levi a little extra thrill. Thinking it over, she took off the robe, too, for easier access.

Tonight her secret siren was taking control.

She got excited just thinking about the moment he'd realize she was naked beneath the nightie. She lit candles on the dresser and thought about putting candles on the nightstand, but sometimes they got a little wild, and she didn't want to take a chance of knocking it off or a piece of clothing landing on it and catching fire. She heard him walking around upstairs, and her nerves prickled.

She turned off the lights and cracked open the door, suddenly nervous about where she should wait. She heard him coming downstairs and debated her options. Lying on the bed? Sitting on the edge of the bed? Peering out from the open door?

His footsteps in the hall made her pulse skyrocket, and at the same time, a sense of calm came over her, because she knew it didn't matter if she was posed or not. He'd love her either way.

She stood just inside the door, and when he pushed it open, his gaze slid down her body so lasciviously, her mouth went dry, her nipples pebbled, and her thighs squeezed together to combat the tingling between her legs.

He closed and locked the door, reaching for her. "Where has *this* pretty little nightie been hiding?"

"I was saving it for a special night."

"Every night is special with you, T." As he lowered his mouth to hers, his hands slipped beneath the skirt, and a low, hungry rumbling sound climbed up his throat, and then she was lifted off her feet and tossed onto the bed, and he was stripping off his clothes. He came down over her with a predatory look in his eyes that sent her body reeling and pinned her hands beside her head, his heavy cock nestled against her.

"So much for my fantasy of seducing you," she said teasingly.

He lowered his face beside hers, brushing the tip of his nose along her cheek. "Baby, you seduce me every time you walk into a room."

Her heart soared as his mouth covered hers, his talented tongue making love to her mouth, delving, probing, sliding along her teeth and the roof of her mouth, as if he wanted to inhabit all of her. She was right there with him, craving his taste, kissing him harder, more passionately. When the broad head of his cock pressed against her wetness, she made an "*Uh-uh*" sound into their kisses, still wanting to be the seducer. He took her in a series of slow, intoxicating kisses, leaving her light-headed as he gazed down at her with so much emotion, it penetrated her skin, cradling her heart.

"*God*, baby," he said in a long, low breath. "How am I going to get through a single night without you?"

All the emotions she'd been holding back rushed forward, and she struggled against them. "Let's not talk about that right now. I wanted to give you a fantasy you'd always remember, and I can't if I get sad about leaving."

He touched his forehead to hers. "Do you have any idea how crazy I am about you?"

"About as crazy as I am about you."

He kissed her softly. "Tell me about this fantasy you've planned for me."

"Tell you?" She hadn't planned on *talking* about it, but she couldn't chicken out now. "You weren't supposed to be on top of me."

He gave her a quick kiss and rolled onto his back, naked

and beautiful, and clasped his hands behind his head. "I'm all yours, baby. Have at it."

"I saw this going differently in my head." She buried her face in his shoulder.

He hiked a thumb at the door. "Want me to go out and come back in?"

"*No.* I just had this whole thing in my head, where I'd crook my finger." She crooked her finger as she said it. "And you'd come closer, and then I'd kiss you and run my hands over your chest, and—"

"Like this?" He took her hands and dragged them down his chest.

"Yes." His skin was warm, and his nipples hardened against her fingers. "Then I'd tease you a little." She shifted so she could tease his nipple with her tongue, and he let out a sexy hiss.

"I do like the way you tease. What else?"

"I'd kiss you like this." She kissed a path down his stomach, slowing to nip at his abs, his muscles flexing against her lips.

"Damn, baby. I *love* this fantasy."

"And I'd take off your sweats and drop to my knees." She lifted his cock off his stomach and dragged her tongue along the crown. Her eyes remained trained on him, loving the tightening of his jaw, the sharp inhalation through clenched teeth as he threaded his fingers in her hair, sending ripples of desire through her. She moved lower, licking the base and along his balls. They tightened against her tongue, and his hands fisted as "*Fuuck*," fell from his lips.

She did it again, and he growled as she sank her teeth into his inner thigh, sucking hard. His hips thrust and he fisted his dick at the base with one hand, his other still tangled in her hair. "*Jesus*, Tara."

Gone was the unsurety she'd felt at first, pushed aside by that secret siren he lured out so often. She moved her mouth over his cock and licked the swollen glans, his every muscle going taut. "Want me to suck it?"

His eyes blazed into her. "I want to fuck your mouth, baby, and I want to do it while my mouth is on you. Lie on your back."

Lust consumed her, pulsing between her legs as she shook her head and whipped off her nightie. "I want to be on top."

She'd never done this before, but she had a feeling she'd have more control on top, and as she moved over him, straddling his face, she had visions of suffocating him and stilled as she fisted his cock. But she needn't have worried. He grabbed her hips, guiding her to his mouth, and *holy cow*. The angle and the feel of his strong hands holding her right where he wanted her magnified every sensation. White-hot pinpricks chased over her flesh as he feasted on her.

"*Don't stop*," she pleaded, and lowered her mouth over his shaft, working him with everything she had. Sucking, licking, stroking, using teeth, tongue, and hands. She licked her hand, then stroked him *tight*. His appreciative, guttural sounds had her riding his mouth faster, harder.

He growled, "You're going to make me come."

Dark desires consumed her, emboldened her. *"Good."* She worked him faster, wanting everything he had to give.

He growled, his hands moving to her ass, spreading her cheeks, his fingertips teasing over uncharted territory, sending thrills whipping through her like a hurricane. She tried to concentrate on making him come as he teased and devoured her, wetting his finger with her arousal and pushing the tip where nothing had ever gone before. Lights flashed behind her closed lids, and she squeezed him tighter, quickening her efforts and moaning around his cock. He did something extraordinary with his tongue, catapulting her into oblivion as his hips thrust—hard—and the first hot jet hit the back of her throat. Neither slowed down, moaning, stroking, licking, sucking, and when she couldn't swallow any more, she pulled his shaft from her mouth, and he came on her breasts. He sucked her clit, pushing that fingertip inside her again, sending her right back up to the peak—and held her there, suspended in a state of ecstasy, her entire being electrified, his hips still pumping his cock through her fist.

When they finally floated down from their high, he guided her back to the mattress and went up on his knees, moving his hips between her legs. His gaze lingered on her breasts, covered in his come. She felt a flush of embarrassment and ran her fingers over the stickiness. The carnal look in his eyes spurred her on, and she lifted her fingers to her lips, painting them with his arousal, and made a show of licking it off.

"God, T. You are my *every* fantasy come true."

"*Same*," she whispered.

He wiped the come from her breasts with his hand and used it to stroke his cock to attention. *So. Freaking. Hot.*

She reached for him as he came down over her, and he laced their fingers together, kissing her softly. His gaze turned serious. "I know you're wondering how this is going to work, and talking about it scares you, so know this—"

"Can we not?" Her voice cracked, fading away.

He brushed his lips over hers. "I *need* to say a few things, and I need you to hear them. I respect your need to face your mother alone, but don't misconstrue that for me not wanting to be there for you, to protect you, and stand up with you."

"I'm not," she said, holding back tears.

"We'll see each other every week. I know you have events planned, but we'll make it happen. I don't care if I get an hour with you, ten minutes, or all night, or if we take a walk, make love, or just sit at the ferry landing. I will make *sure* we see each other every week, okay?"

She nodded, a tear sliding down her cheek. "And Joey?"

He kissed the tear. "And Joey. I love you, T, and I know we've only just begun, and your life is on the island, and our lives are here, but I promise we'll figure this out."

She nodded, tears streaking her cheeks, too full of *them* to speak.

He held her tight as their bodies came together, and she soaked in his strength, his tenderness, his *love*. When he kissed her deeper, *hungrier*, his touches becoming rougher, she knew he was trying to love her worries away, and he'd do it until morning if that's what it took.

Twenty-Three

TARA HAD LEFT Levi and Joey dozens of times, and most of them were fairly seamless, other than Joey's pleading for Tara to stay. That always broke her heart, but Tara would carry that heartbreak and her secret love for Levi onto the ferry, and by the time she arrived on the island, she'd tucked it so far down, all anyone saw was happy-go-lucky Tara. But this time, as Levi put her bags in her trunk and Joey clung to her hand, she felt like her heart was being ripped from her chest. It shouldn't be so hard. Especially after all the promises she and Levi had made last night. But she didn't want to go back and deal with her mother or figure out her life. She wanted to figure out her life *there*, with them, and continue what they'd started building.

Her father had called and given her an out from taking pictures at the clothing drive, and she'd been tempted to accept. But she couldn't build a life with Levi and Joey when her own life was so unsettled. She had to figure out where things stood with her mother, or it would hang over their heads like a rain cloud waiting to burst.

"You're all set, blondie." Levi closed the trunk.

"No." Joey threw her arms around Tara's waist. "Can't you stay? I don't want you to go."

"I wish I could." Tara hugged her, Joey's tears making her tear up, too. "We're going to see each other more often. I promise."

"Daddy said you're going to get an apartment or a house on the island. Will you have room for me?"

"I'll *always* have room for you. I might stay at Aunt Jules's old apartment for a little while. There's only one bedroom, but I'll make sure there's a really comfy couch. Okay?"

She nodded, more tears spilling from her eyes. "*Please* don't go."

Tara hugged her, struggling to keep her own tears at bay. Levi's jaw was tight, his eyes dry but as sad as theirs. She drew back so she could see Joey's face and wiped her eyes. "I had so much fun these last two weeks. I want you to promise me something. I want you to have the *best* day today. Water our plants and maybe spray Daddy with the hose."

Joey nodded, swiping at her tears. "I want you to have a good day, too."

"I will. But I'd better go before I miss my ferry." *Or break down in tears.* She gave Joey another quick hug and looked longingly at Levi as he reached for her.

"Get in here, T." He drew her into his arms, holding her so tight, she was pretty sure he didn't want to ever let her go. He slipped his hands into her back pockets and pressed his cheek to hers, whispering, "I don't know what you've done to me, but this is harder than when I moved away from the island."

Too choked up to speak, she closed her eyes for a moment to ward off tears.

He pressed a kiss to her cheek, and then he gazed into her eyes and slid one hand beneath her hair, his thumb brushing over the spot he'd just kissed. "I love you, blondie."

"*Same*" was all she could manage.

"Call me when you get a chance. Let me know how things go with your mom."

She nodded, and they kissed, a sweet, Joey-appropriate kiss, and then she climbed into her car and started it up, quickly taking a mental inventory to make sure she hadn't forgotten anything. She knew she hadn't, but it helped to stave off the sadness.

At least until she glanced at Joey, clinging to Levi with tears in her eyes and waving. Tara rolled down the window. "I love you both. See you soon."

With a wave, she drove away. Joey ran to the end of the driveway, waving as Tara drove down the street. When Tara turned the corner, tears slipped down her cheeks.

By the time she boarded the ferry, she'd stopped crying, and as they pulled away from the dock, she began her silent pep talk, shoving her feelings down deep as she'd done so many times before. Her phone rang, and she reached into her back pocket for it and pulled it out along with an unfamiliar folded piece of paper. Her mind tiptoed back to Levi sliding his hands into her back pockets. She let Jules's call go to voicemail and quickly unfolded the note.

Blondie, before we got together, my father asked me if I was lonely, and I said I wasn't. It was true, but the last few weeks made me realize it was because when you were around, you brought so much joy into our lives, it held me over between visits. This time everything is different. Now that I know what it feels like to hold you, kiss you, love you, and do dirty things to you (and vice versa), I'm already lonely for you, and you haven't even left yet. As I write this, you're lying next to me in bed, fast asleep. Know I'm with you today as you face your mother, and as you take the first steps in figuring out how to move forward, be sure you're leaving room for me and Joey to walk beside you. XO, Levi

Tara swiped at the tears wetting her cheeks, wondering how she was supposed to figure out her life, when she'd left the best parts of it behind.

TARA TEXTED JULES before driving off the ferry and made plans to meet her and Bellamy at Jules and Grant's bungalow after seeing two properties she'd lined up with Charmaine. She drove to Seaport, remembering the night Levi had taken her out to dinner. Her life had changed so much since then. *She'd* changed.

She wasn't the lovesick girl who had pined after Levi and taken shit from her mother and sister. For the first time in her life, she felt like a woman. She didn't know if it was from standing up to her mother or her relationship with Levi, but she had a feeling it was both.

As she drove toward Gallow Pointe, where the charity drive was taking place, she gave herself a pep talk, mentally preparing to see her mother. The lighthouse appeared in the distance when she rounded the bend, and her nerves flared. She drove under a banner announcing the event, and the Gallow family's bed-and-breakfast came into view. She gripped the steering wheel tighter. The inn was run by Goldie Gallow, a tall, thin, high-spirited eighty-year-old who patterned her attire, shag hairstyle, and heavy use of eye makeup, after Joan Jett, looked more like she was in her seventies, and acted like she was in her thirties.

Goldie had been holding community breakfasts and potluck dinners for island residents forever. Tara had attended those events many times, but as her mother's need for perfection had become more irritating, she'd stopped attending as a guest and had shown up only as a photographer. Hiding behind her camera had certain benefits. It allowed her to catch up with people she didn't get to see very often, while avoiding being dragged into her mother's world of *putting on airs*.

The parking lot by the lighthouse was packed, and the charity event was in full swing. Crowds of people milled about the grassy lawn, some carrying bags toward gigantic donation bins and others checking out the food beneath a white canopy. Children ran around with balloons tied to their wrists and cookies in their hands.

Tara found a spot at the far end of the lot, grabbed her equipment, and headed over to the event. She loved community events where people came together to help others. Her thoughts turned to Levi, working hard to make Autumn's dreams come true. She missed him desperately, but she couldn't afford to get lost in those feelings. She needed all the strength she could muster to get through a conversation with her mother.

With her camera to her eye, she took pictures of children laughing and playing, couples holding hands, and volunteers helping to sort through donations. Her mother was holding court over a group of women by the lighthouse entrance. She was impeccably overdressed in a pretty mauve shift and heels. Tara headed in the opposite direction, taking more pictures of people giving donations. She warmed all over when she saw her father talking with a group of people who looked younger than Tara. She took a few candid shots and would get more when he took his turn at the podium thanking everyone for attending.

She spotted her grandmother talking with Goldie, who deserved a spotlight for all she did for the community, and Goldie's petite bestie, Estelle. Estelle was a pistol. She had thick, curly gray-blue hair and wore red-framed sunglasses. Tara's grandmother looked cute in tan capris, a bright blue top, and matching blue glasses, while Goldie wore black skinny jeans and a purple shirt with a dangerously low neckline and NOTHING'S SEXIER THAN A MAN WHO GIVES emblazoned across her chest. *Gives* was the only word in bold.

Tara took several pictures of them before her grandmother waved her over.

Her grandmother had called her a few times last week, making sure she was okay and commiserating about Tara's mother. Tara had asked her grandmother if she knew why her mother acted the way she did, and her grandmother had said *It's who she's always been*, which wasn't exactly helpful.

"Hi, Gram." Tara hugged her.

"Tara, sweetheart, give Grandma Goldie a hug," Goldie drew her into a warm embrace.

"It's nice to see you both. How are you?" Tara asked as Goldie passed her to Estelle, who also hugged her.

"From what I hear, not nearly as good as *you*," Estelle said.

"What has my grandmother been telling you?"

"Nothing that isn't true," her grandmother said.

"I hear you and Levi Steele are knocking boots," Goldie

said.

Tara gave her grandmother a disapproving look.

"He's a good egg, darling," Estelle added. "A whole lotta man and quite a fine father."

"*Fine* is right," her grandmother added.

Tara was caught between amusement and a little put off that they'd checked out Levi in that way.

"Why do you look like your panties are too tight?" Estelle asked.

"Because I'm trying not to think about you checking out Levi," she said honestly.

"Oh, honey, we check out everyone. Men, women, makes no difference," Goldie said.

"We have to make sure our Silver Island young'uns are getting the partners they deserve," Estelle said.

"Maybe you should open a matchmaking business." Tara was teasing, but they didn't get the joke, because they began brainstorming business names.

"Two for Tea?" her grandmother suggested.

"Too boring," Estelle said. "How about Love Connection?"

"The Love Ladies?" Goldie offered.

"Sounds like a brothel," Tara said.

"That could give Goldie's bed-and-breakfast a whole new clientele," her grandmother said, and they all cracked up.

They abruptly quieted and schooled their expressions. Tara followed their gazes and saw her mother approaching. She stood taller, drawing her shoulders back, readying for battle.

"Tara, honey, I'm *so* glad you made it." Her mother kissed her cheek.

Irritated that she had the gall to act like everything was fine between them, Tara said, "I'd never let Dad down."

"Of course not, and we're so proud of you for taking your responsibilities seriously." Her mother turned her attention to Goldie and Estelle. "Did Tara tell you that our beautiful granddaughter won a skateboarding trophy? We had the greatest time watching her perform her tricks..."

If Tara listened to any more of this, she was going to be sick. "Excuse me. I need to go take pictures."

"I'll help you." Her grandmother fell into step beside her and lowered her voice. "I bet you want to hop the first ferry back to Harborside."

"More than you can imagine."

HER MOTHER KEPT up the act throughout the event, and by the time Tara left, she was fit to be tied. Poor Charmaine probably thought Tara had lost her mind, she was so quiet while looking at the rental properties. Tara was afraid to speak for fear of misdirected anger coming out, and since she'd been seeing red, she hadn't been able to pay attention to the tour of the rentals.

She drove out to Brighton Bluffs and walked along the cliffs, letting the sea breeze kiss her skin, trying to calm down before seeing Jules and Bellamy, but it didn't help. Levi texted to see how the event and her rental appointments had gone, but she didn't want to burden him with her troubles. He couldn't fix them, and although being in his arms would make her feel better, she'd screwed herself over on that one by telling him not to come. So she simply said the event had gone fine, and she'd decided to stay at Jules's apartment for a while. She promised to text when she got settled in for the night.

It was almost six by the time she got to Jules and Grant's bungalow. Knowing she was going to see her besties took the edge off. She parked between Jules's bright yellow Jeep and Bellamy's steel-blue Toyota Camry hybrid and took a moment to just breathe.

A cold breeze swept up from the water as she walked to the porch. She wrapped her arms around herself, remembering how run-down their bungalow had been before Jules and Grant had gotten together and how it had reminded her of the way Grant had seen himself at that time. He'd lost more than his leg with his amputation. He'd lost his brotherhood, the men with whom he'd carried out covert missions, and worse, he'd lost his sense of purpose. Jules had helped him get that back and rediscover his love of painting. Tara's thoughts turned inward. She hadn't felt broken before she and Levi had come together, but she hadn't felt complete, either. Now she felt complete, but a piece of her was broken because of the fight with her mother, and she didn't know if it was fixable.

She lifted her hand to knock, but the door swung open, and Jules and Bellamy converged on her with open arms.

"Finally," Bellamy said.

"We missed you," Jules said. "Are you okay?"

They ushered her inside. "I'm fine."

"How was it seeing your mom?" Bellamy asked.

"Do I need to have *my* mom give her a harsh talking-to?" Jules asked. "Wait. Sit down and relax and then we'll talk. We poured you a glass of wine, and Belly brought snacks."

"Comfort food," Bellamy explained. "Pizza bites and chocolate."

"I love you guys," Tara said.

"Of course you do. We're the best besties a girl could have," Bellamy said as they sat on the couch, with Tara in the middle.

Tara toed off her sneakers and sat cross-legged, telling them how her mother had put on a charade of the perfect family all afternoon and how painful it was. She rested her head back and gazed up at the ceiling. "How can my life be so perfect in one way and so broken in another?"

"I think some things need to break in order to heal in a better way," Jules said.

Tara met her gaze. "Why? It's so painful."

"Because sometimes broken turns into normal, like how your mom makes comments about you, and she doesn't see it—"

"*Wait,*" Tara snapped. "She might not have realized it *before*, but she knows *now*. I made it crystal clear when we were arguing."

"And we're proud of you for doing that." Bellamy put her arm around her and hugged her.

"Thanks. But it didn't help."

"Maybe it's easier for her to pretend it never happened and she'll *still* change her ways," Jules said.

"*Nope*. Before I left she said, 'Next time you might want to wear something a little more fashionable.'" She closed her eyes against the sting of tears. "I don't get it. I'm not a horrible daughter."

"You're an amazing daughter. This is *her* issue, not yours," Bellamy said.

"Then why does it hurt so bad?" She leaned forward to grab a handful of chocolate, then thought better of it. "See? She makes me want to eat my feelings away."

"It hurts because she's your mom," Jules said. "Why don't you talk to her?"

"I'm afraid to. I'm not sure what will come out of my mouth."

"Good point," Bellamy said. "Have you heard from Amelia?"

Tara shook her head. "No, thank God. I don't think I could deal with her right now."

"How was your dad today?" Jules asked.

"Fine. He stood up for me when my mom commented on my outfit. He told her to back off in a way I've never heard him speak to her before. I got the impression things were not great between them, and I feel guilty about that."

"Don't," Jules warned. "My mom says children should never take responsibility for their parents' issues and that what happens between parents often has nothing to do with whatever is going on around them at that time."

"What does that mean? They got along fine before," Tara said.

"You don't know that. You only know what they wanted you to see," Bellamy said. "Look at my parents." Her parents were still in love but had lived in separate homes for most of her life.

"You're right," Tara said. "Jules, would you mind if I stayed in your apartment for a while? It won't be for long. I'm still looking around, but don't think I could stomach sleeping at my parents'."

"Of course. I thought you might want to, so I made you a key." Jules picked up a pink key from the coffee table and handed it to her.

"Thanks."

"Was it hard to leave Levi and Joey?" Bellamy asked.

"*So* hard. He wanted to come with me, but I felt like I needed to prove that I could do this on my own. And now I wish he were here."

"*Aww,*" Jules and Bellamy said in unison, and hugged her.

"Okay, *no.* We're not getting bummed about this," Tara said. "I need you guys to lift me up and make me laugh, not commiserate about how much I miss Levi. Tell me something fun."

"I have some juicy gossip," Jules said.

"Do tell," Bellamy urged.

"Leni told me that Shea just took on *Duncan Raz* as a client." Leni worked for her cousin Shea's public relations firm, and Duncan "Raz" Raznick was a gorgeous A-list actor.

"*Whaat?*" Bellamy squealed. "I heard he had a really bad breakup with that Jacinda chick he was dating."

"I read something about that," Tara said. "She cheated on him with a costar. No wonder he needed a new PR company."

"*Hello.*" Bellamy waved her hand. "Her loss can be my gain. Tell Leni to hook me up with him!"

"You might not want that," Jules said. "Leni told me that he drives Shea crazy. He never wants to do what she tells him to."

They talked for two hours straight, catching up on gossip and circling back to Tara's parents, Amelia, and Levi and Joey. Tara admitted how wonderful it was to truly feel loved. She and Jules commiserated about how much they missed their guys when they weren't together, and Bellamy complained about feeling left out and needing a man, which brought them to Bellamy's submission to the reality show. She hadn't heard back yet but said it could take a long time.

Sometime after the sun went down, Grant walked in and found them chatting animatedly with their feet on the coffee table. He stopped cold, like a deer in headlights. "Oh, uh. Still girl time?" He hiked a thumb over his shoulder. "I'll be working out, Pix. Lemme know when it's safe to come in."

He walked right back out the door.

"Okay, girls. Finish your wine. You gotta go," Jules said hurriedly.

"*What?* Why?" Bellamy whined.

"He's going to *work out.* That means *shirtless.* There is nothing sexier than your brother shirtless and in gray sweats." She fanned her face. "Hurry up. I'm getting hot already."

Tara and Bellamy laughed.

"I feel your pain. I'm leaving," Tara pushed to her feet. "Want help cleaning up?"

"No. I don't mean to be rude, but…" Jules pulled Bellamy up to her feet.

"Hey!" Bellamy complained.

"You'll understand when you find your forever love, right, Tara?" Jules hugged them and ushered them playfully toward the door.

"It feels weird agreeing since I'm with your brother, but heck yeah."

BOTH OF TARA'S parents' cars were in the garage when she got home. Tara's stomach twisted painfully, and she debated playing her mother's game and just letting it go. Could she even *pretend* everything was okay? Levi's voice whispered through her mind. *If you won't do it for yourself, do it for Joey…She learns from you.* She touched the thin leather bands of her bracelet, thinking about Joey having seen the tail end of their argument. If she backed down now, it would have all been for nothing.

She allowed herself to feel the hurt and anger, to carry it like the burden it was. To use it to fuel her determination as she plowed through the kitchen door.

Her mother was sitting at the table, her back to the door, head bowed, resting on her hand. She didn't look up as Tara strode past. Tara told herself not to blow up, not to say a word until she'd packed her things, so she wouldn't have to stick around in the awkward aftermath of their next argument. She tried to steel herself against the hurt of being ignored, and she *almost* made it out of the kitchen, but the argument and today's farce rushed in, and she was unable to hold back. She spun around, snapping, "Where's my fake *hello, sweetheart*? Where's the show you put on for everyone else after saying horrible things to me, and about Levi, and not speaking to me for a week? How do you think all those people would react if they knew the truth about how you treat your daughter? What *then*, Mother? Would you still pretend it never happened?" Tara paced, anger spewing as fast and hot as lava. "I don't know why I've never been good enough for you, but I don't care anymore. I'm good enough for me, and I'm proud of who I am, and I'm proud of who Levi is. And I will *never* treat my kids the way you treat me."

Her mother lifted her face, eyes red and swollen, tears streaking her cheeks.

Tara blinked several times. She'd never seen her mother cry, and the shock of it pulled her out of her own head long enough to see that her mother's clothes were disheveled, her hair was messy, and her eye makeup had streaked down her cheeks. Her mother's mouth hung open, as if she were unable to speak. Tara averted her eyes, and that's when she noticed the empty pint of ice cream lying on its side on the table, a spoon lying in a puddle of melted ice cream.

Panic spread through Tara. She could think of only one

thing that would cause her mother to look like that. "Did something happen to Dad?"

Her mother shook her head. "Other than him not speaking to me? No. He's fine."

"*Grandma?*" she asked frantically.

"She's fine enough to give me hell every freaking day since last weekend," she said flatly. "And don't ask about your brothers—they're fine—and I know you won't ask, but it's not Amelia."

"So, *what*, then?" Tara crossed her arms and realized she was shaking. "You're having your own pity party?"

Her mother shook her head, looking ten years older than she had that afternoon. "I don't want pity. I want a do-over."

"Why? Did something happen after I left the event? Didn't they get enough donations?"

"Not for the event, Tara," she said in an utterly exhausted voice. "I want a do-over in raising my family and being a wife. I hear the things I say, and they're all the things I swore I never would."

Tara's heart hammered against her chest as fresh tears spilled from her mother's eyes. "What are you talking about?"

"There's a reason we rarely see my parents. I only know how to be one person, and that's the person they raised. My mother was a perfectionist. She used to get on my case about everything. How I stood, how I walked, how I talked. *Nothing* was off-limits."

Conflicting emotions rained down on Tara, empathy for her mother and anger at herself for feeling that way. "You're not getting any pity from me. You had a *choice* every time you spoke to me, and you chose to be overly critical."

"I don't *want* your pity," her mother said sharply. "I just want to explain. I know you might never forgive me, but I hate myself for the way I've treated you, and I never saw it. I heard it come out of my mouth, but I told myself it was to help you be the best you could. I rationalized the very thing I grew up loathing."

"But it's only me you do it to," Tara said shakily.

"No, it's not. I do it to your father, too, and I did it to Carey when he needed a reminder."

"You never did it to *Amelia*."

"When I had Amelia, she was so easy. She loved being in the spotlight. She was happy to wear pretty dresses and let me style her hair. And as she got older, I never had to remind her of the importance of putting forward her best image."

"Don't you mean her *fake* image?"

"No. It wasn't fake for her. But then you came along, and you were this sweet, beautiful quiet girl who didn't care if you got dirty and didn't want to impress *anyone*. You wanted to be comfortable and you wanted to be *you*. I should have celebrated that about you, but I was lost. I didn't know how to relate to you. That's a horrible thing to say to your child, but it's true. You hated to slow down enough for me to brush your hair or put bows in it, and you wanted to wear sneakers, not Mary Janes or cute sandals. You wanted jeans and leggings and the things your friends were wearing, and that should have been fine. A relief, even, that you weren't like me. But it was ingrained in my mind that I needed the family to look and act a certain way, and I didn't know how to break away from that."

"Well, that's messed up," Tara said, refusing to give her an easy out. "And I paid the price."

"You're right, and so did the rest of our family, and Levi, and his family, and that wasn't fair of me. I have so many regrets. I didn't want to believe Amelia could be so rotten to you when you were younger. I wish I could take it all back. I wish I had believed you and never given her the chance to be mean to you. Never given *myself* the chance."

Tears welled in Tara's eyes at that admission.

"I promised myself I wouldn't do that to you today. I had a *plan.* I was going to take you aside and apologize and tell you all this, but then we were at the event, and all those people know me as the person I've always been. I didn't know…I fell right back into my old habits. I don't know how to act any other way. But I *want* to, Tara." She pushed to her feet, and Tara instinctively took a step back. Her mother stopped and bowed her head, more tears falling. "I don't blame you for keeping your distance." She met Tara's gaze, and the love in her eyes was inescapable. "I don't know how you turned out to be so lovely when I have been such a shit."

Tears slid down Tara's cheeks at the deep-seated anguish she carried toward her mother and the raw pain in her mother's voice.

"But I'm going to get help." Her mother lifted her chin. "I know you might never forgive me, but I *want* to change, and I want to be a better mother and wife."

Suddenly she wondered if her parents were on the brink of disaster. "Where's Daddy?"

"He's in his office."

"Are you two…breaking up?"

"No. At least I hope not. Your father is not a quitter. He loves me despite my faults, and you should know that he has *always* stood up for you. Not just today. In the past, in private, he *always* tried to get me to say the right things, and I wanted to. But then our days would start and they were chaotic and I'd try…and fail, and I'd tell myself I'd try again tomorrow."

"You didn't always fail," Tara admitted through tears.

"I failed enough," her mother said. "I let you down, and I

let your father down. He saved me when I was younger, and I made all sorts of promises to change. When I had Amelia and your brothers, I truly believed I *had* changed. But then—"

"So it's *my* fault?"

"No, sweetheart, not now and not ever. That's not what I'm saying. I'm saying that I was wrong. I *hadn't* changed. I just hadn't been in a position to be tested. Robert has always done what he was told, and Carey knew how to play the game and walk the walk until he could walk far away from us and get off the island. I know that's my fault, too."

"Carey's a vagabond at heart," Tara said softly. "He'd have traveled all the time no matter what."

"Maybe or maybe not. We'll never know. But I've spoken with a therapist in Chaffee, and I'll be seeing her every week."

"You're serious?" Tara asked carefully. "This isn't just some ploy for attention?"

Her mother shook her head. "The last thing I want is attention. I'm embarrassed by the things I've said and the way I've acted and horrified that I've made my own beautiful, kindhearted daughter feel so bad."

Tara's heart ached for both of them. "Why didn't you ever tell me about how your mother treated you?"

"Because it hurt too badly to talk about it, especially since I was putting on a repeat performance." She closed her eyes and held on to the counter for balance, breathing deeply. When she opened her eyes, she didn't even try to dry her tears.

For the first time ever, Tara saw the woman beneath the steely facade. She saw her mother's faults, vulnerabilities, and to her own shock, her mother's strength, because of all people, Tara knew what it was like to carry a secret that felt bigger than herself and how much strength it took to admit it.

"I'm going to apologize to everyone," her mother promised.

"To Levi, his family, Joey. Please give me a chance to make it up to you. To make it up to our family. Please don't move out."

Tara's heart told her to say okay, that she'd stay and do everything she could to make things better. But she thought of Joey and what advice she might give her in the same situation. Staying might make it easier for her mother, but it would also leave Tara in a situation where she was forced to endure the same treatment while her mother tried to figure herself out. If Joey were in this situation, Tara would not want her to stay. She mustered her courage and said, "I'm glad you're getting help, and I hope things can change. But I'm going to move out, Mom. I'm going to stay at Jules's apartment for now, and I'll find a more permanent solution when I can. But I can't stay here."

"I don't blame you for hating me," her mother said quietly.

"I don't hate you." Tara swiped at her tears. She was sad for all they'd lost and would never get back, and despite everything, she was hopeful for what they might one day have. "I love you even though I hate some things you've said to me and the things you've said about Levi. But it's time for me to be a grown-up, and maybe it'll be easier for you to work through your issues if we put some space between us. I'm going to pack a few things before I leave."

Her mother's shoulders slumped, sadness weighing down her features despite her agreeable nod. "Do you want help packing?"

Tara reached for the olive branch. "Sure, if you promise not to make me feel like my packing isn't good enough."

"I promise." Her mother pretended to zip her lips and throw away the key.

Gifted with a rare dose of her mother's humor, Tara said, "Okay."

As they headed upstairs, Tara's hopeful heart, the one that had been so swept up in Levi, she hadn't been able to hope for much else, led the way.

A LITTLE WHILE later, Tara drove toward Main Street, the reality of her situation hitting hard. She didn't have a home, and she had no idea if her mother was capable of changing. What if she couldn't change? Where would that leave them? A lump formed in her throat. She couldn't go there. She was already mired down with enough for one night, but at the same time, she felt an unexpected flutter of something else. Something *good.* The contradicting sensations caught her off guard, and she looked up at the glow of the old-fashioned streetlights, closed shops, and empty sidewalks. The flower boxes were vibrant with colorful blooms, and the giraffes in front of the Happy End gift shop wore cheery SEE YOU TOMORROW signs around their necks.

And then understanding of that unexpected flutter hit her. Not hard or all at once but soft, like the gradual feeling of the temperature dropping, the sky darkening, and the promise of a new day forming. Only it didn't feel like a promise. It felt like a possibility, and it wasn't just the possibility of one new beginning. It was the possibility of many. For herself, with Levi and Joey, and if the stars aligned and her mother really wanted it bad enough, then maybe they'd have a new beginning, too.

As she parked in front of Jules's shop, she mentally covered those seeds of possibilities with care, patting the soil around them with nurturing hands, and watered them with hope.

Feeling lighter but lonely without Levi there to tell of her awakening, she gathered her purse and computer bag and popped the trunk button on her key fob as she stepped out of the car. As she closed the door, a shadowy figure appeared at the entrance to the alley beside the building. She froze, her heart racing, fingers clutching the keys like a weapon.

"Would you like some help with your bags, blondie?"

Tara's heart leapt as Levi walked into the glow of the streetlamp. She ran to him and jumped into his arms, wrapping her legs around his waist. "You're here! I can't believe you're here." How had he known she needed him?

"I promised to let you fly solo when you faced your mother, but there's no way I'd leave you to deal with the aftermath of all those feelings alone."

"IloveyouIloveyouIloveyou." She kissed his lips, his cheeks, and his lips again, unable to believe he was there. "Where's Joey? Why didn't you tell me you were coming?"

"Joey is staying with Jesse tonight, and he's taking her to school tomorrow. And I didn't tell you because I knew you would tell me not to come."

Tears slid down her cheeks. "I would've, but I'm so glad you're here. I have so much to tell you."

"I have to be on the first ferry out in the morning, but I'm yours all night."

"I hope you've got that wrong. You're *here* for the night, but you're *mine* for much longer."

"Every second of every day, sweetheart."

Moonlight shimmered in his eyes, and with the man of her dreams holding her, her mother's promise, and all those other glorious possibilities waiting in the wings, he sealed his vow with a deep, delicious kiss.

Twenty-Four

"CAN WE GO to the beach when Aunt Tara comes this weekend?" Joey asked as she put on her skating helmet. Levi had picked her up from after-school care and taken her to the park for a lesson with Brent. They were working on another new trick.

"If she's up for it, sure."

It had been several weeks since Joey's spring break ended and Tara went back to the island, and the long-distance relationship was already weighing on them. The Saturday after Tara had left, she'd been booked with clients during the day, and some of them had run late, so he and Joey had gone to the island to see her. Joey was so excited about Tara moving into Jules's apartment, she'd wanted to stay there instead of with her grandparents, which meant the two girls slept in the bed, and Levi had been relegated to the couch. *That* was fun. The next weekend, Cassidy had gotten sick and had asked Tara to take over for a two-day wedding shoot for one of her friends in Connecticut, where she and Wyatt were from. Tara had been booked with her own clients, but she'd managed to juggle her schedule and cover the event for Cassidy, but it meant staying overnight in Connecticut. She called Joey every night at eight o'clock to say *sweet dreams.* Even when she had photography sessions, she managed to take a moment to call, and his little girl ate up the attention.

He'd tried to keep his promise and take the ferry to see her, even if for only an hour each week, but between their work schedules and Joey's school, it wasn't easy and not always possible. While they'd mastered video sex and had even bought hands-free stands for their phones, it was a poor substitute for holding the woman he loved in his arms.

They were *finally* going to see each other this weekend, and he and Tara would have some alone time. She was coming to Harborside, and Joey was going to a sleepover Friday night.

Levi couldn't wait.

"Dad." Joey picked up her skateboard. "Can we spend the summer on the island?"

"I've got to work, baby, but I'll see if you can spend some time there if you'd like."

"Can I stay with Aunt Tara?" she asked hopefully.

She missed Tara as much as he did and talked about her every day. "She works too, babe. But we'll figure something out."

"Okay." She ran over to Brent. "I'm ready!"

Levi took a picture of Joey on her skateboard and sent it to Tara with the text, *Wish you were here.* She responded quickly. *Me too. I'm with a client, but I miss you guys like crazy. Talk tonight?* She added a heart emoji. He'd give anything to hear her voice, but he thumbed out, *I'll call after I put Joey to bed. Love you.* Her response was immediate. *Same.* She added a smile emoji with three hearts around it. That one word never failed to make him long to hear it whispered against his skin. Another text rolled in. *In the words of my favorite niece, long-distance stinks.*

Wasn't that the truth? The night Tara had left after spring break, Joey had been in tears. She'd been overtired and was having trouble accepting that just because Daddy was seeing Tara didn't mean they'd see her every day. She'd buried her face in his chest the way Tara sometimes did and had sobbed, *I'm never having a long-distance boyfriend. Long-distance stinks!*

Later that night, when he'd told Tara, it had broken her heart, too.

HE AND JOEY played a board game after dinner, and when Tara called at eight, Joey told her all about how she'd whipped Dad's butt in Monopoly. Now Levi was reading to her in her room and feeling like an asshole, counting down the minutes until he could talk with Tara in private. He wasn't rushing through reading to Joey, and he didn't sound agitated, but he felt the difference, and he didn't like it.

He hadn't expected to miss Tara in so many ways. Everything felt off without her, from breakfast to outings, dinners, and even putting Joey to bed amplified her absence. If he were in a relationship with any other woman, they'd still be in the getting-to-know-you phase, but he *knew* Tara, and he loved every little thing about her, except the distance separating them. But there was no easy answer for that, and the worst part about it was that as she and her mother navigated their new relationship, he couldn't be there to celebrate the ups and help her through the downs.

When he closed the book, Joey was fiddling with her bracelet. "Dad?"

"Yeah, peanut?"

"Maybe now that you're Aunt Tara's boyfriend, we should find a bracelet for you that Tara's circle fits in, so you're not left out."

"I love that idea, but we should ask Tara how she'd feel about it."

"She'll want you to have it," she said confidently.

"What makes you think so?"

"Because she loves you, and she told me that when you love someone, you always want to be with them. That's why she calls me every night, because we love each other, and that's why she gave me the bracelet. They mean that no matter how far apart we are, we're always close at heart."

Knowing his daughter was not only wholly and completely loved but that *she knew* she was brought a different feeling than being loved, or even being *in* love, and it just might be the most spectacular feeling he'd ever felt.

"You know what, Jo? I think you're probably right about that." He kissed her forehead and picked up her bear. "Where is he snuggling tonight?"

Ten minutes later, with his daughter cocooned by her stuffies, he headed into his room to shower, giving Joey time to fall asleep.

He closed his bedroom door and stretched out on the bed to call Tara. She answered on the second ring, her beautiful face lighting up the screen.

"Hey, blondie. How's my girl?"

"Wishing I was there to tuck Joey in and lie next to you."

"Me too, baby. Nothing feels right without you here. How was your day?"

"Kind of interesting."

"Yeah? With your mom or work?"

"Both. I had lunch with my mom, and it was nice. She's really trying, but she's so worried about saying the right things, it's hard, you know? It's not comfortable yet. I wish I could just tell her to relax and be herself, but I'm not sure she knows who that is anymore. I think that's what she's trying to find out."

"I bet you're right about that. It's got to be hard for her. But I'm glad you had a nice time. That's what matters."

"I think the therapy and the changes she's making are helping her relationship with my dad, too. She asked if I'd consider going to therapy with her at some point. Not now, but maybe in a month or two."

"How do you feel about that?"

"I think it would help. I told her I would, and guess what? I got a lead on a studio rental. It's not officially on the market, and it's not ideal. There's a guy in Rock Harbor who has space above his workshop. I'd rather be in Silver Haven if I can, but I'm keeping it in the back of my mind just in case, *and...*" she said coyly. "I found a cottage I really like. It's not far from town. It's small, only two bedrooms, but at least Jules could have her apartment back. I'm thinking about signing a lease."

"Month to month?"

"No. I asked, but they wouldn't do it. Charmaine said we could try for a year lease, but they'd like eighteen months, which seems weird to me, but their son will be coming to stay with them after that."

"Eighteen months? That's a hell of a commitment."

"I know, but it would free up Jules's apartment."

"She's not using it, T. She doesn't mind."

"Levi, we talked about this. She's just being nice. I'm sure she'd like to have more space to show Grant's paintings and expand her shop. She's been talking about it for months. Besides, I don't like not having a *home*. Most of my stuff is still at my parents' house, and I miss seeing my pictures on the walls and feeling settled."

"I understand that, but wouldn't you rather find something short-term? I know we've got a lot to deal with, between your mom and Joey and our businesses, and there's no easy solution to seeing more of each other, but we'll figure it out at some point. Do you really want to be locked into a long-term lease?"

"I might not have a choice. There aren't that many affordable rentals, much less month-to-month rentals. Everyone who rents by the month charges tourist rates, and I can't afford that."

Fuck. Something's gotta give. "Yeah, I get it. I'll support whatever you want to do. But maybe you should take the weekend to think about it before jumping into the lease."

"That's my plan. I told Charmaine I wanted to talk it over with you this weekend and I'd let her know Monday."

"Great." He didn't have any answers, but at least that bought them a few days.

"Why is your eyebrow twitching?" she asked sweetly.

"Because I *miss* you. I'm like a fucking kid with his first crush. Only love is a hell of a lot more consuming."

"I'm so glad you said that, because all I can think about is being with you and Joey. Last weekend was the worst. Jules said I'm having Levi withdrawals, and I think she's right."

"Leni said the same thing about me having withdrawals

from you. She said I caught love-addicting cooties from my brothers and that I'd better keep them to myself because she can't afford to catch that *bug*."

Tara laughed softly. "I love Leni."

"She's something."

"Guess what else?"

He arched a brow.

"Only one more sleep until we see each other, and I have something special to show you tomorrow night."

"Why make me wait?"

"Because it's something you'll want to strip off me, and it's pretty risqué."

His cock twitched in his boxer briefs. "You woke the viper, blondie. Now you have to model it."

"Oh, does he want to play?" she asked tauntingly.

"How is that even a question? All I have to do is *think* about you and he's ready to go."

"In that case, I guess it's a good thing that I bought three outfits. When I was on the website, I kept thinking about your reaction to my pink babydoll outfit, and I wondered how you'd react to something a little *naughtier*."

"Get your pretty little ass up, because now I need to see you in all three."

She giggled. "Listen to you getting all bossy."

"You like me bossy." She got off on dirty talk, and he was the right man for the job, because with her, he held nothing back.

"What do I get in return?"

He grinned, loving his playful siren. "What do you want?"

"*You*," she said innocently.

"God, baby. You've got me so tied up in knots, I don't

know who I am without you anymore."

"*Same*," she said breathily. "Give me a sec."

He watched her set her phone down and grab a bag from a chair by the bathroom door. As she disappeared into the bathroom, he set his phone in the stand by the bed, imagining her stripping naked, her hair tumbling over her breasts, and slid his hand into his boxer briefs, giving his dick a tug as the bathroom door opened.

She sauntered toward the bed, wearing a black lace choker and a black lace bra that pushed her tits together and barely covered her nipples. Thin black straps rose up from between her breasts, curving around the swell of them to each shoulder strap. A sliver of lace crisscrossed over her stomach, and a black lace thong rode high on her hips, the tiny lace triangle barely large enough to cover her sweet pussy. She turned around and glanced over her shoulder so seductively, his cock jerked.

"You're lucky I'm not in that room, sweet thing, because...*damn*."

She giggled.

"Come closer, gorgeous. Let me see all of you."

Her hips swayed seductively as she came toward the phone and ran her fingers along the edge of her thong and up her hip. "You like?"

"Hell yeah, I like. I'd like to tie you down with those straps and lick every inch of you until you're so needy, you beg me to make you come."

She climbed onto the bed on her knees and slid her fingers into her thong. "What else would you do?"

"I'd tear off that bra with my teeth and suck your tits."

Her eyes became heavy-lidded. "*Yes.*"

"Touch your tits for me. Pretend it's me touching you."

She did, and he pushed off his boxer briefs.

"Let me see you," she said huskily.

He angled the phone and licked his hand, then began stroking himself. "I want your mouth on my cock, baby. I want to feel your lips around me, sucking, and your hand stroking me. I want to come in your mouth, on your tits, and on that sexy ass of yours, and then I want to bury myself deep inside you and come again."

"*Levi,*" she panted out. The tremor in her voice told him she was close.

"I want to lick your pussy, baby, and suck your clit. I want to hear you cry out my name while I fuck you."

"Yes. *More.*"

"Lie on your back and take off that thong."

She did as he asked.

"Spread your legs. Let me see how wet you are for me." When she did, he growled. "So damn beautiful. Touch yourself the way I do."

She did, and bowed off the bed. "*Levi,*" she pleaded.

"Yeah, baby, that's it. *Watch* me."

She looked over, watching him stroke himself, and trapped her lower lip between her teeth.

"That's it, baby. I'm imagining your mouth on me, and I want my mouth between your legs. I want to eat you all night long."

"Tomorrow night. *Promise?*"

"Hell yes, I promise. I'm going to take you six ways to Sunday, and you're going to suck me so good. Move your fingers faster, and use your other hand to squeeze your nipple."

She moaned and whimpered, and he worked himself tighter, faster, until they were both panting, their hips bucking. He grabbed his boxer briefs to catch his come, grunting out, "*T*," as his name flew from her lips, and they surrendered to their mutual ecstasy. Her sinful sounds drew out his climax, until he sank down to the bed, spent but not nearly sated. He needed Tara, to feel her breath on his skin, to hold her and know she was safe in his room, in his arms.

They lay on their separate beds, trying to catch their breath. "God, T. I miss touching you, and I miss kissing you more than you can imagine, but I think what I miss most is just being with you."

"Only one more sleep until we're together," she said softly, in an utterly blissed-out voice that made him miss her even more.

"I'm counting down the hours, baby."

"Same." She yawned. "Levi?"

"Yeah, love?"

"Can you stay on the phone while I fall asleep? I like knowing you're there."

"I can't think of a better way to end the night, except with you here in my arms."

Twenty-Five

TARA DROVE TO the ferry Friday evening, singing along to the radio and dancing in her seat. She had been in the best mood all day, knowing she'd see Levi and Joey tonight. She'd picked up a new book for Joey, and she couldn't wait to see her when she got home tomorrow after her sleepover. This morning, when she'd woken up to Levi's handsome face on her phone—he'd fallen asleep last night while waiting for *her* to fall asleep—she'd had the ridiculous notion to ask if she could wake up that way every morning they spent apart. But since that was too clingy, she'd kept it to herself, and after a few sweet, sleepy exchanges, they'd shared how excited they were to see each other tonight and made plans to take Joey to the beach tomorrow. After the last few insanely busy weeks, it sounded like the perfect day.

She pulled into the ferry parking lot, and a shiver of happiness ran through her. Soon she'd be in Levi's arms. Her grandmother's voice whispered through her mind. *If I had all that you have going for you, I'd be on his front porch wearing nothing but a trench coat and a come-hither smile.* When her grandmother had first said that, Tara couldn't have imagined feeling safe enough to be that bold, but that was no longer an issue. Levi always made her feel safe, and after last night's reaction to her lingerie, maybe she *should* show up wearing a trench coat over one of the other sexy outfits she'd packed.

She parked her car, and as she cut the engine, her phone rang. Amelia's name appeared on the screen, and Tara's stomach seized, her pulse instantly going into panic mode. She'd wondered when her sister would get around to giving her shit about Levi. She stared at the screen, debating letting it go to voicemail, but if she put it off, she'd think about it all weekend, and she didn't want to ruin the little time she had with Levi and Joey.

She took a deep breath, and with her heart pounding like a rampant drum, she answered the call. "Hello."

"Hey, Tara," her sister said casually. "I hear *you're* doing great."

Even though her sister couldn't see her, Tara lifted her chin. "I *am*. I'm happier than I've ever been, and Joey's happy, too. She was really upset when you blew off her tournament."

"I know. Levi gave me hell for that. That's kind of why I'm calling." Amelia's tone was uncharacteristically apologetic. "I *know* how important family is to you and Levi." And there it was, the slightly sarcastic way she said *know*, as if their beliefs were ridiculous but she'd bow to them. "I want to try to fix things with Levi and Joey and make things right so you don't spend your life feeling like you have to make up for my faults."

"Why?" There was always a reason with her.

Amelia sighed. "Because it's the right thing to do, and Joey doesn't need us fighting all the time. I talked to Mom, and she told me everything you said, and I guess I want to make it up to you, too, and what better way than fixing things with the man you *love*?"

Shock and disbelief swept in, and Tara's hopeful heart scooped them up, cautiously asking, "What are you thinking?"

"I'm just off the Cape for a sponsorship gig, not far from Harborside. Mom said you were going to see Levi this weekend, but right now is the only time I can get away. I'm hoping you'll wait to go see him until tomorrow and give me tonight to try to talk to him and work things out. I know he doesn't trust me, and if you're there, it'll be twice as hard to try to talk to him. This isn't easy for me. We don't exactly have a great history of communicating."

Tara was quiet for a beat, thinking about Joey. "You *have* to mean it this time. Joey's too old for you to be coming in and out of her life on a whim. She's heartbroken every time you let her down, and it makes her feel bad about herself, like she's not worth your love." *The way you made me feel.*

"I *know,* Tara. I mean it. Can you just give me *one* night with Levi to make things right for my daughter? It's *one* night. Isn't this what you want? For things to be better?"

Tara steeled herself. "Yes."

"Then just give me tonight. I can be there in half an hour."

"*Fine.* This is probably the best time for you to do it, anyway. Joey is at a sleepover, so she won't be there to witness the argument. I'll call Levi and let him know you're coming."

"Please don't. You know how he gets. He'll be angry before I even get there, and I'll never stand a chance."

She was right. He would. "He's going to ask me why I'm not coming."

"Can't you just tell him you got held up at work?"

"And *lie* to him?" She scoffed. "I don't lie to the people I love."

"Then don't lie. Just say something came up and it's important. *Jesus.* I forgot how *good* you are."

Anger clawed up Tara's spine, but the thought of Joey not having to face the same disappointment for years to come overrode her own disappointment at giving up her one night with Levi. "Fine. But don't mess it up. And don't piss him off. If you're going to make things right, then listen to what he has to say, because he loves Joey, and everything he says is for her protection."

"I'm not an idiot. I know how to play the game. Thanks, *Mouse.*"

The line went dead.

Tara's chest physically ached. She looked longingly at the ferry, the pit of her stomach burning as she replayed the conversation with her sister. Her mother was trying so hard to be more thoughtful about the things she said and how she acted. Could she have tried to get Amelia to change, too? Were the stars finally aligning for her and for Joey and Levi? She sure hoped so as she pulled out her phone to text Levi, praying she was doing the right thing.

LEVI PUT THE wine bottle on the table and lit the candles. Tara would be there any minute. He couldn't wait to see her walk through that door and see the smile that was meant solely for him lift her pretty cheeks and light up the sweetest baby blues he'd ever seen. He couldn't wait to hold her, to kiss her, to hear her voice without miles between them. They had all night alone to do and say whatever, wherever they wanted.

He dimmed the lights and reached in his back pocket for his

phone to see how far away she was. It wasn't there. *Shit.* He must have left it on the charger after his shower. He ran upstairs and found it plugged in by his bed. He saw a missed text from Tara and read it on his way downstairs.

Hi. I'm so sorry, but I can't make it tonight. I love you, and I promise to make it up to you. I'll take the first ferry out in the morning.

His elation deflated like a popped balloon, leaving him feeling ragged and disappointed, the disappointment cutting deeper as he walked over to the table and blew out the candles, feeling like he'd lost his best friend. He knew she'd only cancel if she had no other choice, but that didn't make it suck any less. He began thumbing out a text to find out why she'd canceled, when a knock sounded at the front door. He bit out, "*Thank God,*" and shoved his phone in his pocket on his way to answer it.

As he opened the door, his relief poured out. "You scared me, bab—"

His blood chilled at the sight of Amelia wearing sky-high heels and a formfitting, short-sleeved pale green minidress with a plunging neckline that barely concealed her breasts, slanted hip pockets that seemed to be pointing between her legs, and a zipper that ran down the middle from her sternum to the ridiculously short hem that barely covered her crotch. Her shiny cinnamon hair fell to the tiny zippered pockets above her breasts. Her makeup looked freshly done, and her lips were painted what might be an alluring shade of pink on anyone else, but Levi couldn't see past the conniving blue eyes he'd somehow missed when he'd been a horny teenager.

"Cat got your tongue, big daddy?" Amelia strutted past him, running her fingers along his chest.

Anger roiled in Levi's gut over all the things Amelia had

done to Tara and how badly she'd hurt Joey. "What are you doing here, Amelia?" He remained by the door because he was about to throw her out it. "I told you, no unscheduled visits."

"*Oh*," she said in a practiced shocked and breathy voice. "Didn't my precious sister tell you I was coming?" She walked through the living room as she spoke. "I asked her to. I knew how upset you would get, but she insisted on being the one to tell you."

His eyes narrowed as the pieces of Tara's mysterious cancellation fell into place. "Bullshit. I don't know what game you're playing, but you need to leave."

She rolled her eyes dramatically. "Don't get all grumpy with me. We've got all night, and I want to talk about a few things."

She fluttered her lashes and turned, her gaze catching on the dining room table, which he'd set for Tara, with a vase of red roses and her favorite wine, to go with dinner and dessert from her favorite restaurant. He'd even bought a pretty candelabra, wanting to give her the night of romance she deserved.

But her selfish asshole of a sister walked over to the table and picked up the single red rose he'd put on Tara's plate and brought it to her nose. "Aw, did I spoil your romantic evening? You must be really hung up on Mouse."

"Don't you *ever* call her that again." He closed the distance between them, stealing the flower from her hand. "Whatever this charade is, it's *over*. You want to talk about Joey? Text me, and we'll schedule a time. Now, get the hell out of my house."

She stepped closer, eyeing him seductively, and pressed her hands to his chest. "I'm loving this whole protective-daddy thing you have going on."

He grabbed her wrists, speaking through clenched teeth. "I'm going to say this only once, so you'd better listen. I know how you treated Tara when she was young, and I finally understand why you said that shit after we had sex. You need serious help, Amelia."

The front door flew open and Tara stormed in, eyes blazing.

Levi stepped back, dropping Amelia's wrists like he'd been burned. "Tara, it's not—"

"Don't worry, Levi. I know *exactly* what this is." She stepped between Levi and Amelia, staring down her sister. "You *almost* had me," she said shakily. "I believed you when you said you wanted the night alone with Levi to try to make things better for Joey. But then I thought, you've had *years* to make things better. *Years*, Amelia. I'm nobody's fool. Especially not yours. You know how to *play the game*? Did you think I wouldn't pick up on that? What was your plan? Come in and seduce Levi because I'm in love with him? What kind of person does that, much less to their own sister? Don't you have *enough* without coming back for the man you didn't deserve in the first place? I have never done a thing to you, and all you want is to make me unhappy."

"Oh, *please*." Amelia made a sound between impatience and disgust, and strutted around the room. "Get off your high horse. Do you have any idea what it was like to live in your shadow? To go from being the center of Mom and Dad's world to suddenly being told to be quiet because Tara's napping or that I couldn't go shopping with Mom because *you* didn't want to?"

"I was a *child*," Tara snapped.

"*Perfect Tara. Look at her. She's so cute and so sweet*," Amelia mocked. "You think I didn't hear what people said? You were the one *everyone* liked before you even learned to talk. You had a hundred friends and never had to try, and I had to work for every friend I ever had."

Tears filled Tara's eyes, and her jaw hung open.

"That's *enough*," Levi fumed, pulling Tara into his arms.

"Oh yeah. You even got the guy," Amelia said with a sinister edge to her voice. "Freaking perfect."

"Have you lost your mind?" Tara fumed, tears streaking her cheeks. "You *ruined* my childhood. You made me think I was worthless and taught me to stuff my face to try to feel better. That was *you*, Amelia, shoving food into my hands, saying the most hurtful things you could, all because you were *jealous*? All I wanted was to be *loved*. I wanted a big sister like Jules and Bellamy had, who would love me even if I was a pain sometimes. But I never had a chance, did I? It sounds like you hated me from the time Mom and Dad brought me home from the hospital."

"No," Amelia said sharply. "I hated you before you were even born, when Mom stopped buying me all the cute outfits and started stockpiling them for you."

"Why didn't you hate *Carey*? He's younger than you." Tara's voice cracked.

Amelia scoffed. "He was a boy, not my competition."

"You're *sick*," Levi snapped. "*Dangerous*. You need serious help, Amelia, and I clearly made a mistake by trying to keep you in Joey's life. This is *not* salvageable. I will not allow you anywhere near my daughter again, and stay the hell away from Tara."

"You think Joey's going to allow that? She's going to miss my expensive gifts," Amelia said with an annoying smirk.

"Joey is eight years old. She doesn't make those decisions, and she doesn't need gifts. She needs parents who love, respect, and *protect* her, and that's exactly what I'm doing. She might not understand it now, but one day she'll thank me." He grabbed Amelia by the elbow and dragged her to the front door, opening it with his other hand. "Now, get the hell out of our house, and if I *ever* hear that you tried to contact my daughter, or hurt Tara again, I will get a restraining order. I wonder how *that* will go over with your bloody sponsors."

He shoved her out the door and closed it behind her, turning the lock. He strode over to Tara, who was shaking, and gathered her in his arms. "Sorry, Tara. I had to do it."

"No. *I'm* sorry. She told me not to tell you she was coming, and for a while I actually thought she'd changed, or wanted to."

Levi cradled her face between his hands and kissed her softly. "This isn't your fault. All you did was give her the benefit of the doubt, because that's who you are, and that's who I am, too. I think we've both learned a hard lesson. I'm sorry, T, but I can't let Joey be around her."

"I don't want you to. She's…" She shook her head, at a loss for words.

"*Toxic*. I'm sorry she said those horrible things." He hugged her. "What can I do to help you feel better?"

"Nothing. I'll be okay."

He gazed down at her. "Babe, it's okay not to be fine. That was pretty traumatic."

"Honestly, I'm kind of relieved. Now I know why she hates me. I had no idea she was so messed up."

"That makes two of us. I'll have to figure out how to talk to Joey about it."

"We'll figure it out."

He loved her use of *we*. "Yes, *we* will." He kissed her softly.

"But I don't want to think about it right now. Even though she's been an ass to me and she's hurt Joey, some part of me held out hope that she would change, and now that hope's gone. As okay as that is, it's also really sad. I'll probably fall apart at some point, but Amelia has ruined enough of my life. I'm *not* going to let her ruin the rest of tonight. Unless you need to talk about it now?"

"I don't, but when you're ready, let me know."

She nodded and blew out a breath. "Maybe a little later?" Her brow wrinkled. "Is that okay?"

"Everything's okay, babe." He glanced at the dining room table. "It's not exactly the romantic night I had planned."

"Did I see *roses* and candles?" Her eyes danced with delight. "Levi…?"

"I thought I'd wine and dine you and get you a little tipsy so when I tell you what I've been thinking about, you'd have no choice but to agree."

"Are you thinking about something *that* naughty?"

"No. *Yes.*" He laughed. "But that's not why I was going to ply you with alcohol."

"Good, because you should know by now that there's no alcohol required for *that.* You've turned me into a not-so-secret siren."

"God, I love you." He kissed her. "Baby, I can't hold it in anymore. I want to see you in the mornings and come home to you and Joey after work. I want to have dinners together and tuck Joey into bed together. I can't stand all this back-and-forth. I miss you too damn much. I want you to move in with us. I'll build you a beautiful studio here and buy you one on the island if you need one there, too. I know most of your work and your family are there, and you're just starting to fix things with your mom, but…*Shit.* That's not going to work." He paced. "Why did I think it would? That's asking *way* too much of you. Okay, new plan." His words came fast as he met her confused, amused, and *shocked* gaze. "I've got this, T. I hope you don't think it's too pushy, but Joey and I have to move in with you. The three of us in Jules's apartment will be tight, but we'll get something bigger when we have time to look around. I'll take the ferry and bring Joey to school, and I'll come back for church with the guys. Joey wants to spend the summer on the island anyway, and that's only a few weeks away. *Yes*, this is per…*Damn it.* I can't make that decision without talking to Joey about it. It's too much for a little girl—"

Tara went up on her toes and silenced him with the soft press of her lips. Love shined in her eyes as she said, "I want all those things, too. *Yes.*"

"Yes?" His head was spinning.

"Yes, I'll move in with you, here in Harborside. I don't want to put that commute on Joey, and I like taking the ferry. It'll give me time to edit my photos, and then when I get home, I can focus on the people who really matter."

"Really? It's not too much? If it gets to be too much, we'll figure something else out."

"Nothing is too much if it means being with you guys. That's all I've ever wanted."

"Oh, *baby*!" He pulled her into his arms and kissed her, spinning her around. "She said *yes*!" he hollered, and they both laughed. He kissed her again, and as he set her on her feet, tears slipped from her eyes. "Please tell me those are happy tears."

"How could they be anything else? But have you talked to Joey about this?"

"Who do you think told me to buy you your favorite dessert?"

He lowered his lips to hers, knowing they had a rough road ahead explaining the situation with Amelia to Joey and figuring out their long-term living arrangements. At some point, his tender-hearted woman and trusting daughter would probably fall apart over what happened with Amelia, but he'd be there to pick up the troubled pieces of their hearts and love them back together, because they're all he ever wanted, too.

Twenty-Six

AFTER A BITTERSWEET night enjoying the special dinner Levi had planned, making love, trying to make sense of all that had happened, shedding a few tears, and making love again, the morning brought a brighter perspective and the *promise* of a new beginning.

Tara felt a little guilty for feeling relieved that Levi had put such finality between them and Amelia, but the relief outweighed the guilt, and they enjoyed a lazy morning, loving on each other and eating breakfast on the deck before going to pick up Joey. They decided to celebrate the news of Tara moving in and wait to tell her about Amelia until the time was right. Not that there was ever a good time to share such a thing, but until Joey brought her up, there was no reason to upset her.

They climbed out of the car at Emily's house, and the front door flew open. Joey sprinted across the yard, yelling, "Did she say *yes*?"

Tara's heart nearly exploded, and she knew waiting was the right decision. That kind of genuine happiness was too precious to ruin.

"Yes!" Levi said with the biggest smile Tara had ever seen.

Joey launched herself into Tara's arms, clinging to her. "I love you, I love you, I *love* you!"

"I love you too, cutie, so much!"

"We're going to have breakfast together every morning and dinner every night, and even though you and Daddy are going to sleep in the same room, Daddy said that sometimes we can still have sleepovers, too!"

Tears wet Tara's eyes. "I wouldn't want it any other way."

"Congratulations," Lauren said as she and Emily joined them. "Joey told us your big news, and we're thrilled for you."

"Thanks," Levi and Tara said in unison.

"Tara, can I have a moment?" Lauren asked.

"Oh, sure." She took a step away.

"No, I mean with you and Levi." Lauren touched Emily's shoulder. "Honey, why don't you and Joey go inside and get Joey's things."

The girls ran inside, and Lauren looked a little embarrassed. "Levi, I wanted to apologize for hitting on you so often. I didn't realize you and Tara had feelings for each other, or I never would have tried."

Levi and Tara exchanged a knowing and slightly amused look, because he hadn't realized it, either, and he reached for Tara's hand. "It's okay."

"That's gracious of you, but it's *not* okay. I've been a little overzealous in the flirtation department the last few months, but I'm starting to realize that love can't be forced, and it's not a bad thing to be alone until the right person comes along, so things are going to change. Tara, I hope we can be friends."

"I'd like that," she said, knowing she'd have little time for new friends but still hoping things would change for Lauren. Because even though her sister had proved her wrong, Tara still believed in the importance of having a hopeful heart.

The girls ran outside, and after thanking Lauren and a quick goodbye, Tara, Levi, and Joey piled into the Durango.

"Are we going to the beach now?" Joey asked. "I wore my bathing suit under my clothes."

Tara looked over her shoulder to the back seat and winked. "In one sec. Levi, can I see your left hand, please."

"O-*kay.*" He stretched his hand across the console, his brow furrowed.

"Joey and I had this made for you." Tara pulled the leather bracelet with the flat silver circle that fit around her bracelet, inside which, Joey's heart-shaped bracelet fit, and put it around his wrist. "So no matter how far apart the three of us are, we'll always be close at heart."

He looked at the bracelet, his expression warm and a little overwhelmed. "I love it." He glanced at Joey. "Sorry I dropped the ball, kiddo."

"It's okay," Joey chirped. "I knew you'd forget, and Aunt Tara wouldn't, so I asked her."

"Aunt Tara never forgets a thing." When he turned his devastating smile and sexy brown eyes on Tara, the love in them wrapped around her like an embrace. "I'm glad she never gave up on her feelings for us because Daddy can be a dodo bird sometimes."

She glanced at the little girl who had owned half her heart since the day she'd come into her life and at the man who had owned the other half since Tara was Joey's age and got too choked up to form a sentence, but she didn't need to, because one word said it all. *"Same."*

Twenty-Seven

THE COOL DAYS of May bled into a warmer June, a hot July, and a scorching August, full of adjustments and transitions and more love than Tara ever imagined possible. Gone was the practice of setting an alarm to sneak out of bed, but now they had other things to remember. Like putting on clothes before falling asleep because one of Joey's favorite things to do was bounding into their bedroom in the morning and snuggling with the two of them while she took stock of all their plans for the day. Their lives were full of everyday activities like work, coordinating schedules and playdates, laundry and other mundane chores. But there was also an abundance of laughter, occasional tears, and a multitude of deep conversations. They hadn't heard a peep from Amelia, but Joey had asked about her a few weeks after Tara had moved in, and they'd sat her down and talked about how things had changed. As they'd expected, Joey had a rough time with it and had acted out for a while, but things had finally settled down. They knew it would be an ongoing adjustment that might spike during holidays and other points during her life, and they were thinking about finding a therapist for her to talk to, to help guide her through the transition.

Tara and Levi were also thinking about talking with someone who could help them navigate the rough waters for all their sakes. There was a fair amount of guilt that came with protecting Joey's well-being, and their own. While Tara's brothers and grandmother felt bad that the issues with Amelia had come to such a hurtful end, they supported her and Levi's decision. Her parents had taken it harder. They were sad about the deeper rift that had developed between their daughters, but they weren't pressuring Tara to do anything other than keep an open mind for the future. She and Levi had already discussed that, because as Tara's mother had proven, if a person really wanted to change, they would.

Life had become perfectly imperfect, and even with the rough spots, Tara and Levi were blissfully happy, and Joey had even more to be happy about these days, having gotten her wish to spend the summer on Silver Island. Levi had finished Autumn's house in early June, and he'd picked up several jobs on the island. He had put Joker in charge of his Husbands for Hire crew in Harborside, and for a jovial guy, Joker sure knew how to buckle down when it mattered, and he filled Levi in every week at church. Meanwhile, Levi had been working long hours renovating a house in Seaport, but Tara didn't mind, because she'd gotten to check off one of her childhood wishes. They were staying with Levi's parents for the summer, and in the evenings, while he was working late, Tara and Joey hung out with some of their favorite people, listening to his parents' stories.

It was Sunday, and Joey was on a playdate with Hadley.

Tara had just finished with her morning clients, and she was enjoying lunch on the deck of Rock Bottom Bar and Grill with her mother, grandmother, Jules, Shelley, and Lenore. She'd taken Jules and Grant's save-the-date photos a few days ago, and they were admiring the proofs. Tara's mother looked genuinely relaxed, looking over the pictures with the other ladies leaning in close.

Tara had noticed many differences beyond how her mother had treated her the last few months, which was a wonderful change in and of itself. She hugged Tara every time she saw her and called just to see how she was doing, and she usually had kind or complimentary words to say. Occasionally she had critical moments, but she was quick to catch herself and apologize. In all fairness, there were times when Tara *had* looked tired or could have dressed a little better. But the changes in her mother didn't stop there. She looked and acted younger, happier. Her eyes were clearer, and she gave off a warmer vibe. She was getting along better with Tara's grandmother, and she was closer to Tara's father, too. She'd also begun spending more social time with Shelley and several other women on the island. They'd even convinced her to join them on a Bra Brigade outing, which had shocked Tara. But if anyone knew how the right person—or people—could bring out parts of them they hadn't known existed, it was her.

"I can't believe we get to have a Christmas wedding," Jules said giddily. "I'm already driving Grant crazy with ideas."

"Maybe you should be driving him crazy about a honeymoon instead, so you can work on having grandbabies," Shelley suggested.

"Shell, don't rush them into parenthood," Tara's grandmother advised. "Let them ride the high of being young and in love before they're tied down to strollers and diapers."

"I agree," Lenore chimed in. "They should do exactly what they're doing. Travel, fawn over each other, stay up until three in the morning fooling around, and watch the sunrise, because once you have babies, that stuff gets put on hold."

"Remember how exhausted Levi was when Joey was a baby?" Tara added. "And he had help from Shelley and Steve."

"I'm feeling a little outnumbered." Shelley leaned closer to Tara's mother. "You'll back me up on this, right, Marsha?"

"Oh, no you don't, Shelley Steele," her mother said with a soft laugh, which was music to Tara's ears. "I'm not getting sucked into trying to tell *anyone's* daughter what to do. I've discovered that life is much easier when you let it happen instead of trying to control it."

"Attagirl," Tara's grandmother said. "I'll get you to Pythons yet."

"Oh, goodness, *no*," her mother said, crimson spreading on her cheeks.

There was a round of laughter.

"I was really hoping for a little grandbaby support," Shelley teased. "Next time I'll have to invite Gail and Margot to join us."

"Don't worry, Mom," Jules said. "Grant and I want babies, just not quite yet. We have a *wedding* to plan."

"These save-the-date photos are magnificent." Tara's mother looked across the table at her. "You've got such a good eye, Tara. You've captured the very essence of their love in every shot."

"Thanks, Mom." Tara soaked in the compliment, but it was the warm way she'd said it that had Tara bottling up the sentiment and tucking it away with all her other treasured moments.

"You don't have to look far to see their love," her grandmother said. "It radiates off Jules and Grant the way it does Tara and Levi."

Tara gathered that sentiment, too, although she didn't need to gather those words in order to remember them. She felt it every time she and Levi were together. Her phone vibrated in her pocket, and she pulled it out, hoping it was Levi. He'd said he'd text if he finished early. But it was a text from Charmaine. *You'll never guess what went on the market last night. 800 Gable Place! It's not even in our system yet. I'm heading there to put up a sign. Want to meet me there? It'll go fast.*

"Oh my gosh, you guys." She looked around the table. "My favorite house just went on the market."

"In Harborside?" her mother asked.

"No. It's here, in the older section of Silver Haven. The one at 800 Gable Place. I used to dream of living there."

"Are you and Levi thinking of moving to the island?" Jules asked hopefully.

"Wouldn't that be lovely," her mother said.

"I would give anything to have more of my family living here. Please tell us you're thinking about it," Shelley urged.

"We're not. *Sorry.* We think it's better if we don't uproot Joey from her friends and school." But there was no denying how much Tara was loving being back on the island full-time. Levi seemed happier there, too, and Joey was having a great summer. She'd even had a few sleepovers with some of the Venting Vixens' kids. But having a great summer away from home was one thing. Moving away from friends and her skateboarding coach was a whole different ball game.

"That make sense, for Joey's sake," her grandmother said.

"Moving is hard on kids."

"I know. I really want to see the inside of it, but I should tell Charmaine I don't want to see it so I don't waste her time, right?"

"Why would you do that?" Lenore asked.

"Life's too short to miss out on your favorite things," her grandmother said.

"I agree," her mother chimed in. "There's no harm in going to see it."

Excitement bubbled up inside Tara. "Charmaine did say she was putting up a sign, so she's there anyway. But I have to meet her right now, and I hate to leave you guys."

"*Go*," they said in unison.

"Okay! Thank you!" She popped to her feet and hurried off the deck and toward the parking lot, thumbing out a text to Charmaine. *I'm on my way. Thank you!*

As she drove toward Gable Place, she wanted to call Levi and tell him, but she didn't want to put pressure on him. He was so good to her, and he'd made a huge concession by handing over the management of his business to Joker so they could be with Joey for the summer. But it was too exciting. She had to call him.

"Hey, beautiful. How was lunch? Did they like the pictures of Jules and Grant?"

"They loved them, but I left early. They're still there. The house on Gable Place just went on the market, and I know we're staying in Harborside, but I just want to take a quick look inside. I don't suppose you can take an hour off and go with me, can you?"

"I wish I could, babe, but I'm knee-deep in a kitchen renovation. If you see something in the house that you love, get pictures, and I'll build whatever it is for you in our place."

She grinned as she climbed into her car. *Our place.* Even after three months, hearing it still brought a thrill. "Okay. Love you."

"Love you, too. I'll see you soon."

She drove to Gable Place and was surprised to see the owner hadn't done anything to spruce it up for the sale. It was in the same state of disrepair as it had been at the beginning of April, when she'd stood across the street fantasizing about living there with Levi and Joey, and he'd appeared out of nowhere. She stared at the house she'd spent years dreaming about, with its boarded-up window, broken shutters, and precariously hanging gutters and found it to be every bit as beautiful as she always had. But she no longer had to dream about a life she'd longed for. She was living it, and now she knew it wasn't the house that made a home. It was the people in it.

As she walked through the broken picket fence, Charmaine came out the front door, looking as professional as always in a pretty paisley skirt and white top. Her hair was pinned away from her face, and she had her phone pressed to her ear.

"Okay, just a minute." Charmaine lowered her phone. "I have to take this call, but you can go in and look around. Take your time."

Tara nodded and headed up the porch steps and walked inside. Her breath caught at the expansive foyer. The interior was *immaculate*, with light bamboo floors, high coffered ceilings and gorgeous sand-colored walls with white trim. How could a house look that run-down outside and this good inside? She felt a tingling beneath her skin, as if the house's energy was becoming part of her.

There was a living room to her left, and to the right, a

smaller room, but the large front window made it feel much larger. The foyer opened into a great room with a gorgeous stone fireplace. She pulled out her phone and started taking pictures because there was no way Levi would believe this. She turned to take a picture of the foyer and saw two hanging wooden barn doors, stained with grays and browns to match the floor and the stones in the fireplace. Stunned, Tara took a picture and sent it to Levi with the message. *Can you believe it?*

She pulled open the barn doors, and her jaw dropped at the sight of a queen-size nook just like the one in Levi's house, complete with a mattress covered in the same pretty blankets. The cardboard stars she'd cut out and covered in tinfoil dangled from silver ribbons tied to a bar near the ceiling. The walls were decorated with their sleepy-time pictures and pictures of sunsets, only they weren't taken from Levi's back patio. She turned to look out the back of the house and nearly tripped over Levi and Joey, both down on one knee. Joey was smiling from ear to ear, looking like she might burst, and Levi wore a half-smiling, half-terrified expression. Tears filled Tara's eyes.

LEVI WAS SURE he was going to puke or pass out.

"*Dad*," Joey whispered urgently. "Hurry up."

If only he could remember what he'd planned to say. He cleared his throat. "Tara, sweetheart, you're the first and only woman I've ever loved—"

"That's not the speech," Joey whispered. "*You're unexpected* comes first. *Remember?*"

Tara stifled a laugh.

"Right. Thanks." He took a deep breath and smiled up at Tara. "Everything about us was unexpected. I never felt like Joey and I were missing anything, but now I know it's because you've always been in our lives, and because of that, because of *you*, we never missed a thing. You are the first and only woman I have ever loved, and I know I will love you until I have no breath left to give."

"*Levi…?*" she said in a small voice, tears sliding down her cheeks.

"Baby, I love you—"

"*We* love you," Joey said as they rose to their feet.

"We love you." Levi's voice was rough from nerves. "I know how much this house means to you, but what you don't know is that it has always been my favorite house, too. Charmaine helped me track down the owner two months ago. It's ours, blondie. The yard is just waiting for you and Joey to work your magic, and I've already worked mine in here. It's ready for us to fill with love and hang pictures of our kids on every wall and their finger paintings on the fridge. I want to hear our kids sing into their hairbrushes with you, and, baby, I want to make you laugh and hold you when you cry. I want to be the person you let your guard down with, and trust to be so in love with you, you know without a shadow of a doubt that it won't matter if you lose your hair or gain fifty pounds, because what we have is so much deeper than that."

"*You remembered,*" Tara said with awe.

"Every word you've ever said. You rock my world, T, and soothe my soul, and I will spend a lifetime trying to do the same for you. The studio out back is yours, and Joey wants to go to school here—"

"Dad, you're messing up again," Joey whispered. Then

louder, "We love you, Aunt Tara, and we want to spend the rest of our lives with you. Will you marry us?" She elbowed Levi. "Show her the ring."

Tara smiled as tears spilled down her cheeks, and Levi held up the simple, elegant princess-cut diamond ring he'd had made for her with a single smaller diamond on each of the four sides, giving it a floral appearance, and four diamonds down each side of the band.

"Tara, my love, can you find it in your heart to make me the happiest man on earth and give me the honor of being your husband?"

"In my heart it's always been you," she said through her tears.

"Does that mean *yes*?" Joey asked, and he and Tara laughed.

"Yes" bubbled out with Tara's tears. "I love you both. *Yes*, I'll marry you."

As he slid the ring on her finger, Joey ran to the back door and shouted, "*She said yes!*"

Cheers rang out, and as their families converged on them, Levi drew her into his arms, gazing deeply into her eyes. "I don't know how we got to this magical realm, but I never want to leave."

As he lowered his lips to hers, "*Same*" slipped out.

Ready for More Steeles?

Fall in love with Leni and Raz in WILD ISLAND LOVE

Sparks fly between a PR rep and an A-list actor who want nothing to do with each other.

Leni Steele might be looking for love, but she's definitely not looking to be someone's fake date. Especially not one of the most infuriatingly handsome and annoyingly cocky actors on the planet, Duncan Raz. But when the owner of the PR firm for which she works forces her to walk the red carpet on his arm, she has no choice. Neither wants to be there, much less with each other. They're like oil and water, and he gets on her last nerve. But after a few tequila shots, that's not all he gets on. What was supposed to be one date turns into a media frenzy they can't afford to ignore, and Leni has no other option than to continue the ruse. All the fake kisses furtive glances, and seductive touches eventually start to feel very real. But Raz didn't earn his A-list-actor status for nothing. Is he just doing what he does best? Playing a role? Or is Leni the leading lady in Raz's real-life love story?

Have you met The Wickeds: Dark Knights at Bayside?

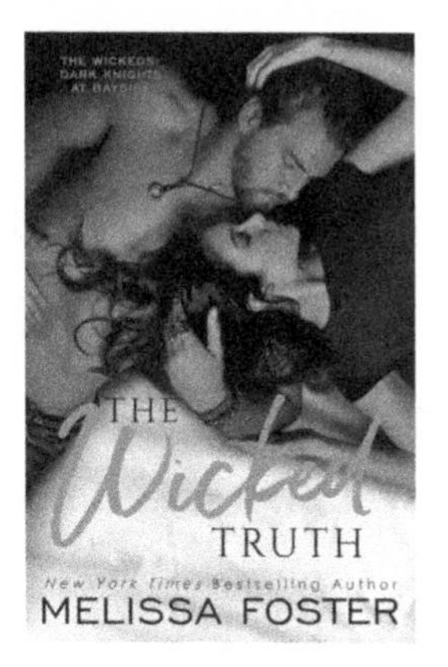

What happens when you're not looking for love, but it walks in the door?

When a mysterious stranger crosses paths with Madigan Wicked, their connection is undeniable, yet neither is open to love. He's on a road to redemption, and she's been hurt before. But love has been known to bully its way into even the most resisting hearts. When the wicked truth of his dark past is revealed, will it be too much for them to overcome?

About the Love in Bloom World

Love in Bloom is the overarching romance collection name for several family series whose worlds interconnect. For example, *Lovers at Heart, Reimagined* is the title of the first book in The Bradens. The Bradens are set in the Love in Bloom world, and within The Bradens, you will see characters from other Love in Bloom series, such as The Snow Sisters and The Remingtons, so you never miss an engagement, wedding, or birth.

Where to Start

All Love in Bloom books can be enjoyed as stand-alone novels or as part of the larger series.

If you are an avid reader and enjoy long series, I'd suggest starting with the very first Love in Bloom novel, *Sisters in Love*, and then reading through all the series in the collection in publication order. However, you can start with any book or series without feeling a step behind. I offer free downloadable series checklists, publication schedules, and family trees on my website. A paperback series guide for the first thirty-six books in the series is available at most retailers and provides pertinent details for each book as well as places for you to take notes about the characters and stories.

See the Entire Love in Bloom Collection

www.MelissaFoster.com/love-bloom-series

Download Series Checklists, Family Trees, and Publication Schedules

www.MelissaFoster.com/reader-goodies

Download Free First-in-Series eBooks

www.MelissaFoster.com/free-ebooks

More Books By Melissa Foster

LOVE IN BLOOM SERIES

SNOW SISTERS

Sisters in Love
Sisters in Bloom
Sisters in White

THE BRADENS at Weston

Lovers at Heart, Reimagined
Destined for Love
Friendship on Fire
Sea of Love
Bursting with Love
Hearts at Play

THE BRADENS at Trusty

Taken by Love
Fated for Love
Romancing My Love
Flirting with Love
Dreaming of Love
Crashing into Love

THE BRADENS at Peaceful Harbor

Healed by Love
Surrender My Love
River of Love
Crushing on Love
Whisper of Love
Thrill of Love

THE BRADENS & MONTGOMERYS at Pleasant Hill – Oak Falls

Embracing Her Heart

Anything for Love
Trails of Love
Wild Crazy Hearts
Making You Mine
Searching for Love
Hot for Love
Sweet Sexy Heart
Then Came Love
Rocked by Love
Our Wicked Hearts
Claiming Her Heart

THE BRADEN NOVELLAS

Promise My Love
Our New Love
Daring Her Love
Story of Love
Love at Last
A Very Braden Christmas

THE REMINGTONS

Game of Love
Stroke of Love
Flames of Love
Slope of Love
Read, Write, Love
Touched by Love

SEASIDE SUMMERS

Seaside Dreams
Seaside Hearts
Seaside Sunsets
Seaside Secrets
Seaside Nights
Seaside Embrace
Seaside Lovers
Seaside Whispers
Seaside Serenade

BAYSIDE SUMMERS

Bayside Desires

Bayside Passions

Bayside Heat

Bayside Escape

Bayside Romance

Bayside Fantasies

THE STEELES AT SILVER ISLAND

Tempted by Love

My True Love

Caught by Love

Always Her Love

THE RYDERS

Seized by Love

Claimed by Love

Chased by Love

Rescued by Love

Swept Into Love

THE WHISKEYS: DARK KNIGHTS AT PEACEFUL HARBOR

Tru Blue

Truly, Madly, Whiskey

Driving Whiskey Wild

Wicked Whiskey Love

Mad About Moon

Taming My Whiskey

The Gritty Truth

In for a Penny

Running on Diesel

THE WHISKEYS: DARK KNIGHTS AT REDEMPTION RANCH

The Trouble with Whiskey

For the Love of Whiskey

SUGAR LAKE

The Real Thing

Only for You

Love Like Ours

Finding My Girl

HARMONY POINTE

Call Her Mine

This is Love

She Loves Me

THE WICKEDS: DARK KNIGHTS AT BAYSIDE

A Little Bit Wicked

The Wicked Aftermath

Crazy, Wicked Love

The Wicked Truth

SILVER HARBOR

Maybe We Will

Maybe We Should

Maybe We Won't

WILD BOYS AFTER DARK

Logan

Heath

Jackson

Cooper

BAD BOYS AFTER DARK

Mick

Dylan

Carson

Brett

HARBORSIDE NIGHTS SERIES

Includes characters from the Love in Bloom series

Catching Cassidy

Discovering Delilah
Tempting Tristan

More Books by Melissa

Chasing Amanda (mystery/suspense)
Come Back to Me (mystery/suspense)
Have No Shame (historical fiction/romance)
Love, Lies & Mystery (3-book bundle)
Megan's Way (literary fiction)
Traces of Kara (psychological thriller)
Where Petals Fall (suspense)

Acknowledgments

I hope you enjoyed Levi and Tara's love story, and I'm excited to bring you more Silver Island love stories. My Silver Harbor series is also set on Silver Island and features the de Messiéres family. As with all my series, characters from each story cross over to other series. If you'd like to read more about Silver Island, pick up *Searching for Love*, a Bradens & Montgomerys novel featuring treasure hunter Zev Braden. A good portion of Zev's story takes place on and around the island, as does *Bayside Fantasies*, a Bayside Summers novel featuring billionaire Jett Masters.

Writing a book is never a solo process, and I'm blessed to have the support of many friends and family members. Although I could never name them all, heaps of gratitude go out to Sharon Martin, Lisa Posillico-Filipe, and Missy and Shelby DeHaven, all of whom keep me sane. A special shout-out goes to Lisa for pulling me through my most stressful moments and somehow managing not to kill me in the process. I'd like to also thank my editorial team, Kristen, Penina, Elaini, Juliette, Lynn, Justinn, and Lee for helping my books shine. And, of course, a world of thanks goes out to my four incredible sons and my mother for their endless support.

I enjoy chatting with fans. If you haven't joined my Facebook fan club, I hope you will. We have loads of fun, chat about

books, and members get special sneak peeks of upcoming publications and exclusive giveaways.
www.Facebook.com/groups/MelissaFosterFans

Meet Melissa

www.MelissaFoster.com

Melissa Foster is a *New York Times*, *Wall Street Journal*, and *USA Today* bestselling and award-winning author. Her books have been recommended by *USA Today*'s book blog, *Hagerstown* magazine, *The Patriot*, and several other print venues. Melissa has painted and donated several murals to the Hospital for Sick Children in Washington, DC.

Visit Melissa on her website or chat with her on social media. Melissa enjoys discussing her books with book clubs and reader groups and welcomes an invitation to your event. Melissa's books are available through most online retailers in paperback, digital, and audio formats.

Melissa also writes sweet romance under the pen name, Addison Cole.